A Woman's Strength

Tessa Hargrave is a survivor. She survived heartbreaking betrayal by a man she desperately loved. She survived an abusive marriage to a man she could never love. She supported herself on her own, raised her child on her own, found her own kind of happiness in a life of her own.

But now it seems she is back where she started, in Yorkshire, England ... in the web of the family intrigue and jealousy that had blighted her childhood and scarred her young womanhood. She finds herself in the grip of a new passion ... and in danger of another that once had held her in such fiery thrall, and is now reaching out to possess her again.

As Tessa struggles against the pull of the perilous past, she can only wonder if she will be wiser and stronger the second time around. Can she survive again ... can she love again ... ?

Homecoming

by

Susan Bowden

A SIGNET BOOK

SIGNET
Published by the Penguin Group
Penguin Books USA Inc., 375 Hudson Street,
New York, New York 10014, U.S.A.
Penguin Books Ltd, 27 Wrights Lane,
London W8 5TZ, England
Penguin Books Australia Ltd, Ringwood,
Victoria, Australia
Penguin Books Canada Ltd, 10 Alcorn Avenue,
Toronto, Ontario, Canada M4V 3B2
Penguin Books (N.Z.) Ltd, 182-190 Wairau Road,
Auckland 10, New Zealand

Penguin Books Ltd, Registered Offices:
Harmondsworth, Middlesex, England

First published by Signet, an imprint of Dutton Signet,
a division of Penguin Books USA Inc.

First Printing, October, 1995
10 9 8 7 6 5 4 3 2 1

Cover art by Robert McGinnis

 REGISTERED TRADEMARK—MARCA REGISTRADA

Printed in the United States of America

PUBLISHER'S NOTE
This is a work of fiction. Names, characters, places, and incidents either
are the product of the author's imagination or are used fictitiously,
and any resemblance to actual persons, living or dead, events, or locales
is entirely coincidental.

In Loving Memory of my father,
KENNETH BOWDEN
(1913–1993)
who might have recognized much of himself
in my portrait of Steven Hargrave

Each life converges to some centre
Expressed or still;
Exists in every human nature
A goal . . .

—Emily Dickinson

Homecoming

Prologue

Vicky Thornton surveyed the scene with a strange sense of detachment. Although it was her own engagement party, held in her own home in the Yorkshire Dales, she felt as if she were watching a movie, set in some exotic locale.

"A fantastic party, Vicky," one of Jeremy's friends shouted to her, his left hand loosely holding his partner, the other grasping a bottle of champagne.

Vicky leaned against the pillar and gave him a nod and a strained smile in reply, knowing that anything she said would be drowned out by the noise of the rock band. Her fingers clutched at the ridiculous little beaded bag that was too small to hold anything but her lipstick and mascara—and a couple of aspirin, which she felt sorely in need of.

This was the first time she'd been with Jeremy's friends, en masse, and she was fed up with them already.

Now she watched, growing increasingly annoyed, as a loudly protesting Jeremy was hoisted onto the shoulders of four of his friends, accompanied by squeals and shouts of laughter.

"Oh, poor old Jeremy," someone shouted to her from the crowd surrounding him. "Aren't you going to rescue him, Vicky? They're about to throw him in the fountain."

"Come on, Vicky. You don't want to miss this." A

couple of girls grabbed her hands and drew her behind the crowd that followed the yelling Jeremy and his captors.

Outside on the terrace, the cool night air struck her bare shoulders and she shivered. Poor Jeremy, if they really were going to throw him in the fountain he'd freeze.

"Don't be a lot of idiots," she found herself shouting. "It's too cold." But her protest was drowned by the shouting and laughter.

"One, two, three ... and in he goes," sang out the crowd. She heard a splash, a yell from Jeremy, and another roar of laughter.

They pushed her forward, someone thrusting a coat into her hands, another a towel. They were dragging Jeremy out of the fountain by the time she reached him.

"Jesus, you bastards," he said through chattering teeth, his breath catching with shock. "I'll get you for this."

"Here's your bride-to-be," someone said, thrusting her forward. "She'll soon warm you up."

Vicky tried to laugh with the rest of them, but found she couldn't. "Here, put this round you," she told Jeremy, trying to pull the coat around his shoulders.

If it had been her they'd thrown in, she would have been furious. In fact, she *was* furious. This wasn't at all the way she'd imagined her engagement party would be. But, despite the water plastering his fair hair and streaming down his face, Jeremy was now laughing. He grabbed the towel with one hand and then dragged her against him, his wet clothes soaking her as well as himself.

"Let's have a kiss," someone shouted. "A kiss, a kiss," everyone echoed.

Honestly, they were like a bunch of stupid kids, Vicky thought. And Jeremy was just as bad. Since his friends had arrived yesterday he'd been acting like a total idiot.

He tried to kiss her, but Vicky pushed him away. "Not here," she told him. She marched ahead of him, back into the house. He flapped behind her, his Gucci evening shoes squelching as he walked.

When she was halfway across the hall, Jeremy caught up with her. He took hold of her arm and spun her around.

"Leave me alone, Jeremy," she said in a harsh whisper. "You're very wet and very drunk." He ignored her, dragging her against him and kissing her hard, his tongue probing inside her mouth, his body pushing against hers.

The flash of a camera startled them. Damn and hell, Vicky thought, what a perfect picture to be in the next issue of *Tatler*!

As Jeremy released her, she looked up and saw his parents, Lord and Lady Ayncliffe, standing behind the photographer, watching them. Beside them were her parents, her mother's beautiful English-rose face flushed with pride, her father's flushed with Scotch.

Her grandparents completed the picture. Her grandmother in her wheelchair, smiling triumphantly. Her grandfather . . .

As Vicky's gaze met her grandfather's he turned away, but not in time to hide his look of disgust. Murmuring an apology, he slowly made his way down the hall, leaning heavily on his silver-handled ebony stick, and went into his study.

Chapter One

Tessa Hargrave received the letter from her Uncle Steven two weeks later. It was nestled among the usual pile of bills and flyers in her mailbox. The sight of the strong pen strokes on the cream vellum envelope brought a sudden rush of tears to her eyes. Dear Uncle Steven. His letters were the only connection with her past life in England.

She stuffed the mail into her bag and unlocked the door to her Westwood town house in suburban Winnipeg. "Are you home, Jason?" she shouted when she'd closed the door behind her.

There was no reply from her son as she went up the open staircase to her bedroom, but that meant nothing. He could have his headphones on. "I swear if I turned on a fire engine's siren in the house, you wouldn't hear it with that noise in your ears," she frequently told him.

The cotton suit she'd worn for her interviews today was wilting, like her, from the heat. It had been a long time since she'd had to go job hunting, but she had to find something to fill in the three-month gap. A week had passed since she'd been laid off from her position as a senior flight attendant with Canada Airways, and still she'd found nothing.

She was luckier than most. For now, at least, her layoff was temporary, but several of her colleagues had been fired. "Necessary belt-tightening" was the term the company had used.

As soon as she'd showered and changed into shorts and a halter top, she went downstairs to the gallery-kitchen. Having filled the kettle and plugged it in, she sat down at the kitchen counter and drew out the letter.

Uncle Steven had written it, he told her, a few days after the party celebrating his granddaughter's engagement to the Honorable Jeremy Kingsley.

Jeremy is Lord Ayncliffe's son, he wrote. *In my opinion, the fellow's a fool, but Camilla and Sybil are delighted at the thought of Vicky one day becoming Lady Ayncliffe and ruling over Ayncliffe Hall.*

Bet they are, thought Tessa. Ayncliffe was one of the finest stately homes in England. But why on earth was a girl getting married at the age of nineteen in this emancipated age?

The thought of Cousin Camilla and Aunt Sybil in cahoots made her feel queasy. She also felt a sudden rush of sympathy for Vicky. With those two for a mother and grandmother, what chance did she have?

The kettle bubbled and then automatically switched off. Tessa made a pot of tea for herself in the small brown teapot, put it on a tray with some of the oatmeal cookies she'd made that morning, and carried it downstairs to the back patio.

Children were playing baseball on the stretch of grass and swinging and sliding in the playground beyond it. Before she sat down, Tessa checked the flower beds she'd filled with bright geraniums and petunias, and edged with blue lobelia. She'd water them as soon as she finished reading her letter.

As she sat on the canvas chair, she smiled to herself, feeling the tension of her day ease away. She enjoyed the sound of children playing, the warmth of the sun on her face, the roughness of the patio bricks she'd laid herself beneath her bare feet.

She picked up the letter again. *I've had a little turn. Nothing to worry your pretty head about, I assure you. I just mention it to explain why my writing is so appalling. Hard to write when you are lying in bed, propped up with pillows.*

Tessa's heart quickened. Oh, God, if Uncle Steven was sick enough to be in bed, it must be serious. Her uncle had never had any patience for illness or doctors ... or going to bed when you were sick. "Good dose of fresh air is what you need," he'd say when she or Camilla had come down with a bad cold or the flu. "Set up the tent and sleep out by the river. That'll soon chase the germs away."

She doubted that Aunt Sybil would allow him to lie out in a tent by the river, or even on the long strip of lawn between the herbaceous borders of Langley. Poor man. Although he had usually slept in his wife's bed, he might now be trapped in the four-poster bed in his own dark bedroom with the tapestry on the wall. He had always disliked that room, but his wife, whose family had owned Langley House for two hundred and fifty years, had designated it as his. "My father used that room, and his father before him," Tessa remembered hearing her say whenever Uncle Steven had complained.

She read on. *At last the house is quiet again. Jeremy's friends threw him into the fountain on the night of the party. Need I say more? I've a feeling my darling little Vicky is making a terrible mistake. She's far too young to be even thinking of marriage, and I don't think she is happy, but I might as well go cry in the wilderness for all the notice that's taken of me. Overpowered by women. It's the story of my life.*

Overpowered by his wife, in particular. *Thank God, I don't ever have to see her again,* Tessa thought.

Dear girl, please come and see me as soon as possible. I am an old man now, seventy-five last birthday, and it is twenty years since I last saw you. Don't wait until the wedding. That would be too late. I am enclosing a money order to cover the cost of your fare. (I had to ask Kevin Taylor, our estate manager, to get it for me.) I have never before asked you for any favors, my dear. This time, please grant your old uncle this one wish. Come to Langley before it is too late.

Twice he had used the words "too late."

Tessa slid her fingers into the envelope and found the bank order. It was for one thousand pounds.

Although the sun was still shining and the children were still playing beyond her little garden sanctuary, she felt as if a wall of ice had risen between her and other living things. How could she return to Langley, when she had vowed, twenty years ago, never to go back?

She shivered. Despite the warmth of the sun on her face and body, she felt cold. Thinking of those things in her past always affected her this way. However much she told herself that the people at Langley House no longer held the power to hurt her, she knew she would be crazy even to consider going back. It had taken her too many years to build up her self-esteem and confidence to risk losing them again.

On the other hand, how could she deny the request of her seriously ill uncle, her father's elder brother, and the only relative who had cared about her when her parents died? *Come, before it's too late.* Perhaps the doctors had given him only a few weeks to live.

She shook her head at the pages in her hand, as if they personified her uncle. "I can never go home again," she whispered, "never."

A shadow fell across the letter. Startled, she looked up. Jason stood behind her, holding a can of Coke.

"Oh, hi, sweetie," she said. "I wasn't sure if you were in or not. Want to join me?"

"Who's the letter from?"

She could lie, of course, but he'd know she was lying. She looked up at his handsome face framed by the distinctive hair.

"My Uncle Steven. It's all about his granddaughter's engagement party. You remember I told you she was marrying the son of an earl?"

"Who cares?"

"You're right," she said, folding the letter and putting it under the leg of her chair. "How did the job hunt go?"

His shoulders hunched eloquently beneath the black Hugo Boss T-shirt. "Rotten."

Holding a conversation with Jason nowadays was like pulling teeth. "No luck?"

He tilted the Coke can to his lips and drank. "They offered me a job with a landscape gardening firm. Minimum wage."

"Did you take it?" she asked eagerly. Too eagerly, she realized immediately.

"I said I wanted something better than that."

"Maybe there isn't anything better." Tessa was careful to keep her voice calm, although she felt like yelling at him.

"I sure as hell hope there is. I'm not going to spend my summer digging flower beds and mowing lawns for five measly bucks an hour."

Tessa took a deep breath. "You're going to have to get something pretty quickly, Jason. Because the lay-off is temporary—we hope—I won't be getting any pay from the airline for three months and even if I find a temporary job it won't pay much."

His eyes met hers for the fist time since he'd come out. "You didn't have any luck today either, eh?"

She shook her head. "They offered me some computer work, but it was only for three days."

"That's tough, Mom." She felt his arms about her neck, his cheek pressed against hers. "I'm sure you'll get your job back."

She reached up to pull his head down and kiss him. "Thanks, love, I really needed that."

He opened the other patio chair and sat down beside her. Only then did she realize that he had something he wanted to tell her—other than news about his rotten day of job hunting. There was an edgy air of suppressed excitement about him. "What's up?"

He looked away. "Nothing. Why?"

"Come on. Tell me."

"Give it a break, Mom."

"Something's up," she insisted. "What is it?"

"It wouldn't work," he muttered.

"What wouldn't?"

"Why bother asking?" His brown eyes flared with anger. "I can't do it, anyway."

"For God's sake, tell me. How can I tell if you can do it or not if you don't tell me what it is?"

He glared at her. "It needs money."

"Oh." Now it was her turn to look away. Money, or the lack of it, had always loomed large in her life, but she'd never before had to go job searching at a time when jobs were almost nonexistent. "Please tell me what it is, Jason. Maybe we can work it out somehow."

He shrugged. "Okay. You remember the camping trip in France Mr. Klassen organized for grades eleven and twelve two years ago?"

"Yes. I thought it might be a great idea, but you said you didn't want to go." What he'd actually said was that he wasn't going on any school tour with a bunch of nerds.

"Yeah, that's right. You and I went to that dude

ranch in Alberta that year, remember? Man, that was a good holiday."

She smiled, remembering Jason and the horses. He'd taken to horseback riding as if he'd really . . .

"Okay, spit it out," she said hurriedly, not wanting to think about John Maltby. Whenever Jason questioned her about his father, she told him as little as she could get away with.

"I was at Jim Shatner's house. He's going on this year's trip. He told me one of the kids had to drop out 'cause he's got mono. Mr. Klassen has to fill the space."

"And you'd like to go."

Jason studied the Coke can he held in both hands. "They'll be high school kids, of course, but, yeah, I'd like to go. Jim and I get on okay. And it may be my last chance to travel for a while."

"What about work?"

"It's only for two weeks, Mom. And I promise I'd work hard the rest of the summer. We'd go the second week of July. That would still give me time for six weeks of work."

"Six weeks at minimum wage isn't going to give you much towards your university tuition fees. And then there's all your textbooks . . . I hate to have to say it, Jason, but there is a chance I might not get my job back, you know."

He crushed the Coke can with both hands. "Shit, don't I know it," he murmured. "I've been asking about student loans."

Tessa was surprised. He'd never mentioned anything about student loans before. Was it possible that irresponsible Jason was beginning to grow up at last? "I hope it won't have to come to that. After all, I've been putting money away for your university for a long time. How much is the trip?"

"What trip?"

"The trip to France, you jerk," she said with a smile, trying to lighten the strain.

"Oh. Two thousand bucks."

A couple of months ago it wouldn't have sounded quite so bad. Now two thousand dollars sounded like a fortune. She was about to say, "Sorry, forget it," when she remembered the letter and, more importantly, the money order from her uncle. A thousand pounds was about two thousand dollars at the present rate of exchange.

"I know you—we can't afford it, Mom, so don't worry about it. It was just an idea, that's all."

"There may be a way," she said slowly.

"Forget it, Mom. You've done enough for me as it is." Jason scraped back his chair and stood up, looming over her. "It's time I looked out for myself instead of you doing it all."

If he had whined and cursed she wouldn't even have considered it, but his newly mature attitude got to her. "There may be a way," she said again. "I'm not sure. I'll have to see about it."

"Shit, I wish I'd never mentioned it." He scooped up his chair, angrily folding it, and stalked into the house, leaving Tessa staring into space.

She could hardly use Uncle Steven's money to send Jason over to France, could she?

But if she went to see her uncle, using one of her two remaining round-trip flight passes, she *could* then pay for Jason's trip with the money. It would solve two problems. Jason's itch to travel and her uncle's wish to see her—and her longing to see him—before it was *too late*.

She'd kept quiet about the passes, knowing that Jason would want to use one over the summer. She couldn't afford the extra money he'd need for expenses, nor did she want to encourage him to goof off. A supervised camping trip was different. The two thousand dollars would cover everything.

The question was, of course, how could she face going back to Yorkshire, to her old home, with all its devastating memories? She closed her eyes against the sun, seeing in her mind's eye the faces of those she had both loved and feared.

For a long time now she'd been feeling a sense of things left undone. Something to do with her age, she supposed. She was nearing forty. A definite milestone. Perhaps it was time she confronted her memories, instead of running away from them. It was twenty years since she'd fled from England. Her uncle was seriously ill. Everything seemed to be telling her that this was the time to go home. And, most importantly, Jason would be safe in France ...

Do it now, she told herself, *before you can change your mind.* She opened her eyes and stood up. For a moment the green and brown world spun around her. Then it settled. "Jason," she called through the open patio door. "Jason!"

"What?"

As his feet pounded down the stairs, she bent to pick up the letter and envelope.

Chapter Two

By the end of the week it was all arranged. Jason would go away with Mr. Klassen's group for the middle two weeks of July. Tessa would use her pass to fly over to England and spend a few days in Yorkshire.

She'd decided not to call her uncle until she reached England. That would give Aunt Sybil and Camilla less time to find a reason for her not to come. Every time she thought of them she felt the old sick fluttering in the pit of her stomach. It made her angry that just thinking of them could still make her feel uncomfortable after all these years.

"Why don't you stay longer in Yorkshire, Mom?" Jason asked her one evening when they were talking about their respective trips overseas. "You haven't been home since you were a kid, almost."

"I was nineteen, about the same age as you when I left."

"Hey, I just thought of something. Why don't I come and join you in Yorkshire for a few days? It would be great to see where you and my father came from."

Tessa felt a rush of hot blood into her face. "You'll be over in France," she told him through dry lips. "You can't leave the camping trip."

"I know that. Just thought I could join you and fly back with you afterwards."

"You're already booked on the return flight with the group, remember? Besides, I'm only going for a few days. Enough time to see Uncle Steven, that's all. I've told you before, I don't get on with the rest of the family. A few days there will be tough enough for me."

"From the little you've told me about your life as a kid, that cousin of yours sounds like a real witch. So does your aunt."

"She was. But she's old now, in her seventies. Anyway, whatever she's like I'm a big girl now. I can stand up to her and Camilla."

"Good. But I'd be happy to come and help you out, if you want. It would be cool to see where my roots are," Jason added wistfully.

"You will, one day," she said, hugging him to her side. "Thanks for your offer of help, love, but I can manage. No, you go and enjoy France. I'll be back in Canada long before you are."

Two nights before Jason was due to leave, Mark Crawford came over for dinner. Jason greeted him with a grunt, as he usually did, and then went out, crashing the front door behind him. He didn't care much for Mark. The feeling was mutual. "He should be over all that teenage rebellion stuff by now," Mark told Tessa frequently. He did so again.

"So you've said before. I don't criticize your children, so kindly leave Jason alone." It was a bad start to the evening.

"Both my kids are working hard, one at a good job, the other doing his—"

"Yes, I know that. Your kids are older than Jason. Besides," she said, her voice softening, "despite your divorce, they've always had a father in their lives. And a damned good father, too."

"Thanks for that, Tess." He bent over to kiss her

cheek as she sat drinking her glass of chilled Chardonnay.

She hated to be called "Tess," it reminded her of the hapless victim of Thomas Hardy's novel. Usually she told Mark, but this time she let it go. She wanted this evening to go well.

Ever since Mark had begun talking of marriage their relationship had changed. Although Tessa enjoyed his company, she didn't want to move into a more serious relationship with him. She'd been trapped in a miserable marriage once. She wasn't prepared to risk going through that ever again.

She thought she'd created a permanently safe, secure life for herself, not having to depend on other people in any way. That was how she liked it. But events of the past few weeks had changed things.

First Mark's proposal, then the news about her job, and now this trip to England and a reunion with the people she'd striven to forget for so many years.

She felt as if she were being shaken up, like a kaleidoscope, so that she was seeing the pieces that formed her present life from a different perspective.

"It's a beautiful night. Why don't we go and sit in the yard?" Mark suggested.

She smiled.

"What's so funny?"

"Nothing. It's just that to me a yard was a sort of paved courtyard at the back of the house where Yorkshire people hung their washing out to dry."

"Bet they use dryers now, with all that rain."

"I bet they do. I keep forgetting that things must have changed there as well in twenty years."

As they stepped out onto the patio, she was suddenly overwhelmed by memories of similar July nights in Wensleydale. Warm evenings, with the sun going down over the fell, the hum of bees as she strolled through the ancient walled rose garden of Thornton

Manor, the ancestral home of the Thorntons, eleven miles from Langley.

It was always Thornton she thought of with warmth, not her own home. Perhaps that was because she'd never thought of Langley as really *her* home, even if she'd lived in it for nine years. Aunt Sybil had made sure that she never felt truly at home there.

As she and Mark sat talking on the patio, part of Tessa remained separate, watching him in a new way. She seemed to be looking at everything in a new way nowadays.

Mark was talking now about the problems of being the principal of a high school in the inner city, the escalating violence in Winnipeg schools. "A couple of years back, kids rarely carried baseball bats or knives. Now it's quite common."

As he spoke, she examined his face. It was a good face. Ruggedly handsome, she supposed it could be called. A Harrison Ford-type face, with a personality to match. Strong, reliable, and conventionally intelligent.

What attracted her to him? she wondered. Perhaps it was his quiet strength, his unswerving loyalty, his reliability. Invaluable assets in a man, nowadays. After what she'd been through with John Maltby, she should be glad to have a man like Mark, shouldn't she? Yet something—perhaps it was just her age—was whispering that it wasn't enough. She wanted to experience once again those intense emotions that poets wrote about, before it was too late.

"Are you sure you wouldn't like me to?"

Tessa started, realizing that she hadn't followed what Mark had been saying. "Sorry. I was thinking that I should go check the casserole. It should be ready. What were you asking me?"

Mark looked slightly pained. "I was asking you if you would like me to come with you, for support."

"Come with me to England, you mean?"

"Yes, of course, to England," he said. "I know you're not really looking forward to going back."

She'd obviously missed a lot of Mark's conversation, if he'd moved from school problems to England!

"You're right about that," she said with a sigh.

She had a sudden vision of Mark in the blue drawing room at Langley, dressed in the check shirt and jeans he wore on weekends. He wouldn't even be at home in the shabbily comfortable but eminently aristocratic Thornton Manor.

The world of her past and her present were not only thousands of miles apart, they were also totally incompatible. "It's like being on a different planet there," she said, trying to explain. "At least, it was, and I don't suppose it's changed that much since I left. I never really felt I belonged there. I'll feel that way even more now, after having lived so long in Winnipeg."

"Why? What's so different?"

"I hate all that class-consciousness they have over there. The 'Us and Them mentality,' my father used to call it. I much prefer living in a society like Winnipeg's, where all the races and creeds mix in together."

"You're being simplistic if you think it works all the time, even in Winnipeg."

"I know. But at least we try to get along with each other."

"You haven't said what you think."

"About what?"

Mark shifted impatiently in his chair. "About my coming with you to England."

"Thanks, Mark, but I'll be fine. I'll be staying only a few days, just enough to see my uncle, that's all. Then I'll come home. But thanks for suggesting it." She gave him a grateful smile. "Sorry I'm not very good company tonight. My mind keeps wandering. I suppose it's the thought of going back after all these years."

"From the little you've told me, your uncle's family sounds like one of those Merchant-Ivory movies you keep dragging me to."

"You're right," she said with a wry grin. "But we're talking about my aunt's family, really. My father's family was just comfortably off, neither wealthy nor aristocratic. My father himself broke away from his middle-class background by becoming a journalist and marrying a working-class girl from Streatham. That caused much consternation in his family, apparently. They'd hoped he'd go into banking, or something equally boring."

"Do you remember them? Your parents, I mean?"

"Not very much. I was ten when they both died in an awful train crash on Christmas Eve." There was an awkward silence for a moment. "I suppose I just blotted everything out."

"Your Uncle Steven," Mark said quickly, trying to fill the gap, "he didn't feel the same way as your father did, I mean about his background?"

"No, not at all. He was the elder brother so I suppose he felt he had to keep up the family name. Besides, I think he liked the privileged life. He married Sybil Faversham, who inherited Langley House from her father. Uncle Steven turned the stables there into a highly successful racing stable."

"Sybil Faversham," Mark repeated. "Definitely a *Masterpiece Theater* name."

"Don't I know it." A shiver quirked Tessa's shoulders.

"It'll be over before you know it," Mark said sympathetically.

"You're right." Tessa gave him a faint smile and stood up. "Let's forget all about it and go eat."

Later, replete with beef bourguignonne and relaxed

with wine, they made love in her bed, with the bedroom door locked in case Jason came into the house unexpectedly.

Mark was a thoughtful lover, always considerate and gentle, stopping to ask her if she liked this and that. But recently she'd felt a yearning for something more—she didn't know what—before it was too late.

There they were again, those words. *Too late.* The words that had been haunting her ever since she'd received her uncle's letter.

The fact that she was lying awake thinking these thoughts, instead of falling into a satisfied sleep like Mark had, disturbed Tessa. She'd had far too much upheaval in her life recently. A sense of order was very important to her. She didn't like the feeling that things were slipping slightly askew.

Once she had visited Langley House and her uncle, everything would settle back into its former pattern and she would be in control of her life again.

Chapter Three

Where Vicky Thornton was concerned, dinner at Langley was always a bit of a production. She often chose to eat a sandwich of cold meat with salad in her workshop rather than having to put on a skirt. But tonight was different. It was the first time in ages that her grandfather was well enough to join them in the dining room for dinner.

Definitely worth putting on a skirt for.

"This is a very special occasion," Vicky said, raising her glass of wine and grinning down the table at him. "Here's to you, Papa."

He bowed his silvery head in her direction. "Thank you, Victoria. I can assure you all that I am not quite on the way out yet."

"Of course you're not," Vicky's grandmother said sharply from the other end of the table. "What nonsense you do talk, Steven. It was just a dose of summer flu."

They all knew—including Papa himself—that it had been far more than that, but Vicky knew that he would never admit to being seriously ill. He despised doctors.

It was her father, as always, who put his foot in it. "I still think you should have told old man Downing to call in a specialist." He sat, sprawled in his chair, staring at the balloon glass of cognac in his hand.

"Oh, shut up, Derek," his wife snapped, giving him

one of her withering looks. "Downing's a perfectly good doctor. He would—"

"Shall we change the subject?" Sybil's basilisk eyes glared down the table. She turned to Kevin Taylor. "I noticed weeds in the standard rose beds, Mr. Taylor, when Victoria took me out for my walk this morning."

Vicky smiled to herself. Trust Grandmother to change the subject by attacking someone. Still, she admired her. She'd chosen a subject that would engage Papa immediately and take his mind off his own health.

He leaned forward. "If you let that creeping Jenny take over, we'll never get rid of it."

"I'll speak to Frank about it first thing in the morning," Kevin said soothingly. "He's been shorthanded this week, with young Brian away."

Beside her, Jeremy shifted impatiently in his chair, obviously bored by the conversation. Vicky slid her hand under the table to grasp his and squeeze it. "We'll go for a walk later," she whispered in his ear.

"No whispering at the dinner table, Victoria," snapped Sybil. "It is extremely discourteous."

"Sorry, Grandmother."

Jeremy stifled a laugh. "What a good, obedient little girl you are," he said in an undertone as the conversation moved on to the gardens in general and aphids on the roses in particular.

"Aren't I?" Vicky agreed. "It's my other self. Comes out when I'm home."

"Not too good, I hope. Your room or mine tonight?"

Vicky flushed. He hadn't even lowered his voice. She was acutely aware of Kevin Taylor watching them from across the table. "We'll talk about this later," she said, drawing her hand away from Jeremy's.

Barton came in and spoke to her grandfather. "There's a telephone call for me," Papa said. "Do you want to see who it is, Vicky? Apparently the woman wouldn't give her name."

Vicky pushed back her chair, glad of the opportunity to escape from the confines of the dining room.

"The portable phone's in the drawing room, Miss Victoria," Barton said.

"I'll take the call in Grandfather's study. The sound on the portable keeps coming and going. I don't think it was designed to work in a great mausoleum like this. Thanks, James."

He gave her a stiff, almost imperceptible bow. As she crossed the hall, her heels clicking on the marble floor, Vicky stifled a giggle. James Barton was a man of no more than thirty who'd chosen to act the part of butler to perfection, although his job encompassed a great deal more than a true old-fashioned butler would have deigned to take on. In appearance the starchy stage butler personified, James was happy to act as a chauffeur, push Grandmother about the grounds in her wheelchair, or even to bathe the dogs, when called upon to do so.

For this perfection of subservience he earned a great deal more money than many professional businessmen.

Vicky went down the corridor to her grandfather's study, which was redolent of leather and the pungent aroma of his pipe. Leaning over the massive desk, she picked up the receiver. "Hallo. Vicky Thornton here."

Silence. For a moment she thought the caller had gone away. Then a woman's voice said, "I would like to speak to Steven Hargrave, please." It was a pleasant voice with a hint of a transatlantic accent.

"I'm sorry," Vicky said, "but my grandfather can't come to the phone at the moment. Would you like to leave a message for him?"

Silence again. Then, "Is he in bed?"

"No, he's not in bed," Vicky said impatiently. "Why

don't you give me your name and I'll get him to call you back?"

"Only if you promise to give him the message yourself."

What an odd thing to say! "I promise," Vicky said, grimacing to herself. Who on earth was this? Maybe it was an American filmmaker wanting to use Langley as a movie set. It wouldn't be the first time they'd been asked.

"My name is Tessa Hargrave," the woman said. "I'm your grandfather's niece."

Vicky gave a long drawn-out "Oh." Then she said excitedly, "Are you phoning from Canada? Papa will be so pleased. He's told me so much about you."

"Has he?"

"There's some great mystery about you, apparently. My mother and grandmother refuse to talk about you. Oh, dear, that does sound fearfully rude, doesn't it? I didn't mean it to come out that way."

"That's all right. I'm the one who ran off with the head stable groom."

"Yes, so Papa told me, only he didn't put it quite so baldly as that."

"No, I don't expect he did. Is he all right? I'd really love to talk to him if I could."

"Of course you can. I only said he couldn't come to the phone because I didn't know who it was. Shall I get him to call you in Canada?"

"I'm not in Canada. I'm in London."

Vicky gasped. "Oh, how wonderful. Will you be able to come up here? Papa would be absolutely over the moon if you could."

"That's why I flew over, so that I could see him. But I'm not quite sure how everyone else will feel about my visiting Langley."

"For heaven's sake, they're not about to turn Papa's niece away because she ran off with the groom twenty years ago. This is the twentieth century, not the nineteenth. Give me your number and I'll get Papa to call you immediately."

"Thanks, Victoria." Tessa gave her the number of the airport hotel.

"Call me Vicky, please. And make sure you come to Langley. I want to meet you."

"I'd like that." For the first time, Vicky heard warmth in Tessa's voice. She'd obviously been very nervous about phoning. Although Papa and his niece exchanged letters, she was sure that they hadn't spoken to each other on the telephone.

"What would we be to each other? You are my mother's first cousin, so I suppose we're first cousins once removed." Vicky laughed. "Too far removed, considering I've never met you."

"Yes, I'm sorry about that. The longer I put it off, the more difficult it became. But when I heard that Uncle Steven was ill, I was very worried. When he wrote to me," Tessa said, in explanation, "he said he was sick in bed."

"He's much better now. We were all terribly worried about him, too. But knowing that you are here, in England, will really cheer him up." Vicky picked up the piece of paper with Tessa's telephone number on it. "I'll go and tell him right away. *Myself*," Vicky added, with a laugh.

"Sorry about that. I must have sounded a bit odd."

"Perfectly understandable, now that I know who you are."

"Thanks for making me feel so welcome, Vicky."

"My pleasure."

"I was really nervous about phoning. Isn't that stupid?"

"Not at all. Wayward niece returns . . . and all that nonsense."

"Exactly."

"I'll go and tell Papa. See you soon. 'Bye."

" 'Bye."

Vicky almost ran down the corridor and across the hall. The family had moved into the blue drawing room for their coffee. "Great news," she said, bursting into the room.

Everyone turned to look at her, apart from her father, who was refilling his brandy glass at the delicate Sheraton desk he used for serving drinks.

"What?" her grandmother demanded.

"Oops, I forgot. I have to tell Papa first."

"What on earth are you going on about, Vicky?" her mother asked, shaking her immaculately coiffed head.

Her grandfather had sat down at the rosewood table by the window, to avoid having to balance his coffee cup on his knee. His hands had become very shaky since this last illness.

Vicky went to him. "She wanted me to be sure to tell you myself." She handed him the crumpled piece of paper with Tessa Hargrave's number on it.

"Who did?" he asked.

"Your niece, Tessa. That's her phone number. She wants you to call her."

His face flushed with pleasure as he took the scrap of paper, holding it close to his eyes so that he could read it.

"She's in London," she announced to the room at large.

"Who is?" her grandmother asked.

"Papa's niece, Tessa Hargrave."

Utter silence met her announcement. The only sounds to be heard were the loud ticking of the long-case clock in the corner of the room and the dogs' snoring. Her grandfather struggled to his feet. "This is the best news I've heard in years," he said, beaming.

"She wants to come here, to see you all," Vicky said.

"She can't come here," Sybil said, her face as rigid

as marble. Both hands gripped the arms of her wheelchair, so that the bones stood out through the translu-
cent skin.

"Of course she can't." Camilla Thornton stood up
and then reached out to the arm of her chair, seeking
support. "It's out of the question." Even from across
the room, Vicky could see how her mother's pupils
had widened, making her eyes appear too large for
her face.

"I don't understand," Vicky said. "Why on earth
can't she come for a visit, when all she did was run
off with one of the stable grooms?"

Jeremy grinned. "Sounds like a rerun of *Upstairs,
Downstairs.*"

"Tessa sounded really nice," Vicky said.

"You know nothing about the situation," her grandmother said. "The girl is not setting foot in Langley."

"Absolutely not," Camilla said.

"She's not a girl. She must be your age, Mother."

Kevin Taylor stood up. "Excuse me, I have work
to do." He strode across the room, raising his eyebrows at Vicky from the doorway before he went out.

The sound of three large raps on the floor from
Steven's walking stick startled Vicky. "When you've
all quite finished," he said, "I wish to remind you that
Tessa Hargrave is my dead brother's child and that
Langley was her home for nine years. I am delighted
that she wants to visit us after all this time. And I
expect everyone to give her the warm welcome such
a homecoming merits."

"You cannot expect me to welcome that girl into
my home, Steven," his wife said.

He limped across the room to the door. "I can and
I do. I am going to telephone Tessa and invite her
to Langley."

"I would remind you that Langley is my family's
ancestral home."

Steven Hargrave's lined face grew as rigid as his wife's. "And I would remind you, my dear Sybil, that it is my hard work with the stables and the money they have generated that has enabled you to keep Langley in the family." He turned abruptly and leaning heavily on his stick, left the room.

"I say, quite a family drama," Jeremy said when the door closed.

"Oh, do shut up," Vicky said to him.

Jeremy swore under his breath. "I think I'll take the dogs for a walk," he said, abruptly standing up.

Vicky grasped his arm. "Sorry. I didn't mean to snap. This must all be very awkward for you."

"You can say that again," he said, returning to his usual good humor. Jeremy rarely held a grudge for long. He smiled at her. God, he was so incredibly handsome that just looking at him made her insides turn over.

"I'll come and look for you outside in a minute," she told him.

He kissed her, pulling her close for a moment before releasing her. She watched him as he rallied the dogs and then led them out through the French windows to the terrace.

"Take me to my room, Camilla," Sybil Hargrave demanded in a querulous voice. "I am far too upset to stay downstairs."

As she rolled her mother's chair across the room, Camilla darted an angry glance at Vicky. She paused in the doorway. "Are you coming up, Derek?"

Only then did Vicky realize that her father had remained standing by the Sheraton desk, frozen in the same position, ever since she had first told them about Tessa Hargrave's call.

Chapter Four

As the train drew in to Northallerton Railway Station, Tessa realized that she was trembling. Then, having dragged her suitcase and carry-on bag to the door, she discovered she couldn't find the handle to open it, and began to panic, thinking that the train would carry her away.

"It opens from th'outside," a man's voice said from behind her. The accent with its prolonged vowels was unmistakably Yorkshire. "Here, let me do it," he said impatiently.

She stepped back as he let down the window to reach the outside handle and then swung open the door.

"Thank you." She bent to pick up her bags, but he already had them in his grasp and lifted them down to the platform. "You'll have to get a cart," he said brusquely, and strode away before she had time to thank him again.

Although she was feeling annoyed at her own incompetence, Tessa smiled to herself as she stepped down to the platform. The man epitomized the mixture of bluntness and kindness that was characteristically Yorkshire.

The weather also was typical Yorkshire. Dark clouds scudded across the sky and a fine rain was falling. As she looked out at the countryside beyond the station's red-brick wall, she saw that the faraway hills were hidden from view by a damp mist. She gave an involuntary shiver, hoping that the bad weather wasn't an ill omen.

Picking up her bag, she started along the open platform, trundling her carry-on case behind her. "I'll make sure there is someone at Northallerton Station to meet you," her uncle had told her. Tessa wasn't sure whom she should be looking for. A uniformed chauffeur or some other worker from the estate? Not, she sincerely hoped, some member of the family.

The thought of driving for almost an hour with Camilla, for instance, and trying to make friendly conversation with her was a particularly daunting thought.

She went down the stairs and out to the car park, experiencing that strange lost sensation you feel when you arrive at your destination and don't know who will be there to meet you.

The few people who had left the London train with her were already getting into their cars or being greeted by friends or relatives.

As she waited, Tessa was suddenly overwhelmed by the memory of arriving at a railway station somewhere in North Yorkshire—possibly this very one—thirty years ago, after her parents had been killed, and not knowing who was there to meet her or, indeed, if anyone would be there. Unlike today, the weather had been very hot. She had been uncomfortably warm in her school uniform of tunic and long-sleeved white blouse and dark green wool blazer. She remembered that a bar of chocolate she'd been given to eat on the train had melted, making her hands all sticky. As she hadn't a hankie or tissues to wipe them on, she'd tried to clean them on the underside of the upholstered seat. That had only made things worse. She had ended up with hands that were both sticky and dirty. What would her aunt and uncle think of a girl who arrived at their house with filthy hands?

At any other time, Tessa might have smiled at the thought of her young, unsure self and of how far she had come since that day, but now the unbidden memory only increased her apprehension.

Coming back to Yorkshire had been a huge mistake. She was seriously considering going to the ticket booth and asking what time the next train left for London when a young woman dressed in jeans, chunky ankle boots, and a dark green rain jacket rushed up to her.

"Cousin Tessa?"

"Yes."

"I thought it must be you. Not very difficult, really, considering there's no one else left." She gave Tessa a swift hug. "I'm so dreadfully sorry to keep you waiting, but the weather's so bloody everyone's crawling along the A684 and I was late leaving, as usual. Follow me." She picked up Tessa's bags and was walking off with them. "I'm Vicky, by the way," she said, over her shoulder.

"Yes, I rather thought you must be," Tessa replied, laughing. She followed Vicky to a Range Rover, to find a muddied yellow Labrador sitting in the passenger seat.

"Get out of there, Regan, you dirty wretch," Vicky said, shoving the dog onto the back seat. "Sorry about that." She handed Tessa an old towel. "Dry the seat before you sit down or your coat'll get all muddy."

As Vicky put her bags in the back, Tessa scrubbed at the seat. That was all she needed, to arrive at Langley House with a dirty coat. Shades of the first arrival.

Then she stopped. What the hell did it matter what her aunt and Camilla thought of her? She was almost forty years old. Independent, with her own home and an adult son. Who cared what she looked like? She tossed the towel onto the floor and got into the car.

"Okay?" Vicky asked as she started up the engine.

"Just fine," Tessa replied, buckling up her seat belt. "It was kind of you to come and meet me."

"Not at all. We didn't want to send just one of the lads to meet you. After all, this is your first time home in twenty years. Daddy said he'd come, but my mother found something else for him to do."

Thank God for that. The thought of being trapped for an hour alone in a car with Derek Thornton made Tessa break out in a fine sweat. "How is Uncle Steven?" she asked.

"A little better, I think. The pain doesn't seem quite as bad as it was." Vicky glanced at Tessa. "It's bone cancer, you know, so we've no idea how long he will last."

Tessa clenched her hands together in her lap. "Oh, God, I didn't know," she whispered.

"I'm sorry. I thought you did. Of course Papa behaves as if there's nothing the matter with him. He loathes doctors. Thinks they're all a lot of quacks."

Tessa summoned up a smile. "He hasn't changed, then. He always thought that. He used to say that sleeping in the open air was the cure-all for everything." She looked at Vicky's hands firm on the wheel, the nails filed short and stained brown. "Do you smoke?" she asked, wanting to change the subject.

"Not anymore. I stopped a few months ago. But don't let that stop you if you want a cigarette."

"No, I don't smoke."

"Then why did you ask me if I did?"

The bluntness of the Yorkshirewoman.

"I just saw the brown on your fingers and thought—"

"Brown?" Vicky held up one hand. "Oh, that's varnish."

"Varnish? Are you an artist?"

"No, I'm a cabinetmaker. I've been french polishing

this morning. I make furniture. Didn't Papa tell you that?"

"He must have done. Sorry, my brain's not working too well at the moment. I'm still trying to adjust to the time change, I suppose. What sort of furniture?"

"All sorts. I'm working with a furniture maker in York, but I also have my own workshop at home and design a lot of things myself. I'm starting to get commissions from friends."

Tessa frowned. "Isn't someone in the royal family a furniture designer?"

"You mean David Linley, Princess Margaret's son? Yes. But I'm certainly not up to his standard yet. I'm only just starting to work on my own designs."

Tessa leaned her head back against the headrest and contemplated the passing hedges and flat fields. They were still to the east of the A1, the old Great North Road that ran from London to Edinburgh. The country on this side of the A1 was flatter, part of the York plain. When they reached the other side, they would be driving into the Yorkshire Dales, with its far more dramatic scenery: steep-sided fells and flat-topped moorland, and fertile, river-fed dales.

But at present, with the mist and rain, Tessa could see little, apart from hedges and rain-wet villages with their distinctive stone cottages.

"Tired?" Vicky asked. "Why don't you have a sleep?"

"I don't want to miss anything."

"Can't see much at the moment. Weather forecast said it will brighten up for the weekend."

"Oh, good." Tessa turned her head to look out the window again, but it was Vicky she was thinking about, not the scenery. With her cap of red-gold hair delineating her heart-shaped face and her mother's aquamarine eyes, the girl was undeniably beautiful. But she was also far more complex than Tessa had expected her to be. The stained fingers of a crafts-woman and the matter-of-fact manner didn't at all fit into Uncle Steven's picture of a young girl being co-erced into a disastrous marriage by her mother and grandmother.

As they sat waiting for traffic lights to change in Bedale, Vicky turned her head to look at her, but said nothing.

"Have I got mud on my face?" Tessa asked, discon-certed by the girl's appraisal.

"No." Vicky shifted gears and started off again. "I was just trying to decide who it is you remind me of. Someone in the family. Can't be my mother. She's as fair as you are dark. It's not coloring, actually. It's more a certain look."

"I have the Hargrave nose, unfortunately. I can re-member Uncle Steven saying when he first met me that he'd know me anywhere, because of the nose."

"How very tactless of him. But then Papa has never been known for his tact, has he?"

They laughed together, joined by the common bond of love for Steven Hargrave.

"I think it must be him you resemble. It's just a way of looking you both have. Sort of a wry, side-ways look."

Tessa's smile faded. "A sneaky look."

"No, not at all. What on earth made you say that?"

"That's what your grandmother used to call it."

"Oh." Vicky glanced at her. "I gather you don't like her."

"She never liked me, I'm afraid. She never gave me the chance to like her."

"I admit Grandmother can be pretty domineering at times, but she's been wonderful to me."

"I'm sure she has. You are your mother's daugh-ter." Tessa immediately wished that she could take the words back.

"Aha, I sense some repressed hostility here."

Tessa shook her head. "Sorry. I must really be feeling tired. It's all water under the bridge. Twenty years have passed. I'm sure things will be very different between us after all this time."

"I knew there must be some mystery about you. Everyone has been acting very strangely since you rang to say you were coming home. Grandmother is barely speaking to Papa and my parents are fighting even more than usual."

"I'm sorry to have caused so much consternation," Tessa said stiffly. "I merely wanted to see my uncle." As she'd feared, the next few days certainly were not going to be a picnic.

"What's the big secret?"

"I beg your pardon."

"Now you're sounding like my grandmother at her iciest." Vicky laughed. "I just meant, why are they all so upset about you coming to visit? No one will tell me."

"I can't think of any reason," Tessa said, "apart from the fact that I married the head groom years ago."

"I knew that part. Is that all?"

"Yes. It definitely wasn't an acceptable thing for me to do. Class distinction, and all that garbage. But I often wonder if they weren't more upset about losing John Maltby than about me breaking the class code. He was a very good stable groom."

"What happened to him?"

Tessa was tempted to reply sharply that it was time to stop the third degree. "He's dead."

Vicky's face flooded with color. "Oh, God, what an idiot I am. I am sorry. I've been inexcusably nosy. I'll shut up now and let you rest. I am sorry, Tessa."

"That's okay." Tessa felt sorry for Vicky. She could remember the tactlessness of youth and the excruciating embarrassment that followed it. "We'd been divorced for years when it happened, anyway. He died in a stable fire in Kentucky."

"Oh, how terrible. But you had your son Jason, at least. That must have made it much easier. You weren't completely alone in a strange country, were you?"

Tessa had to smile at Vicky's eagerness to make everything right. How naive she was! Being left alone in Canada with a child to support had hardly been easy.

"Let's talk about happier things." She leaned forward to look out. "I do believe the weather is beginning to clear."

"There was a strong wind blowing up the dale when I left. That should get rid of the rain."

The fells were ahead of them now, their summits wreathed in cloud and mist. Tessa felt a sudden rush of excitement. She was coming home. Whatever the reception might be at Langley House itself, this countryside, with its erratic weather, its broad dales and sloping fells, the unspoiled moorland where she'd walked alone so often, only the cry of the curlew breaking the profound silence . . . all this was her home.

She hadn't realized until this moment how very much she had missed it.

They drove through the busy market town of Leyburn, across the windswept moor, and then down the steep fellside road that led to Langley. As they descended, Tessa caught a glimpse of the large limestone house and then it was hidden from them by trees and hedges.

Too late now to go back, she thought, fighting panic. When they arrived at the lodge, Vicky pressed a control button and the iron gates swung open for them. They drove down the straight avenue lined with lime trees, drawing nearer and nearer to the house, which stood on a slight rise.

"He must have seen us coming."

"Who?" asked Tessa, her heart hammering in her chest.

"Papa. He's standing on the steps, waving."

"Uncle Steven?" Tessa said incredulously. "But I thought he was confined to bed, so sick he couldn't—"

"Not him. He wouldn't give in that easily."

It was too late to say any more. The Range Rover drew up before the gray limestone mansion, the car door was flung open, and Tessa drawn out. She felt her uncle's tweed-covered arms about her, his mustache brushing her cheek, and breathed in the familiar smell of pipe smoke from him.

She was home again.

Chapter Five

"I can't believe you're really here," Uncle Steven said. "I've thought of this so often, but—" He turned away abruptly to bark an order about Tessa's luggage to a stable lad hovering nearby.

"It's wonderful to be here with you," she told him, meaning it where *he* was concerned at least.

He turned to beam at her, his eyes suspiciously bright. "You're a bad lass to have kept away for so long."

"I know I am, but I'm here now."

"I'm glad you are." He hugged her close to his side, so close that she could feel how little flesh there was on the bones beneath the striped shirt and tweed jacket. "Come on inside and meet the others."

A rush of panic swept over her as he led her up the steps. *I can't do this,* she thought. Then she was inside the vast hall with its black-and-white tiled floor and ornate pillars. She had forgotten how large and very imposing Langley House was. The hall was almost as large as the entrance hall of the Manitoba Legislature, for heaven's sake. Ridiculous to think of only one family living here.

Her aunt and cousin were the only members of that family waiting to greet her. That came as a relief. She wasn't sure she could have coped with everyone at once.

The first shock was the sight of Aunt Sybil in a

wheelchair. The second was that her aunt's hair had turned from jet-black to snow-white. The two things combined to make her seem less intimidating. Then she spoke, and the old fears flooded back. Aunt Sybil's voice had not changed. It was still ice-cold and smooth as silk, with that upper-class intonation that suggested both ennui and superiority.

"Welcome to Langley, Tessa. It has been a very long time." She extended her scarlet-tipped hand to Tessa, but the wheelchair remained immobile, so that Tessa had to go to her.

"Thank you, Aunt Sybil." She bent to kiss the rouged cheek her aunt proffered her. The aroma of Joy, with its cloying lilies-of-the-valley scent, enveloped her, so heavy that she found it hard to breathe.

She straightened up to face her cousin. Camilla had aged, too, of course. There were fine lines around her eyes, but her complexion was still creamy, her hair still golden—although that probably came from a bottle nowadays—and, if anything, she was slimmer than before. Any hopes that Tessa might have had of her cousin having run to fat were disappointed.

"Hallo, Cousin Tessa," Camilla said in her husky voice, the one Tessa knew she had cultivated from the age of thirteen. They touched cheeks and swiftly drew apart.

"How about a sherry?" Uncle Steven asked when he had crossed the hall, leaning heavily on his ebony stick. "You must be dying for a drink after that long journey."

"It's time you went back to bed, Steven," his wife said. "You've been up far too long, as it is."

"I am not going to bed on the day my niece comes home for the first time in twenty years."

Sensing that she was causing trouble already, Tessa jumped in. "I need to freshen up, get out of these damp shoes," she told her uncle. "Why don't you rest for half an hour, then I'll come and find you?"

"Are you sure?"

"Of course."

"You'll wake me if I'm asleep?" He gave his wife a swift glance from beneath his heavy eyebrows to make sure she got the message.

"I'll wake you, I promise." Tessa laid her hand on his arm. "We've a lot of news to catch up with." She could feel the tremor of his arm beneath her hand and knew how it taxed him even to stand here, leaning on his stick.

"I'll send up a decanter of sherry, then. How would that do?"

"That would be lovely."

"Amontillado? I have a particularly good one."

"Perfect." Tessa smiled at him, warmed by his desire to please her.

"I'll fetch James to help you upstairs, Papa," Vicky said.

"I'm not going upstairs. I'll lie down on the couch in the library. You'll find me there, Tessa."

Tessa nodded and watched Vicky help her grandfather across the hall and into the library. "I really like Vicky," she said to Camilla, glad to find something of her cousin that she could like.

No one replied.

"Why don't you take Cousin Tessa upstairs to her room, Camilla?" Aunt Sybil suggested.

"If you tell me which room I'm in, I expect I can find my own way."

"Not at all. I'll take you upstairs." Camilla led the way across the hall, her heels tapping on the floor, her body swaying in the familiar sensual walk. That, too, she had cultivated in her early teens. Tessa remembered watching her practice it in front of the long mirror in the portrait gallery.

"We've put you in the Gainsborough room," Camilla said over her shoulder.

"Oh . . . Thank you. I always loved that room." Tessa was surprised that they would give her one of their finest guest bedrooms. Her own room had been on the third floor, tiny and sparsely furnished. A box room, in effect.

"Daddy wanted you to have the Gainsborough."

"And I expect your mother wanted to put me in my old room." The words were out before Tessa could stop them.

Camilla halted and swung around at the head of the wide staircase, so that Tessa almost collided with her. "My mother would have preferred not to put you anywhere." Her aquamarine eyes glared at Tessa.

Tessa stepped around her cousin. "Such a warm welcome, Camilla," she said, forcing herself to smile. "But, then, it's no more than I expected."

Camilla started off down the corridor, her back straight beneath the close-fitting black dress. "Then you should not have come, should you?"

Tessa caught up to Camilla. She grasped her arm, swinging her around to face her. "Let's get one thing straight from the start, Camilla. I am here only to see Uncle Steven. He told me in his letter that he was ill and asked me to come before it was too late."

Camilla shook herself free and marched ahead again, stopping before the open door of the Gainsborough bedroom. She pushed the door open farther and motioned to Tessa to go inside.

The room was exactly as she remembered it, decorated in blue and ivory to match the coloring of the portrait by Gainsborough of a woman in a chipstraw hat and blue silk dress with a spaniel at her feet.

Tessa's case and flight bag sat in the center of the room, no doubt carried up the servant's staircase by the lad who'd brought them in from the car. They looked rather out of place in this beautiful room. No doubt Camilla traveled with a full set of Louis Vuitton luggage.

"Shall I send for someone to help you unpack?" Camilla asked.

Tessa laughed. "No, you certainly won't." Her laughter subsided when she saw Camilla's surprise. "Thanks for the offer, though. You must remember that I've been living in a completely different world from yours for twenty years."

"An exciting world, I'm sure. You're a stewardess, Father told us." Camilla sounded like the Queen trying to make conversation with one of her lowly subjects.

Tessa bit back her anger. "They call us flight attendants nowadays. Yes, it is quite exciting. I love traveling."

"But I'm sure you can't make much money from it." Camilla crossed the room to one of the tall windows and pulled back the blue silk drapes to let in the light. "There, that's better."

"I manage."

"It can't be easy, though, with a son to take care of and to educate as well. I hear that university is very expensive in North America."

Surely that wasn't a trace of sympathy Tessa was hearing in Camilla's voice? It couldn't be. The light suddenly dawned. "Is that what you're afraid of? That I'm here to wheedle money out of your father for Jason's education?"

Camilla's cheeks reddened. "Of course not. I never said—"

"I know you never said it, but that's what you're thinking, isn't it? You and your mother. You think I'm here for what I can get. Well, let me tell you that I dreaded coming here. It took all my courage to get on that plane. I felt physically sick as we were driving up the driveway. Do you really think—after all that happened to me in this house—that I could come back here just to ask my uncle for money?"

Tessa's tirade seemed to have frozen Camilla. Her face was white, her hands clenched at her sides. "I never said anything about money," she said through stiff lips.

"Perhaps you didn't, but that's what you were thinking, I'm sure. Why else would I have come back to Langley after twenty years? To your mind, money would be the only reason, right?"

Tears swam in Camilla's eyes. She had always been good at that, too. "I don't know why you came back. I don't know how you could." She fumbled in her sleeve and drew out a handkerchief.

Tessa hadn't seen a woman carry a handkerchief for years. How pathetic Camilla looked, dabbing at her eyes with the tiny lace-edged bit of cloth. She felt the anger drain from her as quickly as it had come. "I don't know how I could, either, Camilla. It wasn't easy. To be honest, it was a real struggle for me. I did it for Uncle Steven. I decided that I must see him again before it was too late." She gave a wry smile. "I must say I was really surprised to see him waiting for me on the steps. I thought he'd be in his bed, that he was dying."

Camilla's lips trembled. "He is. But he won't accept it."

"What's new?"

They both smiled involuntarily, joined for a brief moment by past memories. Then Camilla sniffed and pushed her handkerchief back in her sleeve. "I expect he laid it on rather thick to get you here."

"He must have done." Tessa hesitated, and then said, "Don't worry. It will be for just a few days. I'll keep out of your way, I promise you."

Camilla waved her hands in a little gesture of embarrassment. "It's all very awkward. I really don't know what to say to you."

"If you're talking about the past, please say nothing," Tessa said, her voice rising. "I'm here to see Uncle Steven for a few days, that's all. Then I'll be flying back to Canada."

"Do you like it there?" Camilla asked, returning to her royal family act. "In Winnipeg? *Winnipeg,*" she repeated, exaggeratedly enunciating the name. "What a strange name that is."

"It's Indian. Cree. Yes, I like it very much. It's a very cosmopolitan city. Great theater and ballet and opera. And I like living with people who have all kinds of backgrounds; Italian, Ukrainian, Polish . . . In Winnipeg the Brits are just one part of the population."

Camilla looked at her with astonishment. "But I thought Canada was a British colony."

"Well, it ain't so anymore, dear cousin. I hope you don't talk about Canada being a British colony at one of your society dinners. There might be some millionaire Canadian developer or newspaper baron there who would take exception to it."

"The last Canadians I met at a dinner were Conrad Black and Barbara Amiel."

"Exactly so. I don't think a newspaper baron and a famous columnist would take kindly to being called colonials, do you?"

Camilla quickly changed the subject. "Do you have a nice house in Winnipeg?" She was fussing with the drapes at the other window, tying them back with the gold-tasseled cord as she spoke.

"I have a condominium." Camilla appeared baffled by the word. "It's like a maisonette," Tessa explained. "An apartment. Only my particular apartment is on three levels." She looked around the vast bedroom with its exquisite antique furniture. "If you lumped all my rooms together they would fit nicely into this one room, I should imagine."

"How on earth can you live in such a small place? I would find it dreadfully claustrophobic."

"My bedroom in Winnipeg is double the size of the bedroom I had here."

"Oh, surely not." Camilla busied herself with smoothing the padded silk bedcover.

"On the top floor, remember? You used to tell me it was the scullery maid's room."

"Of course, it wasn't. How horrid children can be, can't they?" Camilla's laugh was brittle. She crossed the room to stand by the door, now anxious to get away. "Anything at all you need, just press the bell and Mrs. Whitton will attend to you."

"Whitton? Was she here when I was?"

"No. She took over from old Mrs. Humphreys two years ago. You remember Mrs. Humphreys?"

"Yes. She came here when I was sixteen." Tessa felt a sense of heaviness around her heart. That particular year had been a year of great loss for her.

"She had a heart attack and had to retire. We were very fortunate to find Mrs. Whitton. Not many people want to go into service nowadays. Of course, she's not of the old school. Doesn't like to be given orders." Camilla gave a little smile. "Mother finds that rather difficult."

"I imagine she would."

"But as Mrs. Whitton is extremely efficient, Mother puts up with it."

"That's good."

Now that the subject of the housekeeper was exhausted, neither of them seemed to be able to think of anything else to talk about.

After an awkward moment of silence, Camilla said, "I'm going riding this afternoon. Would you like to come?"

"No, thanks. I never did care much for riding."

"No, that's right. You didn't." Camilla gave her an artificial little smile. "How very strange that is, considering you grew up at Langley," she said. Then she was gone, the door clicking shut behind her, before Tessa could think up a suitable reply.

For a few seconds she stood in the center of the room still staring at the closed door. Then she smiled to herself. She had probably seemed thoroughly obnoxious to Camilla, but at least she felt that she could stand up to her cousin now and give as good as she got.

As she crossed the room to go to the window, Tessa breathed in a waft of Camilla's perfume. Even here in this room, with the door closed, she couldn't escape her.

She struggled to open the sash window, so that she could let in some fresh air, but found it too heavy for her to lift on her own.

Then she remembered the Nilodor deodorizer in her toilet bag. Crossing the room again, she opened her flight bag and found the tiny green bottle. She toured the room, putting dots of Nilodor on the marble-topped dressing table, the oval rosewood table, and the eighteenth-century Italian chest of drawers.

"Oh, Lord," she suddenly said aloud. "I hope it won't mark them." It had been a constant fear of hers, living in this house of treasures, that she would mark or break something.

She felt a sudden longing for the plain servant's furniture of her old room, and for its size. This room swamped her.

"And it's also bloody cold," she said to herself, a shiver running over her shoulders and down her back.

There was a fireplace, but as it was occupied by an open Chinese fan, it was doubtful that it was ever used. At least, not in the summer. Thank God she'd brought warm pajamas.

She knew from experience that even in the summertime there was nowhere colder than an English stately home, with its vast, high-ceilinged rooms and inadequate heating.

She was tempted to have a hot bath—if there was any hot water in the middle of the day—but then decided that she didn't have time. She had promised to go to her uncle after half an hour and that left only fifteen minutes for her to wash and change.

She took off her blouse, skirt, and panty hose—tossing them onto a chair with gilded arms—and went into the bathroom. It had changed, having been completely modernized with fancy ivory bathroom fixtures with gold-colored taps.

She was cleaning her teeth when she heard a knock on the bedroom door.

"Just a minute," she shouted, pulling on the fluffy white toweling robe that was draped over the heated towel rail. She went back into he bedroom. "Come in," she called out. The bedroom door opened. "Sorry, I was—"

A man stood there, tall, heavyset, dressed in casual riding clothes: jodhpurs and tweed hacking jacket. "Hallo, Tessa. Long time no see."

Tessa felt as if she were paralyzed. Her tongue seemed to have stuck to the roof of her mouth. "Hello, Derek," she managed to say. "How are you?" As he came nearer, she quickly held out her hand.

"Oh, well enough, I suppose. Mustn't grumble."

She gazed at him, still tongue-tied. Had he always talked in clichés like this? she wondered. Surely not. It must be embarrassment. She knew that *she* was excruciatingly embarrassed.

He had taken her hand and was holding it between both of his. She drew it away and stepped back from him, her heart beating fast. "I'm sorry. I was just getting changed." She drew up the collar of the bathrobe and tightened the belt.

His face grew redder. "Sorry about that. Bad timing." But he still stood there, his eyes—still very blue—gazing at her. "I wanted—" He cleared his throat. "I wanted to see you alone. Without the rest of them being there."

"I'm not sure that's a good idea." Tessa went to the window by the bed, determined to set some distance between them.

"I can imagine what you're thinking," Derek Thornton said.

Could he? She doubted it. She was utterly shocked by the change in him. At first she had thought Derek was his father, he had become so like him in looks. How could a man who had been so good-looking and debonair and sophisticated have changed so much in twenty years? With his sunburned face and fading red hair he looked more like a caricature of an English squire than the man who . . .

He came to her across the room. "Little Tessa. Not little anymore, though. You've grown into a beautiful, mature woman." His rich voice had always made her think of mellow cognac. Now, it reminded her more of plum pudding. She felt the window at her back, the wooden sill pressing into her waist.

He held out his hands to her. "Have you been able to forgive me, Tessa?"

"Of course I have," she said lightly.

"I was a fool. A bloody fool." He came a little closer.

Okay, buster, she thought, *let's stop it right there.*

"Excuse me, Derek, but I must get dressed. I promised Uncle Steven I'd be down to see him." She looked at her watch. "I'm already ten minutes late."

"It must be a great shock for you, I know, seeing me again."

You can say that again, she thought, and wanted to laugh . . . and cry.

"Could we continue this later, Derek? I really must get dressed."

"I understand. You need a few minutes to collect your thoughts."

She nodded. To her utter dismay, tears filled her eyes and spilled down her cheeks.

That was all the encouragement Derek needed. "Oh, my dear," he said, taking her in his arms. She could smell whiskey on his breath. She shoved against his chest, taking him by surprise so that he almost fell against the bedside table.

"No, Derek," she said, making for the center of the room. "Please leave."

"But we have so much to talk over."

"Leave *now.*"

He shrugged his broad shoulders. "I know how difficult this must be for you. We'll meet again, later, when you're feeling more composed."

It sounded like the farewell of a comic villain. Except that Derek Thornton had once been her hero.

He stood there, staring at her, looking pathetic with his watery eyes. Drawing a checked handkerchief from his pocket, he loudly blew his nose. Then he opened the door, turning to give her a sad smile before leaving the room.

Swiftly Tessa crossed the room to lock the door with the large gilt key. Then she threw herself into one of the wing chairs by the fireplace and abandoned herself to a fit of weeping.

She wept for all her lost dreams, for the wasted years, for her own stupidity. But most of all she was weeping because the smile Derek had given her as he left the room had been the only part of him that had conjured up the man she had once loved so passionately. The man she'd thought she had never stopped loving during the past twenty years.

Chapter Six

Several minutes passed before Tessa was able to compose herself as Derek had put it. She was just pulling on her kelly-green cable sweater when another knock came at the door. Not again!

"Who is it?" she called.

"Vicky."

"Come in." The handle rattled. "Oops, sorry. It's locked. Hang on a minute." Tessa went to the door and unlocked it.

"Papa wondered if you'd lost your way. He sent me to find you."

"Sorry. I got sort of delayed."

Vicky peered at her. "Are you okay?"

"Sure I am. Why?"

"You look like you've been crying."

Tessa turned away. "Come on in. I've just got to brush my hair." She went into the bathroom. Damn, Vicky was right. Her eyes were all swollen and red. That was all she needed.

She added more eye shadow and mascara to try to cover up the signs.

"Ready," she said brightly as she came out of the bathroom.

"I was right. You have been crying," Vicky said. "What's wrong?"

"Oh, just memories crowding in. Let's go, before Uncle Steven sends up a search party for us."

The library had always been Tessa's favorite room in the house. In a day that was threatening to overwhelm her with memories this room—with its book-lined walls and comfortable couches and chairs, and the print stand in the corner—held mainly happy ones for her.

Her uncle was sitting in his green leather armchair by the welcoming fire. "Surely that's not the same chair?" she asked, seeing how worn the leather on the arms had become.

"The same chair as what?" demanded Uncle Steven in his old pedantic style.

"The same chair as you were using when—when—"

"When you ran away from here, twenty years ago? Yes, it's the same one. Your Aunt Sybil complains that it looks shabby, but that's too damned bad. It's taken me all these years to get this one to conform to my body. I'm not about to go through the same process with a new one." He gestured to the sofa with his stick. "Don't hover over me, Tessa. Sit down."

Tessa did as she was told. They looked at each other, neither of them speaking. Then she said softly, "How are you, Uncle Steven?"

"I'm as you see me," he replied. "Sitting in a chair with my feet up on a stool, like a bloody old man."

"I must admit I expected to find much worse. Your letter made me think you were . . . well, that you might be in bed all the time."

" 'The reports of my death are greatly exaggerated,' " he quoted with a dry chuckle. "That's where Sybil would like to keep me, in my bed, out of the way, so I don't know what's going on."

Tessa hesitated, not knowing quite how to put it. Then she plunged in. "You said that I should come and see you before it's too late."

"Precisely. I'm concerned that it's too late already, though."

"What is too late?" she asked, knowing now that he wasn't referring to the state of his health.

"Victoria's marriage to Jeremy Kingsley."

Light dawned. "Is that what you were talking about? Vicky's marriage?"

"Certainly it was. What else would it have been?"

There was no way she could give him the obvious reply. "But what on earth can I do to help?" she asked him. "Vicky and I have only just met. Besides, she strikes me as a young woman who knows her own mind. Certainly not the sort to be talked into a marriage against her will."

"Good in bed."

"What?"

"The fellow's good in bed."

She couldn't hide her smile. "How do you know that?"

"Victoria positively glows when he's here."

"Love can make you glow."

"So can lust. Besides, she told me he's good in bed. And he's damned good-looking, as you'll see."

"Will I? Is he here, then?"

"He will be tomorrow. Usually drives up here at the weekend."

"If Vicky likes him, why don't you?"

"Reminds me of Derek." He looked at her over his glasses.

"Oh." Tessa bent down to pat the brindled spaniel stretched out before the fire.

"Need I say more?" her uncle demanded.

"I suppose not." She hoped fervently that he wouldn't.

"He has the same good looks as Derek once had and the same attitude that women were made just to please him."

Don't say any more, she begged him silently. But now that he was on the subject of Derek, he obviously intended to say a great deal more. "And he's seduced my darling Vicky, just as Derek Thornton seduced you and Camilla."

Tessa kept her gaze fixed on the leaping flames, sick at heart. "That all happened a very long time ago, Uncle Steven. I don't even want to think about it."

"Yours wasn't the only life Derek ruined, you know. He ruined Camilla's, too. He's made her life a misery."

Tessa lifted her head. "Are you asking me to feel sorry for Camilla?"

"You were lucky. You escaped from his clutches. She didn't."

"I was lucky?" Tessa leaned forward, her breath coming fast. "I ran from Derek to an abusive husband, a hellish marriage it took me years to recover from. I also had a child and no money. For my child's sake, I had to get on my feet and stop feeling sorry for myself. And yet you are asking me to feel sorry for Camilla, who's never had to do a day's work if she didn't want to, and whose mummy and daddy are still looking after her, even though she's almost forty years old."

It was his face that stopped her. Not his expression, but the fact that his face was as white as one of the small marble statues on the desk behind him.

"I'm sorry. I should keep my big mouth shut."

He stared at her, his eyes fixed glassily on her, so that she grew afraid. She went to him, kneeling beside the footstool. "I'm sorry, Uncle Steven. I shouldn't have said that."

"Yes, you should. I never realized . . . You never told me that your marriage had been such a bad one."

"By the time I wrote you that first letter, the marriage was over. Did you really think I would write and tell you that John Maltby had been an abusive husband and had run off with every penny I ever earned, leaving me with nothing but his debts? I can just see Camilla and Aunt Sybil reading that and saying, 'Well, it's no more than I would have expected.' "

She thought he would defend his wife and daughter, but he said nothing and sat, one arm hanging beside the arm of the chair, his face averted. "Let's talk about more cheerful things, shall we?" she begged. "Please."

But he wasn't to be moved. "You have been used abominably by this family," he said, fixing his gaze on the fire. "I brought you here for my dead brother's sake. I vowed that I would give you a good life and treat you like another daughter. I failed miserably."

The catch in his throat brought her to her feet. She flung her arms around him and then took his thin face between her hands, forcing him to look at her. "You didn't fail," she said fiercely. "You gave me a home and I always knew that you cared about me."

"No one else did, though."

It hurt her to hear him admit it, even after all these years, but at least he was now telling the truth that had been denied her for so long. "You can't force people to love someone," she told him. "Aunt Sybil didn't want me here. You insisted that I come. That must have driven a wedge between you both."

"You were my brother's only child. What else should I have done?"

She gave him a sad smile. "Sent me to a boarding school, perhaps?"

"I went to one of those places myself. I was desperately unhappy there. I hated playing their stupid sports and preferred walking in the countryside and bird watching. They used to put dead birds in my bed."

She had always thought of her uncle as a figure of great power, inscrutable, invincible. Now that he was telling her about his childhood fears she saw how vulnerable all people were, hiding behind the positions of authority that were imposed upon them.

"Knowing what they were like," he said, "how could I possibly send you away to a boarding school?"

"You were right," she said. "I would have been terribly unhappy." No point now in telling him that she probably would have been far happier in a boarding school than she'd been at Langley. "You gave me a home and a good education."

"And then you fell in love with Derek."

"What a fine way to repay you for all you'd done for me," she said lightly. "I've seen him, you know."

"Derek? When?"

"Just before I came down. He came to my room. That's why I was a bit late."

He frowned. "I hope he didn't make a nuisance of himself. If he did, I'll warn him off for you."

She sat back on the sofa again. "Let's get one thing straight, dear uncle. I'm a big girl now. I don't need anyone to fight my battles for me anymore. Even with Derek." She raised her eyebrows at him. "*Especially* not with Derek."

"Ah, the typical American woman. Free, independent."

"That's exactly what I am and what I intend to remain. Free and independent ... of men, in particular. And I'm a Canadian or *North* American, if you don't mind, not American."

"What did he want?" her uncle asked, ignoring the rest.

"Derek? He didn't really get around to it. I cut him short."

"Good girl. That's exactly what he needs."

"If you dislike him so much, why do you have him and Camilla living here with you?"

"Several reasons. That way I can keep an eye on him and make sure he's treating Camilla properly.

She's like a hothouse flower, you know, my daughter. She's never been very strong, physically. She needs a great deal of care and attention."

You can say that again, thought Tessa.

"It also pleases your aunt to have Camilla living here. She's not as able to get around as well as she used to since she had the stroke and Camilla is very good with her. Far more patient than I am, I'm ashamed to admit."

That surprised Tessa. She had never considered patience to be one of Camilla's attributes.

"Apart from all that, Derek has been surprisingly good with overseeing the race stables. I've made him a full partner and he's taken over a large amount of my work. I employ good men, of course, trainer, stable manager ... the best. So the stables really run themselves, but still I must admit Derek does quite well. Or, at least, he did," he muttered under his breath.

"So you are all one big happy family."

Her uncle gave her a sharp look. "Do I detect a hint of sarcasm there?"

"Not at all."

He shook his head a little and smiled at her. "You have definitely changed from the shy, retiring little mouse you were when you first arrived at Langley."

"I should hope so."

"You always did say what you thought, of course. A surprising characteristic in one so shy. But now you've become positively aggressive."

"I prefer to call it assertive."

"Whatever. I'm not sure I like the American accent, though."

She didn't bother to correct him this time. "I've been in Canada almost twenty years, Uncle Steven. I'm a Canadian now."

"It must have been hard to adapt to such a different life."

"At first it was. Very hard. But I wouldn't exchange it for anywhere else now."

"Not even for Langley?"

"No, definitely not for Langley. All this"—she waved her hands at the walls lined with books, the painted ceiling, the Chippendale desk—"all this is totally alien to me. I could never come back to it." She didn't want to hurt him by telling him how utterly anachronistic she found this house, the family, the entire way of life.

"I'm sorry to hear it," he said sadly.

"Please don't be. I'm here with you now and that means the world to me."

"And to me, too." He cleared his throat, obviously not wanting to dwell on this emotional note. "Now that you are here, what are you going to do to help me with Vicky?"

"Oh, dear," she said with a sigh. "I really don't see how I can help."

"That's why you came, isn't it?" he demanded. "To help me deal with this problem. I asked you to come before it was too late, and you did, thank God. So let's not waste time. What can we do about it?"

Not wanting to risk upsetting him by telling him that she was here because she'd thought he was on the verge of dying, Tessa decided to humor him. "Do you think Vicky doesn't love her fiancé?"

"She thinks she does. I think it's nothing but lust."

"But why on earth would she want to marry him, then? Surely they could just live together."

"He's a fine catch. He'll be an earl when his father dies."

"Vicky didn't seem to me to be the sort of person who'd worry about such things."

He looked at her with astonishment. "Not worry about becoming a countess one day? My dear child, you really are living on another planet. The family is

also immensely well off. They have not only the Ayncliffe estate itself, but properties in London and
Derbyshire."

"So he's handsome, rich, good in bed, and loves
Vicky. I take it that he does love her?"

"Utterly infatuated. Acts like a stupid puppy
around her."

"Infatuation's not love."

"That's what I'm afraid of."

"What do Vicky's parents think of all this?"

"Oddly enough, Derek's not keen on Jeremy, but
he likes the thought of being connected with the Ayncliffes, of course."

"I don't know why. I should imagine the Thorntons
have been landed gentry in Yorkshire far longer than
Lord Ayncliffe's family has."

"You are right there. The Thornton family was a
great supporter of the Yorkists, back in the fifteenth
century. Thornton Manor was built on the land they
were given by Edward IV after he took the throne."
He sighed. "The Thorntons may be an ancient family,
but unfortunately they don't have a great deal of
money left. Anything they had, Derek's father gam-
bled and drank it away, God rest him."

Tessa was about to ask a question, but decided that
this wasn't the time. "But Camilla is all for the
marriage?"

He sighed. "Camilla is swept away by her mother's
ecstasy over the entire matter. Sybil's family has been
landed gentry for more than three hundred years.
They've had Langley for two hundred and fifty of
those years. But they've never been allied with a title
before. This is her big chance."

"I really don't see what I can do if everyone, except
you, is in favor of the marriage, including the future
bride and groom."

Impatiently throwing aside the rug, he lowered his

legs to the floor, groaning as he did so. "All I ask is that you observe them both together. Let me know what you think. And watch Vicky with Kevin Taylor as well."

"Who on earth is Kevin Taylor?"

"He's my estate manager. Good chap. A local man. His father was a Richmond builder. Made enough money to give Kevin a fine education. Cambridge."

"What has he got to do with Vicky?"

"Keep your eyes open and you'll see."

"I feel like a spy."

He beamed at her. "That's exactly what you'll be. My spy."

"I'm here for only a few days, Uncle Steven."

"That's what you said on the telephone. We'll see."

"I'm sorry, but I have to go back to London on Tuesday morning," Tessa said firmly. "My flight leaves on Wednesday."

"I thought you airline people could fly whenever you wanted to?"

"Not in July, we can't. It's the busy season. Besides, Jason is due home in Winnipeg next Thursday. And I have to get back to work." She had no intention of telling him that she had been laid off.

"You should have brought Jason here with you. I'd like to have met your son. I hope he's like you, not Maltby."

Her heart constricted. "Of course he is. One day, we'll come and stay for a long visit," she lied. "Meanwhile, at least you and I have the next three days to enjoy."

"Only three?" He released a heavy sigh. "Ah well, we must make the best of it, mustn't we?" As he struggled to his feet, reaching for his stick, Tessa went to help him.

A knock came at the library door. "Come," her uncle shouted.

A young man put his head around the door. "Sorry, Mr. Hargrave. I thought you were alone."

"Come on in, Kevin. This is my niece, Tessa Hargrave, come to visit us all the way from Canada."

Kevin came across to them. He was of medium height, probably in his late twenties. Pleasant-looking, rather than handsome.

"How do you do, Miss Hargrave," he said, shaking her hand firmly. He had a direct way of looking at you which Tessa took to immediately. "Welcome to Langley."

"Welcome *back,*" her uncle corrected him.

Kevin grinned at Tessa, not at all put out. "Welcome back to Langley."

"What can I do for you?" Uncle Steven asked him.

"It's not that urgent. I can come back later."

"No, let's deal with it now, while it's quiet." Her uncle turned to Tessa. "You can find things to do to pass the time, I'm sure, Tessa, my dear?"

"I certainly can. I haven't even unpacked yet. And I want to walk around the gardens."

"Might be a good idea to put on some boots," Kevin told her. "It's stopped raining, but it's still pretty wet out there. The wooded parts are particularly muddy."

"Thanks."

She crossed the room and was about to leave when her uncle called after her. "And don't forget to put on something extra pretty for dinner tonight."

"Oh, is it something special tonight, then?"

"Yes, it certainly is special."

"What?"

"It's a big celebration. My niece has come home after being away for twenty years."

Tessa's eyes filled with tears. She rushed across the room to fling her arms around her uncle's neck and kiss his thin cheek. "I love you," she whispered, not caring a bit that Kevin Taylor was standing there, pretending to be reading the papers in his hand.

"I love you, too, dearest Tessa." Her uncle patted her on the back. "I meant what I said, though. Put something pretty on. Philip Thornton is coming to dinner and he needs something to cheer him up."

Chapter Seven

After she had left her uncle, Tessa walked for almost two hours in the gardens. The lovely grounds brought her tranquillity and a chance to sort out her thoughts.

The gardens of Langley had been famous since before the Second World War, but it was her uncle who had changed and developed them. He had softened the classic formality of the long garden that stretched from the stone terrace to the little river, a quarter of a mile away. He had also created several smaller, more intimate gardens and little sheltered corners. Tessa remembered that even on the busiest of Sundays—when the gardens were open to the public—she could always find a spot to be alone.

The secluded grotto, with its little waterfall tumbling down the rocks, had always been her special place of refuge.

Today, she seemed to have the gardens entirely to herself, apart from a chance meeting with two young gardeners in mud-splattered jeans, who smiled and said, "Afternoon, miss," when they saw her.

By the time she went into the house again, she felt far more settled and capable of dealing with the evening that awaited her.

When she had first stepped out onto the terrace, dressed in an old waterproof jacket and green rubber boots that were a size too large for her, her mind had teen filled with the thought of having to cope with a formal dinner party with her formidable family. But then she remembered that Philip Thornton would be there. When they were young, Philip, who was Derek's elder brother, had always cast some strange calming spell over them all, like a wise magician, keeping them from getting too much out of hand.

As she began dragging off her muddy boots in the back hall, she planned a long, hot bath scented with the new bath oil she'd bought at the airport. She had plenty of time to wash and blow-dry her hair and, for a change, generally pamper herself.

She was struggling with the second boot, holding on to the door handle, with her back to the hallway, when a voice said, "May I help?"

She spun around, almost falling over, the boot still half on, to find a man standing there, leaning on a long, cane-handled umbrella. His dark hair was brushed with silver at the temples. "Tessa?" he asked with a quizzical tilt of the head.

"Mr. Thornton." The name she had called him until she was sixteen came out automatically. For the first time in years, she felt herself blushing bright scarlet. "It is you, isn't it?"

"I think it is," he said. "Although I do believe we agreed many years ago that you would call me Philip."

So they had. On the day of her sixteenth birthday. It had been the most important mark of her adulthood that the man who was the embodiment of poise and wisdom should have asked her to call him by his first name that day.

She took a deep breath. "I'm sorry, Philip. Give me a minute to get this damned boot off and I'll greet you properly."

"Take your time."

While he turned to put the furled umbrella in the umbrella stand, Tessa managed to drag the boot off.

She hurriedly combed her fingers through her wet hair.

"Was it raining here this afternoon?" Philip asked.

"No, but I was in the beech wood and the trees dripped onto me. The gardens are even more lovely than I remember them. Especially the borders and the rose garden. Uncle Steven has done so much more since I was here. And those rhododendrons he planted when I was quite young are massive now."

She was painfully aware that she was babbling on, in her embarrassment at being caught in such a disheveled state. She wondered if she should kiss Philip or hold out her hand, which was now muddy from the boots.

He solved the problem by taking her lightly by the arms and kissing her cheek. "Welcome home, Tessa. It's about time." It was done in an instant, so smoothly, so easily, in typical Philip style.

She relaxed. "I know. I should have come a long time ago, but I just couldn't get up the courage."

"I'm not surprised. But you were right to come. Steven is very ill."

"I know. That's why I came now." Her mouth trembled. "Vicky told me how bad it is. I like her very much."

"Vicky? I agree. You know that she's engaged to be married?"

"Yes, Uncle Steven wrote and told me." She couldn't tell from Philip's expression what he thought of the engagement. Unlike his brother, Philip Thornton had never been one to allow his emotions to show. And this was certainly not the time or place to ask him his opinion. "I'd love to stay and talk, but I really think I should go and make myself a little more presentable."

"I think you look perfectly fine," he said gallantly. He gazed at her for a moment. "You have changed."

"God, I sincerely hope so. I wouldn't want to be the same person I was when I left here," she said vehemently.

"No. I can understand that you would feel that way. But I sense that twenty years haven't changed you entirely."

What could he mean? For so long she had worked to toughen herself up that she wasn't quite sure who the real Tessa was now. "I'm almost forty, you know," she reminded him. "Quite a different person from the naive girl who ran away from here twenty years ago."

His mouth tilted into that slightly sardonic smile she'd always liked. "And I am fifty. An old man."

She broke into a laugh. "You always seemed old to me, when I was a kid. Someone on a pedestal, ineffably wise. You always had exactly the right answers to everything I wanted to know."

"Lord. You make me sound like some venerable old Greek philosopher."

"That's how I used to think of you, only without the long beard, of course." Her smile died away. "I'm sorry, Philip. I forgot to say how sad I was to hear about your father's death."

"You wrote to me. That was enough."

He had sent her a little note in return. Just three lines, thanking her for having written. For twenty years, she'd had only two notes from him. The other one had been written in reply to the letter she'd sent him about his wife's death from cancer two years ago.

"It must have been difficult for you, losing your father only a year after your wife . . ." Her voice died away as she sensed that he had pulled the shutters down in the old way she remembered, closing himself off. "I just wanted to say it to you in person, that's all."

"Thank you." He glanced at his watch. "Now, I must go to your uncle. He wants to discuss a business matter with me before dinner. We'll have time to catch up later."

"Yes."

He took her hand in his. "It's wonderful to see you again, Tessa."

She nodded, feeling as shy as a schoolgirl, unable to put her feelings into words.

Having released her hand, he stepped back and gave her a little inclination of the head that was the closest thing to an old-fashioned bow a modern man could make, and then strode away.

He hasn't changed at all, Tessa thought. Philip Thornton was still a man of another time, intense, with a strong sense of purpose, but always courteous and kind. A gentleman of the Renaissance rather than the 1990s.

She watched him as he walked down the corridor to the hall, marveling that he still had the lithe figure he'd had when he was thirty. His brother Derek had inherited the auburn hair and height of his father's family, while Philip had the dark coloring of his mother and was a few inches shorter than his brother. But, unlike Derek, Philip had barely changed in physical appearance, apart from the touch of silver in his dark hair and the fine lines about his eyes.

In one other way he had changed. He seemed a little more accessible, less reserved, but then that was probably because they were *both* mature adults now.

As Tessa climbed the wide staircase, she recalled those evenings in the past when she knew that the handsome Thornton brothers were coming to dinner. The feeling of anticipation, of elation, that if Philip were coming she would have someone to talk to, someone to protect her from the constant sniping of the female members of her family. And, later, as she grew older, the sexual excitement at the thought of seeing Derek again. Derek, who had been the first man to kiss her with an open mouth.

She shook her head in an effort to shake those thoughts from her mind. It was all in the past, she told herself firmly. It couldn't hurt her anymore.

On an impulse, she had bought a new dress in Winnipeg, at an exclusive boutique on Academy Road. It had been on sale, but even then it was decadently expensive. She had kept telling herself she should take it back, that she couldn't afford it.

But as she stood in her room, surveying herself in the long oval mirror in its gilded stand, she decided that it had been well worth the money. The dress was made of silk crepe in a gorgeous rich cranberry shade that suited her dark coloring perfectly.

The idea had been, of course, to make Derek realize what he had lost, but when she walked into the drawing room and he came forward to greet her, Tessa immediately wished she were dressed in a neck-to-floor sack.

"You look absolutely ravishing," Derek whispered in her ear and then kissed her fully on the mouth in front of everyone.

She had an almost irresistible impulse to wipe the taste of him away. From the smell of his breath—and the look of him—he'd been indulging liberally in the Scotch since long before the cocktail hour. She felt again that overwhelming sense of disappointment.

Sidling past him, she went directly to her aunt and bent to kiss her powdered cheek. "Good evening, Aunt Sybil."

"Good evening, Tessa. Is your room comfortable enough for you?"

"My room is lovely. Thank you." She didn't know what else to say and her aunt, certainly, showed no sign of wanting to engage her in any further conversation.

"Do you see many changes at Langley?" Philip asked, coming to her rescue.

She gave him a swift grateful smile. "Not yet, but I suppose I'm still trying to adjust. As I was telling Camilla earlier, my entire apartment would probably fit into my bedroom here."

"That's like my place in York," Vicky said from behind them. "I can barely turn around in it."

"It's a hovel," Camilla said disgustedly from the sofa. "I hate to think of you living there."

"It's more than many people have, Mummy. You ought to try living in a cardboard box, like so many of the homeless in the big cities."

"They ought to be working, instead of lying around, taking drugs, and begging in the streets."

Tessa could feel herself tensing up, but before she could say anything Vicky was responding. "There aren't any jobs, Mother. We live in a different world to the one you grew up in. Besides, what would you know about it, living here in a mansion, with everything you could wish for?"

"What nonsense you do talk, Victoria," her grandmother said from her wheelchair.

"It's not nonsense, Grandmother," Vicky retorted, her eyes bright with anger. "It's the truth. But I forgot. This family doesn't like the truth."

Steven's stick rapped on the floor. "That's enough, Victoria. You are forgetting that this is Tessa's homecoming evening. No family squabbles tonight, if you don't mind. Derek, let's have that Pommeroy you got up from the cellar."

"Can I help?" Kevin Taylor came out of the alcove by the window.

As he crossed the room to go to the drinks trolley, Tessa heard Vicky say softly, "Thanks, Kevin."

Watch her with Kevin Taylor, Uncle Steven had said. In fact, it was Vicky who was watching Kevin now as he deftly poured out the champagne into the tall elegant glasses, but Tessa was unable to see her expression. Then Vicky joined him, to take the tray and hand out the glasses.

"Let us raise our glasses in a toast," Uncle Steven said when everyone had been served.

Tessa automatically raised hers. Looking across the room, she caught Philip's smile. Realizing that she was to be the object of their toast, she grimaced at him and lowered her glass.

"I will make my toast a very simple one," her uncle said. "We are celebrating the long-awaited return to her home of my niece, Tessa." He raised his glass high. "Please join me in a toast to Tessa's homecoming."

"Tessa's homecoming," everyone repeated, some more fervently than others.

Only one glass was not raised, one person who did not join in the toast. Tessa saw Aunt Sybil set her champagne glass down with a distinct rap on the table beside her. She could feel the venom in her gaze as it darted across the room at her. Then Sybil was blocked from sight by Vicky.

"Welcome home, again," Vicky said, hugging Tessa. "I'm dying for you to meet Jeremy."

"I'm looking forward to meeting him, too," Tessa said, quite truthfully. Tessa Hargrave, family spy.

"Oh, and you must meet Kevin, our estate manager. Kevin!" Vicky called across the room before Tessa could stop her.

Kevin came directly. "We've already met," Tessa told Vicky, "but, hi again, Kevin."

"Good evening, Miss Hargrave."

"Please call me Tessa."

There was something wary in the back of his eyes.

"It's all right," Tessa said, smiling. "I'm a Canadian, remember? We have a pretty classless society. Although, sometimes I think we go too far the other way. I must admit I loathe being called by my first name by some receptionist in a doctor's or dentist's office. Must be my snooty upbringing."

Kevin responded to her with a grin that lit up his face. She hadn't thought of him as handsome, but Kevin Taylor was a decidedly attractive man when he smiled.

"It's all a load of old nonsense," Vicky said, very decidedly.

To Tessa's surprise, Kevin turned on Vicky. "That's all very fine for you to say, but you'd see how long my job would last here if I called your mother, 'Camilla.' "

"Or how about calling Grandmother 'Sybil'?" Vicky said, giggling. It was all a joke to her, but Tessa could see that it was deadly serious to Kevin.

"It's different for you, Vicky," she said, trying to explain. "You've lived a life of privilege. It's far easier for you to be generous and allow people to call you by your first name. Kevin probably feels that he never knows exactly who he can do that with, so he prefers to be careful about it."

"Dead right," Kevin said.

"I still think it's a load of bullshit," Vicky said. "After all, Kevin went to Cambridge."

A tide of color ran over Kevin's tanned cheeks. "Yes, well, there's no need to go into that."

"Oh, you!" Vicky punched his arm affectionately and went off to fetch more champagne.

Kevin watched her as she crossed the room. Tessa caught the look of open longing in his eyes, before he recollected himself and starting talking politely to her about Langley.

Well, at least she'd learned one thing on her first day at Langley. She wasn't sure about Vicky's feelings for Kevin, but it was patently obvious that Kevin Taylor was very much in love with Vicky.

Chapter Eight

The dinner was served in the formal dining room, one of the finest rooms in the house, with its salmon-pink and gilded paneled walls, and ornate plasterwork ceiling. As she sat down on her uncle's right, Tessa had to adjust to being at a mahogany table that could seat twenty people. She was used to eating perched on a stool at her tiny kitchen counter or from a tray in front of the television.

She also had to readjust to the formality and seeming endlessness of Aunt Sybil's dinners. As it was, excitement mixed with tension had taken away what little appetite she had.

By the time she had been served cold vichyssoise, followed by a plate of finely cut smoked salmon with thin slices of brown bread and butter, Tessa felt that she couldn't eat another bite. Then came the main course, followed by the dessert: a summer pudding served with spoonfuls of thick cream. The meal ended with the presentation of the cheese board, which was more like a cheese *table,* bearing all kinds of cheeses, including a large ripe Stilton, which her uncle tried to persuade her to try.

"You hardly ate anything at all," he complained when they moved back into the drawing room.

"I haven't seen that much food at one meal for years."

"How about an after-dinner brandy, then?"

"I think I'll have one later, if you don't mind. I'm so full, I couldn't fit in even a drink at the moment." The dinner had been a great strain for her. If she didn't escape from them all for a few minutes she would go crazy. "Would you mind if I went for a quick walk just to stretch my legs?"

Philip was helping Derek serve liqueurs. He looked up when he heard her. "I'd like a walk myself. Would you mind having a companion, Tessa?"

"Of course not."

Derek mumbled something beneath his breath and sank down on the sofa, splashing brandy all over himself from the half-filled glass in his hand. Tessa was disturbed by the malevolent glance he gave his brother.

"I'll go and get my coat," she said when she and Philip had escaped into the chilly hall.

"And I'll retrieve my umbrella. Just in case."

She was halfway up the stairs when he spoke again. "Tessa."

"Yes?"

"Are you sure I'm not intruding? You didn't want to be on your own?"

"I did. But that doesn't include you." She gave him a half smile.

He seemed to understand. "I just wanted to make sure."

A few minutes later they stepped out onto the terrace. It was almost dark. The sky still held a faint touch of pink above the clouds that floated across the full moon.

"At least the peacocks quieted down," Tessa said. "I never could understand how such beautiful birds could make such horribly ugly sounds."

"I suppose you can't have everything."

"I suppose not."

They walked in companionable silence across the

wet lawn, listening to the rustlings and twitterings of the evening. As they descended the steps to the lower part of the walk, Philip took her arm. The unexpectedness of his touch sent a dart of electricity through her. He quickly released her, as if he had felt it, too.

"It's rather slippery on those old steps," he said.

"I noticed that this afternoon. Thank you."

As they walked along the wet grassy path, the sweet scents of nicotiana and night-scented stock wafted from the herbaceous borders that hedged them in on both sides.

The silence stretched between them until it became unbearable. Then both of them spoke at the same time.

"Twenty years," said Philip. "It's been a long time."

"So much has changed," said Tessa, "yet so much is the same."

They both laughed, easing the tension between them.

"You were the last person I saw when I ran away," Tessa said. "Do you remember that night?"

"How could I forget it? I tried so hard to persuade you to stay."

"And when I wouldn't, you gave me money and insisted that I take it. I can remember you grabbing my shoulder bag and stuffing pound notes into it."

"It wasn't much, if I recall. Only what I had in my wallet at the time." He stopped and turned to look down at her in the near darkness. "Do you ever regret it?"

"Not the running away part. It was the best thing I ever did. What came after was the big mistake."

"You mean marrying John Maltby?"

"Yes. I must have been crazy. But I suppose he was someone familiar, someone I knew in the big, scary world out there, beyond the high walls of Langley."

They began walking again. "I never did quite understand why Maltby left Langley at exactly the same time you did," Philip said.

"Aunt Sybil fired him for selling information about the racehorses."

"Ah, so that was it." They walked in silence for a while. "It wasn't a happy marriage, I gather," Philip said suddenly, as if he'd been thinking about her and John Maltby.

"No it wasn't." Tessa shivered involuntarily. "That's all in the past now. John's been dead for several years."

"And what about your son, Jason? How old is he now?"

"Nineteen," she replied quickly. "He's about to go on to university."

"Why didn't you bring him here with you?"

She paused, listening to birdsong from the thicket ahead of them. "Oh, surely that's a blackbird. I haven't heard one for years."

"Yes, the evening is a good time to hear them." They stood listening for a moment, almost holding their breath in unison. Then the singing ceased.

"Sorry," Tessa said reluctantly. "What were we talking about?"

"Your son, Jason. I said you should have brought him to Langley."

"Oh, he's off on a special camping holiday in France with school friends. I had only a few days free, so I thought it best to come alone."

"He must be good company for you."

"Yes, he is. Of course, he drives me nuts at times, like all teenagers. But most times he's terrific company. I'll miss him when he takes off, as he must do eventually."

"You were fortunate to have him." There was no mistaking the note of envy in Philip's voice.

"You would have liked children, wouldn't you?" It

felt strange to her to be offering comfort to the man who had never seemed to need help of any kind. She wondered if she could have done so if it were broad daylight. The evening dusk seemed to create a feeling of intimacy between them.

"Yes, it's the one great source of sadness in my life," Philip said. "That I have no one to come after me. No heir to Thornton."

"So a daughter wouldn't have been any good."

"A daughter would have been fine. Her children would have been my grandchildren. Son or daughter, it wouldn't really have mattered, so long as there was someone to love and take care of Thornton Manor after I'm gone."

"I suppose Derek would be your heir." It was the first time she had spoken his brother's name to him.

"I'm afraid so. He'll probably sell it to the highest bidder or turn it into a hotel. Anything to make money," Philip added bitterly.

"But I thought he was doing well at Langley. Surely he has a share in the racing stables."

"He resents not being his own master, I'm afraid. Steven still has the ultimate say in the running of the stables. Besides, Derek spends money like water."

"On what?"

She could sense the tension in him. "I'm sure you don't want to talk about Derek, do you?" he said.

"No, you're right, I don't. I can't believe how he has changed, though."

"Changed? In what way? I don't find him any different."

"Changed in his—his looks," she said hesitantly.

"Ah, yes. Rather gone to seed, has our young Derek." He halted and turned suddenly to look down at her. "That was inexcusable and utterly tactless of me. I was forgetting that you hadn't seen him since he was a young man. Was it an awful shock to you, to see him as he is now?"

She bit her lip. "He'd always been so—so handsome, so dashing. You remember how you made up the name Dashing Derek?"

"Yes, indeed."

"He doesn't look very dashing anymore. He's changed so much, I hardly recognized him."

"We've all changed, grown older."

"Some less conspicuously than others. You've hardly changed at all."

"I trust that is a compliment, Miss Hargrave."

"Yes, it is."

"Ah, but then I recall you said you'd thought of me as always being old."

She laughed. "That was when I was a child."

"You were always a child to me, Tessa."

That was the problem. For a horrifying moment, she thought she'd said the words out loud. She moved away several paces and turned back in the direction of the house. "I'm feeling cold. Do you mind if we go back inside?"

"Certainly." Now he sounded more like the restrained Philip Thornton of old.

They walked in silence across the wet lawn and up the terrace steps. "Tessa," Philip said as they stood by the door.

"Yes?"

"I don't suppose you'd have enough time to make a quick visit to Thornton, would you?"

Relief flooded over her. "I'll make time. You know how much I love Thornton. When?"

"How about tea tomorrow afternoon? I know you'll want to spend most of your time with Steven. He usually has a sleep in the afternoon, so you could slip away then."

"Perfect. What time?"

"I'll pick you up at three. If you like, we could go for a short drive over the high moor."

"That would be lovely." She looked up at him, feeling ridiculously shy again, now that they were standing in the pool of light from the standard lantern by the door. "Thank you, Philip," she said, transported back to her adolescent self. "Teas at Thornton were always a special treat for me. Yorkshire parkin and fat rascals and fizzy ginger beer."

"Would you like to put in your order now?" he asked. "Sorry, I haven't got my order pad and pencil with me."

She laughed. Philip had always made her laugh. Then the laughter died away. "Thank you for coming to Langley tonight. It made it so much easier for me having you here."

"I wanted to see you again. I also realized how difficult this would be for you. It was brave of you to come back."

"I knew I had to."

"It means the world to Steven."

"That's why I'm here."

Philip's hand was on the door handle. They both hesitated. This time it was Tessa who leaned forward to kiss him on the cheek. "Thanks again, Philip."

They drew apart and stood looking at each other. Philip smiled his enigmatic smile and opened the door. "Time we went in, I think. Your uncle will be wondering if we've fallen in the river."

In fact, Steven was just coming out of the drawing room with James Barton as they came into the hall. "Have a good walk?" he asked.

"A bit damp underfoot," Tessa said. "But it was lovely to walk in the garden again."

"You did it already, this afternoon." Her uncle's penetrating gaze seemed to bore right into her.

"I know I did," she said, laughing. "That doesn't mean I can't enjoy it again, does it?"

"Not at all. Never tire of Langley's gardens myself. I'm going to bed."

"Oh. I'm so sorry."

"What about?"

"For deserting you."

"Nonsense. We can spend tomorrow morning together. St. Luke's has its flower festival this weekend. Want to go?"

She hesitated, remembering Philip's invitation. "In the morning, you mean?"

"Certainly, in the morning. Sybil makes me spend my afternoons in bed." He looked from her to Philip. "Why? Did you have other plans?"

"Not in the morning." Why on earth was she being so stupid about this? She felt as if she'd been caught engaging in some clandestine rendezvous. "Philip has asked me to come to Thornton for tea in the afternoon."

"Good. Tell you what. Why don't we go to church on Sunday and see the flowers then? That would give us more time together tomorrow morning."

Tessa hadn't been to church for years. "Are you sure you had planned to go to church on Sunday?" she asked her uncle.

"Of course. Have to make sure He doesn't forget who I am. Especially now. Right?"

Tessa swallowed the lump in her throat. It was the first reference her uncle had made to the serious nature of his illness. "I'd love to come with you," she said, trying to smile. "Who else will be coming?"

"Your aunt, of course. She must be seen at church. Not Camilla, though. She always sleeps in on Sundays. Come to think of it, Camilla sleeps in most days. And Victoria works in her woodshed at the weekends."

"Her what?"

"Her woodshed. That's what I call it. She likes to call it a studio."

"I see." She turned to Philip, aware that he was being left out of the conversation. "I suppose you'll be going to St. Michael's as you're the lord of the manor there."

"I would have been happy to join you at St. Luke's, but I'm reading the Lesson at St. Michael's this Sunday."

"Do you still sit in that side family pew with the carved gargoyles along the wall?"

"Yes. It's not as grand as the Langley box pew in St. Luke's of course. But it was still private enough for my father to be able to sleep there."

"I know. He snored once when I came to church with the family. You could hear him all over the church."

Philip looked down at her with an unfathomable expression on his face. "It seems so strange to see you here, you know. It's almost as if you'd never left. And yet you're very much changed from that girl we all knew."

"We're all going to have to persuade her to stay much longer," Steven said.

"I wish I could," Tessa said . . . and suddenly realized that she really meant it.

"I must go," Philip said abruptly. "Good night, Steven. Tessa, I'll see you at three tomorrow." He started off for the drawing room. "I'll go and say good night to Sybil."

"She went up to bed just after you went out. And Vicky has gone to the pub with Kevin. Only Camilla and Derek in there now."

Philip halted and swung around. "Then I won't bother. Good night again."

They watched him stride across the hallway, his long black raincoat flaring out behind him like a cloak.

"Poor chap," Steven said as the front door closed. He began to cross the hall to the lift.

"Why, 'poor chap'?" Tessa asked, following him.

"He's burdened with appalling death duties for Thornton. I doubt if he can afford to pay them." He pressed the button and the lift door opened for him. "Are you coming up with me?"

"Does it hold two people?"

"Let's try it out." He laughed at Tessa's hesitation. "Get in, you silly girl. Even if I wanted to finish myself off, do you really think I'd risk hurting you?"

Tessa stepped inside after him and the lift started its slow ascent. "Surely Philip's position can't be that bad."

" 'Fraid so. They may be an ancient family, but the Thorntons were never that well off, you know."

"But he must have earned good money as a barrister in London. He was a good one, wasn't he?"

"One of the best. But being a barrister doesn't necessarily mean you earn lots of money. It's American lawyers who make all those big bucks."

Tessa had to smile at his attempt at an American accent.

"You can see I've been watching *L.A. Law,* can't you?"

"I didn't know you got it over here."

"We get *Cheers, Seinfeld* ... even that dreadful *Roseanne,* God help us. Now, where was I? Oh, yes. Philip. When his father fell ill last year, Philip had to give up his London practice and come back to Thornton. He has chambers in Leeds now. Not terribly lucrative, though. He has even talked to me about having to sell Thornton."

Sell Thornton? The thought of it appalled Tessa.

She was about to ask more questions when the lift shuddered to a halt and the door opened. "Nifty gadget, this, eh?" he said, stepping out. "Bet you never thought you'd see a lift at Langley. Had it installed when Sybil had her back surgery. Must admit, I find it pretty useful myself nowadays."

"It's great." They started off slowly down the corridor. "What time shall I come down for breakfast?"

"Early as you like. I'm up at half six every morning. Shall I arrange for Mary to bring you tea?"

"Yes, please. But not at six-thirty, if you don't mind. Make it seven-thirty. I'm still trying to catch up with sleep after the flight over."

"You're as lazy as Camilla," he said with an affectionate smile, and then halted outside his bedroom door.

"Good night, Uncle Steven." She put her arms around his neck and kissed him.

"Good night, dear child," he said. He shifted his stick to his left hand and patted her cheek. "God bless you for coming," he added in a whisper.

He watched her go down the corridor, until she turned the corner into the east wing. Then he went into his room.

"I could hear you mumbling out there," Sybil said from the four-poster bed. Sitting up, propped against several pillows, in her long-sleeved white cotton nightgown, she looked eternally young to Steven. He had never been blind to her many faults, but he loved her despite them.

"I was saying good night to Tessa."

She wagged one scarlet-tipped finger at him. "That girl's still a little troublemaker. I know it. Mark my words, she's going to cause trouble at Langley again."

"She's not a girl anymore, Sybil. She's a middle-aged woman. And a very nice one, too."

"You were always biased when it came to Tessa. I often thought you preferred her to your own daughter."

"I often did."

She pulled herself up straight in the bed, punching the pillows behind her. "That's a wicked thing to say."

"Nothing wicked about it. Camilla could be a pain in the neck. Still can." He slowly took off his coat and hung it carefully on the back of a chair. "Will it disturb you if I sleep in here tonight?"

"Of course not," Sybil replied.

He could tell she was still displeased with him. He slipped off his braces and began to drag his trousers down, his breath coming fast. "God, I'm as weak as a bloody kitten," he muttered to himself, grabbing the chest of drawers for support.

"I'll ring for Barton to help you undress."

"I don't need a bloody dresser. I can manage by myself."

But her finger was on the bell, and in a minute or so, James Barton appeared at the door.

"Help Mr. Hargrave undress," Sybil told him.

"Certainly, madam," James said, coming across the room.

"You all treat me like a bloody invalid," Steven said, glaring at him.

"Not at all, sir," James said. "We all need help in some way or other. After all, where would I be if I didn't have work to do at Langley, eh? Queuing up for the dole, that's where."

Within minutes, Steven was tucked into bed beside his wife, his books and glasses within reach, and James had gone.

"I'm going to sleep," Sybil announced.

"I'll try to keep the light from disturbing you."

"I'm used to it." She did her usual kiss in the air just above his ear and then turned on her side, away from him. "I still say she is going to cause trouble at Langley," were her final words.

Chapter Nine

Although she felt extremely tired, Tessa was too wound up to be able to sleep. She drew back the curtains and sat sideways in the window seat, looking out over the darkened garden, her mind in a turmoil.

In a few short hours at Langley, her entire perspective of the past had been turned upside down. The man she'd thought she loved all these years, the memory of whom had tainted all her relationships, had become a booze-swilling moron for whom she found it difficult to feel anything but contempt.

And what about his brother? she asked herself. Philip Thornton, whose marriage to a society beauty had cut her off from him at the age of sixteen, so that he had become as remote to her as one of the marble statues in the conservatory?

Philip, too, was changed, but not in looks.

Was she the only one to feel the electricity between them? Of course, she was. Philip had been as kind to her as he had always been. No less, no more. She had been the only one to feel the spark of attraction. Possibly a reaction to her shock at seeing Derek so changed. Besides, there was something vaguely incestuous in feeling such a strong sense of attraction to a man whom she had always thought of as an older brother or a younger version of her Uncle Steven.

Then there was her cousin Camilla, whose beauty was still there, but whose ability to hurt her seemed to have diminished, making it more difficult to cast her as the villain of her past.

Only her aunt had lived up to her expectations. Aunt Sybil had not changed. Tessa had felt the malevolence of her gaze from across the room this evening. Despite the passage of twenty years, she had no doubt that Aunt Sybil still hated her.

Shivering, Tessa closed the heavy curtains and then climbed into bed. She had always said her prayers at night when she'd been at Langley. "Be grateful for all you have here," her aunt had often admonished her. "You must thank God every day for giving you an uncle who provides you with food for your stomach and a roof over your head."

She always had thanked God for Uncle Steven, but her prayers for some mark of affection from her aunt and cousin had gone unanswered.

Later, when she'd been older, she had prayed that Derek would notice her. That wish had been granted, unfortunately.

Nowadays she rarely prayed, but tonight she gave thanks again for Uncle Steven, whose affection was as constant and tangible as it had ever been. And she also tacked on the thought that having fulfilled her wish to see her uncle, she would soon be returning to the quiet and normalcy of Winnipeg, even if she didn't have a job. Life at Langley was far too unsettling for her liking.

She awoke the next morning with a heightened sense of expectation. *Today I'm going to Thornton,* was her first thought.

It was Vicky, not Mary, who brought in her early morning tea. She knocked and then bounced into the room, dressed in a grubby sweatshirt and jeans, bearing the tea tray.

"You don't look like Mary," Tessa said.

"Sorry I forgot to put on my black dress and frilly white apron," Vicky said, precariously setting the tray down on a corner of the night table.

"You don't really mean the staff still wears—"

"Of course not, silly. I was just joking. Not that Grandmother wouldn't prefer that, mind you. But she couldn't get anyone to work for her if she tried that one on. She's lucky to have any staff at all. No one wants to go into service nowadays, not unless the pay is worth it. I certainly don't intend to have servants—"

Vicky stopped short, as if she'd suddenly remembered something.

"I expect you'll have to have some sort of help, in a place as large as Ayncliffe Hall," Tessa said.

"Yes, just what I was thinking. They still have a butler there. Must be one of the few old relics left in the country. Totally useless, of course. He's far too old. But they keep him on because he's been there since long before Jeremy was born." She beamed a smile at Tessa. "You'll be meeting Jeremy today. He'll be here later this afternoon. He's meeting me at the Ripon racetrack."

"I'll look forward to that."

Vicky rolled her eyes. "So will I. He's the sexiest hunk in the world." She glanced at the tray. "Got everything you need?"

Tessa ran her eye over the large pot of tea and the plate heaped with homemade biscuits and fruitcake. "Enough to last me all day. Thanks."

"My pleasure. I'm off to do some whittling."

The door slammed shut behind Vicky before Tessa could say any more. She felt as if she'd been woken by a whirlwind. That was one of the joys of being nineteen. All that wonderful energy.

She spent a quiet morning in the library with her uncle. They talked about Vicky and Jeremy. She tried to soothe his fears about the engagement, but that only made him more fractious.

"She's making a big mistake. Someone has to try to talk sense into her. She might listen to you."

"I doubt it, but I'll try. Give me a while. Let me see what I think of Jeremy first."

"Fellow's an idiot."

"Yes, so you said before. But perhaps he has some good things in his character you haven't noticed."

He gave her a look, and she remembered what he'd told her about Jeremy being good for one thing only. Bed.

"I also want to talk to you about your future," he said, reluctantly relinquishing the subject of Vicky and Jeremy.

"My future? What about it?"

"Are you intending to stay in Canada?"

"Of course I am. I'm a Canadian now."

"You wouldn't like to come back to Yorkshire? After all, your roots are here."

"Not anymore, they're not. Apart from you and your family, I don't have a single living relative that I know here."

"Aren't we enough?" he asked rather plaintively.

"You are very special to me, Uncle Steven," Tessa said gently. "You know that. But my home's in Winnipeg now. That's where Jason and I live."

"I never did understand why you chose to live in a city in the middle of the flat prairie."

"It chose us. John got a job at the Assiniboia Downs racecourse in Winnipeg. By the time we were separated, I'd settled in there. It's my home now. Besides, it's not in the middle of the flat prairie. There are lovely lakes and forests just a short drive away from Winnipeg."

"And you have no desire to come back to the Dales?"

She hesitated. "I must admit I'd forgotten how beautiful it is here. I hadn't realized how much I've missed the countryside, the hills . . . Or at least I chose to forget. But there's nothing for me here now, Uncle Steven. What would I do in a remote place like this?"

He met her gaze for a moment and then turned away. "You're right, I suppose. I'd just hoped . . . And you're going away again on Tuesday," he added.

The dispirited tone of his voice made her feel unutterably guilty. "I'll come back again for another visit in the fall," she said impulsively. A rash promise, considering she might not have a job by then. But the leap of happiness in his eyes was justification enough for her white lie.

Steven went for his afternoon rest after lunch. Tessa had been hoping to spend the time with Vicky until three o'clock, but Vicky had gone to Ripon with her parents for the horse racing.

"So it is just you and me," Sybil said to Tessa, after she had rung the bell for the table to be cleared. "Let us go and sit on the terrace and you can tell me all about yourself."

It was not a pleasant prospect.

Tessa pushed Sybil's wheelchair out onto the terrace, and then sat on one of the white wrought-iron chairs that James Barton had pulled out for her.

"I think we should have some Pimms to celebrate this special occasion, Barton," Sybil said. Tessa caught the edge of sarcasm in her voice.

"Certainly, madam."

A few minutes later James brought out a crystal pitcher of Pimms, replete with slices of fruit and cucumber, the ice cubes tinkling as he set it down on the wrought-iron table. He poured the drink into two large glasses, topping them with sprigs of fresh garden mint.

Tessa recalled that she'd had her very first taste of

this uniquely English summer drink at Philip's wedding to Rosamund Ashton. Her first Pimms. Another rite of passage associated with Philip.

She took a sip of the piquant drink and then sat the glass down on the wrought-iron table. "I haven't had a Pimms for years."

"Tell me all about yourself and your son," her aunt demanded.

"There's little to tell, Aunt Sybil. I'm sure you know most of it from the letters I've written over the years to Uncle Steven."

"I know the main things. Your marriage. Going to Canada. Your son's birth. And then your divorce from that awful man, Maltby. Your marriage was not a happy one, I understand?" There was the slightest hint of a smile at the corners of her aunt's mouth.

Tessa looked directly at her. "That's right, Aunt Sybil."

"I'm not surprised, of course. Mixed marriages rarely work."

"We were both white," Tessa couldn't help saying, deliberately misunderstanding her aunt's meaning.

"Don't try to be obtuse with me. You know very well what I'm talking about. Class, Tessa. Class. You married a man of the working class."

Tessa felt the blood rushing to her face. "That's utter garbage. My marriage failed because John Maltby was an abusive husband. It had nothing to do with what you call class."

She had never before spoken back to her aunt. Doing so for the first time in her life made her feel both terrified and strangely elated.

"Look at your own parents. That was a disaster, too."

Now Tessa was really angry. "Don't you dare compare my parents' marriage with mine to John Maltby. My father adored my mother."

"The daughter of a London bus driver," Sybil said, wrinkling her long nose as if she were smelling rotten fish. "She was nothing but a little clerk who thought she'd snared a big catch. But she soon found out she was wrong when your grandfather cut your father off without a penny."

Tessa drew herself up, pressing her spine against the chair. "They managed. Considering he'd never been trained for a profession, my father was a fine journalist. His colleagues told me that at the funeral."

She swallowed hard, fighting back tears at the memory of walking behind the two coffins, dressed in a black skirt and wool jumper that itched terribly. It had rained nonstop, she recalled, so that there were pink worms on the path down to the dreary little graystone church.

"Not fine enough to be able to provide for his daughter, though."

There it was, in a nutshell. The dislike and resentment she had felt all her life emanating from her aunt. But now, she realized with a sudden surge of relief, it could no longer hurt her. She was free of her aunt, independent. Her livelihood no longer depended on being obedient to this dreadful woman.

She leaned forward, closer to her aunt's wheelchair. "Let's get this straight, Aunt Sybil. It's time it was said. You never wanted me to come and stay at Langley, did you?"

The sloe-dark eyes looked at her. "Your uncle wanted it. Therefore, you came."

"Exactly. Uncle Steven wanted to take care of his orphaned niece, but you did not. You resented my presence here."

The hand reached, like a claw, for the tall glass. "You're talking nonsense, as usual."

"No, I'm not. When I came to Langley I had just lost my parents. I had no one in the world other than you and my uncle. I am deeply grateful to Uncle Steven for giving me a home—"

"Langley is *my* home, not your uncle's."

"Yes, and I'm sure you never cease to remind him of it. You always did, even though you probably wouldn't have kept Langley if it weren't for Uncle Steven making such a success of the racing stables."

Sybil set her glass down with a crash on the table. "That's quite enough. I do not intend to sit here listening to your ill-mannered remarks. It is obvious that despite all the fine education we provided for you, you are still your mother's daughter."

"I am proud to be like my mother. And however much education you gave me—and I *am* grateful to you and my uncle for it—you made my life very unhappy here. You encouraged Camilla to think herself above me."

"She was. Her breeding—"

"Don't talk to me about breeding. I'm not one of your smelly dogs. You don't get it, Sybil, do you? You're living in another world. All this nonsense about breeding doesn't matter a damn anymore."

"I don't have to sit here and listen to your Bolshie rubbish."

"No, you don't. May I push you inside?" Tessa felt guilty about the emphasis on the "push" but she felt it was just one small chance to pay this woman back for years of unhappiness.

"No, you may not." Sybil fumbled in the pocket at the side of her wheelchair and produced a two-way radio receiver. "Barton," she shouted into it, "come at once."

Their eyes met and then glanced away. "I'm sorry, Aunt Sybil, but it had to be said."

"How long do you intend to stay here in my house?" her aunt asked.

"As short a time as is possible. Just enough time to

be able to visit my uncle," Tessa replied just as pointedly. "I leave on Tuesday morning."

"Good. For Steven's sake, I shall treat you with the civility you do not deserve. Were it not for Steven, you would not remain here one moment longer."

"That is how it has always been," Tessa said with a wry little smile. "Why should it be any different now?"

She bolted from the terrace, before her aunt could see the tears welling up in her eyes. How ridiculous to be crying over something that had happened so many years ago!

She stood in the corridor, angrily dabbing at her eyes with a crumpled tissue.

"Anything I can do to help?"

She spun around with a gasp. "Philip. You're early."

"Sorry about that. My meeting finished earlier than I'd expected. What's wrong?"

She shook her head, stuffing the tissue back into her pocket. "Nothing. You have a habit of stealing up on people."

"Do I? How very impolite of me. I am sorry."

"That's twice you've caught me in an awkward position. Once dragging off my boots and this time sniveling away like a baby."

"Is it anything I can help you with?"

"No, but thank you, anyway. Actually, it was extremely cathartic. Not the crying, but the cause of it. I don't want to talk about it here," she added, casting a glance down the hallway.

"Would you like to go now?"

"Yes. Yes, please." An involuntary shiver ran down Tessa's spine. The sooner she got away from Langley, the better.

"Good. That will give us some extra time to see the old places."

He was dressed casually this afternoon. Or, at least,

as casually as Philip would probably ever dress, in
a classically tailored houndstooth jacket, open-necked
checked shirt, and gray trousers.

To her delight, he drove her around their old favorite haunts in Wensleydale and Swaledale in his old
dark green Austin Healey convertible, with the top
down.

"It looks exactly the same as the car you had before
I left," she said, gazing at it in ecstasy, before she
got in.

"It *is* the same. They stopped making them in 1967,
I believe, so I kept mine. It still goes exceptionally
well."

Both Thornton brothers had loved performance
cars. But Derek's driving had terrified Tessa. The ter-
ror had added an extra zest to going out with Derek.
It was tremendously exciting. Philip's driving, on the
other hand, had been fast but always controlled, so
that you sat back and relaxed.

They drove to the ruins of Jervaulx Abbey and
strolled through the tranquil grounds, saying little.
Philip had that wonderful gift of knowing when to
speak and when to be silent. As they walked down
what had once been the nave of a large church—now
a stretch of grass with intermittent tombstones to remind them that they were walking on hallowed
ground—Tessa reflected that she couldn't think of
anyone else she would rather be seeing her favorite
places with.

From Jervaulx, Philip drove her through the ancient
town of Middleham, past the Black Swan, where
Derek had often taken her. It used to be—and probably still was—one of the favorite hangouts of the stable lads from the various racing stables hereabouts.
Then they drove past the castle, where Uncle Steven
used to take her. She remembered the tales he'd told
her about the frail boy who had grown up in Mid-

dleham Castle. How he'd become a famous general at nineteen, only to be vilified, later, as King Richard III.

From Middleham, they drove across the low moor and up onto the windswept gallops on Middleham high moor.

Philip pulled the car onto the rough grass and they got out and strolled to the edge of a steep drop, gazing out at the wide dale spread out beneath them.

"You can see Langley quite clearly from here today," Philip said, pointing across the dale.

"It's Thornton I'm interested in seeing, not Langley," Tessa said.

"We'll be there very soon now." Philip looked down at her. "Someone upset you at Langley today, didn't they?"

Tessa shrugged. "Just Aunt Sybil. I shouldn't let her get to me, I know, but I'm afraid she still does."

"It's all in the past. Nothing to do with your present life."

"You're right." Tessa turned to look out again and sighed. "How lovely it is here. I'd forgotten. I suppose I haven't allowed myself to think about it."

Philip leaned his back against the drystone wall and faced her, the wind blowing his dark hair across his forehead. "Would you ever consider coming back to live in the Dales?"

"Uncle Steven asked me that this morning. No. Definitely not. I'm happy where I am." She turned her head away from his searching gaze. "Too many memories here."

"I'm sure there are. I don't blame you. Sometimes I wish I could get away from here myself, but it's impossible for me."

"You could never leave Thornton. You and Thornton are inseparable."

"I might have to." Philip pushed himself away from the wall and strode to the car. "Let's go, shall we?"

he shouted to her over his shoulder, his voice competing with the rushing of the wind.

Oh, God, how bloody tactless of her. She had totally forgotten what Uncle Steven had told her about the horrendous death duties Philip would have to pay. *He may have to sell Thornton,* he'd said.

"Sorry," Philip said, holding the door for her as she scrambled into the car. "I don't mean to rush you, but I know you have to get back for dinner at Langley."

He drove as fast as was possible down the winding lane that led down into the dale. Tessa glanced at his austere profile, the set features, feeling like a child again, worried that she was the one who had caused this dark mood.

They arrived at Thornton's wrought-iron gates in less than twenty minutes, having exchanged only a few casual remarks about the landscape. "Peter might be in." Philip leaned on the horn. "I'm getting lazy in my old age."

"Will's gone, of course," Tessa said.

"Yes, he died several years ago. This is his son. You may remember him." A fresh-faced man with a thatch of fair hair came from the back of the house. Philip leaned his head out the window. "Sorry to disturb you, Peter. Come and meet Mrs.—"

"I use my single name," Tessa said.

"Of course. Sorry. This is Miss Hargrave."

Tessa had to smile to herself. Obviously Ms. was not in Philip's vocabulary. She held out her hand. "Hi, Peter."

"Hi, Miss Hargrave. Welcome back to Yorkshire." Peter was a man in his mid-thirties, soft-spoken.

"Thank you."

Peter opened the gates wide and Philip drove off down the curving driveway. "Peter's my right-hand man here," he said. "He has a degree in horticulture.

I don't know how I'd manage without him. I only wish I could afford to pay him what he's really worth."

Tessa said nothing. She was too busy peering past the tall rhododendron bushes that lined the driveway, straining to catch her first glance of the house. As she leaned forward, her hands gripping the ledge above the walnut dashboard, her heart was beating fast.

Then it was there, as suddenly and dramatically as always, the sunshine turning its limestone walls to gold, the asymmetrical gables and barley-sugar chimney pots giving it a feeling of being an eccentric but eminently lovable old character.

Tessa turned to Philip, tears filling her eyes. She shook her head, unable to speak.

He looked at her, astonished. "I'd forgotten how much you loved Thornton," he said slowly. "I do believe you love it as much as I do."

Chapter Ten

The great hall was one of the chief glories of Thornton. Although it had a heavily timbered roof and dark paneling on the walls, the expanse of tall windows on the southern side made it surprisingly bright.

Entranced, Tessa stood in the center of the hall, looking about her. There was the battered suit of armor in the corner, and there, on a dais, the pair of old chairs she used to think were thrones. In a bright alcove, lit by a full-length oriel window, was a window seat with a tapestry cushion where she had loved to sit and read whenever she'd spent a day at Thornton as a child.

"It hasn't changed a bit," she said at last to Philip, who was obviously enjoying her pleasure. "It's all the same."

"I'm afraid so," he said wryly. "My father wouldn't allow any changes to be made."

"I've never seen the entire house, you know. When I used to come here as a child I longed to go up to the top floor and explore, but I never dared ask."

"Was I such an ogre?"

"No, not you, but I was terrified of your father. He was always so fierce, with that bristling red mustache. And when he spoke he always shouted."

Philip smiled. "I was terrified of him myself when I was young. He really was the epitome of the major general, wasn't he? But as he grew older I discovered that there was quite a vulnerable person behind all that bombast. We became very close during his last illness."

"I'm glad. What about Derek? Did he ever become reconciled with his father?" It was still hard even to speak Derek's name, but each time she did, it became a little easier.

"No. Father never had any time for Derek, I'm afraid. Unfortunately, that never changed."

Tessa had a sudden memory flash of a young Derek standing erect and white-faced as his father roared abuse at him for some minor mishap. Too minor for her even to remember what it was. She had been standing so close to Derek that she could see his hands shaking. She remembered being surprised. Until that time, she'd thought Derek was totally self-confident and in control.

She shook her head to erase the image. "We were talking about seeing the house."

"You shall have the grand tour today. What would you like to see first, the house or the grounds?"

"The grounds. It's such a lovely day, I'd hate to miss it and then find that it was raining later."

"Perhaps you'd like Mrs. Braithwaite to bring us tea first?"

"Braithwaite?" Another new name. "I take it that Mrs. Miller isn't here anymore. Did she die?"

"No, she's still very much alive. Retired to a comfortable cottage on the estate. But Mrs. Braithwaite won't be entirely new to you." Philip smiled. "She used to be Sarah Roper. You remember, she was a kitchen maid at Langley?"

Sarah Roper! A spasm of fear shot through Tessa. "Of course I remember Sarah," she said through suddenly dry lips.

How could she forget her? Plump, jolly Sarah had been one of the few people at Langley who had been kind to her. It was to Sarah she had turned when she had most needed a friend. Tessa ran her tongue over her lips. "And she's your housekeeper now? How did that happen?"

"She was out of work for quite a while after Sybil got rid of her. I asked my mother to employ her here."

Tessa's heartbeat quickened. "Sybil fired Sarah?"

"Yes. As a matter of fact, it was just after you left Langley with Maltby."

How strange, Tessa thought. Why would her aunt fire Sarah after she left?

"I didn't actually leave with John Maltby, you know," she told Philip. "I happened to meet him when I was walking down the road to Leyburn, wondering what on earth I was going to do. He drove past me and then stopped to give me a lift."

"Sybil prefers to think you ran off with Maltby," Philip said.

"She would, of course. Was that really likely, in the circumstances?"

"Hardly. But, then, you didn't stay around long enough to explain, did you?"

"What was to explain? You know what happened. I just couldn't stay at Langley a moment longer."

"You should have come here, as I suggested."

"To Thornton? How could I possibly come and stay with Derek's parents after all that had happened?"

"I suppose you're right. Damn Derek. I shall never forgive him for—"

"You told me yesterday that it was all in the past, remember? Let's just leave it there, okay?"

"Right you are."

"You were telling me about Sarah."

"She was doing very well here. Mother insisted that she get some more schooling. You know how she was about education."

"Yes. Your mother certainly didn't believe that the

working class should know its place, did she? I loved your mother. Behind all that gentleness, she was a very strong person."

"She was, indeed," Philip said softly. "She always enjoyed having you here."

"The feeling was mutual." Tessa could see that even now, several years after her death, memories of his mother were still fresh in Philip's mind.

"I was telling you about Sarah," he said, obviously anxious to get away from the subject of his mother. "Unfortunately, she left us after a few years. She married a wastrel who treated her badly, and eventually she was divorced. When Mrs. Miller retired five years ago, Sarah applied for the position of housekeeper and Father gave it to her."

"Good for him."

"No one wants to go into service now, of course. Besides, most people don't bother with servants anymore. Actually, Sarah was more of a nurse than a housekeeper. That was the year my mother became ill. Sarah helped to nurse her."

Instinctively, Tessa took his arm and gently pressed it. She could feel the tension in him at her touch, but he didn't draw away from her. "I'm glad she had Sarah to look after her."

"So am I."

Tessa's heart had been thumping hard ever since she'd heard Sarah's name, but she knew that this was something she couldn't run away from. "Let's go and say hi to Sarah and then we can have tea later."

Philip looked surprised.

"Sarah was a very good friend to me, when I badly needed a friend," Tessa explained.

He took her through to the big kitchen Tessa remembered eating in when she was young. She breathed in the delicious aromas of ginger and treacle and yeast. Sarah stood at the large pine table, setting out cakes and floury scones on a silver cake stand. She was plumper than ever.

"Hallo, Sarah," Tessa said quietly.

Sarah turned and smiled, but Tessa could see the wariness in her expression. "Hallo, Miss Hargrave."

"Tessa, please, not Miss Hargrave." Tessa went to Sarah and hugged her, feeling the warm solidity of the woman who had been her friend and, she now suspected, had suffered because of it.

They drew apart and stood looking at each other, the embarrassment of the past between them. Had Philip not been there, they might have said more. Perhaps it was a good thing he was there, acting as a buffer.

"I'm so glad you're here, at Thornton," Tessa told her.

"So am I." Sarah glanced at Philip. "Mr. Thornton has been very kind." She still spoke with a broad Yorkshire accent.

"Nonsense," Philip said, embarrassed and probably puzzled by the emotions that were almost tangible in the warm kitchen. "I couldn't manage without you, Sarah." He hurriedly changed the subject. "We thought we'd have a quick tour of the grounds and then have tea."

"Right," Sarah said briskly. She turned to Tessa. "I've made all your favorites: parkin and flapjacks and fat rascals. I hope you're not on some silly diet. Any road, you look as if you could do with some fattening up," she added, casting a critical eye over Tessa.

"I'm certainly not going to diet while I'm here," Tessa said, laughing. "See you later, Sarah."

When they went outside, Tessa was glad to see that the pattern of the gardens had not been changed. They walked through the herb garden, still set out in the style of an old Elizabethan knot garden: small beds of thyme, mint and sage, lavender and rosemary . . . edged with low hedges of golden box.

Then they went down the gravel path, through an arch covered with purple clematis, and into the rose garden.

"What a heavenly smell," Tessa said, breathing in the heady fragrance of the standard and floribunda roses, many of them overblown now that midsummer was upon them. "How I miss the scent of roses!"

"Surely you have roses in Canada."

"Yes, but not in this profusion. And they have to be special hardy ones to be able to survive our severe winters."

Thornton's gardens had never been as formal as those at Langley House. But, although they were far more natural, they had always been immaculately kept. Now, as they wandered back to the wide stretch of lawn, Tessa realized that they looked positively neglected, the dead roses left uncut on the bushes, daisies and patches of clover in the bumpy lawn. The old hand lawn-roller was propped against the toolshed, covered in rust. It looked as if it had stood there, unmoved, for years.

Philip surveyed the lawn. "Pretty shabby, eh?" He had always been immensely proud of Thornton. Now he looked thoroughly miserable, as if he were suddenly seeing the gardens through her eyes.

"How many gardeners do you have now?"

"Just a couple of part-time lads from the village."

"But I thought you said Will's son . . . what was his name?"

"Peter Wilson." Philip smiled. "I remember how you used to love that play on words. Wilson, Will's son."

"That's right. I'd forgotten that. Anyway, I thought you said Peter had a horticultural degree."

"So he does. But his time is taken up with looking

after the grounds of the entire estate. He doesn't have much time left for the garden."

"I wish I could get my hands on it," Tessa said impulsively, then felt herself redden. "Sorry, that was a pretty rude thing to say."

"Not at all. Just honest. I like that. You always said what came into your head, didn't you? It made you rather special."

Tessa grinned at him. "Thank you, sir. I think."

"No, I mean it," Philip said earnestly. "There you were, this shy little girl, always terribly eager to please and—"

"And always putting my foot in it by saying the first thing that came into my head."

"You must admit it did get you into hot water sometimes."

"It certainly did. That's why I loved it when you were home from Oxford. You always managed to get me out of trouble."

"That was only for a year or so."

"Yes. And then you abandoned me by getting married when I was sixteen and going permanently to London."

A shadow seemed to pass over his face, like a cloud blotting out the sun. God, there she went again, mentioning his marriage, with his wife dead for less than two years. He must still miss Rosamund terribly. She'd been so beautiful and he'd loved her so very much that even now Tessa could recall how he'd glowed when he was with her.

"Do you want to see the orchard?" he asked abruptly. "I think that might meet more with your approval. I'm afraid apples and pears make money, but garden flowers don't." There was no escaping the bitterness in his voice.

They walked across the lawn, over the wooden

bridge that spanned the little stream where Tessa had once caught minnows, and into the orchard.

"Should be a good crop this year," Philip said, looking over the fruit trees.

"Yorkshire isn't exactly famous for its fruit growing, though, is it?"

"What do you mean?" he asked, his dark eyebrows drawing together.

Tessa wondered if she were getting out of her depth. She didn't want to jeopardize the delicate friendship that seemed to be blossoming between them, but something told her she must go on. "What keeps Thornton going? Financially, I mean?"

None of your damned business, his expression said. "Mainly sheep," he replied. He gestured with a hazel switch to the fields that lay beyond the wooden paling.

Stop right there, she told herself, seeing how tight his lips had become. *No, don't,* said her other half.

"Is it enough?" she asked.

"Enough for what?"

"To keep Thornton solvent. I know how many landowners have had to do other things to be able to keep their estates. Even the Queen's cousin, Lord Harewood, has opened his house and grounds to the public. I hear he's made a huge success of it."

"Harewood is different. The house is vast, more like a museum. Thornton is a—a home. My home. Particularly since I moved here from London. I couldn't bear the thought of strangers tramping through it every day."

"It might not have to be every day, might it? You could open the grounds to the public in the summer and the house, perhaps, just on the weekends."

He turned on her, his face white. "Weekends are when I derive the greatest pleasure from my home. Sometimes I'm so busy with my practice in Leeds that

I stay in chambers and don't get home until the weekend."

"Yes, I understand. But wouldn't it be better to open Thornton to the public than to lose it altogether?"

There, now it was out in the open.

He was looking at her as if she were a bitter enemy, chilling her with his hauteur. It was a side of Philip that one rarely saw. What a fool she was to have interfered! But now it was too late.

"Steven has been talking to you, hasn't he?"

"Yes."

"He had no right to do so." Philip's voice was ice-cold. "Thornton is my business and no one else's."

Tessa felt wretched, but she knew she couldn't stop now. "Would Derek be able to help?"

"Derek?" Philip's voice rose. "My brother is one of the main problems."

"I'm sorry." Tessa felt tears pricking behind her eyes. "I seem to be putting my foot in it, like I used to do."

"I would be forced to agree with you." Philip gave a crop of nettles a vicious swing with his stick. "But as you are so determined to know all my business, let me tell you, Tessa, that my father left nothing whatsoever to Derek in his will. I am well aware that Derek should get something. In fact, my father said in his will that it was to be my decision. But the only way I could give Derek his share is by carving up the estate. I might even have to sell Thornton."

"I don't think Derek really needs anything," Tessa said in a small voice. "Uncle Steven said he's well provided for at Langley."

"God alone knows what Derek needs," Philip said wearily. "All I know is that for the last few months he has been badgering me for his inheritance, as he calls it. Now he's talking about going to court on the matter." He walked away from her, down the orchard path. "It's clouding over. Let's go in and have that tea, shall we?"

As she followed him back to the house, Tessa knew that it wasn't only the sky that had clouded over. With her prying questions, she had shattered the revival of what she now realized had once been an extremely precious friendship.

Chapter Eleven

The tea Sarah had prepared was delicious, but Tessa was unable to do justice to it. She felt as if she had a large boulder in the pit of her stomach. Philip, always the gentleman, made light conversation, but the warm rapport between them had vanished. In its place was the politeness of two people who had known each other a very long time ago, but who were now strangers.

He took her for the tour of the first floor of the house, but as she saw each room, each painting on the wall, she was constantly reminded of his fear of losing the ancestral home he loved so much—and of her own lack of tact.

Apart from the great hall, the finest room in the house was the long gallery, with its ornate plasterwork ceiling and walls lined with portraits of Thornton ancestors.

In the alcove created by the bay window stood the locked glass case that housed the Thornton Treasure: an exquisitely wrought golden crucifix about eighteen inches in height, studded with two glowing sapphires and a ruby.

"It's still as beautiful as ever," Tessa said after gazing at it in silence for a few minutes.

"Yes," Philip said. "Hard to believe that it's almost seven hundred years old, isn't it?"

Tessa knew its history well. The ancient medieval

cross had been borne by a Thornton ancestor in the Pilgrimage of Grace, the Catholic revolt against Henry VIII that had ended in humiliation and death for so many northerners.

She was about to ask if it was insured, but decided it would be more judicious to resist the impulse.

Philip must have read her mind. "It's not insured. The cost would be prohibitive. However, I did install an alarm system last year."

She nodded, afraid to make any comment that might be misconstrued as criticism.

"Besides, anyone who stole it wouldn't be able to find a buyer. It's too well known." Philip sounded as if he were trying to convince himself.

But there are a great many unscrupulous collectors who wouldn't care if it was stolen, Tessa felt like saying. Again, she resisted the impulse.

Once they had finished the tour of the house, Tessa suggested that she go back to Langley. "I know you're coming over for dinner again tonight, so it's a pain for you to have to drive there and back twice, but—"

"Not at all. You'll want to change for dinner, I'm sure, and I have work to do."

His eagerness to drive her back to Langley was depressingly apparent.

Before she left, she thanked Sarah for the tea. "I hope you'll come back again before you leave," Sarah said.

"I hope so, too," Tessa said. "I promise we'll make time for a chat then."

But as she crossed the courtyard to Philip's car, Tessa doubted that there would be a next time. Indeed, as she cast a last backward glance at the house she wondered if she would ever see it again. She turned her face away to gaze out the window, the rhododendron hedges and then the lush meadows dotted with sheep passing by in a blur.

When Philip had dropped her off at Langley and driven off again, Tessa immediately went to her uncle's study. "I made a total idiot of myself," she blurted out when Steven asked her how the visit to Thornton Manor had gone.

"You certainly did," he said when she told him what had happened. "Philip is extremely sensitive about Thornton at present. You obviously touched a nerve. I blame myself entirely. I should never have mentioned the subject of the inheritance taxes to you."

Tessa was stung by the unspoken reproach in her uncle's voice.

As she made her way upstairs, she cursed herself for having been so tactless with Philip. It wasn't as if she didn't know how much Thornton Manor meant to him. Even after he was married, he came home as often as he could, despite Rosamund's obvious reluctance to be "buried in the wilds of Yorkshire," as Tessa remembered her saying more than once.

For a few minutes she stood at the window, seeing nothing, but hearing again in her mind Philip's cold responses to her probing questions. Then she turned away and tried to concentrate on what she was going to wear for dinner tonight.

"Informal," Uncle Steven had said. But "informal" at Langley used to mean skirts and blouses rather than dresses. In fact, Aunt Sybil had usually worn long dresses for formal dinners, even when it was only family. Tessa decided on a green silk knit top and black silk pants.

She wasn't at all eager to go down. Not only did she have to face Sybil, Camilla, and Derek again, but she suspected that she had now lost Philip as an ally.

For a few minutes she even considered pretending she was sick. How many times had she done that as a teenager? It had never worked, of course. Aunt

Sybil had always insisted she come down for dinner, sick or not.

When she did eventually go downstairs, a hubbub of voices mingling with laughter greeted her from the drawing room. The door stood half open. Drawing in a deep breath, she pushed it fully open and walked in.

"Here she is at last." Vicky rushed over to her and grabbed her by the arm. "I thought we'd lost you. Do come and meet Jeremy. He's dying to meet you."

Tessa found herself before the strikingly handsome Jeremy Kingsley. Over six feet tall, he was like a Greek god, his head covered in flat golden curls, the tanned face emphasizing his extremely blue eyes.

No wonder Vicky's hooked, she thought. All this, allied with wealth and a title. What girl wouldn't be in love with the Honorable Jeremy Kingsley, heir to an earldom?

"This is Jeremy," Vicky said, her eyes gleaming. "Jeremy, meet my mother's cousin, Tessa Hargrave."

"Hallo, Tessa," Jeremy said in a deep voice. As he took hold of her hand, he looked at her with smoldering eyes.

"Hi, Jeremy," Tessa said, and then slid her hand from his grasp. Jeremy was one of those men who liked to prove his masculinity by giving crushing handshakes.

"I'll get you a drink. Gin and tonic, right?" Vicky dashed off, leaving her with Jeremy.

"Tell me what you think of my little Vicky," he said, taking her arm to draw her closer to the window. Jeremy was a toucher. Second point against him. "She tells me you had never met before." He glanced across the room to where Vicky was getting a drink from her father for Tessa. "Gorgeous, isn't she?"

"She's a lovely girl and also very sensible and down-to-earth," Tessa said, setting a little distance between them. "I like that."

"She certainly is," he said, raising his eyebrows. "That's the way I like them. Down-to-earth." He gave a braying laugh.

Oh, yuck! Tessa thought. She looked across the room and saw that her uncle was watching them. She had to suppress a giggle at the expression on his face.

"Here you are," Vicky said. "One gin and tonic. Compliments of my father."

Tessa looked across the room again and saw Derek raise his glass to her. She raised hers back, summoning up a faint smile. God, this place was like a minefield tonight.

"Daddy's in great spirits. Our mare, Galloping Jenny, won the four-thirty at Ripon."

"Oh, how marvelous. Uncle Steven will be pleased," Tessa said, eager to get onto the safe subject of racing. "Tell me all about it."

While Vicky told her about the race, Jeremy couldn't keep his hands off her. He nuzzled Vicky's neck and ran his hand up and down her back as she spoke. "Jeremy!" Vicky complained a couple of times, but not with much conviction.

Tessa wished she'd slap his face. She also wished someone would come over and rescue her. She was finding it difficult to hide her dislike of the Honorable Jeremy.

"Tessa, might I have a quick word with you?"

Tessa turned to find Philip standing behind her. "Of course," she said. Excusing herself, she followed Philip out to the hall.

Her heart was hammering as she waited for him to speak. Then, impulsively, she said, "Before you say anything, I want to apologize for my rudeness this afternoon. I had no right to pry into your affairs."

To her great relief his face relaxed into a smile. "I'm the one who must apologize, not you. I was a boor. After I'd dropped you off, I came to realize that you spoke solely out of concern for Thornton."

And for you, Philip, Tessa said to herself. But then, Philip and Thornton were synonymous.

"What troubles me greatly is the thought that I might have spoiled your visit to Thornton."

"No, no. You didn't spoil it at all," Tessa said. "You were the perfect host. I had a wonderful time. I can't tell you what it meant to me to see Thornton again." She wanted to fling her arms around him and hug him, to banish the anxious expression from his eyes. "Nothing could have spoiled that for me."

"Thank you for your generosity. I'm hoping that you'll be able to find time for another quick visit to Thornton before you leave on Tuesday." His mouth tilted into a smile. "After all, you still didn't get to see the top floor, did you? You must be thinking I'm hiding something up there. I can assure you that I don't have a mad bride shut away in an attic."

"Oh, no, Mr. Rochester?"

They both laughed. Philip was about to say something else when James Barton came out to bang the gleaming brass gong that stood by the dining-room door. "Dinner is served," he intoned when the reverberation of the gong died away.

"That man should win an Oscar for his performance as a butler," Philip said.

"Don't you like him?" Tessa asked as James walked to the dining-room door.

"He's a play actor, not a real butler. Far too obsequious for my liking. Besides, how many people employ butlers nowadays?"

"I'm not in favor of having servants at all," Tessa said.

"Really? You mean you've never employed a cleaning woman?"

"That's different."

"Oh? How so? When you think about it, we all serve in some capacity or other. If someone engages me as counsel to defend them in a murder trial, am I not serving both the solicitor and his client?"

"I suppose so." Tessa smiled. "You always could out-argue me."

"It is my profession, after all," he reminded her. "But I don't mean to disagree with you. In fact, I understand your feelings about servants. It's the old structure of master and servant that you dislike, am I right?"

"Yes." She was thinking particularly of Sarah Roper and Aunt Sybil.

"It's definitely on its way out in England, but there are some places where it is still practiced in a limited way."

At Langley, for instance, thought Tessa.

"But you must remember that even now many people would rather be employed in large houses like Langley or Thornton than be out of work. As long as there is respect on both sides, I see nothing wrong in that."

"I suppose so. I just don't like the concept of giving someone orders, being in a position of power over someone else, I suppose."

"Don't you have to take orders? As a flight attendant, I mean."

"Well, actually, as a head flight attendant, I am usually the one who gives the orders."

"Aha! I rest my point," Philip said with a smile.

"Come along, you two," Steven called out from the door, effectively ending the discussion.

Uncle Steven sat at the head of the table, with Tessa to his right. To her great disappointment, Kevin Taylor sat next to her. Her aunt's design, no doubt. Not that Tessa disliked Kevin, but she had hoped to be able to spend more time talking to Philip.

Time was growing more and more precious now. There were only two days left. What could she hope to achieve in two days?

"You and Philip seem to have made up your quarrel," her uncle said in a low voice to her as they started on the oxtail soup.

"It wasn't really a quarrel. But, yes, I'm glad he still isn't mad at me."

"Mad at me," Steven repeated. "What a strange expression."

"What?" Tessa asked, puzzled.

"Using the word 'mad' to mean 'angry.' Very American."

Tessa knew better than to argue with him about North American expressions. "Vicky told me that your mare won a race today."

Her uncle's face lit up. "Yes, indeed. A splendid race, apparently. I wish I had seen it. She won by four lengths."

"You should have been there, Tessa," said Derek, who was sitting opposite her. "Why didn't you come with us? I asked Camilla to invite you."

Tessa decided not to tell him that she had received no such invitation from her cousin. "I went to Thornton to have tea with Philip."

Derek darted a glance down the table to where Philip sat. "I see. And what did you think of Thornton?" he asked, his voice rising. "Not in very good shape, is it?"

The table fell into an uneasy silence.

"I've always loved Thornton," Tessa replied. "It was wonderful to see it again."

"My father must be turning in his grave to see it so neglected."

Tessa was sorely tempted to say that it surely wasn't Philip who had neglected Thornton Manor, but his father.

"And my poor mother's lovely rose garden . . ." Derek shook his head and clicked his tongue. "Thank God she can't see how it has deteriorated."

The conversation suddenly grew lively again, everyone speaking at once to cover the embarrassment of hearing one brother goad another in public. Looking down the table, Tessa saw how Philip's lips were compressed as he listened to something Sybil was saying to him. Tessa smiled at him, but he didn't see her. If her legs had been long enough to reach under the table, she would happily have kicked Derek hard on the ankle.

"So, what do you think of Victoria's husband-to-be?" Steven asked when James had finished serving her with the salmon en croute and asparagus in a lemon sauce.

Tessa cast a quick glance about her to make sure everyone else was busy talking. "Not much."

"Agree with me?"

She frowned. "I'm not sure. I haven't really seen them together enough. He was obviously feeling amorous. Couldn't keep his hands off her."

"He's always like that. Disgusting."

"She must like it," Tessa protested. "Vicky's not the sort to keep quiet if someone's doing something she doesn't like."

"Sexual infatuation. It'll soon wear off."

"Yes, but how soon?" She leaned closer to him. "That's what you're worried about, isn't it? That it won't wear off in time. That it will happen after they're married."

He nodded miserably, toying with the tiny portion of steamed sole that had been set before him.

"I wish I could help," she said softly, "but there isn't anything at all I can do. Vicky's her own woman. You must trust her to come to the right decision."

"I would, if she didn't have her mother and grandmother constantly filling her ears with nonsense." Steven turned around. "Excuse me a moment, Tessa. Barton appears to have something on his mind."

James Barton had come back into the dining room and was hovering beside him. He bent down and whispered something in Steven's ear. As she watched them, Tessa saw her uncle cast a smiling glance at her. "That's wonderful," he said, his eyes brightening in response to whatever James had told him. "Show him in." James went away. "A big surprise for you."

"For me?" Tessa tilted her head questioningly at her uncle.

"For all of us, in fact."

James came back into the room and then stood aside to let the man following him go ahead. He was tall, dressed in a nylon rain jacket that was soaking wet. He pulled back his hood. Although his hair was wet from the rain, its color was unmistakable: a rich auburn.

An almost concerted gasp came from those at the table, followed by a "Jesus Christ!" from Derek Thornton.

"Hi, everyone," said Tessa's son.

Chapter Twelve

If only this were a movie video, Tess thought, she could rewind the tape and stop it just before Jason entered the dining room.

The eerie silence was broken by everyone speaking at once.

"What the hell . . . !"

"Who is he?"

"My God, he looks like . . ."

And cutting through the babble, Sybil's imperious, "Who *is* this young man, Barton?"

Jason stood by the door, blinking in the candlelight, looking like a large red setter puppy that had bounded in, wagging its tail, only to be given a swift kick.

Feeling extremely sick, Tessa scraped back her chair and stood up. She walked down the length of the table and went to stand beside Jason. "This is my son, Jason," she said, addressing everyone at the table. "I wasn't expecting him to come here," she added with a defiant little smile. She took Jason's arm in a tight grip. "Excuse us, please."

"Just one moment." The voice she had most dreaded to hear came out of the ensuing babble. Derek heaved himself up, pushing back his chair. "Come into the light."

"Who, me?" Jason said. He looked utterly bewildered by the consternation he was causing.

"Yes, you." Derek's voice held an edge of menace. "Barton, switch on the damned lights."

The room was suddenly flooded with light, banishing all the shadows. Jason's hair gleamed even brighter.

"Come forward," Derek said.

"Okay," Jason said with a shrug and walked toward Derek. "What the heck's going on?"

Tessa winced at his insolent manner, but she knew it was induced by the unfriendly reception he'd received.

They stood looking at each other, the older man and the youth, the same height, the same muscular build. Although Derek's red hair had faded there was no escaping the fact that they were of the same blood.

This was the nightmare Tessa had dreaded for twenty years.

"I—I don't understand," Camilla said in a querulous voice. "It's like looking at Derek when he was twenty."

"If you don't understand you must be even dumber than I thought," Derek said harshly to his wife. Camilla sank back in her chair, looking extremely pale. Derek looked past Jason to Tessa, his face ghastly white, mottled with red patches. "Jesus, Tessa, you owe me an explanation."

"I owe you nothing," Tessa said. She could see Philip rising from the table, his face shocked. "Jason, let's go," she said, walking to the door.

"I'm going nowhere," he said defiantly. "I want to know what the shit's going on here."

"Ask your mother," Derek told him. "Ask her."

At one end of the table Sybil sat, staring straight ahead, her fingers smoothing out her napkin.

Steven rose slowly, leaning his fists on the table for leverage. "Derek is right, Tessa. You owe us all an explanation. Who is this boy?"

"I've told you," she said, trying to steady her voice. "He's my son. That's all you have to know."

The voices rose again, a barrage of words attacking her. Then Philip's voice cut through the noise. He had walked past her and gone to Jason. "You appear to be rather wet. Give me your jacket. How about a drink? What would you like?"

Jason looked from Derek to Philip. "Thank you, sir." He shrugged himself out of his jacket. Barton hurried forward to take it from him. "I'd like a beer, if that's possible."

"Fetch the lad a beer, Barton," Steven said, suddenly recalling his duty as a host.

Tessa remained by the door. She was willing Jason to leave the room with her, but he was ignoring her.

"Have you eaten?" Steven asked Jason.

"No, sir, I haven't. Apart from a sandwich on the train."

"Then you shall sit down with us and have some dinner. You interrupted ours."

"I'm sorry," Jason muttered.

"Not to worry. We shall continue with our meal."

"No, we bloody well won't," Derek shouted. "I want an explanation and I want it now."

"Sit down, Derek," Steven said. "We will finish our dinner like civilized people. Then you shall have your explanation."

"I'm leaving," Tessa said.

"No, Tessa, you are not," her uncle said. "You will sit down with us and finish your meal. Then you will talk to Derek."

She glared defiantly at him down the table, angry tears welling in her eyes. Philip took her arm. "I think it might be best if Tessa and Jason were to have their meal on trays in the library, Steven. That way they can have some privacy."

Tessa wasn't sure that she wanted to be alone with

Jason, but she was grateful to Philip, nonetheless. She couldn't stay in this room a moment longer.

A few words and it was all arranged.

"And don't go running off again like you did before," Derek shouted after Tessa as she left the room with Jason.

Tessa felt like running back and punching him in his florid face.

There was a cheerful fire burning in the library fireplace. Jason went to it, rubbing his hands together. "Man, am I cold. Some guy gave me a ride and dropped me off at the gates here. I had to walk up the driveway." He looked around the room. "I can't get over this house. You never told me your family lived in a palace," he said in a reproachful voice.

"It's not a palace."

"Well, it looks like one." He squatted in front of the fire, stroking the two dogs that were stretched out on the hearth rug. "It's like that boring *Brideshead Revisited* show you made me watch a bit of, remember? I never knew your folks had stacks of money." Again, the accusatory tone.

Tessa's stomach pinched. "It wasn't important."

"Not important? But this is where you grew up, isn't it? You never told me you lived in a rich place like this." He leaned forward. "And what was all that about?"

"What?"

"The big guy with the red face. What was he going on about? He sounded really mad at you about something or other."

At that point James wheeled in a food cart, with heated dishes: salmon, tiny new potatoes and vegetables. The food kept Jason quiet for a few minutes. He was obviously extremely hungry. "Tell me who everybody is," he said when he was working on his second plateful.

Tessa took a gulp of the brandy Barton had brought at her request, and felt the warm spirit coursing through her. Then she set the glass down. "The elderly man who asked if you'd eaten was my Uncle Steven. The woman at the other end of the table was Aunt Sybil."

"The wicked witch?"

"Sssh! Watch it!"

"Sorry." He grinned at her, but she wasn't in the mood for humor. "Who was the friendly guy who asked if I wanted a drink?"

"That was Philip Thornton."

"Who's he?"

"Just an old friend of the family. You've asked enough questions, Jason. Now it's my turn. Why did you come here? What about the school trip?"

"Oh, it got to be a big bore, taking us to all these old ruins. And the kids were driving me crazy. Some of them were only sixteen and behaved like geeks."

"You knew that it was mostly high school kids when you booked it."

"I know. But I didn't think it would be such a pain."

"How do you intend to get home?" she asked in a steely voice.

"To Canada? Oh, no sweat. It's all arranged. I told Mr. Klassen that I was going to stay with my mother in Yorkshire and that I'd meet the group back at Gatwick on Thursday."

"And he let you go?"

"He couldn't do much about it, considering I'm nineteen, could he? I thought I could go down with you Tuesday and spend a day on my own seeing London before I fly home."

Tessa felt like tearing into him, but it was too late now. She was overcome with an ineffable weariness. Nothing really mattered anymore.

"You haven't told me who the red-faced guy is," Jason said.

"He's my cousin's husband, Derek Thornton. Philip's brother."

"They don't look like brothers."

"No, they don't." She waited for him to remark on Derek's likeness to himself, but to her surprise, he made no allusion to it. Perhaps it just hadn't occurred to him.

"But then, look at Dad and me. We weren't alike at all, either. He was short. I'm six-one."

"That's right," Tessa said, her mouth dry.

"What was he going on about?"

"Who?"

"This guy, Derek Thornton."

If she were able to spirit him away right now, he need never know. She heard the murmur of voices. "Jason, would you do something for me?" she said, starting up from the chair.

"What?"

"Let's get out of here before they know we've left."

"But I've just arrived," he protested. He frowned. "Are you afraid of them, Mom?"

"No, of course not. I just don't want to stay here a minute longer."

"Why not?"

"Dammit, Jason. Why can't you do what I ask, just this once?"

It was too late. Someone was at the door, opening it. Philip came in.

"Oh, thank God it's you," Tessa said. "Would you drive us somewhere, anywhere, just so we can get away?"

"You can't run away again, Tessa. It's not fair to Derek. Or to your son."

"Not fair." Her eyes blazed at him. "Since when was anything fair in this house?"

"I understand your feelings, but you must stay and tell your side of the story."

"I should have thought it was obvious."

"One factor is obvious. It is your motive for keeping it a secret that is obscure." Philip looked at Jason. "Does Jason know?"

"Do I know what?" Jason demanded. "Will someone please tell me what's going on? I feel as if I've landed in a nuthouse."

"No, he doesn't know. I thought I'd never have to tell him."

"Know what?" Jason yelled. "Would you stop talking about me as if I'm not here and tell me what's going on."

Tessa looked at Philip. "He must be told right away, before you speak to Derek," Philip said. "As you can imagine, it's been hard to keep him from storming in here, but I've persuaded him to wait until I've spoken to you." He went to the door. "I'll wait outside. Let me know when you've finished."

Tessa went across the room to him. "Please stay," she begged him.

"No. This is something between you and your son." His austere expression softened a little. "I shall be here. I'm not going anywhere." He shook his head and sighed. "Oh, Tessa . . . If only you'd told me that night."

He opened the door and went out.

Tessa went back to Jason, who stood before the fire, waiting for her explanation. "Sit down, love. This is going to take a while."

"It's something bad, isn't it?"

"Not bad. Just that . . . that I should have told you a long time ago. To be honest, I was thinking of you when I made the decision not to tell you."

"It's about this man, Derek, isn't it?"

"Yes."

Jason suddenly sank down into the leather armchair. "Shit! I've just got it," he said. "He's my father, isn't he? Not Dad. This ... this guy's my real father."

"Yes. Derek Thornton is your father."

"Fuck!" He stared hard at her. "Did Dad know? Is that why he used to—to beat up on you?"

Tessa felt the old trembling in her stomach. She drew in a deep breath. "Yes, he knew. He had to know. We'd only been married six months when you were born."

"Yes, well he would know, then, of course." Jason's face was set in rigid lines. He looked at her with narrowed eyes, as if he hated her. "Unless you were sleeping with him at the same time as this Derek guy."

She couldn't trust herself to speak for a moment. "That was pretty unkind, Jason, but I suppose I deserve it. Let's cut to the chase, as you always say." She gave him a ghost of a smile. "I was deeply in love with Derek Thornton. We were engaged to be married."

"Then why the shit didn't he marry you?"

"Because he suddenly decided he wanted to marry my cousin Camilla instead."

"You mean he knew you were pregnant with his kid—with me—and he threw you over for your cousin?" Jason said incredulously.

"No, not quite." This was the difficult part, the part Jason wouldn't understand. The part she never quite understood herself. "Derek didn't know I was pregnant."

"How couldn't he know? You must have told him."

"No, I didn't tell him." Tessa looked down at her hands. She'd been gripping them together so tightly that there were white indentations in the skin. "Before I could tell him I was pregnant, he told me he was breaking off the engagement and marrying Camilla. That same night, I ran away from Langley. That's why I never wanted to come back here."

"But why didn't you tell him? Surely he'd never have done it if you'd told him you were pregnant."

Tessa hesitated. Then she said, "I was too proud."

"Proud?" Jason glared at her. "You must've been nuts. If he was the father of your kid he should've married you."

Tessa lifted her chin. "I didn't want to marry a man who didn't want me," she said through trembling lips.

There was another reason as well, but Jason didn't need to know about that now.

"I don't get it. You were engaged to the guy, weren't you? And how did you expect to manage on your own? This was your only family, wasn't it?"

"I wasn't thinking straight. I just ran. Fortunately—or unfortunately—I met your ... I mean, I met John Maltby and later we got married and emigrated to Canada."

"No wonder he drank and beat you up. You used him."

"I suppose I did. But he knew from the start what had happened." And used it against her throughout those five unbearable years together.

"No wonder he hardly ever saw me after you separated. I wasn't even his kid." Tears swam in Jason's eyes.

"Oh, darling." Tessa tried to put her arms around him, but he flung her off.

"Leave me alone."

"You see now why I never wanted to tell you. It's not a pretty story."

"I had a right to know who my real father was."

"Yes, you did. I'm very, very sorry. I've kept this secret so long that I thought you'd never need to know."

He looked around the library, at the shelves of leatherbound books, the hunting pictures on the walls, the antique furniture. "Did you ever think that all this could be mine?" he said belligerently.

"Hardly," she said dryly, "considering all this belongs to my aunt and uncle, not to Derek."

"Yeah, but he's rolling in it, too, isn't he? An English aristocrat."

"Actually, anything Derek has comes from having married Camilla. She is the heir to Langley. If he'd married me, he'd have got nothing in exchange."

"Except a son."

Tessa fell silent. *Please God,* she prayed, *don't ever let him work out that if I'd married Derek, he could have been the eventual heir to Thornton.*

"And I'd have been brought up in a place like this, instead of a crummy two-room apartment on St. Mary's Road."

"It didn't happen. So there's no point in crying 'If only,' is there?"

Philip knocked and came in at the same time. "Derek's growing very impatient."

"I think Jason and I have finished. For now, anyway."

Philip advanced farther into the room. "Would you like a game of billiards, Jason?"

"No, thanks."

"I think it might be best if we leave your mother and my brother alone together."

"Well, that's just too bad," Jason said. "He's my father and I've got a few things to say to him."

Philip glanced from Jason to Tessa. It was impossible to tell what he was thinking from his expression. "I understand. Very well, I'll send him in."

"Philip, wait." Philip turned at the door. "I can't bear the thought of having umpteen one-on-one confrontations," Tessa said. "I want to speak to the entire family at the same time. That way I'll get it all over at once."

"It could turn into a rather nasty interrogation for you."

"That's okay. I can take it. But what about Uncle Steven? How's he bearing up?"

"He's managing. It is a strain for him, though."

"Should I see him alone, do you think?"

"Why don't I ask him first?" Philip's hand was on the door.

"Philip."

"Yes?"

"Thank you."

He gave her a flicker of a smile and went out again.

"He's my uncle, right?" Jason said after a long silence.

"Yes, that's right."

"I like him. It's him you should've been marrying. I bet *he* wouldn't have thrown you over for your cousin."

The thought of Camilla and Philip together forced a smile from her. "That's true. But Philip is ten years older than I am. I was only sixteen when he got married."

"Oh." Jason was about to say something else, then stopped. He walked to the long window and drew back the crimson velvet curtain to look out. It was still raining hard, the rain streaking the window, obscuring the view of the gardens.

Tessa sat by the fire, watching his stiff back, aching to hold him.

After a short while, Philip returned. He came into the room, closing the door behind him.

"I've asked everyone to assemble in the drawing room. Derek wasn't happy about not seeing you alone, naturally, but I persuaded him that it was the best way. Camilla and her mother didn't want to stay, but Steven insisted that they remain."

"Does Uncle Steven want to see me alone first?"

Their eyes met. "No," Philip said.

Tessa swallowed a lump in her throat. "He's very angry with me, isn't he?"

"Angry? Yes, I suppose he is. But more than anything else he feels hurt. He cannot understand why you didn't go to him for help at the time." He walked to the door and then paused, his hand on the door. "I feel the same way," he added.

Tessa looked into the fire, seeing the blazing logs through a mist.

"Come into the drawing room when you're ready," Philip said, and left them.

Chapter Thirteen

The occupants of the drawing room appeared to have separated into couples, each choosing their own little space, conducting conversations with each other in muted tones, as if they were gathered at a funeral.

Not for the first time, Derek resented the way in which his brother had taken charge, shepherding them into the drawing room, despite his demand that he be alone with Tessa. Surely, in the circumstances, it was his right to see her first.

As he propped himself against the bookshelf near the drinks table, he dwelt gloomily on the past, wishing he could go back twenty years. By God, if he could have the chance, he'd make a different choice this time.

"For heaven's sake, stop that constant sniffing," Camilla told him.

"I've got a cold."

"You've always got a bloody cold."

His heart swelled with the injustice of it all. "You tricked me into it. This would never have happened if you and Sybil hadn't tricked me."

Camilla grabbed his hand and dug her nails into it. "Shut up! It all happened a lifetime ago. Too late now to be whining about it. Besides, I don't remember you making much fuss when it happened."

"I didn't know Tessa was pregnant with my son, did I?"

"I doubt you would have cared if you had known."

"You're a lying bitch." His eyes narrowed. "Come to think of it, maybe you knew she was expecting a child and that's why you forced me to break the engagement."

"Of course I didn't know," Camilla said scornfully. "None of us knew."

Vicky and Jeremy had moved away to the French windows that led out to the terrace, but they remained inside, as the rain was still spilling down. "Give me a cigarette," Vicky said.

"I thought you'd decided to stop."

"I have. But I need a smoke now."

He lit a cigarette for her and put it to her lips. "I must say, this is more exciting than a show on the box."

"How can you treat it like a joke? It's bloody awful."

His smile faded. "You're right. It'll be no joke if the papers get hold of it."

"Did you see poor Tessa's face? She looked absolutely ghastly when her son came in. I thought she was going to pass out."

"I'm not really concerned about Tessa. It's the press I'm concerned about."

"Who cares about the press?"

"I do. This could cause quite a nasty scandal for your father."

"To hell with that. It's Tessa I'm sorry for."

"You should be feeling sorry for your father."

"Well, I'm not. He'd obviously been playing fast and loose with both cousins. Tessa, being the poor relation, had to slink off into the night and have her baby all by herself. Can you imagine how awful that must have been for her?"

"From what I've heard tonight, she wasn't alone at all. She hitched herself up to this stable groom, poor chap. I suppose she foisted the kid off on him, pretended it was his."

Vicky frowned. "What I can't understand is why she didn't tell Daddy she was pregnant. I can't believe he would have abandoned her if she had." She stared out at the rain, watching it bouncing on the flagstones. "You realize Jason is my half brother, don't you?"

Jeremy's eyes widened. "Oh, terrific! That's all we need." He opened the French window and flung his cigarette outside. "Now you're going to take your father's bastard to your bosom."

Vicky stared at him as if she'd never seen him before. "You're just thinking of yourself and how this will affect you, aren't you?"

"I'm thinking about *us,* Vicky. I'm also thinking about my father and what he'd say if this mess were to come out in the papers."

Sybil watched them from her place by the fire. "There's Derek and Camilla yelling at each other in one corner and now Vicky and Jeremy are quarreling," she said. "I told you that Tessa would cause trouble, Steven. I was right. What on earth made you bring her here?"

"I wanted to see her before I die."

"What maudlin nonsense. You're not going to die."

Steven looked down at her. "Yes, Sybil, I am. You know damned well that I am. I wanted to see my brother's child again before I did. And there was something I wanted her to do for me."

"And what was that, may I ask?"

"You may ask, but I won't tell you." Steven bent forward to throw another log on the fire, breathing heavily with the exertion. Hell! He got tired so easily nowadays.

"You should let Barton do that."

"Barton's not here, is he?" He looked at his wife, seeking to see behind the mask she usually wore. Most of the time, he found it safer not to look. He loved her so damned much that he had always been afraid of discovering something that could destroy his love for her. But today he was so shaken by Jason's appearance he wanted to know the truth, whatever the cost. "Tell me, Sybil. What did you know about all this?"

"All what?"

"Tessa's pregnancy. Did you have a hand in it?"

"Hardly." She grimaced. "What could I have had to do with Derek getting your virginal little niece pregnant?"

"You know damned well what I mean. Did you have a hand in her running away?"

"Certainly not. All I knew was that Derek announced that he wanted to marry Camilla, not Tessa. The next thing we knew, Tessa had gone."

Steven gave her a long, hard look. "You always hated the fact that Derek and Tessa were engaged, didn't you? You didn't think she was good enough for him."

"The Thorntons are one of the oldest families in Yorkshire."

"But the Hargraves are just middle-class nobodies, right?" He couldn't hide his bitterness. "You never let me forget that, Sybil."

"I've always loved you, Steven."

"Yes, I don't doubt that, but sometimes I think you hate yourself for that little weakness."

She looked up at him. "If I hadn't had you I would have lost Langley. It was you who made such a success of the stables."

He was surprised to see moisture in her eyes. Sybil rarely wept, unless she was furious about something. He stretched out his hand and covered hers.

Vicky came to sit on the sofa. "What a miserable night it is," she said, holding her hands out to the blazing fire.

"Are you all right?" her grandmother asked.

"Yes, of course, Grandmother. Why shouldn't I be?"

Her grandmother was about to speak when the door opened. Philip came in first, and then he stood back to allow Tessa and Jason to go ahead of him.

As Tessa entered the room her heart was beating hard and fast. She felt as if her eyes were covered with layers of gauze, so that she saw only the outlines of people, not their faces.

"Sit down," Philip said, drawing out a chair.

"Thank you, but I'd rather stand."

Jason, still in his sweatshirt and mud-splattered jeans, stood awkwardly by the wall. *Setting a distance between us,* Tessa thought. One face materialized out of the mist: Vicky's. She was smiling at Jason.

"Jason, come and sit by the fire," she called out. "You must be frozen in those damp clothes."

Jason mumbled his thanks but said he was fine where he was.

Tessa felt like an actress who'd stumbled onto a stage and didn't know her lines. She drew in a deep breath and blinked a few times. Suddenly all the faces became clear to her. Derek and Camilla by the bookcases. Uncle Steven and Aunt Sybil by the fire with Vicky. Jeremy standing alone by the French window that led to the terrace. And, of course, Philip and Jason ... All of them waiting for her to speak.

She cleared her throat and tried to smile, but the muscles of her face were too stiff. "I thought it would be easier to speak to you all at once," she began.

"I must say, I think you might have had the decency to speak to me alone first." Derek glared at her across the room.

"I'm not sure you should be talking about 'decency,' Derek. I suppose I should have spoken to you alone. But I didn't think I could cope with more than one explanation. It will be easier if I tell you all at once."

"How very theatrical," she heard Camilla mutter.

Tessa stiffened, but she bit back the angry words that sprang to her mind. Feeling she could speak better on her feet, she stood behind the chair, clutching the back of it for support.

"There's really not that much to tell. As you've already guessed, Jason is Derek's son. He was born seven months after I left Langley. By then I'd been married to John Maltby for more than five months."

She could see Jason's stony face in profile, his damp hair bright, looking so like his father at the same age that it made her heart turn over.

"You all know that I'd become engaged to Derek and that we were going to be married in July." She turned to Jason. "This was April, Jason," she explained.

He turned away from her.

"For a few weeks I'd suspected I might be pregnant," Tessa continued, annoyed to feel her face flushing, as if she were a naive nineteen-year-old again. "On the Wednesday of Easter week I went to a family planning clinic in Northallerton. They confirmed that I was pregnant."

"Why on earth didn't you tell someone?" Steven demanded.

"I was going to tell Derek that evening. You were all here that night. Philip and his wife had come for dinner. They were spending Easter week at Thornton. Derek had driven from London with Camilla."

Tessa stopped, suddenly overcome with the horror of that evening. Then she sensed Philip standing very close behind her. His unspoken support gave her the courage she needed to get this over.

"I told Derek I wanted to speak to him alone. He said that he also had something to tell me. He seemed upset, distracted. Before I could tell him I was pregnant, he blurted out that he didn't love me anymore, that he loved Camilla and wanted to marry her."

"I was a bloody fool," Derek said under his breath, but loudly enough to be heard.

"My first inclination was to tell him about the baby, anyway. But then I wondered if I wanted him to marry me just because I was pregnant. The thought of him loving Camilla when he was married to me was more than I could bear. It would have been a nightmare."

She turned again to Jason, who was watching her. "You see, Jason, I loved Derek very much."

This time Jason didn't turn away from her.

"I didn't know what to do," Tessa continued. "In a few minutes I'd gone from being ecstatically happy at the thought of marriage and a baby with the man I loved, to being a future unwed mother, an outcast. I went to my room, wondering whether I should go to Uncle Steven and tell him."

"That's what you should have done," her uncle said in a gruff voice.

"A few minutes later Camilla came to me and told me how much she loved Derek. I had guessed that already. I knew that she was eaten up with jealousy over losing him to me. I was about to tell her that I was pregnant with Derek's child, but she . . . she . . ." Camilla's face stood out from the sea of faces turned toward her, as if it were illuminated by a spotlight. She cast a terrified look at Vicky.

Tessa hesitated. What was the point? It was all in the past now. Why destroy the last few illusions about her mother Vicky might still have?

"Camilla convinced me that she and Derek really loved each other and that they wanted to be married." Tessa summoned up a faint smile. "I didn't see the point in forcing someone to marry me against his will. I had my pride."

Derek's face grew so flushed that Tessa was afraid he was about to have a stroke. He turned on his wife. "You bitch! You bloody bitch!" He raised his hand. "You had to tell her, too, didn't you? You tricked Tessa like you tricked me."

Camilla stood up and pushed him aside. "I've had enough of this nonsense." She walked across the room, pushing past Philip, and went out.

"She tricked you, Tessa," Derek shouted. "She was lying."

Tessa went cold. She silently willed Derek to keep quiet for Vicky's sake.

"Camilla tricked both of us." Derek's eyes filled with tears. "She deprived me of my son."

"No. You deprived yourself by playing around with another woman when you were engaged to Tessa," Philip said.

"Ah, my upright brother, who never had an immoral thought in his life. That's because you're such a bloody cold fish you wouldn't know how to."

"That's enough," Steven said. "I want to know why you ran away with Maltby, Tessa."

"I didn't run away with him. I was walking along the road to Leyburn when he drove up behind me. He offered me a lift, asked what I was doing. I told him that Derek had broken our engagement. John told me he'd been fired. I didn't know why. At the time I didn't care. I felt so alone and lost that when he suggested we stay together it sounded like the answer to a prayer. Later on, of course, I found out that it was to be my worst nightmare. But at the time I was very grateful. When he asked me to marry him, I told him I was pregnant."

"Are you sure about that?" Jason was speaking for the first time since she'd begun her story.

"Absolutely. Your dad ... John knew before we were married that you weren't his son."

"Shit!"

Tessa wanted to go to him, put her arms around him, but knew that he would just push her off. The thought that she might have lost the one person in her life who truly mattered to her made her feel sick with apprehension.

"That's it," she announced with a defiant little smile. "The entire sordid little story of why Tessa ran away from Langley."

Derek came across the room to her. "Christ, Tessa. Why didn't you tell me?" He tried to put his arms around her, but she pushed him away.

"Because you didn't want me. You wanted Camilla."

"That's not true." He drew her aside, speaking low to avoid being overheard. "I didn't know what I wanted. Camilla was always a turn-on, but she didn't seem to want me until she heard you and I were engaged. Then she came on to me. She was hard to resist. I knew I'd made a mistake even before we were married. But it was too late then. You had gone."

"Ah, well. It's all in the past," Tessa found herself saying. "Come on, Jason. Let's pack up and go home."

"Not before I've had a chance to get to know my son," Derek protested.

A chill ran over Tessa. "He's not interested in getting to know you."

"Speak for yourself, Mom."

Derek gave her a triumphant smile. "See?"

Tessa's throat tightened. "I don't think—"

"Would you like to spend some time at Langley?" Derek asked Jason. "Get to know us?"

Jason looked from him to his mother and then back again. "Yeah. Yeah, I would."

"No, Jason." Tessa turned to give a mute appeal to Philip.

"It might be a good idea," Philip said carefully. "I think it could be important for Jason to know who his father's family is."

Tessa felt trapped, betrayed. If Philip wasn't willing to support her, she was alone. "I don't intend to stay in this house tonight," she said through tight lips. "How could I possibly stay here?" she asked, again appealing to Philip.

"It's still your home." Steven had come to join the group by the door. "I don't think you should run away again."

"I can't stay. Not after all that has happened. It's impossible. Jason, you have to join the school group at Gatwick next Thursday, remember?"

"That's five days away," Steven said. "The lad could spend a few days here and we could get to know him."

Tessa looked across the room to where Sybil sat, seemingly oblivious to all that was going on. "I doubt if Aunt Sybil would be happy about that, in the circumstances."

The basilisk eyes locked with hers.

"Your aunt will be happy to have your son stay with us, Tessa," her uncle said.

"I'd prefer it if you came away with me," she told Jason.

"I'm an adult, Mother. I make my own decisions. I want to stay here. You go. I'll fly home Thursday."

Jason was very angry with her, she could tell that. But not half as angry as she was. "Could we speak alone for a minute?" she asked, gripping his arm tightly.

He dragged his arm away. "Not if you're going to tell me to leave."

"No, I won't do that. Please, Jason."

"Okay." He followed her out into the chilly hall.

"What about work this summer?" she asked him.

"I said I'd be home on Thursday."

"What if you don't come back?" she said, voicing her main fear.

"If I don't it's because I think getting to know my father is more important than earning five bucks an hour."

"Maybe it is. But there's your future to think of. You start university in September."

"Yeah. Well, we'll see. There's some things much more important than university."

Chapter Fourteen

As Jason watched his mother walk away with her uncle, he sensed that things would never again be the same for them. Gone was the simple, uncomplicated life—apart from a few screwups he'd been responsible for—they'd shared since his father's death.

But he hadn't even been his real father, had he?

As he stood in the middle of the hall, feeling totally disoriented, the girl who'd spoken to him came over to him. He'd noticed her when he'd first come into the dining room. She was stunning, probably about his own age, with red-gold hair.

"Hi, Jason. I'm Vicky," she said. "I hope you don't mind." Before he could say a word, she flung her arms around his neck and kissed his cheek. She smelled wonderful.

Automatically he hugged her back.

"I thought someone should welcome you. Who better than your sister?"

Sister! Jason stared at her.

She laughed. "Poor chap. You look absolutely shattered. I suppose you don't even know who we all are."

He shook his head. Where the hell had his mother disappeared to now, when he really needed her?

Derek Thornton approached him. He looked as if he'd been overindulging in something, Jason wasn't sure what. He held out his hand to Jason. "You won't believe it, looking at me now," he said in a slurred voice, "but you are the absolute double of me when I was twenty years old."

Jason took Derek's hand. It was damp and trembled in his. "I guess that's why everyone was so surprised when I turned up."

"Exactly. Rather like seeing a living ghost."

Derek still held his hand. Jason withdrew it slowly, not wanting to seem too abrupt. *Your father,* a voice said in his head. *This man's your father.*

They stood looking at each other, neither knowing what to say.

"I'd always wanted a son," Derek said after a while. He blinked and turned away to blow his nose hard in his checked handkerchief.

Jason didn't know how to respond. Vicky stepped forward and linked her hand in her father's arm. "I was telling Jason that I'm his sister."

Derek snapped his head around to look about the hall. "For God's sake, don't let your mother hear you say that," he muttered.

"Why not? It's the truth." She grinned at Jason. "Come to think of it, we do look alike, don't we, with our red hair?"

"I suppose so," Jason said.

"Let me introduce you to Jeremy."

"Jeremy?"

"Yes, he's my fiancé." Vicky turned to yell, "Jeremy, come over here!" across the width of the hall.

Jason grinned. He liked her. She wasn't at all stuffy like the rest of the family. Yet, somehow, she still seemed to fit into this place, even though it looked more like a museum or art gallery than a home. He supposed it was because it *was* her home.

As Vicky introduced Jeremy to him, everything fell into place. He remembered his mother telling him how

Vicky's grandfather didn't want Vicky to marry Jeremy. Jason could understand why. Jeremy was looking at him as if he were a slug that had just crawled out of the lettuce. "This your first visit to Langley?" he drawled.

Vicky rolled her eyes and answered for Jason. "Of course it is, stupid. Were you asleep when Jason came into the dining room?"

Jeremy gave her a cold look. "I wasn't sure that it was a subject we should be discussing," he told her.

"Why not? Let's face it, Jeremy. Jason is my half brother."

"Not legally, he isn't."

Jason's hands gripped into fists. He felt like smashing one of them into this jerk's aristocratic nose.

"You'll have to excuse him, Jason," Vicky said. "It seems that manners weren't part of his education at Eton."

Swearing under his breath, Jeremy walked away.

"What's the matter with Jeremy?" Derek asked.

"He's being an idiot," Vicky said. "Can someone tell me why on earth we're standing out here in the hall, freezing? Let's go back into the drawing room and have some champagne to celebrate."

Jason looked around. Jeremy was standing in a far corner of the hall, talking in a low voice to Philip Thornton. His mother and her uncle had disappeared into some room down the passage. And the two other women were nowhere to be seen.

"I'm not sure there's much to celebrate," he said.

"Of course there is. Let's do it. How about it, Daddy?"

But even her father wasn't in the mood for a celebration, it seemed. "I want to speak to Tessa," Derek said petulantly. "She should have spoken to me first."

"She was upset. Papa will help to calm her down.

Then you can speak to her." Vicky spoke to her father as if he were a child.

Another man came into the hall. "There's a good fire in the library," he said to Vicky. "Why don't you go in there?"

Vicky gave him a grateful smile. "Thanks, Kevin. Is my grandfather in there?"

"No, he and Miss Hargrave are in his study."

"Okay. Let's move into the library, then. Do you think you could get James to bring in some champagne?"

"Why not?" The familiar smile he gave Vicky puzzled Jason. It was hard to work out who everyone was. He'd thought this man was a servant of some sort, but he seemed far too casual with Vicky to be a servant.

"Great," Vicky said. "Oh, and, Kevin . . . meet Jason."

"Hi, Jason. I'm Kevin Taylor." Kevin held out his hand.

"Kevin's our estate manager," Vicky told Jason. "Runs the entire place."

"Do you?" Jason said, impressed. "All by yourself?"

"Well, hardly that," Kevin said. "I've a few people to help me." He and Vicky grinned at each other.

Jason felt a bit of a fool. Of course the man couldn't manage this huge place all by himself.

"If you like I'll take you on a tour of the estate in the morning," Kevin said. Unlike Jeremy, he didn't seem at all hostile.

"Thanks. That'd be great."

"Like horses, Jason?" Derek asked.

"I don't suppose he's had much to do with them, living in Canada, Daddy," Vicky said.

"As it happens, I have," Jason said. "At least, when

I was a kid. My father used to—" He stopped, ashamed to feel the heat rushing to his face.

"Of course," Philip Thornton said. Jason hadn't even seen him approach. "Your father worked with horses in Winnipeg, didn't he? I remember Steven telling us that John Maltby was one of the best grooms they ever had at Langley. Isn't that right, Derek?"

"Can't remember," Derek muttered, and then turned away. "Vicky's right. It is bloody cold out here. Let's go into the library and have a drink, as Taylor suggested. Then I shall speak to your mother, Jason."

Remembering the expression on his mother's face when she'd walked away with her uncle, Jason wasn't sure that she'd be willing to speak to Derek Thornton. He'd seen that stony look before. No one would find it easy to deal with her when she was in one of those moods.

The whole idea of coming to Yorkshire was to give her a surprise. It had been a surprise, all right, but not the one he'd intended.

Tessa and her uncle had just started to talk when Barton came in with a message from Sybil, to remind Steven that he hadn't had his evening injection. When Barton took him upstairs, Tessa had sat huddled on the sofa, staring at the glowing electric fire, which her uncle had turned on to warm the place. She was wishing herself anywhere but here.

After about fifteen minutes, Steven returned, now dressed in his paisley silk dressing gown. "Now, let's see where we were before we were so rudely interrupted," he said, glaring at poor James, who was trying to make him comfortable in his chair. James said good night, and left the room.

"I was telling you that I had no idea that Jason would even think of coming here," Tessa said. "I thought it was safe for me to come, with him in Europe."

"You should have told him years ago."

"What? What should I have told him? That he was illegitimate? That my cousin Camilla's husband was his father?"

Steven sighed. "There is no need to be quite so melodramatic, Tessa. Maltby accepted him as his son, so he wasn't illegitimate, was he?"

"You know what I mean. Anyway, now you know why I never came back." She pushed her hand through her hair, rumpling it even more. "And I wish to God I hadn't been such a fool as to think I could come back now and get away with it. If I'd stayed in Canada, this would never have happened."

"And you would have lived a lie."

"I've done it for twenty years." She stared at him. "Don't you see? It's not me I'm concerned about, it's Jason. Think how this is going to affect him."

"I believe it has done so already."

"Exactly. Do you know what he said? That other things were more important than university." She drew in a long breath and released it, trying to ease the tension in her shoulders. "I want him to come away with me, now, tonight, before it's too late."

"He's nineteen. Legally an adult. You can't force him to come with you, you know. Why not stay and work it out with him?"

"What is there to work out? Biologically, Derek is his father. That's it. End of story."

"Now you are being naive. Surely the lad will be curious about his father, about his background."

"I can tell him whatever he wants to know."

"Ah, but can he believe what you tell him? That's the question. You've lied to him before about his parentage."

"I did it to save him from being hurt."

"And to avoid getting hurt again yourself?"

"No, not really. Derek will never hurt me again. Especially now, when I see what he has become. I've been through hell because of him ... and because I married John Maltby. But I've learned to live by myself, without depending on a man for my livelihood and my happiness. I shall never again put myself in a situation where that could happen."

"Are you saying that you would never consider marrying again?"

"Damned right I am. Damned right!" Tessa was breathing heavily. "The day I held those divorce papers in my hand I swore I would never, ever rely on a man again for anything."

For a fleeting moment she felt a spasm of guilt as she thought of reliable Mark Crawford, waiting for her back in Winnipeg, but then she swept them away—guilt and Mark—knowing that she had far more important things to deal with at present.

"I suppose I can't blame you," Steven said. "You've been sadly used by the men in your life, including me."

She sank down before him, leaning her arms on his bony knees, which James had covered with a woolen rug. "No. You mustn't say that. It was never your fault. It was mine. Mine and Derek's."

"The bloody man seduced you, for God's sake. You weren't even twenty."

"It was the 1970s, Uncle Steven, not the 1950s." She gave him a wry smile. "I just made the mistake of believing Derek when he said he would look after everything. Living at Langley was like being in a time warp for me. It might as well have been the fifties."

Her uncle turned his head away to gaze into the fire.

For the first time in ages, Tessa forced her memory

back to those months before she had fled from Langley. There'd been no fancy finishing school or even university for her when she'd left school at seventeen. She'd just stayed on at Langley, working in the office. Hardworked and underpaid. Whenever she had tried to break away her uncle had begged her to stay. Now, with hindsight, she realized that he'd been lonely. There had been something about her, perhaps the fact that she was his brother's daughter, that he needed.

She also realized that with Camilla away she'd had Derek to herself when he came home to Thornton on the weekends. A definite incentive to remain in the comparative remoteness of the Dales.

"I blame myself." Her uncle's voice pushed into her thoughts, startling her. "You should have gone away to London. Got some training, more education. You were cut off from life here."

"Oh, I don't know. I had you ... and Derek most weekends."

"That was the trouble. Derek and you had too much time alone together. But I also blame Camilla. She knew you were engaged. Yet as soon as she came back to England she set her cap at Derek."

Tessa had to smile at the old-fashioned expression. "Camilla had always wanted Derek. She hated me for stealing him from her." Tessa sat back on her heels and stared dreamily into the fire. " 'He'll soon get bored with you,' she used to tell me. 'You wait, he'll break off the engagement before you know it.' "

She didn't mention the one factor that preyed on her mind. *She tricked you, Tessa,* Derek had shouted. She couldn't hurt her uncle by asking him about it. As far as she was concerned, it would never be discussed with anyone again. Not with Derek. Not with Camilla. And, most especially, not with Aunt Sybil.

Because she intended to leave Langley and never see either Camilla or her aunt again.

She scrambled to her feet. "I think it's time I spoke to Derek. Then I'm leaving."

Steven's hands twisted agitatedly in the fringe of his rug. "You can't leave tonight. Where would you go?"

"Let's get one thing straight. I'm not going to stay in this house tonight. But I also intend to keep my promise to you, despite what has happened. Jason and I will move into a hotel tonight for a couple of nights. Tomorrow I can join you for church and the flower festival. Maybe Philip would take us for a drive . . ." She broke off and shook her head. "No, that's not a good idea, either. Better to steer clear of him, as well, in the circumstances."

The door opened. "Speak of the devil," her uncle said, to her annoyance, as Philip put his head around the door.

"Are you alluding to me?" Philip asked with a hint of a smile, but his face immediately reverted to its serious expression.

"Tessa wants to move into a hotel. See if you can persuade her to stay on here."

"Please don't try," Tessa told Philip. "I've made up my mind. Jason and I will move out, but we'll stay on until Monday morning, so that I can spend tomorrow with Uncle Steven."

She could see that he understood. "Perhaps it's for the best." For a moment he hesitated. Then he said, "Would you consider staying at Thornton?"

Her heart leapt at the thought. Comfortable, familiar Thornton was just what she needed, but she knew it wouldn't work. How could she possibly stay in Derek's old home? Besides, she was hoping Jason wouldn't need to see Thornton.

"I don't think that would be a very good idea, do you? Not in these rather peculiar circumstances."

"Would you excuse us for a moment, Steven?" Philip motioned to Tessa to go out of the study ahead of him. To her relief, she saw that the passageway and hall were empty. "I'm afraid you may have some difficulty in persuading Jason to come away with you. Derek is encouraging him to stay on at Langley for a while."

"Oh, no. I thought that might happen. Doesn't Derek realize how furious Camilla and Sybil would be? They'd make Jason's life a misery."

He looked down at her in the semidarkness. "Why didn't you tell me?"

"Tell you what?" she asked, knowing very well what he meant.

"That night, when Derek broke off the engagement. Why didn't you tell me you were expecting his child?"

How like Philip, she thought, to avoid the word "pregnant." Not out of prudishness, but because he preferred to maintain the niceties of an earlier, more courteous age.

"I didn't tell Derek," she said belligerently. "Why should I tell you?"

"Because I could have helped you. If you had told me, you could have avoided being involved in what was obviously a marriage of convenience."

Tessa gave him a bitter smile. "It turned out to be anything but convenient."

"I realize that." He sounded almost angry with her. "Can you imagine how I feel, knowing that had I only asked a few more questions, kept you there for a few minutes longer, you might never have met up with Maltby, might never have had to live a life of misery with him?"

She laid her hand on his arm. Again, she felt that spark of electricity she had felt before in the garden. The sooner she got away the better. Everything here was far too complicated.

"Thanks for your concern, Philip. But I'm just fine now. I've organized my life so that I don't have to worry about anything or anyone other than Jason. And that's how I like it."

"Jason's an adult. What will you do when he leaves home?"

"I just wish I'd never come back, that's all," she said, totally ignoring his question. "I can't believe I was so *stupid*." She spat out the word.

"You did it for your uncle. It was his wish to see you before he died."

Her mouth trembled. "You know, with all that's happened tonight I had almost forgotten why it was I came."

"That is why I'm reminding you."

"He said he only asked me to come because he was worried about Vicky marrying Jeremy."

"Did you believe that?"

She shook her head wordlessly, clamping her lips together to hold back tears. "No, not really. He *is* worried about them, but I think that what he really wanted was to see me again."

"Yes." Philip looked down into her face. "That being the case, can you honestly say that you are sorry you came?"

"I suppose not. I just wish Jason hadn't come, that's all."

How often had they talked together this way when she was in her early teens and he an adult, before his marriage? Usually she had felt much better afterward. Now, she knew that no amount of discussion could heal what had happened.

The library door opened, sending a shaft of light across the passage. "Is . . . is that you, Tessa?" Derek's voice said. He leaned against the doorway. "I want to talk to you."

"Oh, God," Tessa whispered. "He's had more to drink, hasn't he?"

"Celebration champagne," Philip said. "I'll come with you. See if I can persuade him to postpone the discussion until tomorrow."

"I won't be here tomorrow."

"Then you must speak to him tonight."

Chapter Fifteen

Derek pushed himself away from the door frame and stood swaying in the shaft of light. "It's high time we had a talk," he said belligerently.

"Yes, I know. Why don't we talk tomorrow, Derek? I'm terribly tired."

"You're not too tired to talk to my brother, the saintly advocate, though."

Oh, God! This was all she needed. An intimate conversation with a pickled Derek.

"Why don't you let Tessa come into the library?" Philip suggested. "It's cold out here."

Derek stood aside to let her pass, but then barred his brother's way. "Not you. This is between Tessa and me."

"I realize that, but what about Jason? Isn't he still in there with you? And what about Vicky and Jeremy?"

"They've gone up to bed. Poor old Jeremy was probably getting randy."

"And Jason?"

"Jason can stay. He's my son." He stared into Philip's face and gave him a malevolent grin. "You didn't know I had a son, did you?"

"No, Derek," Philip said patiently. "None of us knew until tonight."

"Tessa knew."

Tessa sighed. "Let's go in and talk, Derek." She gave Philip a faint smile. "I'll be okay."

"Are you sure?"

"Yes, absolutely." She hesitated and then went out into the passage with him again. "I . . . I wonder if someone could find me a room in a pub or hotel for tonight?"

"I'll see to it. Then I'll drive you there."

"No, I don't want you to have to wait for me. Surely Kevin or James—"

"I'd like to drive you myself. But first we'll have to find you a place. July weekends are usually booked well ahead."

She brushed her hair back from her forehead in a gesture of weariness. She was sure he was about to invite her again to stay at Thornton, but, to her relief, he didn't. "I shall be in the study with Steven."

"Steven? Oh, God. I'd forgotten all about him. I should—"

"Don't worry. I'll tell him you're with Derek. He'll understand." He looked past her into the library. "Are you sure you can manage?"

"Yes. Derek's not the first drunk I've had to deal with."

He looked at her, eyes narrowed. "Poor Tessa," he said softly. "Fortunately, Derek doesn't get violent, just bloody annoying."

"I'll be fine," Tessa reassured him again, and went into the library.

Derek was about to close the door, but Philip held it open. "Do you want to come with me, Jason?" he called through the half-open doorway. "We never did have that game of billiards I promised you."

"He's staying right here," Derek said.

"If you change your mind, Jason, you'll find me in the study." As Philip moved away, Derek slammed the door shut.

Tessa felt trapped. This was her favorite room at Langley, but tonight the book-lined walls and the dark velvet curtains seemed to press in on her, smothering her. A little shiver passed over her shoulders as she sat down on the sofa beside Jason.

"All right, love?" she asked him softly, touching his hand. His brown eyes looked enormous. She could tell that he was feeling shattered. *That makes two of us,* she thought. "We'll be out of here soon," she whispered.

"Jason wants to stay at Langley for a while," Derek said. "We've been making plans."

Tessa squeezed Jason's hand. "You don't have to do anything you don't want to do."

"I told ..." Jason searched for the right word. "I told Mr. Thornton that I'd like to see the stables tomorrow."

"*Derek,* lad. I told you to call me Derek for now." Derek beamed at Jason and then sat down heavily in Steven's chair, the leather protesting beneath his weight.

"I'm going to talk to Derek for a short time," Tessa told Jason. "Then I'm going to move into one of the local pubs. Philip's making the arrangements."

"I want to stay here, Mom. That's what *he* wants."

Her eyes locked with Jason's. "But it's not what I want. You don't understand, Jason. This is my aunt's house, not Derek's. And—I hate to have to say this— she doesn't want either of us here."

Derek leaned forward. "Camilla and I have our own wing of the house. Sybil never comes near it. Completely private. It's our home. Plenty of room for Jason to stay there."

Tessa's patience was wearing thin. "Oh, and Camilla would welcome Jason with open arms, wouldn't she, Derek?"

"Course she would. He's my son."

Tessa closed her eyes for a moment, praying for either a little more patience or for Derek to pass out.

"I get the message," Jason said to her. "No one wants me here, except him. And you don't want me even to speak to him, because of what he did to you before I was born. Where does that leave me?"

"It leaves you coming home with me."

"I want to find out . . ."

"Find out what?"

"All the stuff about . . . him, about my family."

"I can tell you everything," Tessa said.

"Oh, sure you can. Just like you did before, eh?"

"You've a right to be angry with me. But I promise I'll tell you nothing but the truth if you come away with me tonight."

"Let's have another drink." Derek picked up the bottle. "Damn, this one's finished." He looked around. "Where the devil did Barton get to? Ring that bell, would you, Tessa? Then I want you to explain to me why you didn't tell me you were pregnant with my child."

She saw the flush of embarrassment on Jason's face. "Just one more minute, Derek, please." She gave Jason a pleading look.

He stood up. "I guess I should leave you two together."

That was something, at least. "Philip said to come to the study."

"Where is it?"

"I'll show you." She led him out to the passageway.

"See if you can find Barton while you're at it," Derek shouted.

Jason winced. "Is he always this bad?"

"How would I know?" Then, realizing how sensitive Jason must be feeling at the moment, she quickly added, "He wasn't a heavy drinker when he was young. He was healthy, athletic, and very handsome."

Jason tried to smile. "Glad to hear it. I was beginning to wonder about you."

"I expect you were. Thanks, love."

"For what?"

"For taking all this much better than I would have expected you to." She hugged him, but his body remained unyielding, his spine stiff against her hands.

Oh, Jason, my darling boy. Have I lost you?

She released him, swallowing the lump in her throat. "Cross the hall and the study's the second door on the left. They're expecting you."

"Okay." He started off, his shoulders slumped.

"Jason."

He turned. "What?"

"I'm so sorry."

He stared at her for a moment. "Yeah, so am I."

Reluctantly she went back into the library. She had just sat down again when James came into the room, carrying a new bottle of brandy.

"Do you have ESP?" she asked him.

He acknowledged her question with a little smile. "No, Miss Hargrave. Mr. Thornton contacted me on the house telephone."

"Oh, I see." She watched him actually take a few steps backward, as if they were royalty, before he turned and left the room. His stage-butler act annoyed her. His plummy accent was a phony one, for sure.

"Why did you cut your hair?" Derek asked. "I don't like it as much that way. It's too severe, not very feminine."

"It's practical. Easy to look after when you're flying and staying in hotels."

Derek frowned. He'd obviously forgotten what she did for a living.

"I'm a flight attendant with Canada Airways," she reminded him.

"Bloody awful job. Means you're nothing but a

skivvy, really. Could have done better for yourself than that."

Tessa bit down on the inside of her lip. "Without a degree, I was lucky to get it. I love my job," she said sweetly. It was true, even though she might not be doing it again. She swallowed. Better not to think of that now. "You want to know why I didn't tell you I was pregnant."

"That's right." He poured himself another large glass of brandy and took a gulp of it. "Why didn't you? My child, too, after all."

"That's true." At least he couldn't question *that*. "The reason is simple. I was going to tell you. Actually, I was very excited about it. I knew it would mean having to change the wedding date, but I didn't think you'd mind that. I was about to tell you when you hit me with the bombshell that you were going to break our engagement and marry Camilla instead."

"Bloody young fool!" She wasn't quite sure if he meant himself or her. "If only you'd told me, I'd have married you."

"I didn't want one of Camilla's castoffs."

He glared at her, a nerve jumping at the corner of his eye. "It was you I was going to marry."

"Yes, well you'd decided not to, hadn't you? I wasn't about to stick around while you played 'love her, love her not.' "

"She tricked me into it."

"Who did?"

"Camilla. Threw herself at me. Aided and abetted by that witch of a mother of hers. And then, of course, she told me *she* was pregnant."

"I've an idea you didn't need much persuading," Tessa said quickly, remembering the promise she'd made to herself not to discuss the subject of Camilla's pregnancy with anyone. For Vicky's sake.

He opened his mouth to protest, but then took another drink instead.

"Especially when you knew that you and Camilla would inherit Langley," Tessa continued. "Whereas, if you married me you would have to live a pretty mundane life. Find a real job, take on a mortgage, probably not be able to afford to send our kids to a private school. No wonder you chose Camilla."

He looked at her through half-closed eyes. "Christ, you've changed. I don't remember your having a bitchy tongue like this."

She smiled and knew that it was not a pleasant smile. "Life has changed me, Derek. When I left Langley I had to grow up very fast."

"You certainly did. Out of one bed, into another." He leaned across, fingers splayed on his broad knees. "Tell me, sweetheart, how did you like sleeping with a man who stunk of the stables?"

She lifted her head and looked straight into his bleary eyes. "At least he married me."

"If I had known you were pregnant, I'd have married you, too. You didn't give me the chance."

"This is getting us nowhere, Derek. We're just going round and round in circles. Besides, what's the point? It's all in the past. We can't change what's happened."

"There's Jason. My son." Tears filled his eyes. "I've always wanted a son. After Vicky was born, Camilla couldn't have another child. Too dangerous, the medics said."

"But you love Vicky, don't you?"

"Certainly I do. But it's not quite the same, is it?"

Tessa decided not to touch that one. No point in embarking on an argument about sexism.

"Now I shudden—suddenly find I have a son." He grinned at her. "He's the spitting image of me, isn't he? That's why you never came back, isn't it?"

That . . . and other reasons. "Yes."

"Cruel, that was. Very cruel." He was deteriorating fast. In fact, as she watched him, his eyes closed and he began to snore.

"Derek, we're both very tired. I think we've said all that there is to say."

He opened his eyes. "What about Jason?"

"What about him?"

"What's going to happen to him?"

"As far as I'm concerned, Jason is coming home to Winnipeg with me, getting a summer job, and starting university in the fall."

"Want him to stay here for a while. Get to know each other."

"That sounds lovely in theory, Derek, but Jason is already a year behind. He should have started university last year, but didn't have enough credits."

"What does he went to be?"

"God knows," Tessa said in exasperation. "All I care about is getting him into university. Then he can decide what he's going to be later."

His eyes closed again. He struggled to open them. "Want to help."

"I don't need your help," Tessa said through gritted teeth.

"Not you. Him. My son."

"Neither of us needs your help." Her voice was unsteady. "We've managed fine all these years without it."

"Not fair. Didn't know ... about him." His eyes closed again, but this time they didn't open. His mouth hung open and she saw that he had fallen into a heavy snoring sleep.

Her prayers had at last been answered.

Chapter Sixteen

Slowly Tessa got to her feet, hoping that Regan, who was lying in front of the fire, wouldn't bark when she moved. Then she turned and tiptoed from the room.

Philip was standing outside the door, looking like a guard on duty. She laid her finger on her lips and then walked down the passage to the hall. "He's asleep."

"Thank God for that," Philip said.

"My sentiments exactly." She looked away for a moment. "I think enough was said. He probably won't remember any of it, but—" She shrugged and gave him a faint smile. "I told him it was all in the past, anyway." She looked down at her watch, but not registering what time it was. "I thought you'd be playing billiards with Jason."

"He wasn't in the mood, so the three of us talked instead." Philip hesitated. "He tells me that he intends to stay here. For tonight, at least."

"Yes. So I understand. I'm not happy about it, but what can I do?"

"I don't want to cause you unnecessary worry, but I think you should know that he intends to stay on after you've left, as well. I don't just mean for a few days, either."

"Yes, so I gathered from the rather garbled conversation I had with Derek. I just can't get him to see that Jason won't be welcome here."

"And Jason is far too old for you to be able to order him to come home."

"Exactly." Tessa heaved a deep sigh and released it slowly. "What can I do?" she said, her voice heavy with resignation.

"You're still planning to go elsewhere tonight?"

"Yes. Definitely."

"I rang the Black Lion, but unfortunately they don't have a room available. Nor does Mrs. Middlethorpe, who runs a fairly decent bed and breakfast place in the village."

"Damn. Is there anywhere else? I can't stay here."

He hesitated. "You could stay at Thornton."

"No, I don't want to stay at Thornton," she said, her voice rising. She immediately regretted her rudeness. "Sorry, Philip. I'm feeling a bit on edge."

"I'm not surprised. Have you packed your things yet?"

"Oh, God. No, I haven't."

"Then why don't you do that now? I'll go and ring a few more places to see if I can find you a room. I could ask friends, of course, but I thought you'd prefer to be on your own."

She nodded, but found herself unable to speak. Philip was about to say something, but decided against it and went back into the study.

Tessa stood in the center of the hall, feeling rather like Alice in Wonderland growing smaller and smaller, the family portraits and the painted ceiling towering over her.

Steven came out of his study, leaning on Jason's arm. "Must find this young man a room for the night. Then I intend to go to bed myself."

"He could come with me." Tessa frowned at Jason.

"Are you still insisting on leaving Langley tonight?" Steven asked.

"I think it's better if I do." She could see that he

was hurt by her decision. "I'll meet you at St. Luke's in the morning," she said brightly. "Eleven o'clock?"

"Yes." He began to walk to the lift, and then turned around. "Ring me in the morning to let me know where you are and I'll send someone in the car to fetch you."

She went to him and kissed his cheek. "Thank you." She moved toward Jason, but sensing his tension, did not kiss him. *We should be talking, my son and I,* she thought. *We should be together tonight, not apart.* But Jason had set up a wall between them and she knew from experience that it was no use trying to break it down with a sledgehammer. Chiseling worked better with Jason. But chiseling took time, and time was what she didn't have.

Her heart ached as she looked at his bleak face.

"Come along, young man," Steven said, pressing the button for the lift. "I'll find you some pajamas."

"I've got some in my bag," Jason told him.

"I don't see any bag."

"The man who let me in took it from me."

"Barton? Then we'll get him to bring it up in a minute. Let's go."

The lift door closed and they were gone.

Tessa shivered. A draft was blowing across the floor of the hall. *You're a fool,* she told herself. *There's a warm bed for you up just one flight of stairs. You could run up to your room, lock the door, unhook the telephone, and curl up and sleep.*

But this was Sybil's house, she reminded herself. Those were Sybil's ancestors staring down at her from the walls. There were too many unhappy memories in this house for her. She would not stay here one more night.

She suddenly realized that it was not fear that drove her away. She no longer feared any of them. Tonight the worst had happened, yet she had faced up to them and she was still whole. The realization brought a feeling of lightness, as if a heavy burden had been lifted from her shoulders.

The internal conflict died away and then ceased. She was no longer the poor relation, forced to take charity. She could leave Langley tonight of her own free will and pay for her hotel room.

For a while, anyway, she reminded herself. If she didn't get back to Winnipeg and find a new job pretty soon she might very well be a charity case again. But that was merely being maudlin. This return visit to Langley had served to reinforce her determination never again to rely on anyone but herself.

She was halfway up the flight of stairs when Philip appeared. "Success," he said. "I've found you a room in a hotel in Middleham. I'll drive you over."

"Oh, that's great. Thanks so much, Philip. I'll just throw my things into my bag. Won't be long."

Fortunately, she hadn't brought that much, so it didn't take long to pack everything. She checked the bathroom and then the drawer in the bedside cabinet, to make sure that nothing of hers had been left behind. Then, taking one last look at the beautiful but alien room, she went down to Philip.

"You were very quick." He took his raincoat from James Barton, whose expression remained impassive. The epitome of a storybook perfect butler, James made no comment whatsoever on the strange events that had occurred at Langley this evening.

"You're right," Tessa said as she settled herself beside Philip in his car. "He *is* like a stage butler. To tell you the truth, he gives me the creeps. Even old Henchard, who was definitely the real thing, would have had some little comment to make about what happened tonight."

Philip started the car and drove off down the gravel driveway. "He certainly would have. I can remember him telling me, when I was called to the bar, that I must make sure that I rub some dirt into my wig, to make sure it didn't look so white and new."

"Did he really?" Tessa started to laugh and then found she couldn't stop. She scrabbled for tissues in her bag, knowing she was perilously close to tears.

"All right?" Philip asked.

"Yes." She dabbed at her eyes. "It's been quite a night."

"It certainly has."

"I wish Jason had come away with me. Was I wrong not to stay, do you think?"

"Were you running away again?"

She looked at him, puzzled. Then she understood. "No. No, I wasn't. I just wanted to be on neutral ground. But as I was waiting for you in the hall I knew that I wasn't afraid of them anymore."

"Of whom?"

"Sybil, Camilla. Of memories mostly, I suppose. I realized they couldn't hurt me anymore. I have only two concerns now: Uncle Steven—and I'm going to make sure I spend lots of time with him tomorrow— and Jason."

"He is nineteen. And he seems fairly self-sufficient."

"He hasn't been an easy child to bring up. There have been a few problems."

"Being a single parent can't be easy. He appears to have turned out well enough, though."

Tessa drew in a deep breath. "There have been times . . ." She relived the sinking feeling in her stomach when she'd opened the door to two large policemen one night a couple of years ago. It hadn't been the first time, either. That was definitely not something to share with Philip. "But, you're right, Jason is getting his act together nowadays."

"You're worried about Derek's influence on him, aren't you?"

She smiled, remembering how Philip had always been able to hone in on her thoughts when she was young. "Yes, I am."

"Don't forget that Steven's there."

"But he's so ill, Philip. I can't expect him to look after Jason."

"I shall be able to keep an eye on him."

"I can't expect that of you, either."

"Why on earth not?"

It was a question that she couldn't answer.

"I start summer vacation in a couple of weeks. If Jason does decide to stay on, I shall have plenty of time to spend with him. Besides," Philip added, his eyes on the curve of the road ahead of him, "he is my nephew, after all. A member of the Thornton family."

Tears welled up in Tessa's eyes again. This time she couldn't hide them. "Oh, Philip."

He put out his hand to cover hers for a moment. "Trust me. Jason will be fine."

When Tessa's hand stirred beneath his, he squeezed it, but then drew his hand away again to change gear as they drove up the hill to Middleham.

Tonight was Sarah's night off. Philip unlocked the front door and turned off the alarm system. He switched on the lights in the hall, thinking as he did so how woefully inadequate they were. He had recently received estimates for having the house rewired and new lighting installed. The cost had been prohibitive.

He looked around the timber-framed great hall, the oldest part of the house, built in the fifteenth century.

Perhaps it should stay as it was, dimly lit, with shadowy corners. More atmospheric, some might say. It might be rather incongruous to flood the place with electric light. The six heavy chandeliers that hung from the beams on long chains had held dozens of wax candles in his grandfather's time. Candlelight was far more suitable to oak paneling and beams, but candles were completely out of the question nowadays. Far too much work and also forbidden by the insurance company.

It was difficult enough to keep the house reasonably clean and in good repair. Since his father's death, he'd had to make do with Sarah—who did the work of two people—and two part-time house workers. In his grandfather's time there had been a dozen inside servants at Thornton: two cooks, a valet and a butler, scullery maids and chambermaids and parlor maids ... and several outside servants, plus lads from the village who came to work on the grounds.

Philip tossed his raincoat onto the back of a carved oak chair and walked into the small library. He could do with a drink. Tessa had said no to his invitation to have one at the hotel. He had said good-bye to her in the crowded bar and then watched her mount the stairs to her room. Even her back had expressed her weariness. He hated to think of her being alone at such a time.

He poured himself a brandy, resisting the temptation to make it a large one. One heavy drinker in the family was quite enough.

The fire had gone out, leaving a pile of gray ashes behind the fire guard Sarah had placed there for safety. Philip had always hated the sight of a fireplace filled with cold gray ashes. There was something extremely melancholy about it. Stepping over Whiskey, his black-and-white cocker spaniel, he removed the guard and tried to rake the fire to life with the iron poker. But it was no use. The fire was dead and he didn't have the energy to relight it.

He picked up the brandy glass. As he was about to drink from it, he looked up at the portrait of Rosamund that still hung above the fireplace. It had been painted when they became engaged, twenty-five years ago. She was dressed in a white frothy ball gown, her blond hair in a pageboy style, just brushing her bare shoulders. The artist had captured perfectly her typically English beauty: the large blue eyes, the milk-and-roses complexion.

What the artist hadn't caught in Rosamund's bland expression was her insatiable greed. Greed for power, for sex, for jewels and couturier clothes and money.

"Here's to you, my sweet," Philip said, holding the glass up to her. "If it hadn't been for you, I might have been able to pay this damned inheritance tax on Thornton."

He downed the brandy in one gulp. He could understand why people of other nationalities flung their glasses against walls or into the fireplace after making a toast. It would be a very satisfying thing to do at this moment, but hardly the correct behavior for an English gentleman.

"At least it saves me a large bill for replacement glasses," he said aloud to himself with an ironic smile. Humming a few bars of Gilbert and Sullivan's "He Is an Englishman," he switched on the standard lamp by his armchair and sat down.

What an evening! He was too weary at present to work out all the possible repercussions. What interested him most was his own reaction to the sudden appearance of Tessa's son. The swift jab of shock had been followed by a feeling that everything had at last fallen into place. He realized that Tessa's marriage to John Maltby had always troubled him. It had never seemed quite right. Not because of the difference in class, but because he found it hard to imagine the naive and sensitive Tessa and the coarse John Maltby together.

She wasn't the same naive Tessa anymore, of

course. *A hard nut to crack.* The phrase came unbidden into his mind. Her life had hardened, toughened her. She had assumed a hard shell. Too late now to find out what lay beneath.

Too late for anything, he thought. Sometimes, when he was feeling in low spirits—as he was now—he felt that everything he'd cared about had become blighted. His marriage, his parents and his brother, his profession, and—most especially the thing he loved most— Thornton itself. Yet he was pragmatic enough to realize that upon closer examination, most of these calamities had been beyond his control.

It was his father who had brought Thornton to the brink of disaster. His father who had been a bad influence on Derek. His mother's long illness had been nobody's fault. And as for his profession, he had been on the verge of taking silk—the crowning achievement of his profession at the Bar—when his father had become ill and Philip had had to return to take care of what was left of Thornton Manor.

His marriage to Rosamund was another matter entirely. No one had forced him into that. He had fallen madly in love with her and nothing could have stopped him marrying her. He knew within three months that it had been a terrible mistake, one for which he had been paying for the rest of his life.

Now, here was another blighted life. He had always felt a particular affinity for Tessa Hargrave. He remembered his first sight of her, a shy, skinny child, her brown eyes huge beneath the overlarge school hat. She'd been ten. He, twenty.

It wasn't just pity he'd felt when he saw her. Although there was much to pity: a young girl, instantly orphaned by her parents' shocking death, brought to live with an aunt who didn't want her and a cousin who was thoroughly spoiled. It was the sense of other-worldliness about Tessa that had attracted him to her.

That, strangely juxtaposed with her habit of speaking her mind that always got her into trouble, had drawn him to her.

It appeared that the harsh reality of her life had obliterated the otherworldliness entirely. A good thing, probably. Otherwise Tessa might not have been able to cope with the adversities she had been dealt.

He wished with all his heart that he had done more to help her, asked more questions on the night she'd run away. But, if he remembered correctly, he'd been worrying about a bitter quarrel he'd had with Rosamund. There had been many of those. Now it was too late.

It seemed to Philip, as he stared into the ashes, that all the good things, the exciting possibilities, lay far back in the past, in his youth. It was easy enough now to look back and say, "If only," but that was looking at the past through romantic rather than pragmatic eyes. Perhaps that was preferable, however, to contemplating the empty future.

He thought for a moment about what it would be like if Jason were his son rather than Derek's. Then he laughed aloud. "What a fool you are!" he told himself. Now Tessa would be leaving Yorkshire, most likely forever, carrying away with her only sad and bitter memories, and there wasn't a bloody thing he could do about it.

Putting on his reading glasses, Philip picked up his copy of *The Oxford Book of English Verse* and began to read.

After only a few minutes, he took off his glasses and rubbed his eyes. Carefully marking his place with a leather bookmark, he set the book down and shifted in his chair, turning toward the fireplace with its lifeless fire.

Whiskey came to him, pushing his cold, wet nose

into his hand. When Philip didn't respond, the dog whimpered for a moment, and then rested his head on Philip's knee, gazing up at his master's averted face with soulful eyes.

Chapter Seventeen

The breakfast room at Langley was strangely deserted on Sunday morning, the porridge and kippers, bacon and sausages ... all lying untouched in their heated containers. Everyone appeared to have eaten breakfast in their bedrooms or to have slept in.

Everyone, that is, except Derek, who had recovered miraculously and was pounding on Jason's door at eight o'clock, shouting that it was a marvelous day and he was waiting to take him to the stables.

In fact, Derek was dressed in riding gear and determined to take Jason riding across the moor. When Jason heard this, he leapt out of bed, everything else forgotten in his excitement. The first time he'd been on a horse was as a small boy when his father had taken him riding at Assiniboia Downs. Strange, Jason thought as he quickly showered, that this other father—his *real* father—should be the one to take him riding again.

Sybil had also risen early, to help Barton tend to her husband, who had passed a wretched night.

"She certainly turned out to be her mother's daughter, didn't she?" she said to Steven as she passed him his cup of coffee. "I told you before, breeding will out."

Steven swung his pajamaed legs over the side of the bed. "I told you before," he said, "that I don't wish to discuss it."

"And there's that fool Derek entertaining her by-blow as if he were royalty. In my house, too!"

Steven pounded his fist on the side table. "Damnation, Sybil. I won't have you calling Tessa's son a by-blow. She was engaged to Derek at the time and he *is* Derek's son, there's no mistaking that. Do you realize what Tessa must have gone through when she ran away from Langley?"

His wife pursed her red lips and turned away.

Better not to pursue that subject, Steven decided. "Whatever I think of Derek, I must say I admire him for having taken the lad under his wing."

"What about Camilla? Have you no consideration for your daughter's feelings in the matter?"

"I intend to have a few words with Camilla before this day is out. There's something about Tessa's story that is very peculiar. Very peculiar, indeed."

Sybil quickly changed the subject by telling Steven that today's *Sunday Times Magazine* contained an article about English rivers. A few minutes later she sought out her daughter.

Camilla was still in bed, her face layered with night cream.

"Take that stuff off," her mother ordered her. "I refuse to talk to a woman who looks like a cream puff."

Cursing to herself, Camilla yanked some tissues from the box in the frilly container by her bed and wiped the cream away from her face. "What do you want, Mother? You know how upset I am. Why did you have to wake me so early?"

"Upset you may be—and every right to be so, with the revolting way your father's niece has behaved—but I want to hear what Derek's intentions are to this bastard of his."

"I have no idea. I haven't seen Derek this morning. All I know is that Barton put him to bed in his own room last night. Apparently he fell asleep in the library."

"You speak as if that's an unusual occurrence. Honestly, Camilla, I still cannot understand what you ever saw in the wretched man."

"You thought he was right for me."

Sybil's dark eyes opened wide at this. "I beg your pardon," she said in a quelling tone. "I certainly did not. I had much higher hopes for you. There was the baron: Jimmy whatsit . . . Trubshawe, Trevanix . . . ? He'd have married you had you shown him the slightest hint of encouragement."

"For God's sake, Mother. He was a heroin addict."

"Then what about that tall fellow? I can never remember names. Beresford, Pennyforth . . . something like that."

"He was charged for gross indecency with a minor several years ago."

"More fool him, to get caught. I'm sure the girl was no better than she ought to be."

"It was a boy, Mother," Camilla said in a withering tone.

"Oh. Oh, well. Best that you didn't marry him, I suppose. But I still think you could have done better than Derek. No title. And a younger son, too. But you just had to have him. If I recall, you said you'd die if you couldn't have him." Sybil's tone was caustic. "He doesn't look worth dying for nowadays, does he?"

"At least he's the heir to Thornton."

"Much good that will do, with those horrific death duties. I don't think Philip can afford to pay them. Keep that under your hat, though. Your father said I was not to tell anyone."

Camilla's pale skin grew even paler. "He *has* to pay them. What would happen to the estate if he couldn't pay them? Derek has his heart set on having Thornton for himself."

"If Derek doesn't stop demanding his share—when his father didn't even leave him anything specific in his will—there may not be any Thornton for him to inherit. You can't get blood out of a stone."

"Derek couldn't bear to lose his ancestral home. The Thorntons are one of the oldest landed families in the country."

"Not much use being an old landed family without an estate to go with it, is there?"

"I had no idea things were so bad. After all, Philip had a highly successful career as a barrister before he left London."

"He had. But your father-in-law had already run Thornton Manor into the ground. And you must remember that Rosamund had very expensive tastes."

"Oh." Camilla contemplated her pink nails. "Poor Philip. He loves Thornton more than anything else in this world."

"Poor Philip bedamned. He was a fool to have married one of the Vernon girls. Anyone could have predicted the outcome. They've ruined all their husbands. Just think, Camilla, if you had married Philip instead of Derek, you would have been mistress of Thornton now."

Camilla wasn't sure if her mother was laughing at her or not. "I'd rather be at Langley, thank you."

"I am sure you would. You wouldn't be waited on hand and foot at Thornton. There aren't any servants left there, apart from that wretched Sarah Roper. If you were Philip's wife you'd probably be scrubbing floors and cooking meals yourself."

Camilla gave a theatrical shiver at the thought. "A slight exaggeration, I think, Mother. Anyway, I would remind you that Philip is almost ten years older than me. I was only sixteen when he married Rosamund.

There was never any thought of marriage between us, so please drop the subject."

"It's all beside the point now. In any event, Philip was never particularly interested in you."

Camilla flung back the bedclothes. "Excuse me," she said in a cold voice and went into the bathroom.

Seething with anger, she turned on the tap and washed off the residue of the face cream. Her mother could be extraordinarily cruel at times. What she had said was true, of course. But Philip's disinterest had made him even more attractive to Camilla when she was an adolescent. Even now, she found herself strongly attracted to him. She had tried in little ways to show him so, but Philip seemed to have decided to become an ascetic monk since his wife's death. Or else he was conducting a highly secret affair. The subject was widely discussed in the county, but no one could discover anything that might point to one particular woman.

"Poor Philip," she said again when she came back, tying her azure silk dressing gown around her. "He's still such a good-looking man, but he seems so lonely. What a shame he and Rosamund didn't have any children." She flung herself into a chair and crossed her legs, the folds of her dressing gown falling back to reveal slim bare legs.

"Honestly, Camilla, sometimes I don't think you have a brain in that beautiful head of yours. If Philip had had a child, Derek would no longer be heir to Thornton."

"What good does it do him, anyway? Philip's much fitter than Derek. He's unlikely to die for another thirty years. And you've just said yourself that he may have to sell Thornton. Even if he does keep it, all we'll inherit is debts and even more death duties to pay." Camilla drank down a glass of her special high-vitamin drink and grimaced. "Derek is worried that Philip might marry again."

"I should think that's highly unlikely after his experience with Rosamund. You know what she was like. I doubt he had much more than a year of happiness with that woman, if that."

"I often wondered why he didn't divorce her. He had ample justification."

"Didn't want to wash his dirty linen in public. Philip Thornton has extremely antiquated ideas about chivalry," Sybil said dryly. "And he has always been starchily proud, as you know. Rosamund loved him in her own selfish way. He just wasn't her sort of high-flyer." Sybil laughed. "Can't quite see Philip at sex and drug parties, can you?"

"What on earth would you know about such things, Mother?"

"I know what goes on. I'm not senile yet." Sybil rolled her wheelchair closer to her daughter's chair. "Camilla."

"What?"

"I want you to be very careful."

"Careful about what?"

"About Derek. Make sure you discourage this blossoming relationship with Tessa's son."

"I certainly don't intend to encourage it, Mother. You should know that."

"Yes. I understand how mortifying it must be to know that Derek fathered a son on Tessa and not on you."

A flush of red crept up Camilla's neck. "I don't want to talk about it."

"You can't ignore it. What you must do is be alert for any suggestion from Derek that he legally acknowledge this . . . this Jason. You don't want to see Vicky supplanted, do you? Or your money frittered away on Tessa's son? I would remind you that your father and I won't be here forever to take care of you. Especially not your father." Sybil rolled her wheelchair away to gaze out the window.

Camilla's eyes filled with tears. "Don't, Mummy. I can't bear it. How will we manage without him?" A sob caught in her throat.

"We shall manage very well." There was a long silence before Sybil turned her wheelchair around again. "Your father is leaving Langley in an excellent position. I just want to make sure that it remains that way. Just think what John Thornton did to that lovely estate with his drinking and gambling. When he inherited Thornton, it was one of the finest estates in Yorkshire. Now look at it."

Camilla saw the connection. More and more she realized that Derek had become his father's son. "A chip off the old block," her father sometimes said in a scathing tone. She felt panic rising at the thought that her father would soon die and that her mother might not last very long after him. How in heaven's name would she be able to manage Derek and keep the Langley estate solvent without her parents there to guide her?

"If Derek as much as hints at giving this young man any settlement, trample on the idea," her mother was saying. "Remind him whose house this is and who provides him with everything."

Camilla decided it was high time she came to Derek's defense. Her mother's constant criticism of him always held a veiled attack on her daughter's choice of a husband. Sometimes not so veiled. "Derek has worked hard for Langley," she said sharply. "At times, you treat him like some indentured servant."

"Utter nonsense! He has a partnership in the stables, plus free living accommodation. It pays him to stay on your right side, as he well knows, or he'd be thrown out on his ear."

"No wonder he resents his position here."

"He'd better not talk of resentment to me, or I'll give him reasons for resentment!"

Camilla knew that there was no point in arguing with her mother. Like Margaret Thatcher in her prime, Sybil always won arguments and usually left her opponents intimidated and exhausted. Secretly, Camilla feared her mother. There was a ruthlessness about her that was disturbing. *Thank God she's my mother,* she thought. She wouldn't want to be an enemy of hers.

Not for the first time, Camilla thought about Tessa growing up, unwanted, at Langley, and felt a rush of sympathy. And guilt.

Sybil directed her wheelchair to the door and then asked, over her shoulder, "Have you seen Victoria this morning?"

"No. Why?"

"I just wondered," her mother said and wheeled herself from the room before Camilla could ask any more questions.

Sybil halted outside Vicky's door. She was about to knock when she saw a hotel DO NOT DISTURB sign hanging on the doorknob. Although Jeremy had been given his own room, she knew that he was usually to be found in Vicky's room in the morning. She smiled to herself. "That's all right, then," she murmured to herself, and made her way to the lift.

In fact, it was Vicky who had hung the sign on the door, as Jeremy was still sound asleep in her bed. Vicky herself had left the house before eight o'clock and was working in her workshop, savagely whittling away at a new piece of elm.

She was furious with herself for having succumbed to Jeremy's lovemaking last night. He'd behaved like a moron over the whole scene with Tessa's son. So much so that Vicky had actually torn off her engagement ring and flung it at him. It had hit him right in the face. Jeremy had gone very quiet and pale, and then apologized to her for being so negative about her half brother. Then he had started to make love to her, and she couldn't resist him. Her anger turned in an instant to rampant desire and they'd ended up thumping away on the floor.

"Right above your grandfather's study," Jeremy had reminded her afterward and went off into peals of laughter. Vicky hadn't thought it was that funny.

Sometimes she wondered if Jeremy was some sort of exhibitionist. He wanted to make love in the strangest places, the open air—particularly the moors—being his favorite turn-on. Vicky didn't share his choice of location. Mainly because of the hazards on the moor: thistles and sheep dung ... and hikers in strong boots coming upon one unexpectedly. But she went along with it, not wanting to be told she was a prude. Secretly, she preferred a more romantic setting, but Jeremy was more into rugged than romantic.

As soon as she'd calmed down, Vicky began working on her favorite piece, a lovely beech wood lap-desk she was making for her grandfather's birthday. His health had deteriorated so rapidly that she'd decided not to wait for his actual birthday, but to give it to him as soon as she could finish it.

She took up the plane. As she felt the wood smoothing beneath her fingers, her worries about Jeremy eased away. Yes, he was a terrible snob, but that came from his upbringing. She'd have been the same way had she not had Papa to set her right. Once they were married, she'd make sure that Jeremy changed, too. She just wished that her grandfather liked Jeremy a little more, that was all. He just didn't see his good side: his kindness to animals and children, his zany sense of humor, his canniness with money ... She tried to think of Jeremy's other attributes, but came up empty. Papa wasn't interested in the obvious things: Jeremy's gorgeousness, his prowess in bed—or on the moors. Besides, despite her determination to be a modern woman, the thought of being exceedingly rich, being able to bask in the sun in Mustique or St. Lucia in the winter, or to ski at St. Moritz, was extremely inviting.

The Countess of Ayncliffe. It sounded wonderfully impressive. Far more exciting than plain Mrs. Taylor or something like that.

She had seen the other side of life when she'd worked as a volunteer at a women's shelter in Newcastle. The appalling poverty and degradation she had found there had shown her quite another aspect of England, one that was far removed from Gainsborough paintings and hunt balls and food hampers from Fortnum & Mason's.

She sensed that Tessa had seen more of that side of life. The thought saddened Vicky. She liked Tessa. She also knew that her parents had been a major cause of Tessa's unhappiness and hardship.

Preferring not to dwell on this, she thought instead about Jason. She had always wanted a brother. Not a sister. A sister might have turned out like her mother and that would have driven her nuts. But Jason seemed like her sort, even if he was sort of shell-shocked by all that happened last night. If he did stay on, she could get to know him better.

A shiver ran down her spine. She didn't like to admit it, even to herself, but she thought it would be better if Jason didn't stay at Langley. She'd seen her grandmother's expression when her gaze rested on Jason. Vicky had learned a long time ago that it was best not to cross Grandmother when she looked like that.

Slow footsteps approached. She quickly dragged an old sheet over the desk and went back to her whittling.

"Ah, there you are," her grandfather said.

"How did you get here by yourself?"

"Kevin helped me," he said abruptly, obviously hating to be reminded of his inability to get around by himself these days. "I thought you were still asleep, but Hazel said she'd given you some tea in a vacuum to bring down here with you."

"That's right. Want some?"

"No. I've just had a telephone call from Philip. He had a strange request."

"Is it about Tessa? I hope she's okay."

"She's meeting me at St. Luke's in an hour."

"What about Grandmother?"

"She refuses to come to church if Tessa is to be there."

"Oops! So, what happens now?"

"Tessa is leaving for London tomorrow morning. Whether your grandmother likes it or not, I am going to church with my niece. Afterwards, we shall see the flower festival together."

"La Grande Dame will be furious."

"Then she'll have to be furious. Kevin's going to pick Tessa up from Middleham at ten-thirty. How about coming to church with us?"

Vicky was about to say, *You must be joking,* but then remembered that there might not be too many more opportunities to go to church with her grandfather. "Why not?"

"Good girl." He looked especially pleased. In fact, he was positively beaming. "Better go and put on a nice frock, then."

She gave him a smiling frown. "What's the big deal?"

"I was telling you. Philip rang me."

"And?"

"He wondered if we'd be able to come to lunch at Thornton after we've been to church."

"Who's we?"

"That's the touchy part. The lunch is for Tessa, as it's her last day in Yorkshire, and her son, of course. But—"

"But he doesn't want Jeremy to come, right?"

"That's not what he said. He merely suggested that it should only be people with whom Tessa would feel at ease."

"That cuts out Grandmother and Mummy and Daddy as well, then. How's Philip going to explain not asking his own brother to this farewell luncheon?"

"Ask him, not me."

"Is it all to be a big secret?

He gave a little half smile. "Better that way, don't you think?"

She grimaced. "You're right."

"We'll just say we're taking Tessa and Jason out for lunch. That's the truth, isn't it?"

"Damned right, it is. Jeremy can go riding with Daddy. He won't insist on coming with me."

"Jeremy didn't like Tessa, eh?"

"I can drive us," Vicky said, ignoring his question.

"I've already asked Kevin to do so." The taut skin over his cheekbones became suffused with color. "I need his help getting in and out of the car, you see."

"Yes, of course you do," she said briskly, knowing that he didn't like to be helped by a woman. "Well, Kevin's not one to gossip. Our secret will be safe with him. Frankly, Papa, I wouldn't get in a stew if it does come out."

Her grandfather frowned. "Wouldn't want to cause trouble. Not very comfortable, if you know what I mean."

Vicky knew very well what he meant. The fallout from one of Grandmother's moods could make every-one at Langley feel extremely uncomfortable. It spread from the attics to the stables, permeating everything and everyone.

"Philip's right," she said cheerfully. "After all, if it is Tessa's last day here she should be surrounded by people who care about her."

Steven's worried expression vanished. "So glad you like her, Vicky. She's had a tough life, you know."

"I know she has. But if I were you, I wouldn't worry about her now. I think she's quite capable of handling anything that's thrown her way."

"Even this last bombshell? Jason, I mean."

She took his arm and slowly led him down the path from her workshop. "I know she's worried about leaving Jason here, but I should think she's also glad her big secret's out at last. I would be. It must have been hell keeping it to herself all these years."

"Do you think that Jason will stay on after she goes?" Steven asked her as they came out of the coppice and crossed the velvety lawn.

Vicky could sense his concern. He knew his wife better than any of them did. "Daddy really wants him to stay for a while, but . . ."

"Feeling a bit jealous, are you?"

She smiled. "No. I suppose I should be, but I'm not. I haven't seen Daddy this animated for ages. It's done him good."

"You said 'but.' "

"To be honest, I'm hoping that Jason will go home with Tessa."

Steven looked at her and then away again. "You're right. I was looking forward to getting to know Tessa's son, my dear brother's grandson. But I don't think he'd be made to feel very welcome at Langley by—"

"I know what you mean," Vicky said, intervening to avoid him having to spell it out.

"Understandable, of course. Your mother and

grandmother will feel . . ." He waved his hands in the air, unable to say the words.

Guilty, Vicky said to herself. *That's what they should feel. Bloody guilty.* At least her mother should. And, knowing her grandmother, Vicky was sure she'd had some hand in it, too. Camilla rarely did anything without consulting her. Vicky was certain that things would have been the same, probably worse, twenty years ago.

"We'll keep Jason well away from them," she assured Steven. "But he shouldn't stay more than a few days."

"You're right. Safer to send him home to Canada before anything happens."

As Vicky held the terrace door open for him, she was struck by the spookiness of his words. Surely her grandfather didn't think that any actual harm would come to Jason if he stayed on at Langley, did he?

Chapter Eighteen

Sarah had never known Philip Thornton to be in such a state over what was, after all, just a simple Sunday lunch. She'd come in late last night after going out to the pub for a few drinks with Bill Tennant. It was past midnight and the place was so quiet she'd thought Philip had gone to bed.

Then, just as she was sitting in the kitchen having a cup of cocoa, she heard him yelling, "Lunch! That's it. Sunday lunch!"

It gave her such a start. She thought he was drunk or gone crazy. But she'd never seen him worse for wear with drink, and although that wife of his was enough to have driven him crazy while she was alive, he'd certainly never shown any signs of it.

She ran out of the kitchen, to meet him in the screen passage. "Is everything all right?" she asked.

"Yes, yes. Sorry to have yelled like that. I didn't even know you'd come in." He smiled his attractive, one-sided smile. "I'm sorry to spring this on you without any warning, Sarah," he said, "but do you think we could manage a Sunday lunch? Something very simple." He ran his hand through his hair, ruffling it. "Damn! The butcher won't be open on Sunday, will he? What about Campbells in Leyburn, do they open Sundays? Or I could drive to the Safeway in Ripon, if it's open."

"I've a couple of legs of lamb in the freezer," she

told him calmly. "All I need to do is pod some peas and do some roast vegetables and I can easily throw together a pudding of some sort. Don't you worry about it. How many for?"

"I'm not sure yet. Possibly five or six. I'll pod the peas for you."

He would have done, too, Sarah thought as she washed and chopped the leeks. At the moment he was setting the table with all the best china and crystal. She'd called in one of the girls from the village to help her, but he'd insisted on doing the table himself. Said it was a very important occasion. Tessa was going home to Canada tomorrow.

Sarah had heard in the pub last night that Tessa Hargrave's red-haired son, Jason, had turned up at Langley, the spitting image of Derek Thornton. Word got around fast in the Dales.

Poor Tessa. Sarah didn't envy her, knowing what sort of reception she'd have had even before the lad arrived. She'd have given a tenner to have seen the old witch of Langley's face when she saw Derek's son turn up in her hallowed halls.

Yes, that must have been quite an eyeful. Sarah smiled. Strange to think that she was the only one who'd known that Tessa was pregnant with Derek Thornton's child.

Or was she? She'd never been quite sure about that. But she had her suspicions, all right.

When it was time to leave for church, Jason and Derek still hadn't returned from their ride. Vicky could see that her grandfather was growing extremely anxious. He hated being late for church.

"Why don't you and Kevin go and pick up Tessa?" she suggested when Kevin had helped Steven into the Range Rover. "I'll take my car. That way I can stay on for a few more minutes in case Jason and Daddy get in."

"But you will come to church, won't you?" Steven asked anxiously.

"I'm not likely to have changed into a skirt for nothing, am I now?" Vicky quipped, leaning into the car to give him a quick hug. "You go on." Kevin started up the engine. "And don't start the service without me," she shouted as they began to move.

As they drove away, the wheels crunching on the gravel, she looked at her watch. Less than fifteen minutes, that was all she had. Even then, she'd have to drive like hell to get to St. Luke's on time.

She drove around to the stables and sat waiting. She was about to drive away when she heard the jingle of harness from the paddock behind the stables, and then her father's voice shouting for someone to take the horses.

Vicky scrambled out of the car and ran to the paddock. Her half brother had just dismounted and, having passed his mount over to one of the lads, was walking slowly to the gate in the fence. "Jason!" she yelled. "Get over here."

He tried to move faster, but she could see he was having some difficulty. "Stiff?" she asked with a grin when he reached the gate. "Obviously a greenhorn."

"You can say that again. Jeez, I'm sore."

"Get in the car," she said hurriedly under her breath as she saw her father approaching.

"What?"

"Don't ask any questions. Just get in."

"But I'm covered in dirt," he protested.

"Who cares. Get in." She shoved him into the passenger seat just as her father got to them. She started up the engine and then leaned out the window. "Hi, Dad. Just have to show Jason something. We'll be back in a few hours."

Her father opened his mouth to protest, but she drove off, wheels screeching, hoping to God she hadn't spooked any of the horses.

Jason hurriedly buckled up his seat belt. "Is this a kidnapping?"

She grinned at him. "Sort of, yes. We're going to church."

"Yeah, right. Well, you'd have to kidnap me to get me to go to church."

"That's what I thought."

"Seriously, where are we going?" Jason asked, as they raced through the Langley estate, past fenced fields, and then out through the lodge gates.

"I am being serious. We're going to church. Kevin and my grandfather have gone to pick up your mother from the hotel, and we're all meeting at St. Luke's."

"I can't go to church dressed like this. Besides, I stink."

"You can say that again." Vicky glanced at Jason and saw that his face was bright red. "Sorry, that was mean of me. Don't forget I'm a country girl. I'm used to my men smelling of sweat and horses." She glanced at him again. "You've got mud on your forehead. There's a packet of wipe things in the glove compartment."

"What's all this about?" Jason demanded as he scrubbed his face with the damp wipes. "Your father's going to be mad at me leaving like that."

"Don't worry. I'll explain to him later."

"You'd better explain to me first."

"Okay. Here's St. Luke's," she said, pulling up with a screech of brakes. "I'll just park first. Then I'll tell you what's going on."

She found a place on the side of the road that ran parallel with the river, and switched off the engine. "We've got three minutes," she said, glancing at her watch.

"Do I really have to go in?" Jason asked.

"Yes, you do. This will be the first church service I've attended with my brother."

Jason stared at her and then, to his dismay, felt tears filling his eyes.

"Here," Vicky said gently, taking the packet from him. "Let me do this." She wiped his face clear of dirt. "That's better. Philip has asked us to lunch at Thornton, a sort of farewell for Tessa, but—for obvious reasons—there are certain people who can't be there. Like my parents, for instance. And certain people who must be there. Like you. Tessa promised Papa that she'd come to church with him this morning. So here we all are."

She opened the car door and got out. "We've got one minute. Let's make a run for it."

By now totally confused, Jason did as he was told and sprinted along the narrow road, down the path to the church, pausing at the open door to whisper, "Are you sure jeans are okay?"

"You know what the rector of St. Luke's always says?"

"No."

"What we want in St. Luke's is bottoms on seats," she said in a plummy, high-pitched voice. "We don't care what they're covered with."

"You made that up."

"Cross my heart, I didn't," Vicky whispered and dragged him inside the church.

It was unlike any church Jason had ever seen. The stained-glass windows were set high on the walls, so that the interior was dimly lit. The air smelled damp and musty. The flagstone floor beneath his feet was uneven. Everything spoke of extreme age.

"I expect Papa told them to hold the service for a few minutes," Vicky whispered.

Jason looked at her, wondering if she was pulling

his leg, but her expression was quite serious. She smiled at the usher who greeted them at the door and then led Jason down the side aisle, smiling broadly, giving little waves to people in the congregation.

Talk about a grand entrance, Jason thought. He could hear lots of mumbles and whispers as they made their way down. He felt his face go fiery red, sure that everyone was making comments about the way he was dressed.

To his surprise, Vicky passed the end of the first row and didn't sit down there. Instead, she led him up two worn stone steps, into a boxlike place with a carved screen around it and faded red velvet curtains that were drawn back. His mother and her uncle and Kevin Taylor were already seated there.

"We made it," Vicky whispered. She slipped into the seat beside Kevin, leaving the seat at the front for Jason. He felt like he was in one of those side boxes in an old-fashioned theater. To his amazement, he saw Steven Hargrave give the priest or rector—whatever he was—a nod, and the show got going.

His mother squeezed his hand. "Thanks for coming," she whispered.

He grinned. "I wasn't given any option."

She gave him a puzzled little smile as she handed him the Book of Common Prayer.

How strange to think that I'm sitting here, Tessa thought, *in the Langley private pew with my son at my side.* The last time she had sat here, Jason had been a microscopic speck inside her body. Overcome by the thought, she reached out her hand to touch his. He looked at her and then gave her hand a hard squeeze.

The old, familiar words of the Anglican service were still there, unchanged. As she read the half-remembered words of the general confession one phrase in particular sprang out at her: *We have left undone those things which we ought to have done.*

She had at last done what she ought to have done years ago, but all it had brought her was further unhappiness. Now she was likely to lose the only precious thing she had left: her son.

As the congregation read the psalm, Tessa prayed her own personal prayer. *Lord, please let Jason come home to Canada with me.*

Once the service was over, there was still the ordeal of meeting the rector and being introduced to people, some of whom remembered her from the time she had first come to Langley.

Then there was Jason to worry about. No doubt word had already been spread by those who worked at Langley House. He was introduced as her son, but no one who knew Derek could mistake Jason for anyone but his son.

No one actually said so, of course, but as they admired the bright summer flowers massed around the altar for the flower festival and the arrangements of ribbons, wheat and flowers decorating the ends of the old oak benches, the buzz of scandalous excitement in the church was unmistakable.

Tessa's face was stiff from smiling and pretending to be delighted to meet all these old gossips. Her heart was heavy with dread at the thought of leaving Jason behind in Yorkshire when she left. She had only one last speck of hope: that Philip would be able to persuade Jason to return to Canada.

As she followed Steven outside, she felt a hand slip into her arm. "Are you okay?" Vicky asked.

"Not really."

"I'm not surprised. Load of old vultures, aren't they? One of them asked me point-blank who Jason was."

"What did you say?"

"I told them he was my half brother. Do you mind? Surely it's best to tell the truth."

"I suppose so," Tessa said with a sigh. "But that won't please your mother."

"Oh, that's too bloody bad."

Tessa looked at Vicky's flushed face. How on earth had two people like Derek and Camilla created such a remarkable, forthright person? she wondered. "When is your birthday, Vicky?" she asked on impulse.

"April the fifteenth. Why?"

"Oh, I just wanted to write it in my diary," Tessa said, scrabbling in her bag, "so I can send you a card."

April fifteenth! Vicky had been born a whole year after Camilla had told her she was pregnant with Derek's child. Now she had the proof. Camilla had lied.

She tricked you, Derek had said. She had, indeed. How satisfying it would have been to confront Camilla with the unassailable truth, but to do that last night would have hurt Vicky terribly. And what good would that have achieved? Perhaps she should have tackled Camilla about it later, but she'd wanted to have positive proof first that Vicky had been born more than nine months after Camilla had said she was pregnant.

Now that she knew the truth, the thought of leaving Jason in that house of lies disturbed her even more. They'd probably make up more lies to try to turn him against her. No, he *must* come home with her.

"Are you all right?" This time it was her uncle who was asking her.

"A bit tense, that's all. The flowers were lovely, though. Well worth coming to see."

"Thank you for making the effort, darling. It can't have been easy for you, with all those gossips staring at you. But it's all for the best, I think, especially with Jason wanting to stay on for a while."

Tessa gripped his arm. "I don't want him to stay on at Langley."

"No, you're right. It's best if he stay at Thornton, I think."

"I don't want him to stay in England at all," Tessa said. "It's . . ." She had been about to say *It's not safe,* but she couldn't very well say that to Steven, could she? He was Sybil's husband, Camilla's father. "I want him to come home with me."

"Let's see what Philip thinks." He patted her hand and drew it through his arm.

Chapter Nineteen

"Well, Jason," Steven said. "You've seen your first English stately home. Now you're about to see another one."

They were all crammed into the Range Rover, with Kevin following behind, driving Vicky's Honda.

"Thornton's nothing like Langley House," Tessa said.

Her uncle chuckled. "You always did prefer Thornton, didn't you?"

"Did you, Tessa?" Vicky asked, slowing down to turn into the lane that led to Thornton. "Why?"

"Langley's your home, Vicky. Let's not make comparisons."

"Langley was your home, too."

"Yes, of course it was." Tessa turned her head to look out the window. As they approached the gates, her heart was beating fast. The gates stood open for them. She'd hoped that Jason would never see Thornton, but now she was eager to see his reaction to it.

As they drove along the winding driveway, she anticipated that first sight of the house, holding her breath for the moment before it burst into view. Then it was there: limestone walls the color of creamy moorland honey, the flagstoned courtyard bathed in golden sunlight. And there, too, was Philip, standing in the doorway ... now coming forward to greet them.

"I always feel a bit strange driving up to Thornton,"

Vicky said. "We should be clattering in on horseback, shouldn't we? Strange that I never feel that way about Langley."

"Welcome to Thornton, Jason," Philip said as he helped Steven from the car.

"Thank you, sir." Jason stood by the car, looking about him. His mother was right. This place was nothing like Langley House. Langley was like a huge museum, with its flight of wide steps up to the entrance. Here, you just walked in at an ordinary door. Well, maybe not so ordinary, he thought as he drew nearer. It was obviously very old, made of thick slabs of wood strengthened with iron.

He followed his mother inside and found himself in a passage, facing a wall of carved and paneled dark wood.

Then they were in a large open hall that also seemed to be a sitting room of some sort, with a little gallery at one end and a massive stone fireplace at the other, and great lights hanging from the ceiling beams on long chains.

It was like an old knights-in-armor movie. And there was one—the suit of armor, anyway—standing in a corner of the room. "Wow!" Jason said.

"Is that bad or good?" Philip asked, smiling.

"I'd no idea places like this still existed." Jason looked around again, his eyes shining. "You're right, Mom. It is better than Langley." He made a face. "Sorry about that," he said to Vicky. "It's just . . . just different, that's all."

"That's okay. No need to apologize. Don't forget that this was my dad's home, too. He grew up here."

Oh, God, Tessa thought. She wished Vicky hadn't said that.

Jason stood in the center of the hall, turning slowly on the spot, as if he were in a trance. "This was my father's home," he mused to himself.

"That's right," Philip said softly. "It was. That's why I wanted you to see it." He put his arm lightly around Jason's shoulders. "You shall have the guided tour after lunch."

"Like it?" Tessa asked Jason as they followed Philip out to the terrace for prelunch drinks.

He took a moment to reply. "*This* could have been my house, right?" he said in a harsh whisper.

Tessa's heart sank. "No, I'm afraid not. Philip is the elder son. He was the heir to Thornton."

"Who gets it when he dies?"

"For heaven's sake, Jason."

"Who?" Jason demanded urgently.

"His children would inherit."

"Does he have any?"

"No."

"Then, who?"

Tessa glared at him. "His brother Derek."

"That's what I thought."

She separated herself from him, determined not to continue this conversation about Thornton. The exchange between them had already put a blight on her enjoyment of what would be her last visit here.

She was surprised to see that Philip had invited Peter Wilson to join them. He was bringing him over to meet her now.

"Tessa, you met Peter for only a moment at the lodge yesterday. I've asked him up for a drink so you can meet him properly. I'm just going to fetch the drinks. What will you have?"

"A Tio Pepe, please."

"Ah, you've changed your tastes, I see. You used to drink sweet sherry."

"I'm twenty years older," she reminded him.

He gave her a strange frowning look for a moment and then went away.

Peter sat down beside her. "So, Miss Hargrave,

what do you think of Thornton? You must see a great
many changes in twenty years."

"I'm afraid so. Not good ones, either."

Her bluntness surprised him. "How do you mean?"

"Not so much in the house," Tessa hurriedly said,
feeling that her impulsive reply might be interpreted
as a criticism of Philip. "It seems much the same as
it was. It's the grounds that have really changed."

Damn! Now he'd be thinking she was criticizing *him*.

Peter sighed. "You're right. They need a great deal
of work and expenditure to return them to their former glory." He fell silent.

"There just isn't the money to do that, is there?"

"Money for what?" Philip had returned with their
drinks. Tessa shot a quick look at Peter, whose face
had reddened with embarrassment.

"We were talking about the scheme to help the hill
farmers keep their farms," he lied.

"Ah, yes," Philip said. "A brilliant scheme, but, as
you say, Tessa, it is hard to find the money necessary
to keep the farms going. Excuse me, I must help Sarah
with the drinks."

"Thanks," Tessa said under her breath when Philip
was out of earshot. "That was a close thing."

"He's very sensitive on the subject," Peter explained.

"Yes, I know." Tessa looked around to make sure
Philip wasn't nearby. "I've already been in his bad
books for suggesting he open Thornton to the public."

Peter whistled. "You're braver than I am."

"No, it was a case of a fool rushing in, I'm afraid."
She traced the rim of her cut-crystal sherry glass. "He
loves Thornton so much. I think it would kill him to
lose it."

Lunch was a merry affair, with good British food
superbly cooked and served. The old dining room
looked as it had when Tessa was a girl, the long oak

table and sideboard and linenfold paneling all gleaming from what had obviously been—from the smell of beeswax—a recent polishing.

"You must have been up all night," Tessa said to Sarah when she helped her clear away the plates the cold curried prawns had been served on.

Sarah grinned at her. "Nearly. He announced this lunch when I got in at midnight. Bit of a rush, but we all mucked in and got it done. Just cover the leftover bread and butter with some plastic wrap, would you? I'll have it later for my tea. I love it with fresh honey."

"Are the hives still active?"

"Aye, but I tell Mr. Thornton he'd make a sight more money from it if he'd have Thornton Manor labels made for the jars. That's the sort of thing sells things nowadays."

"You're right," Tessa said with a sigh. "He just doesn't like to think of his home as a commercial concern."

"He may have to," Sarah said cryptically, "or else." She picked up a huge serving dish. "Go on back. I'm about to serve the main course."

"Let me help. I'm not used to being served, you know."

"Too bad. This lunch is in your honor."

"I wish you could eat with us," Tessa said impulsively, and then regretted it, in case it would seem like further criticism of Philip.

"If it makes you feel better, I was invited to, but I told him I'd be far too busy to be able to enjoy my meal. So you can go on in and sit down with a clear conscience."

Tessa smiled at Sarah. "I'd like to talk later."

"Aye, we'll do that. You could take this dish of vegetables in, if you want. Watch out, it's very hot. I'll bring the roast so he can start the carving."

As she ate the superb meal, Tessa watched Jason

talking to Philip. She didn't remember having seen him this animated for ages. She felt a warm thrill run through her at the sight of them together. Uncle and nephew. How strange that seemed. For some reason she had never thought of Philip and Jason as being related. Possibly because Jason resembled Derek so much.

Now Philip was drawing Jason out, asking him questions, as he used to do with her when she was a shy, lonely child, making her feel important, as if someone really cared about her opinions.

"You're very quiet," Uncle Steven said.

Tessa started. "I'm sorry. I was just thinking how good Philip is with Jason."

"I know Philip doesn't show his feelings easily, but he's very excited about finding he has a long-lost nephew."

The warmth Tessa had been feeling turned to ice. "That's great, as long as he doesn't suggest that Jason stay here. His home is in Canada. He starts university in the fall."

"Yes, yes, we've heard all that before," Steven said irritably. He pushed his plate of mostly untouched food away. "I think the lad should stay and see a bit of his own country."

"This isn't his own country, Uncle Steven. Canada is. I should prefer it if you didn't encourage him, *please*."

She was dismayed at the thought of fighting with her uncle at what was probably their last meal together.

"We'll see what Philip has to say about the matter."

Tessa had to bite her bottom lip hard to avoid telling him that it wasn't any of Philip's goddamned business.

Dessert was a choice of hot sticky toffee pudding or raspberries with pouring cream. "Thornton raspberries," Peter announced. "I picked them myself this morning." Unable to resist either dessert, Tessa had a little of each.

The meal ended with an assortment of cheeses that made her mouth water just looking at them: Brie and Camembert, the local Wensleydale cheeses—both the usual white and the creamy blue—and, in the center of the cheese board, that king of English cheeses: a whole Stilton, ripe and pungent.

By the end of the meal everyone was in a mellow mood, too full to do much more than stretch out or amble around the grounds. As she sat on the terrace, drinking her second cup of coffee, Tessa saw Vicky and Kevin walking through the walled rose garden and then disappear. She wondered how Jeremy had reacted to being told he wasn't invited to this lunch. Not very well, she imagined. She'd failed miserably in her supposed quest to separate Vicky and Jeremy. Now it was too late.

"Are you asleep?" Philip asked.

Tessa opened her eyes. "Nearly. Not quite, though."

"How about a liqueur?"

"I couldn't drink another drop. Or eat another crumb. I seem to have done nothing but eat since I arrived in Yorkshire. That was the most marvelous meal." She stood up. "I must go and help Sarah do the dishes."

"We have a dishwasher."

"Now, that's a typically male remark. Since when did you put your Spode dinnerware in a dishwasher?"

"True. But you are my guest. Guests do not wash up or 'do the dishes' as you say."

"I promised Sarah we'd have a chat. This would be an ideal time for it."

Philip's expression grew serious. "It would also be an ideal time to discuss Jason. Vicky and Kevin have gone for a short walk and, to ease your mind, Peter is helping Sarah tidy up in the kitchen."

"You have it all planned, don't you?" Tessa said, an edge to her voice.

"I'm sorry. But you can't put it off any longer, can you? Not unless you change your mind about leaving tomorrow morning."

"No, I won't do that." Tessa found it hard to meet his gaze. "It's time I went home."

He stood there, his face composed, as always, but his thumb was moving back and forth across the back of the ancient Thornton ring that bore his coat of arms. "Are you sure you haven't come home?" he asked softly.

Her eyes widened, her head tilting in an unspoken question.

"To Yorkshire, I mean. Don't you feel that old pull that the Dales exert on their own people?"

"It never meant the same to me as it does to you. My memories of the Dales are not the happy ones you have."

"Perhaps not. I had the feeling that you loved it as I did. The countryside, I mean."

"Yes, I love it in a nostalgic sort of way, but Winnipeg is my home now. That's where my life is, where my work is. That's reality. Reality is being where you can earn enough money to pay the bills, not mooning on about the countryside and the old ways. They're gone, Philip. They're not here anymore. It's time you realized that and stopped living in the past."

She knew immediately that she had gone too far. The shutters were down again, his face drawn and pale. She wanted to cry and knew she must not. She gripped her hands together, so tightly that her nails bit into her palms. "Oh, Philip, I'm so sorry. I had no right—"

"You had every right," he said, giving her a tight little smile. "No doubt what you say is true. Perhaps I find it hard to accept that materialism now rules the world. I believe it was Stevenson who said that materialism would be the downfall of civilization. Nowadays, love of the land and of the past that shaped us all is deemed to be of no importance whatsoever.''

"That's not what I meant. You're being deliberately obtuse. What I meant was that you have to be able to change, to compromise, if you want to keep these things. Of course they're important," Tessa said fiercely. "We must fight hard for them, that's all. Don't tell me that your ancestors didn't have to compromise a little to be able to hang on to what they believed in. If they hadn't, Thornton wouldn't have stayed in the family."

His dark eyebrows lifted. "You want me to be like the Vicar of Bray, you mean? He changed his religion to suit the times so that he could keep his living."

"Something like that," Tessa murmured, knowing how angry he was.

"I'm sorry to disappoint you, Tessa, but I'm not about to compromise my principles, sell myself to—"

"No. You'd rather sell Thornton," Tessa blurted out, "than do what everyone else has had to do, share it with others. Share it with the common people whose sweat and rents helped to build and maintain it throughout the centuries. What makes me laugh is that they're willing to pay their hard-earned money to see all these stately homes and gardens when many of them live in rotten little flats with tiny rooms."

"Perhaps that is why they are willing to pay. They need to know that there's still some beauty left in this miserable world."

"Exactly." Tessa's breath came fast. "But you don't want them to see such places. You prefer to keep Thornton all to yourself."

"Hey, what's going on? I could hear your voice from the kitchen, Mom."

Tessa and Philip looked around quickly, to see Jason standing in the doorway.

"We were engaging in some friendly discussion," Philip said.

"Didn't sound very friendly."

"Your mother was giving me a lecture on the rights and freedoms of the common people." Philip looked at Tessa. "At least, that's what I think it was."

Tessa sighed. "Not really, no. But it doesn't matter." If he chose to lose Thornton because of his stiff-necked pride why should she bloody care?

"You said you'd show me over the house, Mr. Thornton," Jason said. "Is this a good time?"

"I think it's a perfect time. By the way, with your mother's permission, I should like you to call me Philip."

"Okay." Jason hesitated. "I've got another idea for . . . for later on. Maybe. But I don't know if you'd like it."

"Run it by me." Philip glanced at Tessa and gave her a half smile. *You see, I do know some modern expressions,* his eyes said.

"Maybe . . . one day I could call you Uncle Philip."

Tessa felt tears stinging her eyes as she saw Philip's look of complete surprise turn to a warm smile. "I'd like that very much, Jason."

He and Jason stood looking at each other with all the inherent awkwardness of the situation. Then Philip clapped Jason on the back. "Let's get going on this tour, shall we?" He turned to Tessa. "Will you join us, Tessa?"

The swift change of his voice from warm and enthusiastic to cool was unmistakable. Once again, their friendship seemed to have foundered because she had dared to argue with him about Thornton.

Chapter Twenty

As Philip showed them over the house, Tessa was surprised by Jason's enthusiasm. She'd always had to drag him to museums and art galleries.

"Enjoying yourself?" she asked him as Philip went to open the shutters in the long gallery.

"It's fantastic," he said, his eyes shining.

"You don't think it's like a museum?" she asked, curious to know why he was enjoying Thornton so much.

"No. It's not." He thought for a moment. "This is someone's home. All this stuff belongs to one family. And you can tell how much he ... Philip loves it. I think that's the difference."

Tessa knew that Philip had heard what Jason had said, but he didn't comment. "Come and see the Thornton Treasure," he said, leading them to the glass case. "Watch out," he warned as Jason leaned closer. "If you touch the top of the case it triggers the alarm. Wait a minute and I'll deactivate it. There's a button hidden away beneath the case that turns the alarm off. Here, let me show you."

They both crouched down so that they could see the underside of the case. "See this panel here?" Philip asked. "It looks exactly the same as the others, but it's not. Slide it along and there's the button. There, now you can open up the case and see the cross properly."

Jason did so and gazed down at the ancient jeweled crucifix. "Wow! This is something else. Is it gold?"

"Yes, but its chief value is in its age and its history, its provenance."

"What's that?"

Tessa listened with only half an ear as Philip explained to her son what provenance meant. The more time they spent together, she thought, the harder it was going to be to persuade Jason to return to Canada at the end of the week.

"I hate to cut this short," she said suddenly, "but I really think it's time we thought about getting away. Uncle Steven must be needing his usual afternoon rest."

"Uncle Steven is fast asleep in one of the guest bedrooms," Philip said. "And the plan is for Sarah to serve you some tea before you leave."

"Thank you, but I couldn't eat another bite. I don't know if Vicky will want to stay that long, with Jeremy—"

"Vicky said that she would drive back with Kevin after a short walk. They may have left already."

"Oh." She tried to avoid looking at him. "But I haven't said good-bye to her."

"It's not likely that she'd let you leave without saying good-bye. I expect she'll come to the hotel later."

"I sincerely hope so." A feeling of sadness washed over Tessa at the thought of having to leave all the people she cared for so much.

"If you'd prefer to go back to the hotel now, I can drive you there." Philip gave her a glimmer of a smile. "I don't want to keep you here against your will."

"It's just that I . . . we have packing to do. And Jason has to go back to Langley to fetch his stuff."

Jason straightened up. One look at his face and Tessa knew immediately that she was about to have a fight on her hands. "No, Mom. I don't have to fetch my stuff. I'm not coming to London with you tomorrow. And I'm not coming on Thursday, either."

"Oh, Jason, be reasonable. I know you're enjoying yourself, but there are so many reasons why you can't stay."

"Name them."

"You have to get a summer job. You have university to register for."

"Yeah, yeah. I know all that."

"And you won't be welcome at Langley."

"Who says?"

"I say."

"Derek said—"

"I've told you before. Derek isn't the only one at Langley. There are Camilla and Sybil to think about. They'll make your life miserable."

"That's garbage. You were just a kid when you were there. It won't be the same for me."

"Forgive me for intruding into a family discussion, but your mother's right, you know, Jason."

Tessa gave Philip a grateful smile, relieved that he was taking her side. Having seen the camaraderie between them, she felt that Jason might heed his advice.

Jason opened his mouth to launch his protest, but Philip hadn't finished.

"I think you should come and stay here with me. You could stay for the rest of the summer, if you like."

Tessa's smile vanished. A sudden rush of anger took her breath away. "I . . . I can't believe what I'm hearing."

Philip looked surprised at her outburst. "I mentioned before that I would be happy to have Jason stay at Thornton and you seemed quite pleased about it."

"I thought you meant for a few days, until he had to join the summer party at Gatwick. Not for the entire summer. You know how important it is that he comes home next week."

"I believe that it may be even more important for Jason to find out where his roots are."

"That's right," Jason said. "That's what I want to do."

"For God's sake, Philip," Tessa said in a low voice. "I thought that you, at least, would have more sense than to encourage him with this nonsense."

"I can understand why you'd be worried about him staying at Langley. I can't for the life of me understand why you'd worry about him staying here."

"You'll be working. You told me yourself that the courts don't close until the end of July."

"I can commute to Leeds most of the time. On those nights when I have to stay there for a case, Peter frequently moves into the house. And Sarah's here, as well."

"Hey!" Jason said, raising his voice. "Have you forgotten about me?"

"How could we forget you?" Tessa said. "It's you we're discussing."

"Well, you can quit discussing me. I've made up my mind. I'm nineteen, Mom. I can do what I want."

"No one can ever do what they want without considering the feelings of others, Jason," Philip said. "Never forget that."

"What will you do for money?" Tessa asked, determined to ignore Philip. She didn't care about what he thought anymore. This was between her and Jason and must be thrashed out here, now.

"I'll manage."

"How?" Tessa insisted. "If you don't come back with the school group your plane ticket is nonrefundable and will be of no use to you."

Jason glared at her, his chin thrust out. "I'll use one of your free passes to get home."

"No, you won't. You know damned well that I've been laid off. I've only got one pass left."

"Laid off?" Philip repeated. "From your work? You didn't tell me that."

"I didn't tell you a lot of things." Tessa blinked away angry tears. "Now I suppose everyone in the Yorkshire Dales will know I'm unemployed."

"Not from me, they won't."

"It's only temporary," Jason said. "You'll get your job back, Mom. You know you will."

"That's not important now. What's important is that you get a summer job to help pay your university fees."

"I'll find something here," Jason said.

Philip glanced at them both. "There are dozens of jobs needing to be done around Thornton. I should be happy to employ Jason for the summer. Then, I'll make sure he gets on that plane back to Canada in time for starting university. We can discuss his plane ticket later," he added hastily, before Tessa could speak. "How would you like to work at Thornton?" he asked Jason.

Jason's face was radiant. "Geez, I'd love it. I guess I'd be able to see Vicky and . . . him . . . Derek a bit as well, wouldn't I?"

"I think that could be managed," Philip said dryly. "But you'd have to hold to your side of the bargain. I'll expect you to work hard. Then, back to Canada without complaints whenever your mother says so, is that understood?"

"Absolutely." The face Jason turned to his mother glowed almost as brightly as his hair. "What do you say, Mom?"

Tessa knew that she had been well and truly defeated. "It looks as if it's all been taken out of my hands," she said through pinched lips.

"Jason. Would you be good enough to go and tell

Sarah that we'll be down for a cup of tea in ten minutes?" Philip asked.

Jason looked from Philip to his mother and shrugged. "Sure."

"Forgive me for having interfered," Philip said as soon as Jason had gone, "but I think he needs to have time to get used to us. If you drag him back to Canada against his will, he could be so resentful that he might never forgive you."

Her stony silence forced Philip to press on.

"He's had a bad shock. Don't forget it's less than twenty-four hours since he found out who his real father is. He needs time and space to work things out."

"It's a bit late for that now, isn't it? What good will it do him?" Tessa demanded. "All that will happen is that he'll become used to a way of life that can't possibly continue when he gets back home."

"I think you may be surprised to see how much good it will do. As for the way of life, I intend to work him extremely hard here, so that he realizes what running an estate like this entails. But I shall also make sure he has some recreation. Wait and see, we'll have him playing cricket in no time."

Philip's attempt to introduce a little lightness into the conversation met with no response from Tessa.

"And I give you my word that no harm will come to him. Where Derek and Langley are concerned, I mean."

"I can't bear the thought of losing him," she said impulsively, and then immediately regretted it.

He made a slight movement toward her, but then, sensing her resistance to him, stilled. "I do understand, you know. Perhaps you have been close to each other for too long. All children must make a break from their parents at some time. Otherwise, neither side can get on with their lives ... just look at Camilla and Sybil."

Although his tone was gentle, his words wounded her inexpressibly. He made her sound like a clinging, overprotective mother. This time she couldn't stop the tears.

Philip moved to her, but she put up both hands to ward him off.

"God, how I hate to see you cry," he said, helplessly shaking his head. "One day, I hope you'll understand why this was the best thing to do."

She dragged her arm across her eyes, furious with herself for having lost control. "I don't think I'll ever be able to forgive you for taking Jason's side against me. You always used to be my friend. Now I feel you're my enemy."

He flinched as if she had struck him. "I am deeply sorry that you feel that way. It was never my intention to upset you, Tessa."

His expression was unfathomable. She knew that he probably was sorry. She hated the fact that his essential Englishness stopped her from lashing out at him. If she did, she knew that he would not respond, but merely retreat further into his shell.

She had never felt quite so wretchedly alone. Even in the darkest times there had always been Jason. Now she had nothing, no one. "I want to go back to the hotel."

"I'll drive you there as soon as we've had tea."

"No, I want to go now. Immediately. And I'd like Peter to drive me. Or Sarah. Yes, Sarah." She sounded—and felt—as if she had a high fever.

Now Philip looked deeply troubled. "What about Jason . . . and Steven?"

She hurried away from him, along the corridor, down the stairs. "I don't know. I can't think." She went into the dining room. "I can't remember where I put my bag," she said distractedly.

He grabbed her arm, turning her to face him.

"You're terribly upset. It's no wonder, with all that's happened. Why don't you lie down and rest? I'll get you a brandy."

"I don't want a bloody brandy. I want to get back to the hotel and be by myself."

"I can't let you go away like this, Tessa." He tried to draw her closer to him.

She snatched her arm away. "I must. Would you please find someone other than yourself to drive me?" She took in a deep breath, striving to calm down. "Then I'll call later and see if Jason and Steven can join me in the hotel for dinner."

He was very pale. "Just Steven and Jason?"

"Yes."

"Very well. I'll tell them that's what you want. Although I should think that Steven will be too tired to go out again tonight."

"Then I will have to go to Langley to say good-bye to him."

He left her in the dining room. She felt totally shattered, as if she'd been beaten, but the bruising was all on the inside.

He returned in a few minutes, holding her handbag. "Sarah will drive you. She's just getting her car." He watched her as she searched in her bag for a tissue. "Are you sure you won't change your mind?"

"Absolutely. Would you tell Steven I'll call him at Langley, to arrange—"

"No need. I'm here." Tessa turned quickly. Steven was standing in the doorway, holding on to Peter's arm. "Sorry I slept. One of the privileges of old age, being able to sleep in the afternoon. What were you going to arrange with me?"

Tessa hesitated. "I thought I should get back to the hotel, do some packing, as I'm leaving early tomorrow morning."

"You're leaving now?"

"Yes."

"You can't leave now. Peter tells me that Sarah's laid on some tea for us."

Tessa gave him a faint smile. "I couldn't eat another bite after that huge lunch."

"Speak for yourself. I intend to have my tea. And I want you here while I have it."

Once again, Tessa felt that she'd been outmaneuvered. She couldn't possibly quarrel with her uncle on her last day with him.

Steven looked from Tessa to Philip and then gave a little shiver. "I'm feeling cold," he said querulously. "Always feel that way after I've slept."

"There's a fire in the library, Steven," Philip said. "I'll get Peter to settle you in there. Then you and Tessa can have some time by yourselves. I'll have the tea sent in to you." He went to the door.

"Would you mind telling Sarah—" Tessa began.

"I'll let her know you're staying for a while," Philip said and left the room.

Leaning heavily on Peter's arm, Steven walked to the library. There, he was made comfortable in the chair by the fire. Tessa noticed how gentle Peter was with him, tucking his rug firmly around him, but not fussing in any way. Uncle Steven hated to be fussed over. Then Peter left him and Tessa alone together, closing the library door behind him.

"I think this is my favorite room in Thornton," Tessa said, eager to break the silence between them.

She looked around. Thornton's library was far smaller than Langley's, but also far cozier. Like many of the rooms in Thornton, the library had a low ceiling. Its walls were lined with books, apart from the fireplace wall, which was paneled in oak and smoke-stained from the stone fireplace that had been there for several centuries. It was a room that invited you in, its comfortable chairs with their worn covers asking to be curled up in with a good book.

But today the library seemed stuffy to Tessa, far too warm. She wished she could open a window to get some air.

"What's happened with you and Philip?" Steven asked. "You could cut the atmosphere between you with a knife."

Tessa looked down at the copy of *Country Life* she had picked up from the table. "Philip took Jason's side against me."

"What about?"

"About him not coming back to Canada with me. He invited Jason to stay at Thornton for the summer."

"Is that such a bad thing?"

"Yes, I think it is." She leaned forward. "I couldn't say it to Philip, but Jason is already realizing how much better off he might have been if I'd married Derek. His life as Derek's son would have been vastly different. He knows that."

"So?"

"I don't want him to get used to a lifestyle he could never have in Canada."

"He knows that. He's a bright lad."

"When he sees how Derek and Philip live he's bound to feel resentment. Not just about fate in general, but about me not marrying Derek."

"So it's your guilt we're talking about here, not just Jason's welfare."

She gave him a direct look. "I suppose so. Although I don't see why I should be the one to feel guilty."

"It wasn't just pride, was it?"

"What wasn't?" she replied, deliberately obtuse.

"The reason for your not telling Derek you were pregnant that night."

She felt her face redden beneath his intent gaze. "I was so angry with him, I didn't want to marry him anymore. For the first time I saw him as he really was. It was quite a shock, I can tell you.''

"There was something else. You spoke to Camilla later on, didn't you? Before you ran away. What did she say?''

"Oh, only that she was very much in love with Derek. Had always been so. That he'd only turned to me because she was away in Europe. Which, in retrospect, was probably the case.''

"Nothing else?''

"Nothing else," she lied. "I wasn't about to marry a man who loved my cousin. Just think what a hell my marriage would have been.''

He sighed heavily. "Too true. Camilla has reaped her own just reward.''

"Don't be too hard on her," Tessa said, thinking of his feelings. After all, Camilla was his only child. "Once she came home from Europe, it was Camilla Derek wanted. I should have realized . . . but by then it was too late.''

"Now you're worried that Jason will turn against you.''

"No, not me so much. I'm concerned that if he stays here he'll find it difficult to settle into the only life he can have. One where he has to work for every penny he gets, with no inherited wealth or property. Philip says he'll make him work hard at Thornton, but every day he spends here will remind Jason that this beautiful old place and all its grounds could have been his one day.''

Steven studied her face for a while before speaking again. "I'm sorry to say that I agree with Philip. Jason will feel even more resentful if you insist that he return with you to Canada.''

"So you're all against me," Tessa said, her voice bitter.

"No, we're thinking of you just as much as we are

of Jason. You've raised this young man all by yourself. Now you must let him go so that he may find his own way in life. You cannot force him to come home with you against his will, unless you intend to coerce him by threats of withholding help for his schooling, or something of that sort. Which reminds me. Before I forget, I want to speak to you on that subject. I'd like to help you with Jason's university expenses and I won't take no for an answer. Any sort of disagreement is bad for my health, my doctor tells me," he added as Tessa was about to protest.

Tessa had to smile. "Oh, Uncle Steven. I don't want to disagree with you about anything. I'm so sorry. I seem to have brought you nothing but trouble ever since I arrived." She drew in a deep breath, releasing it in a sigh. "I know that I, myself, feel in an absolute turmoil, so God knows what it's doing to you."

"I am absolutely fine, so you may stop worrying about me. Anything that brings you here to see me, for however short a time, and that enables me to meet your son as well, cannot be all bad. Now, stop trying to lead me away from the subject of helping Jason."

"I don't want to have any sort of disagreement with you," Tessa said firmly, "but I will refuse to discuss it."

"Very well. Then we shall consider the offer made and accepted, and pass on to another subject we can discuss. My granddaughter, Vicky."

"I don't seem to have helped at all there, either."

"I'm not so sure about that," Steven said, frowning. "If only you could have stayed on a little while longer, who knows what influence you might have had on her."

Tessa was fed up with having to feel guilty about everything. "Well, I have work to return to," she said briskly.

"Is there any chance of your getting over to England again in the near future? I'm not wanting to pressure you, of course. I'm sure you have your own life. Including, perhaps, a special man?" he suggested hopefully.

"There is a man, but he's not really special, if you know what I mean."

"He's not the Right One."

"No, he's not," Tessa said, suddenly realizing that this visit had brought her to that conclusion, at least. The knowledge that she would have to tell Mark when she got home was not much of a consolation.

"So, there is no one of importance in your life, apart from Jason."

How very bleak it sounded. "No. No one at all. I told you before, I prefer to remain independent, unattached."

"It is no wonder that you're afraid to lose Jason," he said gently. "But you cannot hang on to a son forever, you know."

"I hope you don't mind me saying that I rather resent the suggestion that I rely on Jason for companionship. Philip said much the same thing."

"Good Lord. He really was asking for trouble, wasn't he?"

"Yes."

"That's because he cares about your well-being, my dear, as do I."

Tessa had no wish to discuss Philip with Steven—or anyone. "I assure you that I have a very full social life and many friends, both male and female."

"I am very glad to hear it. So, what do you think?" Steven asked.

"About what?"

"Will you be able to pay us another brief visit?" He leaned toward her, eagerness animating his thin face. "Perhaps you could come just before Jason has to leave. Then you could travel back together. I'd be very happy to pay for your plane fares."

Tessa thought of the one solitary flight pass she still had left. "We'll see about that. I'd love to come back and see you again." She gave him a wry grin. "That way I could make sure Jason comes back with me."

"Exactly."

"Promise me one thing, though."

"What is that?"

"That you won't tell anyone that I intend to return."

"Very well. It will be our secret."

She hated to lie to him, but she knew how important it was that he thought he'd be seeing her again. Unless she got her job with the airline back, there wasn't a chance of her being able to fly over to England again. She'd be starting some new job and wouldn't be able to get the time off.

At least, she *hoped* she'd be starting a new job.

Later, after tea, when they said their final good-bye before he got into the car to drive back to Langley, she clung to him, finding it hard to let him go.

"Are you sure you wouldn't like me to come to Langley with you?" she asked.

"No, I think this is the best way. I hate long, drawn-out good-byes," he said in her ear as he hugged her tightly against his tweed jacket. "By the way, Vicky said she was driving you to the railway station tomorrow, so you can have a nice chat with her on the way." He gave her a warning nod. "You know what I mean."

She knew, all right. The thought of tackling Vicky about Jeremy was not a pleasant one.

"Yes, I know. I'll do my best. I promise."

"Good-bye, my darling," he said. Then, abruptly to Peter, "Let's get going."

The engine turned over and the Range Rover moved

off. A blurred face, a hand raised in farewell, and he was gone.

She stood for a moment, watching the space where her uncle had last been, as if hoping he would materialize again. For some reason she didn't cry. She had the feeling that she would do all her weeping later, when she was alone in her hotel room.

She turned to Philip, who stood silently by. "Such a short visit," she said, for something to say. Shorter even than she'd planned, but she couldn't face going back to Langley again. All her business there was at an end.

"I'm sure that it proved worthwhile for both of you, however short it was." How formal he sounded. Like a polite stranger.

She nodded, not trusting herself to speak. The sun that had shone most of the afternoon had now clouded over. There was an oppressive feeling of an approaching rainstorm in the air.

"How about a drink?" Philip asked.

"Thank you, but I'd rather get back to the hotel now, if you don't mind."

The awkwardness between them was tangible. Where once their conversation had been easy and friendly, it was now stilted and cool.

"Would this be a bad time for Sarah to drive me?"

He gave her a long look. "Not at all. I'll go and get her, and then I'll call Jason. He's in the stables, looking at our three remaining horses. Excuse me."

She watched him go back into the house. The thought of never seeing him again after today was as oppressive as the weather.

"Sarah will be happy to drive you. Jason asked if I could drive him to your hotel later," Philip told her when he came back.

"Fine. Who looks after the horses now?" she asked for something to say . . . and then wished she hadn't.

"We all muck in," he said. "Peter, myself, a lad from the village . . . even Sarah sometimes."

"I expect Jason would enjoy working in the stables." It took a great deal of effort to say it, but she hated to feel this chasm between her and Philip. "He's always been great with horses."

"I'll remember that." He gave her a fleeting smile and then held out his hand. She took it and felt the warmth of his grip, then it was gone. "I wish you a far happier life than the one you've had so far," he said softly. "It sounds trite to say that I also wish I'd been able to help you more, both in the past and now, but I do."

Then why the hell didn't you? she wanted to cry out, instead of taking Jason's side against her. But she merely said, "Thank you. And thank you for looking after Jason."

"I'll make sure he catches whatever plane you decide he should be on."

"I know you will."

"I'll drive him over to Middleham later. Would six o'clock be all right?"

"Six would be fine."

They both hesitated. It was like their first meeting, three days ago, only far worse. Then, it had been a mixture of shyness and warmth of feeling. Now their mutual hesitancy marked the gulf between them, their coolness toward each other.

When Philip kissed her cheek, it was a mere brush of his lips, but she flinched from the kiss, filled with a deep sense of betrayal.

Chapter Twenty-one

For the first few minutes of the drive back to Middleham, Tessa said very little other than thanking Sarah for the terrific lunch and tea and for driving her. Sarah respected her need for silence, driving her little Ford Fiesta slowly and carefully along the upper Leyburn road.

At any other time, Tessa might have welcomed the leisurely pace, but today she just wanted to get back quickly to the hotel, to be by herself.

"Sorry I'm not being very friendly," she said at last as they crested Bellerby Moor.

"That's all right," Sarah said. "Can't be easy leaving your son behind."

"No, it isn't."

"Bet you wish he'd never come, right?"

Tessa nodded. "It was quite a shock when he turned up."

"I hear Mr. Derek's right chuffed about having a son."

Word spread quickly in the Dales, thought Tessa. "Yes, he seems very happy about it. But Camilla and Sybil aren't 'chuffed' at all, I can tell you."

"Doesn't surprise me."

Tessa glanced at Sarah, who was staring resolutely ahead of her, her plump hands clutching the steering wheel. "Sarah, I know it all happened years ago, but I need to know. Did you tell her I was pregnant?"

"Tell who?"

"Camilla ... or my aunt."

"No, I didn't," Sarah said calmly. "But she knew, all right."

Tessa's heart beat faster. "Who did?"

"Your Aunt Sybil."

Tessa turned in her seat. "Are you sure? Did she actually say so?"

"No, she didn't. But I could tell by her eyes that she knew. That's why she got rid of me, so as I wouldn't let on to Mr. Derek that you were expecting."

"Oh, Sarah, I'm so sorry."

"Well, you needn't be. Although she wouldn't like to hear me say so, she did me a kindness. Best thing I ever did was to get away from that place."

"Did she give you any reason for firing you?"

"She just said that my loyalty hadn't been given entirely to my employer ... meaning her, of course."

"Do you think Camilla knew as well?"

"I don't know. You'd have to ask her yourself."

Tessa gave a harsh laugh. "I'm not likely to do that now, am I? Did you know that after Derek dumped me, Camilla told me she was pregnant? That's when I decided to run away. I knew there was no hope at all for me with Derek if she was going to have his child."

"I knew she wasn't expecting. She'd had her period that same week."

Tess gasped. "Oh, God, Sarah. *That's* probably why Sybil fired you. Because you knew Camilla wasn't pregnant and Derek might change his mind if he found out that she had lied to him."

"Aye, but Sybil knew you were pregnant. I'm sure of it. Either way, I knew more than was good for me, so she got rid of me."

"God, she's a wicked woman."

"Aye, you're right there. Never underestimate the Witch of Langley, that's what I say."

That night, in the snug little room with its flowery chintz quilt and chair covers, Tessa slept fitfully. She'd had a light supper in the Black Swan with Jason. They'd both had a pint of the local Theakston ale and steak-and-kidney pie, but Tessa had eaten only a few mouthfuls.

She was overwhelmed with a sense of mission unaccomplished. The fact that she partly blamed Jason for this hadn't made for an easy meal together. Although she knew that this was not the time for recrimination, it was there in her mind all the time as she spoke to him about his future and her past.

If only you hadn't come here. If only. If only ... The words kept repeating in her brain.

Jason had hugged her when they parted, and promised that he'd be back home in good time to register for university. She believed him, but she knew that even one month at Thornton could change him forever.

If it had been one of the little stone cottages in Leyburn, with tiny dark rooms, she told herself at twenty past three in the morning, he might have been happy to get back to their own bright and modern apartment in Westwood, Winnipeg. But nothing could compare with Thornton Manor.

Lucky dog! The words came out of the darkness, perhaps wafted through the open window with the screech of an owl from the ruins of Middleham's ancient castle that stood beyond the market square.

She had to admit to herself, as she tossed back the blankets and quilt that were designed more for the chill nights of midwinter than those in warm July, that she envied Jason. A month in Thornton, away from job hunting and the searing prairie heat and the ugliness of the billboards and signs along Portage Avenue, sounded like heaven. No wonder Jason had been eager to leave her to get back there last night.

She hadn't come out to the car. She and Philip had said their farewells already. She stood inside the hotel entrance, watching the car turn and drive away, feeling as if her heart had been attached to it with a tow hook and was being wrenched from her chest.

"How are you feeling?" Vicky said to her when she arrived at the hotel the next morning. "You look dreadful."

Tessa had to laugh. "Thank a lot. I feel it. It was too hot last night to sleep."

Vicky gave her a searching look over her sunglasses, but said nothing. She picked up both of Tessa's bags. "This all?"

"Yes. Same as I brought with me."

"That's awful. You've come all this way and didn't even get a chance to shop." Vicky put the bags in back of the Range Rover as Tessa climbed into the passenger seat.

"Philip was going to give me a jar of Thornton honey," Tessa said suddenly as Vicky drove down the road to Leyburn. "He must have forgotten."

Quite unexpectedly, she found herself crying and couldn't stop.

"Oh, Tessa." Vicky put out a hand to squeeze Tessa's. "Do you want me to drive over to Thornton and get some honey for you?"

Tessa shook her head, but couldn't speak. She gave a little sob and searched unsuccessfully in her purse for a tissue.

Vicky grabbed some from the box on the dashboard and handed them to her. "Here."

"Thanks." Tessa sniffed and blew her nose. "It wasn't really the honey. It was why he forgot."

"I gather from Papa that your second visit to Thornton wasn't exactly a wild success."

Tessa smiled through her tears. "You can say that again. This entire visit has been a bloody disaster."

Vicky turned onto the Bedale road. "Oh, I wouldn't say that. Papa is delighted to have seen you and he's also terrifically excited at the thought of Jason staying on."

"Is he?" Why hadn't she thought of that aspect of it?

"Of course he is, silly. First young man in the family and all that nonsense."

"I hadn't thought about it like that. I must say the men have accepted Jason remarkably well, considering . . ."

"You can't really expect my mother to be quite so magnanimous, can you? After all, you've given my father what he always wanted: a son."

"Does it bother you, Vicky?"

"Am I jealous, do you mean? Not really. I like Jason. Trouble is, being around my parents at the moment is like being in a war zone."

"I'm sorry about that."

"Don't be. It's not anything new, really. Besides, it was their fault in the first place, wasn't it?"

"How's Jeremy?" Tessa asked, anxious to change the subject.

"He's fine. We're going to drive back to the city together when I get back. I have to prepare some stuff for an exhibition there at the end of the week."

"How exciting! I wish I could be there."

"I wish you could, too. Are you sure you wouldn't prefer to drive to London with us?"

"No thanks," Tessa said. "I need the time to myself, just to think."

"I have an idea," Vicky suddenly said after a pause. "Why don't you stay on in London? You could stay with me in Jeremy's flat in Mayfair and do some shopping. Maybe take in a few shows."

"That's so kind of you, Vicky. I do wish I could, but I can't. I have to get back to work."

"What a shame. We'd love to have you stay with us."

"You might, but I'm not so sure about Jeremy. Did he mind about lunch yesterday?"

"Wasn't too happy about it, but we had a good evening together, so that was okay."

This was a good opening, but Tessa wasn't sure she was in a fit state to have a serious discussion with Vicky. Besides, she'd made such a hash of her own life, what right had she to interfere in someone else's?

Do it for Uncle Steven, she told herself.

"Are you getting excited about the wedding?" she asked.

"Are you kidding? Every time I think of it I feel like barfing."

"Oh, why?"

"All that silly nonsense of dresses and veils and page boys and invitations. If I had my way we'd just run off and get it done in a registry office."

"Why don't you, then?"

"Because Mummy and Grandmother would never speak to me again if I did. Come to that, nor would Jeremy and his family. So that idea's out."

"Not getting cold feet, are you?"

"No, of course ..." Vicky's voice died away. "You don't think I should marry him, do you?" she asked, aggressively changing gear.

Tessa was taken aback for a moment. "I don't even know Jeremy. We just met for that short time on Saturday."

"Forget Jeremy. You think I'm too young to get married, don't you?"

"Yes, I do." At any other time, Tessa might have been a little more diplomatic, but her emotions were too raw to be able to pretty up her feelings. "I can't imagine why you'd tie yourself down at nineteen, however great the guy might be."

"Grandmother says I could lose Jeremy, if I asked him to wait."

"Surely not. After all, he's still a young man."

"He's five years older than I am."

"That's nothing. He's in love with you, isn't he?"

"Yes, he is. But he's a big catch, if you know what I mean. Heir to an earldom, pots of money, and gorgeous to look at as well. You can imagine how quickly he'd get snapped up if I let him go."

"Do you really want to be a countess, Vicky?"

"Wouldn't you want to be, if you had the chance?"

"God, no. I'd hate it."

"Would you, really?" Vicky sounded surprised. "Grandmother says it would be the achievement of a lifetime."

Tessa shivered, remembering what Sarah had told her yesterday. "Does she?" Although her head was splitting, she tried to choose her words very carefully. "I think achievement is something you do by yourself. Creating a beautiful piece of furniture is an achievement. Winning the marathon is an achievement."

"Beating out all the other talent in getting Jeremy was certainly an achievement, in my book," Vicky said defensively.

"I suppose it was."

"When I was a kid, Grandmother always used to tell me that it was up to me to bring a title into the family. In more than two hundred years, no one in our family has ever had a title. I think poor Mummy feels that she was a bit of a failure that way."

Poor bloody Mummy should have gone out and

found a title, then, thought Tessa, *instead of stealing other people's fiancés.*

"That must have made you feel very pressured to marry someone with a title."

"Bloody right. Fortunately I got the best." Vicky grinned across at Tessa.

"As long as you're sure, that's all that matters," Tessa said.

"And if I'm not, I can always get out of it, can't I?"

This was the first time that Tessa had ever heard a hint of doubt in Vicky's voice. "Just remember that divorce in this sort of family can be a lot more messy than it would be for Mr. and Mrs. Smith. You've got to think about those properties and possessions. There could be all sorts of pressure on you not to do it."

"Oh, heaps of our sort of people get divorced nowadays. Even in the royal family, as you know."

"Yes, but it's still messier and much more public. If you're even thinking about divorce as a way out of a marriage, you should make sure, before you marry Jeremy, that you know it's definitely what you want to do."

"Thanks for the advice, but it really is what I want to do." Vicky suddenly slowed and swerved over the center line. "Oops, just missed Peter Bunny there. I hate to squish them, don't you?"

Tessa knew that their conversation about marriage was over. If she had managed to sow seeds of doubt in Vicky's mind, she had achieved something, at least. She was relieved to see that Vicky wasn't upset by her plain speaking. She had no wish to alienate absolutely everyone she cared about before she left Yorkshire.

When they reached Northallerton Station, Vicky dropped her off and then went to park the car. As Tessa stood on the station platform, the warm wind ruffling her hair, she thought about all that had happened since her arrival at this same station. It was hard to believe that it had been only three days ago. So much had happened in such a short time. She had learned that her aunt and cousin were mere mortals and no longer had the power to hurt her. She had seen her beloved uncle and made him happy by her visit.

These were the positive results of her homecoming. These, plus her growing affection for her cousin's daughter. But although she had gained a new friend in Vicky, she was mourning the loss of an older, long-cherished friendship.

And it was very possible that she had also lost her son.

Vicky came rushing up to her. "Phew! That was close. The train's just coming. I had to park in a no-parking zone. There weren't any spots left."

"Oh, Vicky, don't do that. Quickly, let's say goodbye now. I'd hate you to get a ticket."

She hugged Vicky and Vicky hugged her back, holding her tightly. "I'm going to miss you so much," she said.

"Me, too," Tessa said.

"Promise me you'll try to get over for the wedding."

"I'll try. It might not be easy, with work and everything."

"I won't get married unless you're there," Vicky warned as the train pulled in with a screech of brakes.

That's a deal, Tessa was tempted to reply.

"You work with an airline. You'll get here, I know it. I want Jason there as well." Vicky hugged her again. "I love you, Tessa. Thanks so much for coming." She swung one of the bags up the steps and into the train.

"Love you, too," Tessa said as she climbed into the train, carrying her other bag. "Look after Jason for me."

"I will."

A whistle blew, doors were slammed, and the train started off. Tessa leaned from the window to wave. As the train gathered speed, Vicky's last words came to her on the wind.

"Thanks for giving me a brother!"

Chapter Twenty-two

Vicky's mind was seething as she drove back to Langley. She hadn't let on to Tessa that Jeremy had been furious with her for making him late in leaving for London this morning.

"Can't Barton or Taylor drive her?" he'd said. She'd told him that Tessa had been treated badly enough, without having a stranger drive her to the station.

"Then what's wrong with your father doing it?" Jeremy made things even worse by adding in a sarcastic tone, "*He's* certainly no stranger to her."

It ended by her slamming out of the house, yelling, "Go to London on your own. I don't need you to frigging drive me."

Unfortunately, she met Kevin as she was running down the steps. "Trouble in paradise?" he said, giving her one of his knowing grins.

Vicky muttered something rude under her breath and drove off, her wheels churning up gravel.

Now, as she drove back, she was thinking of her conversation with Tessa. She was the first woman in her family to question her engagement to Jeremy. Vicky had written Papa off as being an old fuddy-duddy, and she had very little respect for her father's opinions, but Tessa was different. Tessa was younger and more with it. She seemed surprised—no, dismayed was the word—that someone should get married at nineteen. She also, Vicky could tell, disliked Jeremy.

For the first time since their engagement, Vicky allowed herself to list the things that she, too, disliked about Jeremy. His arrogance. His lack of sensitivity to other people's feelings. His inability to appreciate the arts in general. (The only pictures he liked were those of dogs or horses.) His racism and classism. (Was there such a word?) He made her cringe when he treated waiters or salespeople as if they were an inferior species from another planet.

But she felt that she was beginning to exert a strong influence on him. He had already changed in many ways. She was sure that he would continue to change, to mature, under her influence. After all, it was tough growing up wealthy and spoiled, heir to an immense estate, knowing that you would one day be an earl.

Besides, she had promised her grandmother and mother when she was a child that she would marry a prince for them. When she'd brought Jeremy home to Langley for the first time, she'd whispered to her grandmother, "Not quite a prince, Grandmother, but he will be an earl one day."

From that day on she had been treated like something very precious. Nothing else she had done had ever met with this sort of approval. She'd been a bit of a tomboy as a child and run rather wild as a teenager. She'd grown used to being told that she was behaving like "a common hooligan" and admonished to try to be "a lady, like your mother."

Then, when she'd discovered, quite by chance, what it was she wanted to do for the rest of her life, she'd had to fight tooth and nail to be apprenticed to one of the leading cabinetmakers in the north. Only by threatening to leave home for good, never to come back at all, did she get her own way.

However successful she was in her profession, she knew that it could never please her mother and grandmother. Not even if the Queen herself commissioned a piece from her!

Jeremy was the magic key to their wholehearted approval.

She left the car by the stables and was about to go looking for Jeremy when her father came out of the tack room with Jason.

"Got away all right, did she?" Derek asked.

"Yes, Daddy. I saw her right onto the train." She spoke gently, seeing the dark circles beneath his eyes. Despite his pleasure at finding he had a son, this had all been a great shock for him, she knew.

"I wish she had let me drive her," he said, his lips quivering. "I'd like to have spent a little more time with her."

"I know you would, but it would just have caused more problems with Mummy, wouldn't it?"

He walked away, muttering beneath his breath.

"Was she really okay?" Jason asked. "She was acting really weird last night."

"She was fine, Jason. Honestly," she said, seeing the doubt on his face. "I think she's doing the right thing. It's much better for her to get away from all the rotten memories. Once she's back home, she'll be able to distance herself from it all."

"That's what she said." He scuffed at a tuft of the grass with his toe. "But I know I've screwed things up for her. She was mad at me for staying on."

"Oh, she'll get over it. Once she's back at work—"

"That's the problem. She's been laid off from the airline. She hasn't got a job to go back to. That's one of the main reasons I'm worried about her."

"God, how awful for her. She never said anything about it to me."

Jason shrugged. "No, I guess she wouldn't want to.

Shit! I should've gone back with her, shouldn't I? Instead of letting her go all alone."

Vicky put her arm around Jason. "I'm sure she'll be fine. Go and find my dad. Cheer each other up. By the way, are you staying here or at Thornton?"

"Thornton. Philip said it was okay. It was his idea. Your father's not too happy about it, though."

"No, he wouldn't be. But you'll be better off staying at Thornton. It's only a few miles away, so you can spend lots of time here during the day. Keep Thornton as a safe haven." She raised her eyebrows at Jason. "If you know what I mean."

"Yeah, I know. Mom said it was best, too."

Vicky looked at her watch. "Blimey! I'd better go and find Jeremy before he explodes. See you toward the end of the week.

"Yeah." Jason grinned. "Wish you were staying."

"Some of us have to work for a living. Not all of us are lazy do-nothings."

"Speak for yourself. Philip's got a list a mile long for me to start on tomorrow."

"Glad to hear it. Bye, little brother."

"I'm older than you are," Jason said indignantly.

"Sorry about that. Here comes Kevin. Jeremy's probably sent him to look for me. I'm off."

"Your sweetheart's on the warpath," Kevin said when Vicky reached him. "Your mother's busy buttering him up."

"Let's hope she succeeds. I'd rather drive to London by myself than with Jeremy in one of his moods."

"I don't know what you see in him."

"So you've said before. Please don't say it again."

His cheeks flamed. He turned his face half from her. "I'm sorry. I try not to . . . but I can't stand the thought of your marrying him and then him making you unhappy."

"If that happens, I can deal with it."

Kevin grasped her by the upper arms. "I care about you, Vicky. You must know that. You're not bloody blind."

"I care about you, too, Kevin," Vicky said softly. "We've been friends for years."

His hands gripped her more tightly. "That's not what I mean, and you damn well know it."

"What the hell's going on here?"

At the sound of Jeremy's voice, Kevin released Vicky and stepped back from her.

"What's going on?" Jeremy demanded.

"Kevin and I are having a fight, that's all," Vicky said.

"Didn't look much like a fight to me." Jeremy darted an angry look at Kevin, who was standing there with an infuriating grin on his face.

"Well, it was," Vicky said, feeling like smacking Kevin. She gave him one of her dark looks, and walked away from both men. "Are you coming, Jeremy?" she said over her shoulder.

"In a minute," he replied, looking at Kevin.

She went back and slipped her arm through his. "Come on. Let's go. We're late enough as it is."

"That's not my fault."

"Course not. It's mine." She pulled Jeremy away, feeling the tension in his arm.

"I'd like to knock him down."

"I'm sure you would, but that would be terribly unfair. You're far taller than he is." She had to stifle a giggle as she remembered that Kevin had been a lightweight boxer for Cambridge. If it came to a fight between them, he'd probably have Jeremy on the ground in less than a minute.

The fact that she rather relished that thought made her feel decidedly uneasy.

* * *

As Philip was driving to Leeds he felt a heaviness in him that seemed to drag him down. He tried to concentrate on the facts of tomorrow's case, but however hard he tried, somehow they eluded him.

He had woken just before dawn that morning, probably because of the raucous predawn chorus of birds coming in his open bedroom window. He'd lain awake for several minutes, hoping that he could get back to sleep. Eventually he became so tense he decided to get up. No point in lying there, worrying about something he could do nothing about.

There had been no telephone call from Tessa last night. He'd hoped that there might have been, but it was foolish of him to expect her to call. He had obviously made her very angry by taking Jason's side, but he was still sure he'd done the right thing. The lad would probably have caused her a great deal of trouble once she got him home. Occasionally, he'd caught a wild glint in Jason's eyes that reminded him of several horses he'd known ... and of Derek at the same age. Tessa had hinted that she'd had some trouble with Jason in the past. Considering Derek was his father, that wouldn't surprise him at all.

He'd thought of calling her himself before she left the hotel this morning, but what was the point? What could either of them have said that would change the way she felt? Tessa was furious with him for having supported Jason in his wish to stay on in Yorkshire and obviously felt that he'd betrayed their old friendship by doing so. And he resented her attitude about Thornton. No one, not even Tessa, had a right to dictate to him what he should do with Thornton. What he resented most was her suggestion that he was some sort of ultraconservative aristocrat because he didn't want hordes of people trampling through his home every day—not even just at weekends.

As he sped down the Al, dressed in his dark gray

three-piece suit, ready for his meeting with the solicitor and his client in his chambers, Philip reflected that
the quiet and, admittedly, rather boring life he had
led since his wife's death had been revitalized by Tessa's visit. Whether that was good or bad remained to
be seen.

"So . . . she's gone," Sybil said to Steven as they sat
out on the terrace after lunch.

"Who's gone?" Steven asked.

"Tessa, of course."

"Well, you could have meant Vicky, you know."

"Vicky will be back on Friday. Tessa, thank heav-
ens, will not."

"I'm very sorry to see her go. It was far too short
a visit."

"I said she'd cause trouble, didn't I?" Sybil nodded
at him, her dark eyes bright as a robin's.

"I think you knew a bloody sight more about all
this than you're telling me."

"Nonsense." Sybil leaned forward to pat his rug-
covered knee. "I've never had any secrets from you,
my love."

He took her hand in his, and then released it. "I'm
too tired to argue with you." He closed his eyes, leaning back in the wooden deck chair that Barton had
wheeled out for him. The sun was pleasantly warm on
his face, but although he wouldn't dream of saying so
to Sybil, he would rather be in his bed. Not that she
would allow him to stay there. Every morning she
arrived at his bedside to rally him, and he responded,
for her sake.

Nowadays he felt mortally tired. Something deep
within him wanted to be left alone, to be allowed to
separate himself from the world. This summer—his
last summer—was too bright. He wanted gray skies,
gray clouds, gray everything, to match how he felt.

The sun was too golden, the grass too green, the sky too blue. It hurt him to look at them.

Even his favorite poets no longer gave him solace. Reading them made him feel too much. And feeling meant pain, both mental and physical. He knew that it wouldn't be long before he was confined to bed, with a morphine drip in his arm. Every day he prayed to God that He would release him before that time came.

"Did you hear what I said?" Sybil's voice intruded into his thoughts.

Steven opened his eyes. "Sorry, darling, must have dropped off for a moment."

"I was saying that I don't want that young man in the house."

"You mean Jason?"

"Yes. I don't want him in the house. I don't trust him. He has a shifty look about him."

The wave of anger that engulfed Steven made him feel weak. "What a bloody awful thing to say! I would remind you that the lad carries my family's blood in his veins."

"Mixed in with a lot of other rubbish. And upbringing is important, as well."

"I thought breeding was all, where you were concerned."

"There are other considerations. I'm appalled that you don't seem to be considering Camilla's feelings at all in the matter."

"The less said about Camilla and this matter, the better. But I must insist that Jason be made welcome at Langley whenever he comes here. Although Philip has asked Jason to stay at Thornton with him, Derek has every right to have the lad over here whenever he wants. I'm pleased with Derek."

"What on earth for? I thought you were furious with him for what he did to your darling niece."

"He's behaved very well over this," Steven said, choosing to ignore the snide tone Sybil used when she spoke of Tessa. "So he should, of course, considering his despicable behavior twenty years ago. But that's all water under the bridge. I'm pleased with the way Derek's taken the lad under his wing."

Sybil lifted her face to the sun. "Let us hope that he is never given cause to regret his misguided benevolence."

Chapter Twenty-three

The worst part of coming home for Tessa was taking the down escalator at Winnipeg Airport, watching all those upturned faces of people waiting to meet passengers, and knowing that there was absolutely no one there to meet her. Flying was her job, so she wasn't used to people meeting her, but this time was different.

It was her own fault, of course. She had plenty of friends who would have been very happy to have met her had they known she was coming home, but friends would have asked questions about her trip. Questions—and the answers they necessitated—were just what she didn't need. And Mark wasn't expecting her to fly in until tomorrow evening, so he certainly wouldn't be at the airport.

Thank God for that, at least. Mark Crawford was the last person she wanted to see at the moment.

When she opened her front door and stepped inside she felt a sense of refuge. She loved coming home. The smell of basil still lingered from the batch of pesto sauce she'd made and frozen before she'd left. Her first instinct, as always, was to check the answering machine. But this time she decided to wait until she'd settled in. Telephone messages would connect her with the real world.

They might also connect her with those she'd left

behind in Yorkshire and she couldn't bear to think of them or she might break down.

But once she had changed into shorts and a T-shirt, she couldn't resist checking the machine. There were only three mundane messages: Westwood Library to say the book she'd reserved was in. Eaton's to say the bra she'd ordered—her favorite—had been discontinued. Sally Murdoch to see if she'd be in town for a baby shower next week.

A chilling sense of loneliness stole over her. She was also acutely aware of how very small the apartment seemed after staying at Langley. Normally she would have loved this feeling of coziness, but tonight it made her feel as if she were trapped in a prison cell.

Determined not to allow herself to sink into a gloom, she made a salmon-and-cucumber sandwich and a tall glass of iced tea, and carried them outside to her little patio.

Although it was past seven in the evening, the heat was still intense. From the nearby field came the usual summer sounds of kids playing baseball: shouts, laughter, the whomp of the bat on the ball . . .

We'll have him playing cricket in no time. She started, the plate almost sliding off her lap. It was as if Philip were right there beside her, repeating the words he'd said about Jason.

She was engulfed in a wave of nostalgia, of a longing for the people she'd left in England, and for England itself. At least, for the Dales country that to her meant England.

She missed the lush greenness. The grass spread out beyond her patio fence was dry, scorched by a too-hot sun. She missed the beauty of the old houses. Langley, grand and stately, a symbol of the prosperous Georgian era in which it had been built. Thornton, the ancient home of an ancient family, gentle and warm and welcoming.

As the taxi had driven her home from the airport, Tessa had thought that the buildings that lined Portage Avenue had never seemed quite so ugly to her before: the strip malls thrown up without any sense of order or aesthetics; the car sales places, festooned in gaudy balloons and flags; the Safeway shopping center, flanked by the huge parking lot, covered with row upon row of cars.

The American dream . . . flourishing in its northern neighbor.

Tessa was well aware that England had more than its share of ugliness in the wastelands of the big cities that had, with the Industrial Revolution, spawned the very blight that had swept across North America. But she had left the Dales less than twenty-four hours ago and it was there that her memory dwelled.

She was just tired, she told herself. She went inside, sliding the glass door closed and snibbing it, the cool air a relief after the heat outside. She looked at the unopened bags sitting in the middle of the floor and decided that they could wait until tomorrow. In fact, everything could wait until tomorrow. Including phoning Mark.

She put the glass and plate into the dishwasher and went to bed.

"Why didn't you call me when you got in?" was Mark's response when Tessa finally plucked up enough courage to call him the next day in the afternoon. The hurt in his voice annoyed her.

"I was dead tired. I am sorry, but I just couldn't stay awake. Can you come over?"

"Sure. I'll be there in half an hour."

That's too soon, Tessa wanted to shout down the receiver. As she replaced it, her heart was pounding. This was going to be really tough, but it must be done right away, or they'd slip back into the unbalanced relationship they'd had before she'd gone to England.

She dashed around the living room, tidying away clothes she'd left draped over the chairs, wishing that she could somehow make it larger, not quite so intimate. She'd thought about taking Mark outside, but it would be difficult to tell him that she couldn't see him anymore with the nosy Pattersons sitting with their yappy dog on the other side of the low fence. Joy Patterson was quite likely to yell hello and ask them over for a drink of orange Kool-Aid. "Come and tell us *all* about your trip," was her favorite mode of invitation, even if Tessa had just made her hundredth routine flight to and from Toronto.

She was about to put out some cheese and crackers she'd picked up at Safeway that morning when she heard the mailman putting mail in her box. She went to the door and collected the post—just bills and flyers except for one letter with the Canada Airways logo. Her heartbeat quickened as she tore the envelope open. She read the letter and then reread it, not sure that she had quite taken it in properly.

Dear Ms. Hargrave,

I have been trying to get in touch with you by telephone, but you must be away. I did not leave a message as I wanted to make sure I spoke to you in person. You will be happy to hear that we have decided to reinstate several of our senior flight attendants, including yourself, commencing September 1. Please would you contact me as soon as possible to confirm that you will be returning to Canada Airways.

Tessa stared down at the letter. She was no longer out of a job, unemployed, redundant. All those miserable words were what she no longer was. She would have yelled for joy, but the coming meeting with Mark dampened her enthusiasm a little. All she said was a fervent "Yes!" accompanied by a punch of her fist.

Mark came dead on time, as always. "God, it's good to see you," he said as soon as she'd opened the door to him. Before she could move away he put his arms around her and kissed her. "I've really missed you."

She pulled away and led the way into the living room. "I've been away less than a week."

"Seemed like a month to me."

Tessa glanced away, to avoid seeing the look of hunger in his eyes. "Would you like a beer . . . or iced tea?"

"The tea would be fine. Whatever you're having. I'll come and help," he said as she went upstairs to the gallery kitchen.

"I don't need any help." Tension sharpened her voice.

"Okay, okay. Are you still tired?"

She answered him from the kitchen. "Yes. The trip was quite a strain."

"I can see that."

His aggrieved tone annoyed her. In fact, everything about him annoyed her. How could she ever have gone out with this man, never mind slept with him?

Her realization that she felt this way should have made her feel happy that she was splitting with him. But, instead, she was swamped with guilt. She had used Mark. He'd been her defense against loneliness, against facing up to herself . . . and her past. Now that she had made her visit to the past and blended it into the present, she knew that she must work it all out by herself, however painful the process might be.

As she set the glass of iced tea in front of him, he shifted on the sofa to make room for her, but she sat in the chair across the room from him.

"Tell me about your trip," he said. "How did it go?"

She looked down at her glass, swirling it, making the ice tinkle. "It wasn't easy."

"I bet it wasn't."

"I got a lot of stuff sorted out. But then a whole lot of new stuff came up."

"Can you be more specific?" Mark said in what she called his schoolteacher voice.

"I'll do my best. But to do so I have to tell you some things you don't know anything about. About Jason, for instance."

"What did Jason have to do with your trip overseas?"

"A good question." She gave him a wry smile. "Just as I thought I had everything sorted out Jason turned up at—"

The telephone rang.

"Have you got the machine on?" Mark asked.

"Yes, but it could be . . ." She let the sentence trail. The machine had run through its message.

"Hi, Mom. I'm just—"

It was Jason. Tessa jumped up and grabbed the phone. "Hi, love."

"Philip and I were wondering how you were," Jason said. "I told him you'd be fine, but he wanted to make sure your journey home was okay. He began to get worried when we didn't hear from you."

Tears rushed to Tessa's eyes. She swallowed, and then said, "It's so great to hear your voice. Tell Philip I'm just fine. How are you doing?"

"I'm sore all over. Peter and I were mending a stone wall all day. Geez, that's hard work, lifting those stones."

"I bet it is." She liked the thought of Jason working on one of the traditional drystone walls in the Dales.

"Did you know he was gay?"

"Who?"

"Peter Wilson."

"How do you know?" Anxiety sharpened her voice. "Did he do something?"

Jason laughed. "No, Mom, of course he didn't. If he had I'd have knocked him out with one of those stones. I thought he might be and Sarah told me he was. I really like her."

Tessa was having trouble following Jason. "What did Sarah tell you?"

"That Peter was gay. She called it 'queer.'"

"Does that bother you? Working with him, I mean."

"No. Why should it? I feel sorry for him. Not because he's gay, of course, but Sarah said he has a lover stashed away in a cottage somewhere. He thinks no one knows about it, but Sarah knows because the local doctor told her."

"I see. Does Philip know?"

"About him being gay? Yes. But Sarah says she thinks Peter's worried that Philip might find out about his lover and give him the boot because of it."

"Oh, I see." Somehow she didn't think that it would bother Philip, but then Philip was frequently unfathomable, as she'd learned to her cost this past week. She decided it was best just to change the subject. "You seem to be getting on well with Sarah."

"Sure am. Man, is she a great cook."

"Ah, so that's why. How's . . . how's everyone there?"

"Great. Philip won his case."

Tessa couldn't help smiling. Jason spoke about Philip as if he'd known him for years. "That's good. Is he still in Leeds?"

"No, he came back yesterday evening. He's taking me to a sheepdog show tomorrow."

"Great," said Tessa, feeling very envious. The world

of sheepdog trials seemed a long way away from suburban Winnipeg.

"And Derek's taking me to the horse races at York next weekend."

Mark put his glass down on the table with an audible click.

"I have some great news to tell you, love," Tessa said. "Then I must go. Mark's here."

"Oh, is he?" Even across thousands of miles Jason's tone reflected his feelings about Mark. "What's the news?" he asked suspiciously.

"I've just had a letter from the airline. I get my job back in September."

"Wow! I knew you'd do it. The airline would fold without you. Way to go, Mom."

"Thanks, love. I knew you'd be pleased "

"I sure am. Wait till I tell Philip and Derek."

"You're really enjoying yourself there, aren't you?"

"I am. I love it here, Mom, but . . ." Tessa could sense his hesitation down the line. "Have you forgiven me?"

"For what?"

"For deciding to stay on here, even though you didn't want me to."

"It's okay with me, so long as you get back in time to register for university."

"I will. Well, I'd better go. Have to be up at six tomorrow. Bye, Mom. Oh, by the way, Philip says to send his good wishes."

"Is he there?"

"No, he's watching the news on the telly. He told me to bring the phone up to my room so that I wouldn't be disturbed."

And so that he didn't have to talk to her, thought Tessa. "Say hello to him for me, please."

"I will. Bye, Mom. Love you."

"Love you, too." She put down the receiver and returned to her chair.

"That's terrific news about your job," Mark said.

"It certainly is. The letter arrived just a few minutes ago. It certainly takes a load of worries off my mind." Tessa hesitated for a moment, and then said, "You must be wondering about that call."

"It was obviously from Jason. He's due back on Friday, isn't he? Is he still in France?"

"No, he's staying with his uncle."

"*His* uncle? You mean your uncle, surely. Jason's great-uncle."

"No, I mean Jason's uncle, Philip Thornton."

Mark shook his head. "You've lost me."

"It's a bit complicated." She took a drink from her glass and began telling Mark what had happened.

"So you can imagine," she said when she'd come to the end of her story, "what consternation Jason's arrival caused."

Mark looked bewildered. "You kept this a secret from me all this time," he said, shaking his head. "I just can't believe it."

"No one knew. Not even Jason." She was annoyed that he seemed to consider himself badly done by because she hadn't told him.

"Why didn't you tell me?"

"You're not listening, are you, Mark?" Her voice rose. "I told no one. My husband was the only man who knew who Jason's real father was."

"He must have been quite a guy to marry you, knowing that."

Tessa's head snapped up. She stared at Mark.

"What?" he asked. "Why the funny look?"

At first she didn't reply. Then she said slowly, really talking to herself, "That was the strange thing. He wasn't 'quite a guy' at all. He was a bastard. I never could fathom why he would marry me. I decided it must be because he felt that a married man was more likely to be accepted as an immigrant."

That was what she'd always told herself, but now she wondered if there was something else behind it. She shook her head, her mind too befuddled to be able to dwell anymore on the past.

"You seem to be off in a dream world," Mark said. "Want to share your thoughts with me?"

"Sorry. I can't."

"Apparently there's been a lot you couldn't share with me."

"I'm sorry." What more could she say?

"You don't even want to share your past life with me."

"It isn't just you, Mark. I kept my past a secret from everyone, for a good reason. Now you know why."

"You've told me about Jason, but now there's something else you're keeping from me."

"I'm sorry, but it's just not any of your business." Mark was really beginning to get to her. And she hadn't even broached the subject of their splitting up yet!

He looked deeply hurt. "I get the message. I don't think I know you anymore. This trip has changed you."

"Yes. Yes, it really has. I'm sorry, Mark."

"You just need a little time and space to get back to your old self again." He gave her a little reassuring smile, but his eyes were filled with anxiety.

"I won't ever be that old self again. That wasn't really me. It was half of me. The other half lay hidden in my past."

"Sounds very Freudian." He leaned forward. "Maybe you should go for counseling. That would help."

"I don't need counseling, Mark. I'm fine. I just need

time to work things out and get them into perspective. You were right. Time *and* space are what I need."

"Meaning?"

Now comes the tough part, she thought. "Meaning, I'm very fond of you, Mark, but ... but I need to be just me for a while."

"Sure. I understand that. I'm happy to give you time. Wish it wasn't in vacation time, though," he added ruefully.

She got up and walked to the window. "I'm talking about a permanent break, not a temporary one." She tried to say it gently, but the words were too brutal to be softened.

He came to her, put his arm around her. "You've been through a tough time, honey. I just wish I'd been there to give you support. Time heals all, you know."

She stood within the circle of his arm, her body rigid. Then she shook her head from side to side, her eyes brimming with tears. Slowly, very slowly, she drew away from him and went to stand behind her chair.

"Is it another man? Is that what it is?" he asked.

The age-old reaction of rejected men. Another man, they could understand. To be rejected for some nebulous reason was incomprehensible.

She hesitated. Was there another man? In a way, she supposed, there was. Someone unattainable, remote. An ideal who'd always been on a pedestal, beside whom everyone else—even his handsome brother—had paled.

He didn't exist, of course. Reality was a man filled with pride and stubbornness, a man who remained firmly rooted in the past, despite the fact that disaster faced him if he didn't change.

"Have you fallen for someone else. Is that it?" Mark was shouting. Mark rarely shouted.

"No, Mark. I haven't fallen for someone else. I just don't think our relationship is going anywhere."

"And whose fault is that?"

"Mine. I kept telling you that I didn't want to get married again."

"Who cares about marriage? We could just live together. That's okay by me."

"You know it isn't." She wished she could connect with him, but even his eyes avoided hers, as if he were afraid of what he would see in them. "Anyway, it's not just that." She swallowed a lump in her throat. "I've been using you as a shield against loneliness."

"We all do that, especially at our age. What's wrong with that?"

"What's wrong with it is that it's false, dishonest. We pretend to feel more for someone than we really do, just to keep a warm body beside us."

"Is that all I was to you, a warm body?"

She gave him a ghost of a smile. "A good friend with a warm body."

"Thanks a lot. You really know how to make a guy feel good, don't you?"

"My lack of the right sort of love for you doesn't make you any less of a man, Mark. It's not your fault. It's mine."

"You're a choker, that's what you are."

"A what?"

"A choker. That's what they call sports people who never win."

"I thought that was a loser."

"No. A choker is someone who has all the potential to win and chokes at the last hurdle or hole or whatever."

She gazed at him, both stung and surprised at his analogy. "You're probably right. My past experiences have made me afraid of any sort of commitment. I prefer to be alone rather than risk failing again."

"I wouldn't desert you or beat you."

His simple statement brought tears surging to her eyes. She clapped her hand over her mouth. "God, I know that, Mark. I know that so well. That's what makes this so difficult to do." She drew in a deep breath and let it out on a shuddering sigh. "You're a good man. You deserve a lot better woman than me. Someone without all the baggage I'm still carrying. I know there's the right woman out there for you."

"I think you're the right one for me."

"I know you do, but you're wrong. I know it sounds like an old cliché, but one day you'll come to me and thank me for this."

"That's not likely." His lips compressed in an attempt to hold back his pain and anger.

Tessa sighed. "We're not getting anywhere arguing like this. We're just going around in circles. The bottom line is that from now on I can think of you only as a friend. If it's easier for you to break off entirely, then that's what we'll do."

"I can't be just a friend with you."

"I understand that. I really do."

He opened his mouth to start in again, but she shook her head. "No, Mark. No more, please."

Tears swam in his eyes. She'd never seen Mark cry. Her instinct was to rush to him, to wrap her arms around him, but she resisted it.

He crossed the room without another word. His feet moved down the hall. The door opened . . . and then closed quietly.

She was totally, utterly alone.

She would start back at work in September, but for now the summer stretched endlessly and emptily ahead of her.

Chapter Twenty-four

Jason had never worked quite so hard before. He was often in bed before ten o'clock, a very unusual occurrence in his other life in Canada. His body ached and his hands were cut and bruised, and he could never scrub the dirt completely out of his nails. But ... what the heck! And he really did think that his pecs were starting to develop very nicely, with all that stone heaving and fence repairing. Which was great, as he'd met this terrific girl who was working at the Langley stables during the summer vacation. Gillian Pailthorpe, her name was. Jill for short.

He tended to spend most of his weekdays at Thornton and his weekends at Langley. It worked well that way. Vicky was often home on weekends and he got on well with her. Unfortunately, Jeremy usually came home with her, which was not so good. Jeremy was an arrogant jerk. Jason failed to understand what Vicky saw in him, apart from his obvious good looks. And she just didn't seem the sort who would go for looks only. Sure, he had pots of money and the title as well, but so what? Jason much preferred Kevin, who couldn't hide his feelings for Vicky, although he tried to, mainly by being rude to her.

When he was at Langley, Jason spent a good deal of his time with his great-uncle Steven, with whom he got along extremely well. But he kept out of the way of both Camilla and Sybil, slipping out through one of Langley's many exits when he saw one of them coming. He did it mainly to avoid trouble for the people at Langley whom he liked: Vicky and Steven . . . and his father.

His relationship with Derek was a strange one. Derek was totally unpredictable. One day he'd be all over Jason, wanting to take him riding, pushing ten-pound notes into his jeans pocket. Other days he'd freeze him out, treating him like one of the lowliest stable lads.

"Take him as he comes," Uncle Steven had advised him when Jason had told him how Derek's attitude upset him. "It's just his way. He treats everyone like that."

But although Jason suspected that Derek's moods came from the booze or whatever it was he was on, he didn't like being screwed around that way. So he found himself spending less and less time with Derek, and more with Philip.

With Philip, he always knew exactly where he stood. If he didn't like something Jason was doing, he told him straight, without any shouting or name-calling. He was the first person to treat Jason like an adult, not a kid.

After three weeks at Thornton, Jason began to dread going home to Canada. He knew he'd given his word that he'd be home in time to register for university, but the thought of being shut away in a stuffy classroom for a minimum of three years gave him a griping gut.

He broached the subject very tentatively one night after he and Philip had been to the White Boar for a pint of Theakston.

"Less than two weeks before I have to go home," he said when Philip had parked the Austin Healey, which he'd promised Jason he could drive next time they went out.

Philip deactivated the alarm, unlocked the back door, then reset the alarm again. "So soon? The time has flown."

"I've been here three weeks."

"Have you really?" Philip studied Jason's face in the dimly lit back hall. "I've enjoyed having you here. You've been good company."

Jason swallowed. "Could we talk, do you think? I know you've got work to do. Books and things. But I . . . it would help if I could talk to you."

"Certainly. Come on in to the study."

"I'll make it quick."

"Not to worry. I'm not in the mood for working on the accounts, anyway. Too depressing." Philip gave Jason a fleeting smile and opened the study door, gesturing to him to go in.

Jason went in, breathing the now familiar aromas of stale pipe smoke and old leather that permeated this most masculine room. Although he knew that Philip didn't smoke, a row of pipes stood in a wooden rack on the mantelpiece. "They belonged to my father and grandfather," Philip had told him. *My grandfather and great-grandfather,* Jason had said to himself.

In a modern house, the pipes would have been thrown out years ago, but here they remained, to be added to the stuff that had accumulated at Thornton over five centuries.

As the weeks had passed, Jason made it a point to examine and touch everything at Thornton. Nothing was barred to him. *This belongs to my family, and this . . . and this . . .* he thought, hugging the sense of belonging close to him, like a kid with a security blanket.

"Whiskey! Get down from there," Philip told his dog, who slunk down from the rug-covered sofa, ashamed to have been caught by his master in a forbidden place. Philip shoved aside the pile of papers that he'd left on the table and then switched on a bar of the electric fire. "Bit chilly in here."

Jason had been perpetually cold since he'd first come to Thornton. These old stone houses were more than "a bit" chilly. "Couldn't you install a central heating system?" he asked.

Philip sat down in the old office chair, behind the desk. "I could—and I would—if I had the money to do so."

Jason grimaced. "Sorry."

"No need to be. I know it's hard for you to understand that someone who has a good profession and a famous old house with an estate of many acres hasn't the money to put in a much-needed heating system, but that's how it is. Apart from this crippling inheritance tax I still have to pay on the estate, Thornton Manor costs a tremendous amount to maintain. So there's nothing left for any improvements, I'm afraid."

"Couldn't you sell something? The paintings, for instance?"

Philip gave him one of his enigmatic smiles. "Our ancestors, you mean?"

Jason felt ashamed for having even mentioned the idea.

"Even if I did want to get rid of them, they aren't worth a great deal. I'm sorry to say that our family wasn't particularly interested in encouraging the great masters to paint them. They believed in giving the work to the local daubers."

"What about the Thornton Cross? It must be worth a bomb."

Philip's face tightened. "It is indeed, Jason. Possibly as much as a million pounds, I should imagine."

"Wow! Haven't you thought of selling it?"

"I might have thought of it, but the cross has been part of the Thornton family since the fifteenth century. Our ancestors must have endured far worse threats than an inheritance tax and yet they managed to preserve the Thornton Treasure for their descendants. Surely, I must do the same."

"You could sell it to a museum. That way everyone would be able to see it, not just you."

"You sound like your mother," Philip said, his voice suddenly cool.

"Sorry. It just seems a shame that something so beautiful can't be seen by everyone. After all, that Pilgrimage of Grace thing you told me about, when a Thornton carried the cross, wasn't it some sort of uprising of the common people against the King? So the cross is kind of a relic of the ordinary joe's history, isn't it?"

"I must admit I had never quite thought of it that way," Philip said dryly.

"If it got stolen, you'd get the insurance, wouldn't you? You could hire a professional to steal it. Then the thief'd be rich and so would you."

Philip frowned. "Let's change the subject, shall we? What was it you wanted to speak to me about?"

Jason shifted in his seat, suddenly unsure of himself. He felt himself going red and bent to pat Whiskey, to hide it. "I don't want to go back to Canada," he muttered.

Silence. He looked up to find Philip's gray eyes speculatively gazing at him.

"I thought we had been through all that at the start. We made a bargain. You could stay on, with the understanding that you would go back to Winnipeg in time to register for university."

"I don't want to go to university."

" 'Want' doesn't come into it. We all have to do things we don't want to do. You need some further education to make sure you will have a profession."

"Going to university doesn't guarantee a job. You

said yourself that there's lots of people out of work who have university degrees."

"I did. But that means that not having one makes it even more difficult to find a job."

"I'm not academic material."

"Who told you that? You're a highly intelligent young man."

"That's nice of you to say, but I'm not much good at books and papers." Jason looked down at his nails and stretched his hands toward Philip. "I can never get them truly clean. I *like* that. I love the work I've been doing here."

Philip leaned back his head, pinching the bridge of his nose. "You mean you would like to be a farm laborer, or some such thing, all your life?"

"No, of course not. But I do like working on the land. I'd love to have Peter's job . . . or Kevin's."

"Peter went to college and took his degree. Kevin was at Cambridge."

"Yes, but I wouldn't mind all that studying, if it was the work I like doing," Jason said. "Can't you understand that? It would be different, then."

"Have you thought about becoming a veterinary surgeon? Working with animals, that's a good and extremely lucrative profession. I'm sure it would be in Canada, as well."

"Oh, I love the animals, especially the horses, but . . . but . . ." Jason struggled to put his feelings into words. "It's the land. *This* land. I don't want to leave it. I know it's not mine." He felt the blood rush into his face. "But I feel it." He banged his chest with his fist. "I feel it in here." His eyes filled with tears. "Oh, shit!" He turned his face away, willing himself not to cry.

Jason sensed that Philip had risen from his chair. He felt his hand gripping his shoulder. "I'm sorry," he whispered.

"So am I." Philip sat down beside him on the small sofa. "You've been dealt a rotten hand, Jason. But it's up to you to make sure that you don't let your sense of being badly treated drag you down, get you off on a wrong course."

"That's easy to say. Not so easy to do, without money. I bet you and Derek go through more money in a month than Mom and I would have in a lifetime."

"A slight exaggeration, but I know what you mean. Despite all my financial problems, I have lived a privileged life. Will it make you feel better to know that it's unlikely to last, that I shall probably have to sell Thornton Manor?"

Jason buried his hand in Whiskey's fur. "No, that makes me feel much worse. You've got to keep it, Uncle Philip," he said fervently. "It's ours. It belongs to the Thornton family. You can't sell it. Just think, one of those awful leisure center people might buy it."

Philip sighed. "I have thought. That's why I'm addling my brains at night, trying to find a solution."

"Yeah, and here I am bothering you with my little problems. Sorry."

"Not so little. I realize that. Give me some time to think about it, Jason."

The fact that Philip would even take time to think about it was a great encouragement to Jason. He stood up. "Okay. Thanks." They exchanged smiles. "I'm going to make myself some hot chocolate. You want anything?"

"No, thank you. I'll make myself some tea later, if I'm still awake. Good night, Jason."

"Good night, Uncle Philip. And . . . thanks."

"No promises, mind. After all, you gave your mother your word that you'd come home."

"Yeah, I know. I don't want to let her down."

"Don't worry anymore about it tonight."

"Okay, I won't."

And he probably wouldn't, thought Philip as the door closed behind Jason. Having Jason around the place had proved to be a great tonic. He was a constant reminder of the perpetual resilience of youth. One minute down in the slough of despond, the next bouncing back up again.

Philip wasn't sure, however, that there was any solution to Jason's current dilemma. There was no doubt that he was growing more and more attached to the Yorkshire Dales and to Thornton Manor in particular. But this could be nothing more than the feeling one had at the end of a holiday, the reluctance to return to the daily grind of work.

Perhaps Tessa had been right, after all. Perhaps Jason should not have stayed in England. It might have made him even more restless and resentful than he had been before.

Well, he couldn't think about that for now. He had to go over the July figures Peter had given him. Although, if they were in the same sort of a mess that the June ones had been in, he might have to send them all to his accountant. God alone knew what was wrong with Peter. He had always been extremely efficient, but for the past few months his mind seemed to be on another planet.

Sighing, Philip opened up the accounts book, but the figures jiggled before his eyes. Even when he put on his glasses, he found that he couldn't concentrate.

Damn Jason for putting thoughts of the Thornton Treasure into his mind. Now he couldn't get rid of them. He kept seeing the jeweled cross rising up before him, hanging in the ether, like one of Macbeth's daggers.

Chapter Twenty-five

It was Sarah who discovered that the Thornton Treasure was missing, when she was dusting the long gallery. Philip was having guests for lunch on Sunday and she hadn't gone over the paintings with her long-handled feather duster for ages.

She was actually polishing the heavy carved oak chest that stood at the end of the gallery—the one they said was the wedding chest of one of the Thornton brides hundreds of years back—when she suddenly felt a shiver run down her back. She turned with a sense that something was wrong, but she wasn't sure what. Then she saw it. Or, at least, she didn't see it. The glass-covered case was closed, the purple velvet lining unruffled—still bearing the imprint of the heavy gold cross—but the cross itself was no longer there.

"He must've taken it for repair or a valuation or summat like that," she muttered to herself, her heart galloping. "He should've told me. Give me quite a turn to see it gone."

Despite her certainty that Philip must have taken the cross for some good reason, Sarah felt extremely anxious, so that her morning was wasted. "I'll give him a piece of mind," she said to herself in the kitchen as she stirred the pot of Scotch broth she'd made for lunch earlier that morning.

"Who, me?" Jason asked, having heard her muttering as he came in from the top field.

"Oh, Jason. I'm right glad you're back. Maybe you know what's happened to the cross. Did Mr. Philip say he was taking it with him to Durham, do you know?"

"The cross? He didn't say anything about it."

"It's not there."

Jason stared at her. "It must be."

"It's not. I was up dusting the gallery. Then I noticed that it was gone."

"Maybe Philip took it somewhere for a valuation," Jason suggested, remembering their conversation last Monday.

"Well, if he did, he certainly didn't tell me."

"I'll go take a look." Jason raced up the wide stairs, taking them two at a time. He ran down the length of the gallery to came up short in front of the glass case. Sarah was right. The cross was gone. His heartbeat boomed in his ears.

He tried to lift the glass case, but it had returned to its locked position. He bent down and pressed the secret button that released the latch, but then realized that there was no point in opening the case. Obviously, the cross was not there.

He went downstairs again, this time very slowly. As he went along the screen passage he heard Philip's voice from the kitchen.

Please, God, let him have taken it, he prayed.

"Who has been in here today?" Philip demanded in a tone that Jason had never heard from him before. He spun around when Jason entered. "Ah, there you are, Jason. What do you know about this?"

Jason felt his face flush beneath Philip's searching gaze. "Nothing. I haven't been near the gallery for days."

Philip continued to look at him. Jason knew that he was thinking about what he'd said on Monday. What *had* he actually said? He couldn't even remember much of it now.

"It was in the case on Monday night," Philip said. "I saw it there before I went to bed. Have you brought any friends into the house since then?"

Jason shook his head. He felt that everyone was looking at him, suspecting him of something terrible.

Philip swung away from him. "What about you, Mrs. Braithwaite?" he asked Sarah. "Any friends been here, in the house, since Monday night? Tell me the truth, please. This is a very serious matter." His words came like staccato gunfire.

"The only person who was here was my sister and her lad on Wednesday morning, for a cup of coffee."

"Your sister's son is Tom Abbott, right? He'd be about, what, seventeen?"

"Sixteen." Jason sensed Sarah's growing resentment. "You surely don't suspect Tom of stealing the treasure, do you, sir?" she asked.

Philip's eyes, when he turned to look at her, were the color of lead. "Until we find out what has happened to the cross, everyone must be under suspicion." Philip looked across the kitchen at Peter, who was standing by the Aga stove. "Has this been reported to the police?" he asked him.

"No," Peter replied. "Not yet. I just heard about it myself, a minute or so before you arrived."

"Then I must ask you not to report it."

Peter frowned. "Not to?" he asked.

"I don't want it reported," Philip said abruptly. "I want it to be kept quiet for now. If this was to get into the papers it could cause an immense scandal." He glanced at Jason, and then shook his head.

He thinks I did it, Jason thought. *He thinks I stole the cross.* All at once, the rich aromas of food in the kitchen made him feel sick to his stomach.

"Let's go and take a look," Philip said to Peter. He strode past Jason, brushing against him, but making no sign of having done so. It was as if he didn't exist.

Even Sarah was looking at him strangely. "You don't think I took it, do you?" Jason demanded.

She shrugged. "Been there for years and none of us took it before, did we?"

Hot tears rushed to Jason's eyes. "Shit! You know I wouldn't steal the cross. What the hell would I do with it?"

"Sell it. Whoever's taken it will make a lot of money from it."

"Well, I didn't take it. But I suppose everyone will think I did, just like you and Philip." Misery swept over him.

A search was made of the entire house, including the outside buildings, but there was no sign of the cross anywhere. Having given strict instructions to them not to speak about it to anyone, "That applies particularly to you, Sarah," he warned, Philip drove directly to Langley.

"Shall I come with you?" Jason had asked, his face pinched with anxiety.

"No, I think it's best that you remain here," Philip had told him. "Keep looking around the house. There may be somewhere we've missed."

Philip realized as he drove fast along the familiar road, taking all its bends and curves automatically, that he was running a risk in telling those at Langley the news of the theft. But it must be done. It was that or go to the police. He fervently hoped that it wouldn't have to come to that.

He asked for Steven when he arrived, to be told by James Barton that he was in bed.

"Can I be of assistance in any way, Mr. Thornton?"

"No, you can't," he was told. "Except to tell me where my brother is."

"He's in the stables. Shall I—"

"No, thank you." Without saying any more, Philip went up to Steven's room, his heart heavy.

He was met at Steven's door by Sybil, barring his way with her wheelchair. That bloody intercom, he thought, seeing the gadget in her hand. Barton must have called her on it.

"Steven is resting," she told him. "He had a very bad night."

"I'm sorry to hear that, Sybil, but I must see him."

She didn't budge. "I'm sorry, too, Philip, but I cannot permit you to upset Steven, whatever the reason."

"Who is it, Sybil?" Steven's voice wafted through the doorway.

"It's Philip," she answered. "I've told him you're resting."

"Poppycock! Send him in."

Sybil's dark eyes narrowed at Philip, but she moved away from the doorway. She was about to wheel in after him when Philip said, "I'm sorry, but this is a very private matter. I must speak to Steven alone."

Sybil's crimson mouth set into a thin line. "Make it quick, then. I shall return in exactly ten minutes."

Philip waited, watching her move down the corridor, to make sure she didn't remain outside the door. Then he went into Steven's bedroom, closing the door behind him.

"Sorry about that," Steven said. "Sybil's getting to be a pain in the neck. Like a bloody bodyguard." He was extremely pale and his face seemed to be all fine bones, hardly any flesh.

"I can't blame her. She's right, really." Philip cleared his throat. "But this is something I must discuss with you in private."

"You look awful man. What's happened?"

"The Thornton Treasure has been taken."

Steven's eyes widened. "What do you mean, 'taken'?"

"Just that. Sarah found that it was missing this morning."

"Good God! Was it a burglary? Did they smash the case?"

"No. There's nothing broken. The alarm didn't go off. It had to be an inside job." Philip's gaze met Steven's. They both remained silent for a moment.

"Have you any idea who?" Steven asked. "Could it be Sarah?"

"She had her sister and that young scamp of a nephew in for a visit this week. But he wouldn't have known how to open the case."

"Unless Sarah told him how."

Philip paced restlessly to the window, looking out over the manicured lawns. "I don't really suspect Sarah. She wouldn't know how to get rid of it."

"Unless someone had paid her to do it."

Philip still stood by the window, his back to the bed. "No, I don't think it's Sarah, Steven. I wish it were. It might make things less complicated."

"You never did insure the blasted thing, did you? I kept telling you this could happen."

"The cost of insurance was totally prohibitive. I had to take the chance. Besides, what use would the money be, with the cross gone?"

"You ask me that, with those damned inheritance taxes hanging over you like Damocles's bloody sword."

Philip spun around. "Are you suggesting that I took the cross?"

"I know you didn't, but I should imagine others might think so. Like Derek, for instance."

"Ah, yes. Derek would, of course."

"He'd never have openly agreed to your selling it, but I daresay he wouldn't mind sharing in the proceeds of the sale, which would be private, of course, to avoid publicity. Reported it to the police, have you?"

"No, I damn well haven't. And I resent your insinuation that I might have stolen the cross myself."

"Sorry. Just testing the waters, so to speak."

"The reason I haven't reported it to the police is that I want to avoid a scandal. If this was to get out ..."

"Yes, I understand." Steven leaned back against his pile of pillows. He suddenly appeared to have shrunk to half his size. "You suspect Jason, don't you? My God, that would destroy Tessa."

"I suppose it could be Jason, but I don't think it is. The person I suspect is someone who has both means and motive *and* the know-how to be able to sell it."

Again, they looked directly at each other. "Was he at Thornton this week?" Steven asked in a hoarse voice.

"The cross was there on Monday night. He visited me on Wednesday."

"To see Jason?"

"Well, that was his excuse, but he soon asked to speak to me privately and then started demanding money, as usual."

"Was he on his own there, at any time?"

"I can't remember, but he has the keys, of course. He can get in anytime he likes. After all," Philip added bitterly, "Thornton Manor was Derek's home as well as mine."

"Dear Christ," Steven said in a low voice. "It's not as if I don't pay him well."

"Don't start blaming yourself, Steven. This has absolutely nothing to do with you."

"Don't be bloody ridiculous. The man's married to my daughter. He's my grandchild's father. It has a great deal to do with me."

"I wouldn't have troubled you with this, but I need your advice. You know Derek as well as anyone. Is he capable of such a thing, do you think? If I accuse him, and he didn't do it, he will never forgive me for it. After all, he is my brother."

"He must be made to give the cross back. You must confront him with it immediately."

"That's what I thought, but I didn't want to do it without asking you first. Thanks, Steven. I'm truly sorry to have had to worry you over this."

"You did the right thing. Go and see him immediately. Let me know what happens."

"I will."

As soon as Philip had left, Sybil came in. "What's happened that Philip has to barge his way in here against my wishes?"

"The Thornton Cross has been stolen."

Sybil's hand went to her throat. "Oh, my God! How terrible!" She wheeled herself to his bedside. "Was it really necessary for him to worry you with it, though? You look worn out."

Steven felt worn out. His entire body ached and he longed to be left alone. "Yes, it was. He's convinced that Derek stole the cross."

"Derek?" Sybil's mouth hung open for a moment. "What utter nonsense! How could he suspect his own brother of such a thing?"

"He does. And I think he's right. Derek's been acting very strangely recently."

"Nonsense! I'm afraid that Philip is showing his true colors. He has always disliked his brother. You know that. Derek was his mother's favorite and Philip resented him because of it."

"Don't spout that psychological mumbo-jumbo to me. Philip has every reason to suspect Derek. As he said, he has both means and motive, and he could find a private buyer."

"I'm sorry, darling, but Philip is obviously using Derek to cover up the true culprit."

Steven's eyes narrowed. "Who is?"

"Jason."

"Why would Jason do such a thing?"

"He comes from bad stock on both sides. You remember we had to turn Maltby off?"

"Your brains are getting addled, Sybil. Maltby wasn't even Jason's father." Steven felt an uncomfortable tingling in his arm.

"Not genetically, perhaps. But Jason grew up with him. No doubt he was influenced by the man. Jason sees this beautiful, extremely valuable object. He knows exactly how to get at it. He's there in the house all the time, after all."

"And what the hell would he do with it when he's got it?" Steven demanded, his heart pumping fast. "The only people he knows are us and the people at Thornton."

"I hear he's been seen with a few of the village lads. Tom Selby and that gang of layabouts. They were the ones who were suspected of breaking into the rectory, remember?"

Steven stared at her. The tingling had become a dull but insistent ache in his shoulder and arm. "Are you sure?"

"Would I say so if I wasn't."

"If it were true," he said slowly, "it would break Tessa's heart."

"I do believe you'd rather have it be your own daughter's husband than Tessa's son."

Steven wasn't sure what to believe anymore. He was too weary to think about any of it. His ears were filled with a roaring sound, like waves tumbling on a shore, and the dull pain was now like a vise gripping his arm.

"Steven? Are you all right? Steven!" His wife's voice came from a long way away.

He tried to smile at her, to assure her that everything was the way he wanted it, but the pain was too extreme to say anything. He wanted to thank her for their life together, for her part in relieving him of a long, undignified dying, but all that came from his mouth was a low moaning. She was calling him again, but her voice sounded even farther away, as if it were coming from the far side of the stream at the foot of the garden.

Now her face hung directly above his and he felt the weight of her body across his. He wondered for a moment how that could be, considering she was in her wheelchair, and then her face wavered and faded away.

"So you suspect me of stealing it," Derek said again, glaring at his brother.

They stood confronting each other in the open meadow beyond the stables. If Philip had hoped that Derek would confess to the theft immediately, he was to be disappointed. Derek's face was bright red with fury.

"I am asking you if you took it," Philip said.

Derek's hands formed into fists. "I've a good mind to knock you down."

"Do so, if you wish. I don't care what you do, so long as you tell me the truth. I haven't reported it to the police. No one need know."

"Don't be so bloody sanctimonious. 'No one need know.' No one, except everyone at Thornton and Steven and Sybil here. You have discussed it with Steven, haven't you?"

Philip said nothing.

"Yes, I thought so. You and Steven have always been in cahoots against me."

"Do you give me your word that you didn't take the cross?"

"Damn you! Yes, I do. I swear I didn't take the bloody thing. I wish I had now. If you didn't take it— and you say you didn't—then someone who doesn't deserve it will get the money from it. Money I badly need."

"To pay for cocaine?"

A nerve flickered at the corner of Derek's eye. "What the hell are you talking about?"

"For God's sake," Philip said wearily. "It's obvious."

"I may take a few drinks more than I should, but cocaine? Don't be bloody ridiculous."

"Why do you think I suspected you of taking the cross? The signs are all there: the watery eyes, constantly running, sore nose. The mood swings. I also know that Steven has been extremely generous with you financially and it costs you nothing to live at Langley. So you must be using the money somewhere."

"Gambling," Derek said.

"Perhaps, but that isn't it, is it, Derek?"

Derek shoved his hands into the pockets of his riding britches.

"There are clinics you can go to," Philip said. "Private places that keep it quiet. You must go, Derek. You owe it to Camilla and to Vicky."

"I'll think about it," Derek muttered. "But I swear I didn't take the cross."

"Then who did?"

"It must have been Jason."

Philip looked hard at Derek, until he turned his head away. He was about to ask him a question when James Barton came running across the field, shouting.

"It's Mr. Hargrave."

Philip started toward him.

"Mr. Hargrave's had a bad turn," James said when he reached him, panting for breath. "Looks like a heart attack."

Chapter Twenty-six

Tessa was about to go out to meet friends for lunch in Osborne Village when the telephone rang. When she picked it up and heard Philip's voice at the other end of the line she knew immediately that something was very wrong.

"Has something happened to Jason?"

"No, no. It's Steven. I'm sorry to have to tell you, he's had a heart attack."

"Oh, God! Is it serious?"

"He's been unconscious for the past few hours," Philip said. "The doctors are not sure he'll come out of it. I thought you'd want to know."

Tessa thought of her remaining flight pass, and the fact that there'd be many more now that she'd be starting work in a couple of weeks. "I'm coming over."

"Are you sure? There's little hope of his regaining consciousness."

"I'd still like to be there. Then Jason and I can fly back together."

"If you could get a flight to Manchester, I could pick you up at the airport there."

"I don't want to give—"

"This is no time for polite platitudes," Philip said curtly. "I want to meet you."

"Thank you. I'll call you back as soon as I know what flight I'll be on. Are you at Langley?"

"Yes. I just got back from Northallerton Hospital. Derek's waiting at the station for Vicky to arrive."

"Philip."

"Yes?"

"Thank you for calling me."

"Why wouldn't I? You're Steven's niece." His voice sounded strange, abrupt. Surely he wasn't still angry with her after all this time?

"How's Jason?"

"He's here with me now. I'll put him on."

A pause, punctuated by the murmur of voices, then Jason came on. "Hi, Mom." He sounded very subdued.

"Are you okay? I guess it's pretty sad there with Uncle Steven so ill."

"I'm fine. I'm glad you're coming over. If you hadn't been, I was planning to call you and say I was coming home."

"Oh. I thought you were coming home next week."

"Yeah, well things have changed. But now you're coming I can wait to come back with you, can't I?"

"That's right. I'll call again when I've got my flight set up."

"Make it soon, Mom." Tessa was reminded of Jason calling her from school with a gashed leg when he was nine. She was surprised that Steven's heart attack had affected him this much.

Throughout the day, as she arranged her flight to Manchester via Toronto, and then rushed around paying bills and canceling appointments, cleaning out the fridge and packing, she was haunted by the sense that something else had happened, something that concerned Jason himself.

The feeling stayed with her, building and building, so that the flight across the Atlantic seemed to drag on unmercifully.

When she came out from customs, to find Philip

standing in the front row of those waiting for passengers, she wanted to run into his arms. His face brightened when he caught sight of her, but as she walked toward him, she saw that he was looking extremely tired. His face had always been aquiline. Now it appeared positively gaunt.

When he bent to kiss her cheek, she wanted to throw her arms around him, hug him close, take away his tangible tension, but she knew that this was neither the time nor the place to do so.

"Jason didn't come with you?"

"No. We both thought it would be easier for you to rest as we drove back. He's fine, though. He and Sarah are planning a splendid lunch for you."

She hadn't the heart to tell him that the last thing she felt like doing was eating. "And Uncle Steven? Is he still unconscious?"

They were standing in the center of the arrival hall, people shoving against them, weaving luggage carts around them.

"Let's get out of here," Philip said. "We can walk to the car park. That would be far quicker than bringing the car around to pick you up."

He hadn't answered her question. As they made their way to the car park, Philip carrying her bags, both of them remained silent: Philip wrapped up in his own thoughts and Tessa too afraid to repeat her question.

She waited until Philip had stowed her bags in the trunk and then asked him again, "Is Uncle Steven still unconscious?"

This time there was no avoidance. He looked directly at her, his gray eyes filled with compassion. "I'm sorry. I didn't want to tell you in the airport. Steven died last night without regaining consciousness."

She stared at him, willing the words to go away. Then her face crumpled. "Oh, Philip."

His arms went around her, holding her tightly against him, one hand stroking her hair, her cheek. "The doctor said he didn't suffer," he said after a little while.

Tessa drew away and looked up at him through streaming eyes. "He said he didn't want to live on if it meant he was bedridden and drugged."

"Exactly. It was what he wanted."

Philip drew a folded white handkerchief from the breast pocket of his jacket. Instead of handing it to her, he tenderly wiped her face with it, as if she were his child. Then he opened the car door for her.

Tessa clambered inside, automatically doing up her seat belt. The inside of Philip's car was like a leather-scented cocoon, enfolding her.

"I'm sorry," Philip said. "I wanted to get you away from the crowds so I could tell you. I didn't even ask you if you wanted a coffee or anything before we started off."

"We had breakfast on the plane. I'd just as soon we got home as soon as possible."

As soon as she'd said it, Tessa realized that now Uncle Steven was dead she no longer had a home in England. The tears started flowing again.

Philip handed her the handkerchief and then took her hand in his, squeezing it.

"I'm sorry," she said after blowing her nose. "I just realized I could never stay at Langley again. Even though I never really liked the place, it was my only home in England. Now I have nowhere to go."

"You will stay at Thornton," Philip said, "where your son is."

"Are you sure?"

"I think I already told you that between you and me, especially at such a time, there is no need for artificial politeness. Yes, I'm sure. You will make Thornton your home for as long as you please." He started the engine and then glanced across at her. "You wouldn't prefer to lie down in the back, would you? There's a rug there."

"No, I want to stay here, with you. I can sleep sitting up."

As soon as they were on the motorway to Leeds, Philip turned on a compact disc of Mozart's piano concertos, and Tessa drifted in and out of sleep, sometimes awakened by a lively rondo, only to be lulled off to sleep again by an andante of such loveliness that it induced more weeping.

Her sleep was shallow, mixed with the music, the purr of the engine, and the occasional blare of horns. Philip drove fast in the outer lane, swiftly passing the slower vehicles. Sometimes, when she awoke, he made some comment to her, but it wasn't until they were driving along the winding road north of Ripon that Tessa sat up and started to look around her. The hay was cut, much of the barley and wheat stacked in golden bales in the fields they passed.

"It's hard to believe that almost a month has gone by since I was last here. Yet, here we are in the middle of August already."

"We've had good weather this summer. The harvest is going well."

"It's strange, isn't it? Whatever happens, however catastrophic the world's events, certain things remain the same. The seasons. The weather. Seeding and reaping. It all goes on much the same, all over the world."

He gave her a smiling glance. "That's why I prefer to live in the country. It helps to maintain one's sense of proportion."

"When is the funeral, Philip?" she asked as they drove up the hill just past the Masham turnoff.

"Next Monday."

"But that's a week away."

"So? There are numerous arrangements to be made."

"It seems such a long time to have to wait. How is everyone taking it? Sybil, especially."

"She seems bewildered by it all. I think she thought she could keep Steven alive just by the sheer strength of her will."

"Yes. Aunt Sybil always liked to play God. Sorry," she added hurriedly, realizing how catty that had sounded, "but I find it hard to feel anything but animosity for a woman who can be so cruel and unfeeling, unless it suits her to be otherwise."

"She genuinely loved Steven."

"I know that. And he, for some strange reason, adored her. Yet I believe he was well aware of her failings. He just chose to ignore them."

"There was great sexual magnetism between them, despite their age."

"Maybe that was what kept them together." Tessa shivered. Just talking about Sybil made her feel uneasy. "How is Camilla?"

"She has taken it very badly. You know how much she cared for her father."

"Poor Camilla." Tessa was quite surprised to realize that she genuinely meant it. Stuck with Derek for a husband, a domineering tyrant for a mother, her beloved father now dead, and few outside interests other than buying clothes and wintering in Mustique, Camilla's life seemed horribly empty. "At least she has Vicky. How are the wedding plans going?"

"We shall have to see if Steven's death will bring about any change." Philip glanced across at Tessa. "Between you and me, there are signs that she is cooling off Jeremy."

"Thank God for that. Uncle Steven couldn't stand the thought of her marrying him."

"Well, we shall see what happens now. Steven

dropped a few hints to me that he'd asked you to intercede with Vicky when you were here."

"If you remember, I didn't have much chance," Tessa said wryly. "Too many other things happened. But we did speak about it when she drove me to the station."

They both fell into a strained silence, remembering the rift that had been between them then, Tessa recalling her sense of betrayal and her deep sadness. "I must apologize," she managed to say after a little while.

"For what?"

"For being so angry at you for taking Jason's side against me."

He didn't respond. She thought at first that it was because they were about to turn in through Thornton's open gates, but when she glanced at him she could see that his face was unnaturally taut.

"Perhaps you were right," Philip said at last.

"You're keeping something back from me." She grabbed his arm. "Something awful has happened to Jason."

Philip shifted into low gear and then pulled over to the side of the driveway. "I must admit I've been putting this off, but you have to know. The Thornton Cross has been stolen."

"Stolen? Oh, God!" She gave him a searching look. "And you think that Jason stole it?"

"No, I don't. I think Derek did, to pay for his drug habit."

"I . . . I didn't know he was on drugs. I thought it was just booze. Has he admitted it?"

"The drugs, yes, but not the theft. He insists that he knows nothing about it."

"Do you believe him?"

"Somebody took the cross." His aquiline profile was as adamant as a Greek statue's.

"What do the police say?"

"The police don't know. In the circumstances, I felt it was better not to bring them into it."

A cold lump settled into the pit of her stomach. "What does Jason say about it?" she asked at last.

"He says he knows nothing about it. I believe him."

"But no one else in the family does, right?"

He looked straight ahead of him, through the windshield, and then sighed. "I'm afraid not. Even Derek suspects him. Which is natural, I suppose, considering Derek is my chief suspect. But it wounds Jason to think that his own father would suspect him of a crime."

The lump in Tessa's stomach grew colder and heavier. "Was anything broken? Did it seem like a normal break-in?"

"No. It was obviously an inside job, done by someone who had easy access to the house and who knew how to unlock the case."

"That includes everyone at Thornton, of course, and most of those at Langley. What are you doing about it?"

"Making discreet inquiries that are leading absolutely bloody nowhere." In his frustration, Philip slammed open palms on the steering wheel.

"Meanwhile, everyone at Langley suspects Jason of the theft," Tessa said, anger sharpening her voice. "No wonder he sounded so down when I spoke to him yesterday. I thought it was just because of Steven's heart attack." Her hand went to her throat. "Oh, my God, Philip. Did Steven know about this, about the Thornton Treasure having been stolen?"

His face grew even more rigid. "Yes. And I was the fool who told him. I blame myself for his death."

She took his arm in both her hands. "You mustn't," she said fiercely. "You couldn't have kept quiet about it. He had to know. He was terribly fragile. I am sure that any little shock would have affected him in the same way."

"Perhaps, but I was the one who brought him the news. I thought he'd taken it so well, Tessa. When I left him with Sybil he seemed quite calm. A short while later Barton told us that Steven had suffered a heart attack."

"It was a great blessing that he did. He wanted to die before he became an invalid, having to rely on others for his every need. You must not blame yourself." Her hand slid down to take hold of his.

His response took her by surprise. He turned and pulled her to him. This time it was definitely not the staid kiss of an old friend, but one of great need, bruising the softness of her mouth.

Oh, God, it's happened at last, she thought, her mouth opening beneath his. Then all thoughts vanished as her hands moved behind his head, pressing him closer. As their mouths met in mutual hunger, Philip's hands caressed her breasts, and she felt herself become exquisitely sensitive to his touch.

It ended as suddenly as it had begun. His hands dropped and he moved back from her, leaving her feeling cold and frustrated . . . and very much alone again.

He looked at her, his eyes dark as charcoal. "I must apologize," he said stiffly. "The last couple of days have been rather a strain."

Tessa felt like laughing and crying at the same time. "Don't apologize. I didn't mind at all."

"I took advantage of you. Trapped here in the car."

Tessa felt like yelling at him, *For God's sake, Philip. You didn't rape me!* But she knew that Philip still had some way to go before he realized that she was no longer the child she had once been. Perhaps it was time to give him a jolt in the right direction.

"I'm almost forty now, Philip," she reminded him.

"I've been married to an abusive husband and lived to tell the tale. I've dealt with amorous drunks and roving hands on numerous flights. I know how to look after myself."

"I am sure you do. I just regret my bad timing, that's all. I took advantage of your vulnerability."

"I'd like to inform you that no one, including you, Philip, takes advantage of me unless I want them to."

He looked at her, obviously surprised, and then his mouth tilted into that delicious one-sided smile of his that had always made her insides quiver. "I shall remember that," he said.

"Please do."

Their eyes met in a look of a promise made, but deferred to a more favorable time. Then Philip started up the car again.

Chapter Twenty-seven

The ancient church of St. Luke's was crammed with people for Steven Hargrave's funeral. So much so that they'd had to leave the wooden doors open so that those who couldn't get in could hear the service. They clustered around the entrance, straining to hear the familiar and sonorous words of the Burial of the Dead.

"The Lord gave, and the Lord hath taken away," intoned the rector.

Such simple, blunt words, Tessa thought as she sat in the family pew beside Vicky, who was weeping into a large handkerchief. Jeremy sat on her other side, rather stony-faced.

The coffin was directly in front of them, draped with an old flag that had been in the family since a Captain Hargrave had brought it home from the Battle of Waterloo. It was hard to believe that Steven Hargrave lay, stilled forever, inside it.

His spirit, Tessa knew, had flown off long ago, and was probably fishing in the Ure or the Swale at this instant, shouting into the ether, "Come on out! Far too nice a day to be inside."

It was Philip who gave the eulogy. As she watched him make his way to the pulpit with his habitual grace, Tessa found herself smiling. Not at all the thing to be doing, grinning away at her uncle's funeral, but despite the strain of the last few days, she felt that there had been a subtle change in the relationship between her and Philip. Whether anything would come of this change, she had no idea. Certainly there had been no repeat of the intimacy they'd experienced in the car. But, then, everything seemed to be in limbo during those days leading up to the funeral, including Philip's investigation into the theft of the cross.

"He acts as if it doesn't matter anymore," Jason had complained to her the day she arrived. "He forgets that everyone thinks I took it."

"He hasn't forgotten," Tessa assured him. "It's just that the funeral is the most important thing at present."

She knew how important it was to Jason to have the mystery cleared up. He fretted about it constantly. "How can I go back to Canada with this hanging over me?" he'd asked her only last night.

Tessa worried about that herself.

Philip's message was simple but eloquent. He had a vibrant speaking voice, but used it without the bombast that other barristers frequently employed. In a few brief sentences, he captured the essence of Steven Hargrave so well that he had everyone smiling at the memory of this well-loved man.

Her eyes brimming with tears, but still smiling, Tessa turned to Vicky and they locked hands. Then she turned to Jason and took his hand, wanting to include him. It had meant a great deal to Jason when Philip had told him that Steven did not think he had taken the cross.

When Philip came down the aisle to return to his seat, he glanced across at her. She gave him a warm smile and mouthed, "Thank you," to him.

Steven was buried in St. Luke's churchyard. As Sybil threw a handful of earth on the coffin, a sheep detached itself from the small flock that was grazing in the longer grass and wandered over to stand behind her. How Steven would have loved that! thought Tessa.

Sybil seemed to have shrunk since Steven's death. She sat, a tiny figure, slumped in the wheelchair. All her vitality now seemed to be concentrated in those dark eyes, which darted fire at Tessa and Jason across the open grave.

Later, when everyone but members of the family had left Langley, Steven's solicitor asked them all into the library for the reading of his will.

"His will?" Tessa said to Vicky. "Can't it wait until tomorrow?"

"It was Papa's wish, apparently. He wanted to have it all done in the one day, so that people could get on with the business of living. Those were his own words." She gave Tessa a tremulous smile. "Sounds exactly like him, doesn't it?"

"It certainly does." Tessa gave Vicky a hug. "I decided that he was off fishing during the funeral and urging us to hurry up and get outside."

Vicky hugged her back. "I'm so glad you flew over. Having you here means a lot to me."

Tessa found herself unable to speak for a moment, then she said, "Thanks, Vicky. Your grandfather was a very important person in my life."

Plain wooden folding chairs had been set out in the library, making it look rather like a board meeting of some sort. It seemed not only inappropriate, considering this had been one of Steven's favorite rooms, but also unnecessary as there already was an abundance of comfortable leather and upholstered chairs in the library. Tessa suspected that it was James's idea of what was appropriate for a will-reading.

At first she had been reluctant to join the others, but Mr. Charing, the solicitor, informed her that she was a beneficiary and should, therefore, attend the reading of the will.

Mr. Charing was the epitome of the country solicitor, dressed neatly in a dark gray suit, his glasses perched on the end of his nose. But Uncle Steven had once told her of his lawyer's passion for Gilbert and Sullivan operas. He was a leading light in the local G and S company, playing the comic roles of the Lord Chancellor and the Major General.

Now, as she sat waiting nervously for him to begin, Tessa had a slightly hysterical vision of Mr. Charing turning Uncle Steven's will into a patter song.

She had always thought that her uncle relied upon his wife for his financial support, but it seemed that he'd been a canny investor and had amassed a fair amount of personal money during his lifetime. He left most of it to his "beloved wife, Sybil, to continue our work in making Langley House one of England's showplaces." Camilla would inherit all, of course, upon her mother's death. She was admonished to "remember that Langley is not only your inheritance, but also your responsibility. One that I know you will not take lightly, but will carry out well."

Tessa saw Camilla's face crumple at that, and her eyes became streaked with mascara.

No mention had yet been made of Derek.

To Vicky, Steven had left his small collection of exquisite Elizabethan miniatures, with the understanding that they remain on view at Langley for as long as the family owned it. He also left her a letter, which she was not to open until she was by herself.

Vicky raised her eyebrows at Tessa when she heard this. When Tessa saw how Sybil's lips had clamped into a thin line she suspected that Steven's letter to Vicky was a surprise to her.

"Now," said Mr. Charing, pushing his glasses up to the bridge of his nose with one finger, "we come to Mr. Hargrave's niece, Tessa Hargrave. She, too, has a letter from Mr. Hargrave, but he requested that I read this letter aloud, so that everyone present at the reading of the will would be able to hear it."

Tessa felt that every eye in the room was looking at her. She lifted her chin and looked directly at Mr. Charing.

" 'My dear Tessa,' " Mr. Charing read. " 'Throughout the years, you have endured—and valiantly survived—difficulties that might have defeated a less courageous woman: a broken engagement, the loss of your home, an abusive husband, the subsequent divorce, and rearing a son by yourself. Despite all these, you steadfastly refused to take from me the financial assistance I frequently offered. No doubt you would still continue to do so, even after my death. I am, therefore, leaving you Kirkby House, a modest Georgian house I own in Middleham.' "

Tessa heard a murmur and something that sounded like "Damn!" but she continued to stare straight at Mr. Charing.

" 'As my only brother's only child,' " Mr. Charing continued, " 'it is fitting that you have this house, as it was a favorite holiday home for the Hargrave family when they first came to the Dales many years ago. This small bequest comes with my gratitude to you for having brought great pleasure to me during those years you lived at Langley and for those few days we spent together in July. My hope is that it will bring you pleasure and, in some small way, help to atone for the wrongful acts members of my family have committed against you.' "

The words of the last sentence hung in the air, greeted by a stunned silence.

Oh, Uncle Steven, I wish you hadn't, Tessa thought, squeezing her eyes shut. This very public rebuke was going to make things even more awkward for her. And yet . . . somehow she felt a sense of justice having been done. It was just that this was not the right time to have done it.

Mr. Charing hurried on to the next part of the will. " 'To Jason Maltby, the son of my niece, Tessa, I bequeath a sum of money to be determined by my trustees in consultation with Jason and Tessa for his further education.' "

This time the protests were more open. "Disgraceful!" Sybil said. "He's a common thief. Steven made this will before he knew that."

Tessa felt Jason move. She grabbed his arm to drag him down, but he shook her off and sprang to his feet. "I didn't steal the cross!" he shouted, his face almost as red as his hair. "You've no right to say I stole it. Uncle Steven knew I didn't."

"It was the theft of the cross that killed him," Sybil said. "You, young man, are the cause of my husband's death."

"That's not fair, Grandmother," Vicky cried out.

Mr. Charing tried to restore order in what was fast becoming a debacle. "Please. I beg you to remember the occasion of our meeting here."

Philip rose to his feet. "Before you resume the reading of the will, Mr. Charing, I wish to say something to everyone assembled here. The theft to which you have alluded, Sybil, and which I had asked not be discussed while I pursued inquiries privately, did not of itself bring about Steven's death. Forgive me for saying so, Sybil, but we all knew that Steven had no more than a few weeks to live. Steven knew that himself. You knew it. Therefore, to make wild accusations of this sort achieves nothing but hurt for those involved."

Sybil glared at him. "He might have lived on for a while longer had it not been for the shock."

"He might indeed. But he didn't want to live on, as you well know. We talked about it frequently. So whatever caused his sudden heart attack, it was a blessing."

Philip looked straight at Sybil. She blinked rapidly and then turned her head away from his direct gaze.

"What I must tell you all," Philip continued, "is that I am convinced that it was not Jason who stole the cross, and so was Steven."

Derek dragged himself to his feet. "No, you think I did it. You accuse your own brother of stealing what is legally his." He clutched at the chairback in front of him, his body swaying.

"Gentlemen, gentlemen," Mr. Charing said, trying to make his voice heard.

"For God's sake sit down, Derek," Camilla said wearily. "You're making a fool of yourself."

"What's in the will for me?" he shouted, slapping her hand away. "What did Steven leave his be—beloved son-in-law?"

"Really, Mr. Thornton," Mr. Charing said, outraged. "This is highly inappropriate."

Tessa felt as if she were at the Mad Hatter's Tea Party. She stood up. "I think it best if my son and I were to go now and leave you to read the rest of the will to the immediate family, Mr. Charing." She turned to Jason. "Let's get out of here," she said quietly.

"That's right," Derek shouted. "You've got what you wanted, so you can go now. That house was to be Vicky's, not yours."

"I don't want the bloody house," Vicky cried.

Tessa saw the hurt in Jason's eyes. The man who was his father had been revealed to him today in his true colors. She ached for him, but perhaps it was better this way.

She moved from the row of chairs, but then turned to face them all again. "I'm leaving Langley now. Before I do, I promise you all that I won't be back. My only reason for coming here was Uncle Steven. Now that he's gone, I need never set foot in this house again."

"Good riddance," Sybil muttered beneath her breath, but everyone heard her.

"Langley House holds too many unhappy memories for me and I refuse to dwell on them anymore."

Tessa was tempted to say more, but this was not the time to do so. Besides, it had all been said before. With Jason following behind her, she marched from the library into the hall.

Chapter Twenty-eight

Out in the hall, Tessa drew in several deep breaths to calm herself.

"Boy, were you great in there," Jason said admiringly.

She squeezed his arm. "I'm sorry about Derek, love."

He shrugged. "I'm fine. I know what he is."

The library door opened and Philip came out. "Are you all right?"

"I feel great," Tessa said. "All the chains that bound me to this place have been taken off, thank God."

"I'm sorry I can't drive you home yet. As an executor I have to be there for the entire reading. And Kevin is a beneficiary in the will so he can't drive you. Perhaps Barton—"

"I'm perfectly happy to walk around the garden. A sort of farewell. You understand."

"Of course I do. As soon as I've finished I'll come and find you." He gave her a little grin. "You made a marvelous exit, by the way. I wanted to applaud."

"I'm glad you didn't. It was embarrassing enough in there."

"Indeed it was. I admire your singular restraint. I could tell that you were bursting to say more, but wisely did not. It could have turned into a regular slanging match."

Philip was about to go back into the library when the door opened and Camilla came out. She looked from Tessa to Philip. "Are you leaving?" she asked.

"I'm going for a walk," Tessa said. "Philip is staying for the rest of the reading."

"I'd like to speak to you."

"To me?"

Behind Camilla's back, Philip raised his eyebrows at Tessa. "Good luck," he mouthed and went back inside.

"Yes," Camilla said. She glanced at Jason. "Alone, if you don't mind."

"Jason, do me a favor, would you?"

"What?"

"I could do with something to eat. I didn't eat a thing at the reception. Would you go to the kitchen and get some sandwiches or cakes and take them out to the terrace? I'll join you there in a few minutes."

He glanced at Camilla. "Are you sure?" he asked Tessa.

"Yes. This won't take long." Tessa turned to Camilla. "Where?"

"Let's go to my bedroom."

Tessa would have preferred somewhere more neutral than Camilla's pink, heavily scented room, but she followed her cousin upstairs. "Shouldn't you be there for the rest of the reading?" she asked when Camilla had thrown herself onto a chaise longue and indicated that she sit in the pink brocade chair opposite.

"Why? It's only all the extras. I know what I'm getting: Langley and all the responsibilities. You heard what Daddy said in his will."

"I should have thought you'd be glad to get Langley."

"Then you're quite wrong. I loathe the bloody place. I also loathe living in the Yorkshire Dales, in the middle of nowhere, where all everyone talks about is fishing and shooting and sheep. I want to live in London, but I'm trapped in this rotten museum in the wilds."

Tessa looked at her, suddenly realizing what it must be like to be saddled with a huge estate and the responsibility for running a stately home when all you wanted was a flat in Mayfair and a life of going to nightclubs and the theater. She refused to feel sorry for Camilla, though.

"Has Steven left anything to Derek?" she asked.

"Just an interest in the stables, much the same as he already has, really. Anything else has to come from me. Which means," Camilla added bitterly, "that I won't ever be able to get rid of him." She crossed her legs, which were very thin, and picked at invisible lint on her black silk dress.

For the first time in her life, Tessa saw how unhappy her cousin was. She used to think she had everything her heart could wish for. Now she saw that her life was an utterly empty one. Even Vicky hadn't turned out the way she wanted her to be. Instead of a pink-and-white debutante, she'd got a carpenter with stained fingers for a daughter.

"What was it you wanted to speak to me about?"

"You said you were never coming back to Langley."

"That's right. Now that Steven's gone, there's nothing for me here."

Tears filled Camilla's eyes. "I know what you mean. I miss him terribly."

For one impulsive moment, Tessa felt like taking Camilla into her arms, but she knew that she'd be rebuffed, so resisted the impulse. "We shall all miss him. Your father was a very special person."

Camilla swallowed. Tessa saw the movement in the thin throat above the strand of flawless pearls. "Once you return to Canada, I don't suppose we shall ever meet again."

"I doubt it very much. I'm flying back to Canada with Jason at the end of the week."

"What about Philip?"

"What about him?"

"I thought there might be something between you two. I've seen the way he looks at you."

"That's your vivid imagination, Camilla. We're just good friends." As soon as she said it, Tessa laughed, recognizing the clichéd response. "I mean that. We've always been friends."

"I know. I always envied you your rapport with Philip when we were young."

Tessa couldn't believe her ears. "You envied me?" she said, her voice rising.

"Yes. You used to talk away together about things I couldn't care less about, books and poetry and things like that. Philip treated me as if I were some bimbo."

"I'm sure Philip never treated any woman as if she were a bimbo," Tessa said hotly.

"Oh, I don't mean he made advances or anything of that sort. You know Philip. Always the gentleman." It sounded as if Camilla would have preferred him not to be. "He just never talked to me the way he did to you. He treated me like a child."

"But we *were* children to him, Camilla. Don't forget, he was ten years older than we were."

"I know that," Camilla snapped.

"You still haven't told me what you want to talk to me about."

Camilla looked down at her pink nails. "It's hard to know where to start," she murmured.

"Is it about the past?"

"Yes."

"Then it's best forgotten. I don't want to talk about it."

"If I shan't see you again," Camilla said, almost

inaudibly, "I want you to know that I knew nothing about it."

"About what?" Tessa was beginning to grow impatient.

"About your pregnancy. I'd never have taken Derek away from you if I'd known you were pregnant."

"I don't believe you."

Camilla stared at her. "You must. It's the truth."

"Your mother knew about it."

"How do you know that?"

"That's why she fired Sarah. Sarah was the only person at Langley who knew I was pregnant. At least, I thought she was the only one. Somehow, Sybil found out. She fired Sarah because, I suppose, she thought Derek wouldn't marry you if he found out."

"I didn't know that," Camilla whispered.

For the first time, Tessa began to think that Camilla might be speaking the truth. She felt chilled all over at the thought of Sybil's hellish conniving.

"If you're speaking the truth, then I take it that it was Sybil's idea to pretend to Derek that *you* were pregnant with his child."

Camilla looked surprised—and concerned. "I didn't think you'd realize—"

"Not hard to work out, when Vicky tells me that she was born a year after your marriage."

Camilla got up and walked to the fireplace, pausing to adjust a fragile Dresden shepherdess on the mantelpiece. "It was Mummy's idea. She said it would be the best way to ensure that Derek would break off the engagement with you."

"Why was she so keen on your marrying Derek? I thought she wanted you to marry a title."

Camilla stood before her, slim and elegant. "I told her I'd kill myself if I couldn't have Derek. She believed me."

"And would you have done?" Tessa asked her coldly.

"I was so jealous of you, I might have. I ranted and screamed. My penniless cousin had snared both the Thornton brothers, two of the most eligible and good-looking men in England."

"Camilla, you're forgetting that Philip was married to Rosamund at this point. He'd married her when we were sixteen. He wasn't even living in Yorkshire then."

"Yes, I know. But to my mind, Philip had always preferred you to me. When he used to come home for vacation from university it was always you he sought out to talk to. Then, when I came back from Switzerland, it was to find that you were engaged to Derek. I felt like killing you!"

"Poor Camilla. You'd always had your own way about everything, hadn't you? I can see how it must have been quite a shock for you."

"You're enjoying this, aren't you?" Camilla glared at her.

"No, as a matter of fact, I'm not. I always thought of myself as the victim of Langley House, but I begin to see that you were also a victim. Your mother raised you to think that you could have everything you wanted. And when there was something you couldn't have, she lied and plotted to make sure you got it."

To Tessa's surprise, Camilla did not respond with any kind of defense of her mother. Tessa stood up. "I think we've said all we need to say."

"There's one more thing I don't think you know about."

Tessa sighed. She didn't really want to hear any more. "What's that?"

Camilla played with her rings, turning them round and round her fingers. "I wasn't going to tell you, but you might as well know it all. Your meeting with John Maltby that night wasn't an accident."

"What do you mean?"

"My mother sacked him that afternoon."

"I know that. He told me."

"What he probably didn't tell you was that it was all part of Mummy's plan."

"What was?"

"The sacking. John finding you on the road. Marrying you. Taking you to Canada. It was all part of the plan. Her plan."

Tessa's body seemed to have turned to ice. Her breathing became so shallow, she felt she was going to pass out. "You mean the ... the meeting, the getting married, the emigrating ... *all* of it was planned in advance?" she said, her breath catching in her throat.

"Yes." Something in Tessa's expression must have frightened Camilla, because she cried out, "Oh, Tessa, I'm so sorry. I knew nothing about it. Nothing at all until later, when Mummy told me he was blackmailing her."

"You mean John *blackmailed* her from Canada?"

"Yes. She kept sending him money, but he'd demand more, threatening to write and tell Daddy if she didn't pay him."

Now Tessa knew the secret source of John's money. And she also knew the reason for John's sudden proposal to her.

"I told her she'd done a terrible thing." Camilla was crying now, no longer caring that her makeup was ruined, her mascara running down her cheeks. "She said that she'd done it all for me, to make me happy. Happy? Christ! I knew even then that I'd made a big mistake in marrying Derek. You can imagine how I felt when she told me what she'd done to make that marriage possible. She said she'd made sure you were out of the country. What she never told me was why she wanted you so far away: that if you remained single and in England, you could still come back to Langley with Derek's child. It wasn't until Jason arrived here that night that I realized why she'd done it." Camilla was distraught now, her arms clutching her stomach, as if she were in severe pain. "She never told me you were pregnant. I didn't know."

Tessa went to her. She put her arm around her, making her sit on the chaise longue and then sat beside her. "Come on, Camilla. It's all in the past," she said, pushing tissues into her hand. When Camilla continued sobbing, Tessa wiped her face herself, trying to soothe her. "It's all over now.

Camilla sniffed inelegantly. "How can you forget, or forgive?"

"I can forget by living my life to the fullest now. And I can forgive you, because you were manipulated by your mother. But, you're right, I can never forgive Sybil for what she did to me. John Maltby was an abusive husband, Camilla. Your mother condemned me to several years with a man who hit me, until I wised up and kicked him out. It's a wonder he didn't tell me then and there why he'd married me, but I suppose he thought that he'd better keep quiet while Sybil was still a source of income for him. I hate to have to say this, especially on the day of your father's funeral, but your mother is an evil woman, Camilla."

"I know." Camilla's fingers tore a tissue into strips. "But what can I do about it? She's too strong for me."

"Maybe she is, but there is something you can do to stop her making one more person in the family miserable for life."

"What?"

"I want you to tell Vicky everything you've told me. Everything, mind."

Camilla's eyes opened wide in horror. "I couldn't tell her. She'd hate me if I did."

"No, she wouldn't. In fact, I think she'd understand you a lot more than she does now."

"No, no, I can't. Mummy would never forgive me if I told Vicky."

"Forget Sybil. Who cares if she doesn't forgive you? Think about it. What harm can she do you now? In a few years she'll be dead and Langley will be all yours to do whatever you want with. You could even sell it." She gripped Camilla's hands tightly in hers. "Look at me." Camilla obeyed her, as if mesmerized. "This marriage to Jeremy would be a disaster. Vicky's far too young to be getting married. She should be traveling, working, seeing the world, broadening her mind. Then, and only then, can she decide whom she wants to share the rest of her life with. She finds Jeremy sexually attractive, that's all."

"Like me with Derek," Camilla whispered.

"Exactly. Tell her that. Tell her that it doesn't make for a good, solid marriage. That's why your father was so worried about Vicky."

"I know he was, but I also knew how much Mummy wanted someone to bring a title into the family. I'd failed her with that. Vicky would be able to fulfill my mother's dream. Did you know that my grandfather, Mummy's father, refused to speak to her again when she told him she was going to marry Daddy?"

"Why?"

"Apparently he said that Steven Hargrave was a middle-class commoner and that he would no longer consider her his daughter if she married him. She defied her father, but he kept his promise and never spoke to her again."

"That's appalling, but it doesn't excuse Sybil's behavior. When you think about it, she became a replica of her father, manipulating other people's lives."

"Well, at least she didn't refuse to speak to me when I wanted to marry Derek, although she wasn't at all happy about it. But you can see why we both felt that Victoria could fulfill the family wish for a title."

"For God's sake, who cares about that crap anymore? Are you saying that you'd sacrifice your daughter's happiness just to fulfill your mother's sick dream?"

"I love Victoria," Camilla protested.

"Then it's time you did something to prove it. Talk to Vicky. Tell her about yourself and Derek. You can do it without affecting her feelings about her father. Besides, she has no illusions about him, and she's pretty tough."

Camilla gave her a faint smile. "Much tougher than I am."

"She's had to be to withstand you and Sybil. There must have been a hell of a battle with Sybil when Vicky said she wanted to be a furniture designer."

"I knew she wanted it very much. I couldn't understand why, but it was what she wanted to do, so I stood up to my mother and took Vicky's side."

"Remind Vicky of that when you talk to her. Show her you're on her side."

"Why do you want me to tell her about Mummy and you . . . and John Maltby? Is that absolutely necessary?"

"Absolutely. Vicky must know how insanely manipulative your mother has been. She's bright. She'll realize that if Sybil did it with me and Derek and you, she can do it with her. And if she doesn't realize it, then it's up to you as her mother to point it out."

Camilla sat curled up at the end of the chaise longue, shivering. "I'm afraid. I'm afraid of my mother."

Tessa touched her hand. "No need to be. You can stand up to her. I think you'll find she won't be as strong now that Steven is dead. In a way, he shielded her from all the consequences of her actions. Whatever she did, he loved her blindly, unreservedly. He's not here to do that anymore."

Camilla's hand slipped over Tessa's. Tessa steeled herself not to draw away. "If only I'd had the chance to get to know you properly when we were young," Camilla said. "We might have been friends. We could have been like sisters."

"We might," Tessa said. "But then, even sisters quarrel and envy each other." She stood up. "Forget the past, Camilla. It's gone. Your daughter's future is what matters now."

Camilla's tear-ravaged face brightened. "I'll do it. I owe it to Daddy."

Tessa grasped at this. "Exactly. If you were able to persuade Vicky to end this engagement or even just to postpone the wedding for a while, your father would be at peace. It was the one thing that bothered him. In fact, can I share a secret with you?"

Camilla's lips quivered. "I'd like that."

"One of the main reasons he wanted me to come and visit him was because he was so worried about Vicky's engagement to Jeremy."

"Really?" Jealousy reared its head again. "He could have talked to me about it."

"No, I don't think he could have. You would have gone straight to your mother if he had. He knew that she'd soon persuade you that the marriage was the best thing for Vicky . . . and the family."

Camilla sighed. "I suppose you're right."

"So, take my advice. Tell Sybil nothing and Vicky everything." Tessa went to the door. "Good-bye, Camilla."

Camilla got up, straightening her crumpled skirt. "Good-bye, Tessa. I envy you."

Tessa smiled. "What, again?"

"I envy you your freedom."

"You can be free, too. Take Vicky traveling somewhere. Just the two of you." The thought that Vicky would loathe the idea crossed her mind, but she ignored it.

"That's a marvelous idea." Camilla stood up. "Tessa."

"Yes."

"I'd like to kiss you good-bye, if I may."

"Certainly." Tessa moved toward her cousin. Camilla was about to peck her on the cheek, but Tessa put her arms around her and hugged her. "Good luck."

"I'm going to need it."

"You can do it," Tessa said, and stepped out into the upper hallway.

As she ran down the stairs, feeling the polished banister smooth beneath her hand, she felt a huge wave of relief.

When she reached the foot of the wide staircase she looked around the hall, with its black-and-white marble flooring and gleaming white columns, thinking how she had always felt chilled by its formality and hard, shining surfaces. She smiled to herself, feeling like some sort of anarchist about to blow the place up, metaphorically speaking, of course.

"Yes!" she shouted, not caring who heard her, at the same time raising her fists high in the air.

Chapter Twenty-nine

Jason was waiting for her on the terrace, with a half-demolished plate of cakes and sandwiches.

"I thought you said you'd be a few minutes," he said, licking cream from his fingers.

"Sorry. It took longer than I thought it would."

"Was it a real catfight?"

"No, not at all." Tessa poured herself some tea and then replaced the cozy on the teapot. "Amazingly enough, we parted quite amicably."

"You're joking."

"No, I'm not. All in all, it was a very satisfying conversation. Pass me those scones, would you?"

"Have you thought about what you're going to do with it?"

"With what?" Tessa asked, spreading strawberry jam on her scone.

"With the house your uncle left you, of course."

"Oh, that. I haven't had any time to think about it."

Jason looked at her as if she were in her dotage. "I would've thought you'd be freaked out. I mean, to be given a house here, in England. It'd be cool to live here, wouldn't it?"

Cool was what Tessa suddenly felt. "Not really," she said, giving him a half smile, "considering my job and home are in Canada."

"Couldn't we use it like a summer home or something? Maybe rent it out when we're not here?"

"I suppose we could, but it sounds like a lot of hassle to me." Tessa picked up a brandy snap and played with it, transferring a few pieces to her mouth. "I don't know why he left the house to me. He knew I couldn't live here."

"Maybe he was giving you a subliminal message."

Tessa looked over her sunglasses at Jason. "If he was, it's so subliminal I don't get it."

"Maybe he knows you really love it here, in Yorkshire. The way I do. It was just Langley you hated."

"Maybe that's it, Dr. Jason Freud. Who knows? All I know is that we can't stay here. I don't see any airlines here in the Yorkshire Dales, do you?"

Jason pushed back the white wrought-iron chair, so that its legs scraped on the paved terrace. He went to the head of the stone steps and stood, looking out over the expanse of smooth green lawn spread before him. "I want to stay here."

"What, at Langley?"

He turned around. "No, of course not. No one here wants me. No, I meant I want to stay in England. In Yorkshire, if possible."

"Doing what?"

"Working. Like I'm doing now, at Thornton."

"You mean working as an odd-job man, a farm laborer?" She knew it sounded like a put-down, but she couldn't help it.

For once, Jason didn't yell back at her. "No, that's just part of it. I'd like to do a job like Peter's, in charge of the estate."

"You said that before. Remember, I told you that Peter has a degree."

"Okay, I'll get a degree, if that's what it takes."

"And . . ." Tessa had been about to say, *And how will you do that?* when she remembered. So, she gathered, from the "gotcha" smile on her son's face, did

Jason. "I suppose you're thinking about Uncle Steven's bequest to you."

"Yeah, I am."

"I think he meant that to cover education in Canada."

"He didn't say so, did he? There's no reason why I couldn't study here. Philip said there are sure to be jobs in estate management in a few years time. He also said he could do with the help at Thornton, if he was able to keep it."

"So you've already discussed it with Philip?"

"What's this you've discussed with me?" Philip appeared at the terrace doors.

"Jobs in estate management."

"Ah, I see. I take it we're talking about Jason's wish to stay in England." He flinched theatrically. "Do I duck now?"

Tessa frowned. "Why?"

"Because the last time we had this discussion, you were furious with me for taking Jason's side."

Hearing voices in the drawing room, Tessa got to her feet. "It seems I won't be able to take my walk after all. Do you think we could continue this conversation back at Thornton?" she suggested, already moving to the steps. "Or do you still have work to do here?"

"It can wait. Charing has gone, so there's nothing else for me to do officially. Not now, anyway. I promised to come back and see Sybil tomorrow."

"I'd like to have said good-bye to Vicky, that's all, but after the funeral we arranged that she'd come over to Thornton tomorrow for a visit, so I suppose it doesn't matter."

"I have to say good-bye to everyone myself. Why don't you and Jason go to the car? Go the back way, across the lawn and then through the stables. I'll tell

Vicky you'll ring her this evening, to make arrangements for tomorrow. Will that be all right?"

"Thanks, Philip. I don't think I could face them all again."

She walked with Jason across the lawn, passing the croquet hoops stuck in the grass, the mallet stand by the toolshed. They could be the same ones they'd used when Steven had taught her to play croquet almost thirty years ago.

God be with you, she said silently. The older version of "Good-bye" seemed much more fitting for this occasion. Only, of course, it was the other way around. Steven was with God. If, as he'd often told her he believed, heaven consisted of what one had delighted in during one's life, his spirit would be flitting around the Dales, fishing in the becks and rivers, pottering in the gardens at Langley, frequenting the sheepdog trials and the race meets.

"What are you thinking about?" Jason asked her when he saw her smiling to herself.

"Steven."

"Sad thoughts?"

"No, not at all. Very happy ones. Especially now."

"Why, now?"

"Well, for one, he's no longer suffering. And, secondly, I think I've maybe been able to set the ball rolling in solving one of his greatest worries. If it succeeds, I shall be very happy."

"What was it?"

"Can't tell you. Not yet, anyway. I can't tell you unless it works out."

"That's not fair."

"Sorry about that. It concerns someone else."

That someone else was hailing them at this very moment. "Wait," Vicky cried as she raced across the lawn toward them. "Philip gave me your message," she said when she reached them. "I just wanted to make sure you're okay."

"I'm fine."

"Mummy said she wants to talk to me right away, which sounds horribly ominous. I wondered if it had anything to do with what you and she were talking about in her room. You were up there for ages."

"If you're going to ask me what we talked about, I can't tell you."

"She's full of secrets today, Mom is," Jason said.

"Sorry about that. But I will tell you that it was a good talk. I think we ended up understanding each other far better than we've ever done."

"Wow! I wonder what she wants to talk to me about."

"Can I give you a bit of advice?"

"Of course."

"Whatever she tells you, please listen to it all and think very seriously about it. It will be hard for her to tell you, because part of it shows her in a bad light, but not all."

Vicky's smile faded. "You know what it is, don't you?"

"Yes, I do."

"Can't you give me a hint?"

"No, although some of it concerns me, this is between your mother and you. All I can do is ask you to listen—and learn."

"Sounds like heavy-going stuff," Vicky said nervously. "Couldn't she have left it until another time? I'm not sure I can take any more today."

"I don't think she could pluck up courage again to tell you, if she postponed it. So, go now. Will I still see you tomorrow?"

"I hope so. I suppose it depends on Jeremy. He wants to drive back to London tonight. He says he's had enough."

For once, Tessa could sympathize with Jeremy, but it seemed singularly boorish of him not to stay to support Vicky. "Why don't you call me, then? Let me know what your plans are. I just don't want to go back to Canada without seeing you again."

"You are going back, then?"

"Certainly I am. I don't have to go right away, though. I start work again on September first. I'll probably spend a few more days here before I leave."

"I thought you might think of staying now that you have a home here."

"You mean the house Steven left me? I am sorry about that. Was it really going to be yours?"

"Not to my knowledge. That was just Daddy being stupid and vindictive. Silly ass."

"Would you like it? I haven't even seen it yet."

"Hey, wait a minute," Jason said. "Your uncle left it to us. I wouldn't mind having a place to live here."

"I didn't know you were staying on, Jason," Vicky said.

"Not so fast. Nothing's decided yet." Tessa caught sight of Derek coming down the steps. "Excuse me, folks, but I'm getting out of here. Don't forget to call me, Vicky. And don't forget what I said about your mother."

Vicky watched her father approaching across the lawn. "I'm off, too," she said, suddenly sprinting ahead of them, around the corner. "I'll go in the other way."

Tessa and Jason walked fast to the garages. Philip was waiting for them by the car. "Can you make a quick getaway?" Tessa asked. "Derek's on the warpath."

"With pleasure, madam." Philip slid into the driver's seat and turned on the ignition. They purred out of the stable yard just as Derek came around the corner.

"Phew! That was close," Tessa said, fanning herself with her hand. "The last thing I wanted was an altercation with Derek."

She laid her head back against the soft leather and closed her eyes.

"What do you think about us keeping the house?" Jason asked Philip.

Tessa turned around to glare at Jason. "I forbid any discussion of this house until tomorrow, at least."

"Mom!"

"You heard me."

"If you like," Philip said, "I'll take you to see Kirkby House tomorrow. I have the keys. It has a holiday tenant for August, but I'll explain that you're the new owner."

"I don't really want to see it," Tessa muttered.

"I think you should, even if you do decide to sell it."

Tessa shook her head and sighed. "Oh, all right, but no more discussion about it tonight, please. I'm too tired."

Philip glanced at her. "It's been a strain."

"It has. But there have been good things, too."

She leaned her head back again, but this time kept her eyes open so that she could enjoy watching the scenes she loved passing by: sloping fields edged with drystone walls, high above them the rolling moors that had turned purple now that the heather was blooming. Then the drive along the narrow, winding lane that led to Thornton.

The shadows were lengthening, so that when they reached the house the old stone walls were dappled with sun and shade. Above the back door, plump white roses grew, their sweetness perfuming the air as they went inside.

Sarah came out of the kitchen to greet them. "How did it go?" she asked.

"Not too bad," Tessa said. "But it's been a long day."

"Why don't you go and have a bath?" Sarah suggested. "There's lots of hot water. Then I can serve you all a light supper in the library."

"I couldn't eat another thing," Tessa said.

"Speak for yourself," Jason said. "Is it that game pie you were making this morning, Sarah?"

"Aye, it is."

"Great."

Tessa rolled her eyes. "He's perpetually hungry." She moved away to the foot of the stairs.

Sarah looked from her to Philip. "Come on, Jason, I need some help here with the veggies."

They went into the kitchen and shut the door.

"How about a brandy to take up with you?" Philip asked.

"Sounds great, but I'm afraid I might fall asleep in the bath. It must be reaction, but I suddenly feel absolutely exhausted."

He moved closer. "As you said, it has been a long day." He brushed her hair away from her forehead. Tessa held her breath for a moment ... and then she was in his arms, too tired to resist. If she had wanted to, which she didn't.

At first he just held her close, stroking her hair, her head against his chest, so that she could hear his heart beating fast. She thought that she could stand there forever, Philip's arms about her, the dark beams of Thornton's old hall above her.

Then, the grandfather clock in the corner began to chime. Tessa lifted her head to look into his eyes, until his face came so close that it blurred. Groaning deep in his throat, he dragged her against him and kissed her.

It was as if they'd waited a lifetime for this kiss. The last one had been a kiss of impulse and need.

This one had a sense of rightness. She was in the house she loved, being kissed by the man she loved. Then hall and house faded away and all Tessa knew, as Philip's mouth moved over hers, was a blissful feeling of this being ordained.

They were so lost in each other that neither of them heard the kitchen door open . . . and then close again.

"They're kissing," Sarah said, grinning at Jason.

"It's about time," Jason replied, and then went back to scrubbing new potatoes in the sink.

Vicky was utterly shaken by what her mother had told her. She left her mother's bedroom and walked down the back staircase, not wanting to meet anyone, particularly Jeremy, until she'd had time to think.

It was a good thing Tessa had warned her to be patient and listen, because some of what her mother had told her had seemed so incredible that she'd had trouble following it, never mind believing it. Coming so soon after her beloved Papa's burial she felt shaken up, actually unsteady on her feet.

She knew that her grandmother was a domineering matriarch, but in her wildest dreams she could never have suspected her of such terrible things: hiding the fact that Tessa was pregnant from everyone, paying John Maltby to follow Tessa and actually *marry* her, making her mother pretend that she was pregnant to trap Derek Thornton into marrying her.

Vicky began to understand why her father treated her mother the way he did. He must have found out pretty soon after their wedding—if not before—that she wasn't pregnant at all.

But it was Grandmother who had planned it all, schemed against Tessa, deprived Jason of his father and his birthright.

And, as her mother had pointed out, it was Grandmother who had brought her and Jeremy together.

Jeremy's grandmother was one of Sybil's best friends. God knew when they had arranged all of it, plotting together like two old hags around the cauldron.

Vicky knew that she'd been blinded by Jeremy's looks and charm. But she'd discovered recently how that charm came and went, depending on whether she was dancing attention on him or not. He'd also become resentful of her work, ridiculing it, calling it her "chiseling."

She walked past the fountain, remembering the night of her engagement, and then took the path, kicking at loose stones as she went. Although some of her friends didn't care much for Jeremy—and Papa had thoroughly disliked him—it was Tessa who'd made her realize that it wasn't just Jeremy but the whole idea of marriage at her age that was crazy.

Now she knew the entire truth. She'd been manipulated, used to fulfill this archaic dream of her grandmother's that a title must be brought into the family. Which, as she'd just discovered from her mother, was something Grandmother herself had been expected to do, and had failed. Of course, Vicky had known about this before, but now that she knew that her grandmother's mind was warped, it made a hell of a difference to her entire perspective of the thing.

"I've been a bloody fool," Vicky said to herself as she walked into the copper beech wood.

Today she must come to a decision. It had to be today. Papa was gone, but she knew—just as Tessa had—that his spirit lived on.

The envelope Papa left her had contained a brief note to say that Mr. Charing held a bank draft for ten thousand pounds in her name to help her establish an independent lifestyle. That way, if her parents refused to help her, she had something to get started.

Papa had thought of all the angles, she reflected. She owed it to him to come to some decision today.

Do it now, he was whispering in her head, *so that you can get on with your life.*

The sex with Jeremy had been great, but even that palled when you thought that the man you were doing it with was an egotistical idiot.

Being rich would be great, too, except that money didn't seem to bring people much happiness. She thought of her mother and poor dead Rosamund Thornton, both spending money like water, and both the most dissatisfied women she had ever known.

"I bet I get more pleasure out of planing a piece of wood than they did out of spending a thousand pounds," she said aloud to herself.

And being a countess would be a big bore, always being on show and having to go to stuffy balls and open new hospitals and schools . . . or whatever it was that countesses did. Not her thing at all.

"Vicky!"

Damn, there was Jeremy now, looking for her. It was too soon. She hadn't had time to work things out yet. Suddenly, as she heard Jeremy crashing through the wood, she decided to be a fatalist. Things would work themselves out, she decided.

"Where the hell have you been?" Jeremy demanded, his fair hair blown across his face by the evening breeze. "I've been tramping around looking for you everywhere. Look at my shoes." He held up one foot to show his shoe covered in dust and mud.

"Sorry," she said lightly. "I needed time to myself."

"You might have said."

Had he always sounded this petulant? she wondered.

"You would have wanted to come if I did."

"I was looking for you to see when we could get away. I want to drive back to London tonight."

"I told you, I don't want to go back yet. You go, if you want to. I want to stay and work on that commission for a bureau that Christopher gave me."

"For God's sake, you promised to come with me to London and then to come to Ayncliffe for the shooting next weekend."

"I hate shooting. I hate the noise. I hate seeing birds soaring up into the skies one minute, then plummeting down dead the next."

"Don't be so bloody ridiculous. Everyone shoots. I haven't noticed you not liking to eat those dear little birds."

"Just because I like eating roast beef doesn't necessarily mean I like working in an abattoir, does it?" she said belligerently.

He stared down at her. "What's got into you today?"

"My darling Papa was buried today, Jeremy. Or have you forgotten?"

"That's over now. He'd want you to get on with your life."

"I agree. But it depends on what that life is, doesn't it?"

He grabbed her by the arm. "Come on up to the house and get a drink into you. That's what you need. Then we can decide whether we should go tonight or first thing tomorrow."

She shook herself free. "You aren't listening, are you? I said I don't want to go to London. I want to stay here and work. Remember?"

He narrowed his eyes at her, his chin jutting out. "You're just being bloody-minded."

"Because I don't want to do what you want to do? That's bloody-minded, is it?"

"I know what you need." Jeremy glanced around and then looked at her, his eyes gleaming.

"What?" she asked warily.

He bent his head. "You need a good fuck," he whispered in her ear. "That'll make you feel better." He looked around the shadowy glade, the leaves whispering in the breeze.

"This was one of my grandfather's favorite places," she said slowly, her eyes never leaving his face. "He loved to sit here, sheltered by the trees, watching the ripples in the stream."

"Good for him," Jeremy grabbed her and, catching her behind the knees with his leg, toppled her off balance so that she fell onto her back. Usually she laughed when he did this. Today, she didn't.

His weight was on her, his hands groping her. "Get off me, Jeremy," she said, her voice cold.

"Not bloody likely. You've put me off for a week. I need my oats."

His mouth covered hers. She felt like throwing up all over him. "I don't want to do it here, Jeremy," she said through gritted teeth. "I've told you why."

He was trying to drag her skirt above her knees, his knee forcing hers apart. Fear suddenly flooded over her. She'd never felt afraid of him before, but then he'd never had to force her before.

"I don't want to do it here." She was fighting him off now, her hands pushing at his chest, trying to shove him away. "I'd much rather do it in bed. Let's go back to the house." Fear made her voice shake.

"Much more romantic here. Bet your Papa had it off with one of the parlor maids a few times here. That's probably why he liked the place—"

Summoning up every ounce of strength, Vicky had managed to free one hand. She drove her nails like talons down his face, at the same time bringing her knee up hard into his crotch.

He let out a yell that startled the birds from the trees and then doubled over. "You bitch!" he roared. "You bloody bitch."

He made a grab for her, but she eluded him. Heaving up the long, straight skirt of her black dress, Vicky tore through the wood and down the grass path between the herbaceous borders.

Then she burst out onto the lawn, sobs tearing at her chest.

She saw Kevin coming around the corner from the stables. He saw her. He started to run. She slowed to a walk, tears pouring down her face.

Kevin came closer. "Jesus, Vicky. What's happened to you?"

"Don't touch me, please, Kevin. I don't want to be touched."

His hands fell to his sides. "Of course not." He lifted his head, his eyes fixing on something behind her. She knew it must be Jeremy. "That bastard. It was him, wasn't it?" He was about to take off across the lawn.

Vicky grabbed his arm. "Do something for me, Kevin."

"I'm about to do it, if you'll just let me go."

She hung on to his arm. "No. You can wait here for me, but I want to do this myself." Kevin tried to drag his arm away. "Kevin! Keep out of this, *please.*" She was yelling at him as if he were deaf.

Kevin was shaking with anger. "He needs a bloody good thrashing."

"Certainly he does, but this is something I have to do myself, okay? If you want to help, you can stay here to make sure he doesn't do anything to me."

Kevin was breathing heavily, glaring at Jeremy, as he approached.

"So you ran off to your lover boy," Jeremy said. His face was bleeding. Vicky saw with great satisfaction five red tracks raking down his cheek.

Slowly she drew the diamond engagement ring from her finger and held it out to him.

"Here. Hold on, now," he spluttered. "It was just

a bit of fun we had. Get rid of your lackey there and we'll kiss and make up."

The ring fell from her fingers into the grass at his feet.

"I haven't decided yet whether or not to charge you with attempted rape," she said, her words measured and cool, although her heart was into high gear. "No doubt the bruises on my legs and arms and the scratches on your face would be enough evidence to corroborate my accusation. *Earl's son charged with sexual assault.* I'm sure your daddy wouldn't be too happy about reading that in the newspapers, would he? Nor would your mummy."

"It's a load of rubbish. Everyone knows we've been sleeping together since before we got engaged."

"There's quite a difference between sleeping together and forcing me to have sex in my own garden on the day of my grandfather's funeral. The *Sun* would have a field day with that one, wouldn't they?"

"You can't break off our engagement just because of a little quarrel."

"I certainly can." She walked away from him, toward the house. "See? I just did."

Kevin followed her, keeping himself between her and Jeremy. When she reached the stone steps up the house, she turned. Jeremy was on one knee scrabbling in the grass for the ring. "Would you mind packing the Honorable Mr. Kingsley's clothes into his case, Kevin, and bringing it down to his car," she said in a voice that carried all the way back to Jeremy. "He won't be coming into the house. And kindly make sure that all the staff is informed that he is not to be permitted to enter."

"With pleasure, Miss Thornton," Kevin's little bow of the head was the response of the perfect servant. His wide grin, however, was not.

Chapter Thirty

Tessa was woken the next morning by a shaft of sunlight coming through the gap in the curtains. For a moment she wondered why on earth she should feel so content, considering her uncle had been buried yesterday and she'd learned a few more diabolical facts about her aunt.

Then she remembered. She stretched luxuriously on the bed, a honey-sweet warmth stealing through her veins.

She and Philip hadn't stayed for long out in the hall last night. They'd come to their senses fairly quickly and realized that they should call a halt, before Sarah or Jason found them necking like a couple of teenagers.

During the rest of the evening it had become increasingly difficult to maintain a normal conversation when they were both longing to be alone, to explore each other both mentally and physically. At least, Tessa was. And so, she realized when she caught him looking at her with a smoldering expression that gave him away completely, was Philip.

A few minutes after they'd all said their good nights to each other and gone to their rooms, Philip came to her bedroom door. "Would you like to come in?" she asked him.

He hesitated, and then said, "No. I think not."

"Oh," she said, taken aback. She tried to hide her

disappointment. It wasn't only because she wanted him to make love to her, but she was also afraid that if they left everything in limbo until tomorrow, somehow the magic might have evaporated and they'd be back to normal. Good friends, but not lovers.

Philip took both her hands in his. "I want this to be perfect. I don't want to make a wrong move," he explained. "Can you understand what I mean?"

"Not really."

"Let me try to explain. I've know you since you were a child. Because of that, I've been fighting my strong attraction to you ever since you came home. I'd been like an older brother to you for so long that it felt terribly wrong to think of you as a mature woman." He smiled. "Does that sound crazy to you?"

She shook her head, her concern ebbing away. "Not at all. It's a bit like incest, isn't it?"

"Well, not quite, thank God." He smiled. "It just takes some getting used to, that's all. Changing our perspective of each other." He took her face between his hands and gazed into her eyes. "I think I've always loved you in some way or other, Tessa. It's like one of those mythical loves that keeps changing shape but continues for eternity."

Tessa felt tears gathering against her eyelids. "I know," she whispered. "I've always loved you, too, Philip." The confession made her feel suddenly very shy with him. "It nearly broke my heart when you married Rosamund, you know. Until then, I'd always hoped that you'd wait for me until I grew up."

His hands pressed against her face. "God, I wish I had. How very different both our lives might have been had I not married Rosamund."

"I cried the entire night after your wedding. You looked so right for each other, so beautiful together that I thought I'd die just looking at you."

He released her. "Appearances can be deceptive," he said, his mouth twisting into a wry smile.

"What do you mean?" she asked, frowning.

"Never mind. It can wait. Is it too late for us now, do you think?" His anxiety was palpable. It gave her a feeling of infinite power that Philip Thornton, the man she had loved since she was a child, wanted her.

Slowly she shook her head from side to side. "No, it's not too late." She lifted her hands to pull his head down, his hair springy against her fingers, and kissed him again.

They'd parted reluctantly at her door, agreeing that since they'd waited for each other for more than twenty years they could wait just a little while longer.

Now, as she lay in bed, the warmth of her memories of last night began to cool, as thoughts of all the intricate problems that faced them both flooded over her.

The Thornton Treasure was still missing, with Derek and Jason still suspects. Philip was still burdened with a massive inheritance tax, as well as the maintenance costs for Thornton Manor. Most of all, their homes, their professions, their very *lives* were separated by the Atlantic Ocean and half of Canada.

"Is it too late for us?" Philip had asked her. Tessa, overwhelmed by feelings of love for him, hadn't been able to see any reason why they couldn't be together for the rest of their lives. Now, in the bright light of morning, she wasn't so sure.

She wished she could rewind the clock back to the time Philip had left her last night. Knowing how they were both longing for each other, it would have been so easy to persuade Philip not to leave her alone. The consummation of their love might have made things a good deal more concrete than they appeared to her now that she was fully awake.

When she went downstairs, she found Philip in the kitchen, eating breakfast with Jason and Peter. It ap-

peared to be a working breakfast, as r...
plaining a spreadsheet of figures that Philip had in
front of him.

When she came in, Philip pushed the paper aside
and stood up. They exchanged smiles. "Good
morning."

Tessa suddenly realized that everyone was watching
them. "Morning, all."

"You're up early," Philip said. "Join us for breakfast." He drew out a chair for her and waited for her
to sit down.

"Just coffee and toast, thanks."

Anyone observing them might have said their behavior was quite normal, but Tessa could read the
flash of warm amusement in Philip's eyes, the tender-
ness in the curve of his mouth. She, in turn, hoped
that he knew that just seeing him made her knees feel
weak. She felt like a besotted schoolgirl.

The kitchen seemed to have gone very quiet, as if
they were all holding their breath, waiting for her or
Philip to speak again. Sarah set a pot of coffee in front
of her.

"Hi, Sarah. How are you?" Tessa realized that she
sounded a bit too hearty, but the silence was getting
to her.

"Fine, thanks. Brown or white toast?"

"I'd like some of that terrific multigrain bread, if
you have it." Tessa looked across the table at Philip
and Peter. "Please don't stop work for me. I'm happy
just to sit here and not talk. It takes me a while to
wake up."

Peter scraped his chair back on the red-tiled floor
and stood up. "We're finished," he said abruptly. "I
have to go into Leyburn later this morning. It's market
day. Anybody need anything?"

"I'd like some haddock from the fishmonger's van,"

 ᴕarah said. "It's going to be another warm day, so take the cooler with you to keep it fresh."

"I'd love to come and see the market," Tessa said.

"You wouldn't like it much," Peter said. "Almost impossible to park in Leyburn on market day." He spoke curtly, almost rudely, which surprised Tessa.

"Hang on, Peter. I'll come and check that broken paling before you go to Leyburn," Philip said. He turned to Tessa. "I'll be back in about half an hour. Then we can talk about going to see your house today."

"You haven't forgotten that Vicky's coming over sometime this morning?" Tessa reminded him. Vicky had phoned yesterday evening, saying she had something important to tell Tessa, but wouldn't say any more. Tessa was extremely eager to hear what had happened between her and Camilla.

"No, I haven't forgotten. I don't need to be here for her visit, do I?"

"No. Definitely not."

"Good. Then we'll go and see Kirkby House this afternoon. Maybe even fit in a visit to Leyburn Market, as well, if you like." Philip squeezed her shoulder as he passed behind her.

Tessa looked up to find Jason grinning at her. She narrowed her eyes at him, but said nothing. Jason jumped up to join Philip, and all three men left by the kitchen door.

"Sleep well?" Sarah asked as she washed dishes in the old-fashioned ceramic kitchen sink.

"Yes, very well, thanks." Sensing that Sarah was fishing for information, Tessa swiftly changed the subject. "What's biting Peter? He's a bit surly today, isn't he?"

"Peter? He's got some personal problems." Sarah looked uneasy.

"I've noticed he's been very quiet. Maybe he's working too hard."

"He's not the only one. All of us at Thornton are carrying more than our load. That's not a complaint against Mr. Philip, mind," Sarah added hastily. "He works harder than any of us. It's just that there's too much to do for the staff he's got."

Tessa sighed. "I know. It's an awful problem. I don't know how he's going to solve it. I daren't even mention it to him."

Sarah hesitated and then said, "It might help for a start if he got rid of Peter."

Tessa looked at her, surprised. Then she remembered what Jason had told her about Peter. "Because he's gay, Sarah? Surely that doesn't affect his job capabilities?"

"No, not because he's gay. It's because his mind's not on his work, that's why. You just said yourself that he was surly. That's exactly what he is."

"But it just doesn't seem like him. I thought he was very pleasant when I met him last month. I remember how kind he was to my uncle when he came here."

"He's got a lover hidden away in a cottage in Coverdale," Sarah said, her voice sinking to a whisper.

"So?"

"I don't think Mr. Philip knows."

"Even if he did, I doubt if he'd mind."

"He might, if he knew what's wrong with him."

"What's wrong with whom? Peter or his lover?"

"Good question!"

All at once, Tessa realized what Sarah was trying to tell her. "Has his lover got AIDS?"

Sarah nodded. "That's what they say in the village. From the way Peter's carrying on, I think it's true."

"Maybe it's just a rumor."

"No one's seen the man. And the doctor visits once a week, regular."

"He could be ill with anything. Just because he's gay, it doesn't have to be AIDS, you know."

"Most likely, 'tis. All things considered."

"If you're so concerned, why haven't you told Mr. Philip about this?"

" 'Cause I gave Peter my word I'd not let on that he had a lover nearby. He's desperate afraid he'll get the sack."

Tessa got up. "You're a kind soul, Sarah," she said. She sensed Sarah's desire to let Philip know, despite her promise to Peter. Perhaps that was her reason for telling Tessa, so that she'd pass the word on to Philip. She went to the sink and began drying the dishes Sarah had washed.

"Leave those. They can dry themselves."

Tessa kept on drying.

"That was a lovely service yesterday," Sarah said.

"It was, wasn't it? I thought Philip's eulogy was particularly good."

"Aye, he caught Mr. Hargrave right, didn't he?" Sarah squished washing-up liquid into the greasy frying pan. "How did the rest of it go?"

"Rather well. By the way, I have something to tell you."

"What?"

"I've found out that Sybil did know I was pregnant. That was why she sacked you. To keep you quiet." Tessa looked up from her drying. "I am sorry, Sarah."

"Don't you worry your head over it. It's all water under the bridge now. Any road, she did me a big favor. But how did you find out?"

"Camilla told me."

"Camilla?" Sarah repeated incredulously.

"Yes. She was in a chatty mood yesterday." Knowing what a gossip Sarah was, Tessa wasn't about to tell her the worst of it. "I thought you should know, considering you were the one most affected by it."

"Thanks. Somehow, it makes me feel better."

"That's why I told you. Thanks for being such a good friend to me when I really needed one."

"You're welcome. You always treated me right, you did. Not like that stuck-up Camilla."

Tessa grimaced, but said nothing. She didn't want her feelings about Camilla broadcast around half of Yorkshire. "I'm going up to make my bed."

"What's happening between you and Mr. Philip?" Sarah's question caught Tessa just as she was going out the door.

"Why do you ask?"

Sarah shrugged. "I thought there might be summat going on, that's all. He hasn't proposed yet, then?"

Tessa felt her face grow warm. "No, he hasn't."

"Bet you he will."

"If he does, it's all going to be very complicated."

"Why?"

"I live in Canada, Sarah. That's where my work is, too."

"You'd have enough work, and more, here at Thornton Manor, if you married him," Sarah said dryly.

Instead of discouraging her, Sarah's warning gave Tessa a jolt of excitement. "I would, too, wouldn't I?"

"Aye, you would that. The house hasn't had a proper mistress looking after it since Mr. Philip's mother fell sick. That Rosamund was useless. All *she* could do was spend his money."

Tessa was beginning to realize that Philip's marriage hadn't been at all the ideal union she'd thought it was. "It wasn't the house I was thinking about so much as the entire estate," she said, half to herself.

"What about the estate?"

Tessa smiled. "We'd have to see, wouldn't we?" She hurriedly escaped before Sarah could do any more prying.

*   *   *

Vicky arrived at eleven o'clock. By ten past eleven, Tessa knew the outcome of Vicky's conversations with Camilla and then Jeremy. From what Vicky told her, she gathered that the conversation with Jeremy had been more action than talk. Vicky didn't go into complete details, but Tessa could tell from the dark circles under her eyes and her tension that it had been very nasty.

"He showed me what he was really like," Vicky said as they sat drinking coffee in the sunny morning parlor. She stirred her coffee round and round and then looked up at Tessa, her mouth trembling. "God, Tessa, what an idiot I've been."

"Not at all. You were besotted with him. It just made you blind, that's all. We all go through that some time in our lives. I did with Derek. And so, apparently, did Philip with Rosamund."

"Mummy told me that Rosamund made him desperately unhappy."

"So I understand, although Philip and I haven't actually talked about it. I didn't know, you see. I thought it was a wonderful marriage, that Philip must be devastated by her death." Tessa summoned up a smile. "It shows how easily we can be mistaken about people, doesn't it?" She glanced at Vicky's left hand, which looked bare without her engagement ring. "What will you do now?"

"Mummy wants me to take a trip somewhere with her." Vicky grimaced. "I'm not sure that's such a good idea, but I might just do it. Then I intend to move out of Langley and find a permanent place of my own. It's time I lived my own life and made my own decisions."

"Will you live in York or London?"

"Neither. I'll finish my apprenticeship in York, of course, but I'm thinking of setting up a proper workshop and studio somewhere in Wensleydale. I know that London's supposed to be the place to be. I love it for a riotous weekend, but I don't really like living there."

"The country girl at heart."

"I never thought I was. Anyway, if my stuff's good enough, people will come to me, wherever I am. I'd like to have lots of space for a workshop and some sort of showroom, and I can't afford that in London." She looked at Tessa, her lovely eyes showing her vulnerability. "It's all going to be a big change."

"You can do it. Does your grandmother know yet that you've broken the engagement?"

"No. Mummy offered to tell her for me."

"You're joking!"

"No, I'm not. Amazing, isn't it? Mind you, that was last night. She'd probably have had cold feet by the morning. Anyway, I told her I'd tell Grandmother myself."

"But you haven't done it yet."

Vicky laughed. "No. I'm the one with cold feet." Her expression sobered. "I'm going back to tell her right now."

"And Jeremy?"

"He got the hell out of the house last night. I think he was scared that Kevin might set upon him. You should have seen Kevin, by the way. He was like a ferocious bull terrier. He'd have gone for him and torn him apart if I'd let him."

Tessa was tempted to say, *Good for Kevin,* but she knew that Vicky must still be hurting from her realization that the man she'd loved was a jerk. Emphasizing that fact would only make her feel worse. "I think Kevin's in love with you, Vicky."

"He is. He told me so last night. I suppose I've known it all along." Vicky sighed. "More complications. I feel like running off to a desert island."

"What did you say to him when he told you? Or is that none of my business?"

"Of course it is, you silly thing. I told him I really liked him, but that I didn't want to get into any sort of serious relationship with anyone for a long time. He said he'd be willing to wait, but meanwhile he'd be happy to be just a friend."

"That won't be easy for him."

"I know. That's one of the reasons I think it's a good idea for me to get away for a while and let everything cool down. What about you, Tessa? There's something between you and Philip, isn't there?"

Tessa grimaced. "Is it that obvious?"

"Oh, you're both very proper and restrained, but I could tell after the funeral that something was going on." Vicky tucked her feet under her on the sofa. "Come on, cousin mine. Give."

"There's nothing much to give, really. Except that I'm in love with him."

Vicky squealed. "And that's nothing much?"

"I've always been in love with him, Vicky," Tessa said very quietly.

"I thought it was Daddy you loved?"

"I suppose he was the next best thing. Philip had married Rosamund. Derek was Philip's brother."

"Oh, that's so romantic. All these years, pining for Philip. I can't blame you, really. He's still very dishy."

"I haven't exactly been pining for him," Tessa said dryly. "After all, until a few weeks ago, I hadn't seen him for twenty years."

"Love eternal," Vicky said in a swooning voice.

Tessa slapped her hand. "Oh, stop it." They both laughed.

"But you've only told me about you. What about Philip? Has he declared his love?"

"Sort of."

"Sort of? What exactly does that mean?"

"God, you're as nosy as Sarah."

Vicky giggled. "No one could be as nosy as Sarah. Has she been asking questions, too?"

"Sort of. I didn't tell her much, though."

"You can tell me. I am your cousin, after all."

"Once removed cousin."

"Whatever. We're soulmates. Has Philip actually proposed?"

"No, he hasn't. But I suppose you could say we've made the first move."

Vicky's eyes rounded. "Oh? Sounds promising."

Tessa shook her head. "You're impossible. Philip is always very much the gentleman."

"Too bad."

Tessa laughed outright. "Last night I thought that, too." Her laughter died. "But now, I wonder. There are so many problems still to solve."

"Like what?"

"I was listing them all in bed this morning. The theft of the Thornton Cross—"

"I'm sure Daddy took it. He's probably hocked it in some pawnshop."

"That's what Philip thinks, too, I'm sorry to say. Or that he's sold it to some private collector, which would be infinitely worse. But until it's found, it leaves a cloud hanging over Jason."

"How could Jason get rid of it? He doesn't know anyone here."

"There's rumors he was hanging around with some bad kids," Tessa said in a low voice.

"I doubt that. Jason's not that sort. Besides, he knows Philip would be down on him like a ton of bricks if he did anything. He thinks Philip's a bit too strict and starchy, but underneath he really respects him."

"Anyway, Philip will have to go to the police if it doesn't surface soon, and that could be really nasty."

"What other things are standing in your way?"

"Thornton Manor itself. Those damned inheritance taxes. Philip doesn't know where to find the money for them. When I brought up the subject in July, he froze me out."

"He's an old fuddy-duddy when it comes to Thornton. Langley's been open to the public for ages."

"Yes, but only at certain times of the year. Langley's stables are its main source of revenue. Thornton would have to have some drastic changes to keep it going."

"I can't quite see Philip turning it into a safari park, can you?"

"No, I can't. That's the problem. And he won't even let me discuss it with him."

"When he asks you to marry him, you'll have to make that a stipulation of accepting: that he'll be willing to discuss Thornton with you."

"How can I accept, Vicky? My life and job are in Canada. His are firmly rooted here."

"So what? Love is more important than all that stuff."

"Is it, Vicky?" Tessa's voice was grave. "Can you imagine what it would be like to give up your work, your independence, after managing very well on your own for fifteen years? The thought terrifies me."

They gazed at each other. "It's strange, isn't it? We're both scared," Vicky said. "You of losing your independence, and me of getting it."

Instinctively, they both leaned forward at the same time to hug each other.

"Besides," Tessa said, "this is all taking things a bit too much for granted. Philip hasn't asked me to marry him."

Chapter Thirty-one

As Vicky drove back to Langley, she went over several different ways of broaching the subject of Jeremy with her grandmother. In the end, she decided that a straightforward statement was the best way. She'd field the questions afterward.

As soon as she'd parked her car, she went inside the house. "James," she called, "where's my grandmother?"

James came from the dining room, clad in a striped apron, his cloth for cleaning silver still in his hand. "She's up in her bedroom, Miss Victoria."

"Thanks." Vicky started up the stairs.

"She doesn't want to be disturbed," James warned her. Vicky ignored him.

When she reached her grandmother's room, she knocked on the door. "Come in." The voice sounded weaker, but it still held that imperious note that could make Vicky's stomach cramp.

She put her head around the door. "Hi, Grandmother. Sorry to bother you, but I need to talk to you."

Her grandmother lay in the large bed, a tiny figure swamped by lace-edged pillows. "I told Barton I did not wish to be disturbed."

"Don't blame him. He told me. But I have to speak to you."

"Help me up."

Vicky went to her grandmother and heaved her up, so that she was able to sit back against the pillows. Her body was as slight and fragile as a bird's. But the dark eyes were still as piercing as ever.

Vicky perched on the side of the bed, only to be told, "I can't abide people bouncing on my bed. Pull up a chair."

Vicky did so. "Are you all right? Have you got everything you need?"

The dark eyes stabbed at her. "Don't be a fool, girl. I'm crippled and I've just lost my darling Steven. Does that answer your question?"

Vicky swallowed. "I'm sorry." She looked around the pink-and-ivory room, at the crystal dressing-table set and the silver-backed brushes she had always coveted as a child, anything to avoid seeing those eyes.

"Well, out with it, girl. You wanted to tell me something. What is it?"

Her grandmother's bluntness inspired Vicky to counter in the same way. "I've broken my engagement to Jeremy." She held up her bare left hand, fingers splayed, to make her point clear.

The eyes stared at her without blinking. "Why?"

"Because I don't love him anymore, Grandmother."

"What rubbish! Romantic love doesn't last, anyway. What you have with Jeremy is much more important."

"Had. And what was that?" Vicky demanded.

"Your breeding. You are both from old families. You have the same backgrounds. You are ideally suited to each other."

"What you're talking about is not two individuals," Vicky said heatedly, "but representatives of a certain class of people. The way you talk, we might as well be horses for breeding purposes."

"Quite right. That is exactly what I mean. Such marriages invariably last longer than those based on romantic love."

Vicky's face burned. "And what about your marriage? Was that for breeding purposes only?"

Her grandmother's eyes narrowed to thin slits. "How dare you talk of my marriage, with my husband newly in his grave." Vicky recoiled from the venom in her voice. "My marriage was one in a million. You couldn't hope to aspire to such a marriage."

Vicky's chin went up. "Oh, but I do. And that's why I don't want Jeremy. He's shallow. He's boring. He's stupid. All he's interested in—all he's good at, actually—is sex. And I found out that if he can't get that when he wants it, he tries to take it, anyway."

"Aha! So that's the reason. What did he do?"

"It doesn't matter. I dealt with him."

"You're still a child when it comes to men. Just because you've slept with Jeremy, you think you're so experienced. He is probably the only man you've slept with, isn't he?"

"How many men did you sleep with, Grandmother?"

The eyes flashed. "How dare you!"

"Exactly. It's none of my business, is it? Just as my private life is none of yours."

"You are making a grave mistake. You have acted impulsively and will rue it. You will never find a match like this one. Such wealth and status. And the chance to become a countess of the realm. All of that, all of that thrown away, because of a childish whim. Because you didn't know how to manage stupid Jeremy."

"Because I didn't want to be raped."

"Raped!" Her grandmother's voice was filled with scorn. "You've been sleeping with the man for months. Don't talk to me about rape."

"I don't care if I've been sleeping with him for years, or even if we were married. I will not be forced into sex."

"All this feminist, newfangled nonsense." Sybil's scornful eyes suddenly grew cold. "Tessa has had something to do with this, hasn't she? I see her hand in it. Her coming back to England has ruined everything."

Vicky matched coldness with coldness. "Don't speak to me about Tessa. I'm surprised you can even mention her name after what you've done to her."

"What do you mean? What lies has that woman been spreading?"

"She doesn't need to spread any lies. It's the truth that's spreading."

"Don't believe a word she tells you. She is a compulsive liar. Always has been."

"I know all about your interference in Tessa's and my parents' lives. So, I'm warning you, Grandmother, stop interfering in mine."

"I know a great deal more about the world than you do."

"Actually, I don't think you do." Vicky was both appalled and elated to be saying such things to her grandmother. "You've lived a cushioned existence all your life. You've never had to earn your living or take the tube to work every day or do your own cleaning, like normal people."

Sybil glared at her. "I've had to run a large estate, oversee staff, help your grandfather make the stables turn a profit. I'd like to see your average woman do all that."

"True," Vicky conceded, "but that still doesn't mean you know a great deal about the world, does it?"

"I object to your arguing with me. It is ill-mannered. Does your mother know about your decision to break your engagement?"

"Yes."

"She said nothing to me about it this morning," Sybil said in a querulous tone.

"That's because I said I wanted to tell you myself."

"How could she look me in the eye this morning and not even mention it?"

"I've just told you why. Besides, Mummy isn't a puppet with you holding the strings. It's time she lived her own life. After all, she is going to be the sole owner of Langley one day." Impulsively Vicky sat on the side of the bed and grasped her grandmother's hand. "Don't you see, Gran? By cosseting her and ordering her around, you've deprived her of her ability to make her own decisions. If you don't stop now, she'll never be able to run Langley by herself. You've sheltered her so much from the real world that all she thinks about is the latest Emanuel ball gown or whether her new hair color suits her."

"Are you suggesting that I have been a failure as a mother?"

Vicky felt like laughing aloud. What a monumental understatement! "Let's just say, you've overprotected my mother and manipulated people in a rather misguided attempt to make her happy. I expect it became a habit with you, after a while." She looked directly at her grandmother. "You tried to do it with me, but I've had enough, okay?"

Sloe-dark eyes clashed with aquamarine. Then Sybil turned her head away. "What are the Ayncliffes going to think?" she said, her crippled fingers plucking at the silk quilt.

Vicky bent to kiss her wrinkled cheek. "Who the hell cares?" she said and left the room.

Tessa telephoned Vicky after lunch. "How did the big meeting go?" she asked her on the phone.

"Pretty scary. But I told her. My mother has been given the royal summons. She's with Grandmother now. Poor Mummy, she looked positively green when she went upstairs. I was just getting out of the house when you rang."

"Why don't you come with us to see this house Uncle Steven's left me?"

"Great idea. I'll be right over. I may even be asking Uncle Philip for a bed for the night. Grandmother's probably going to order James to throw all my things out into the driveway."

Uncle Steven had described Kirkby House as modest. Tessa supposed it was modest, if one was to compare it with Langley or Thornton. It had been converted into three holiday flats, each containing ample space for a family. The rooms were large, with high ceilings and sashed windows, with lovely views of the dale and the fells beyond.

"It's a great house, but what on earth am I going to do with it?" Tessa asked Philip as they stood on the top floor, looking out over Wensleydale, the River Ure meandering through its meadows.

"You could sell it. The market in the Yorkshire Dales is very good at present, especially for a period house like this. It's in first-class condition. You could get possibly two or three hundred thousand pounds for it."

"I don't know. I could really do with the money, of course, but somehow I hate to part with the house, when Uncle Steven left it to me. And it has a connection with my father, as well. I think Steven wanted me to keep it, don't you?"

"That must be your decision," Philip said gravely in his best legal manner.

He was being deliberately noncommittal. In more ways than one, Tessa thought.

"Mind you, the income from holiday lets is quite considerable." Philip showed her the figures Mr. Charing had prepared. "This is a very popular tourist area, as you know. All three flats were let almost the entire year last year, including over Christmas."

"That would mean I'd have some extra income coming in fairly regularly, wouldn't it? Yet I could still keep the house, until I decided what I wanted to do with it. Of course, I'd need some sort of agent to look after it for me, wouldn't I?"

He looked at her circumspectly. "Why?"

"For looking after the rentals. I can't look after it from Canada, can I?"

Silence stretched between them until she felt the very wallpapered walls vibrate with it.

"Ah, yes. I see." Philip moved to the head of the stairs. "I'm sure Mr. Charing would be happy to help you with that."

As she followed him down the stairs, Tessa was tempted to kick him. After all that had happened between them, she expected him to show a little more emotion when she talked of returning to Canada.

Vicky and Jason were enthusiastically exploring the garden and the disused stables. "You could almost build another house here," Vicky said.

"I doubt that you'd be able to get planning permission for that," Philip said.

He seemed to be in a particularly pedantic mood today, Tessa thought.

The garden was large, with an overgrown rockery and several fruit trees, one of them laden with dark red plums. "It needs quite a bit of work." Tessa felt a stirring of excitement. She'd love to get her hands on it. She could see in her mind's eye how lovely the rockery would be if it were rebuilt and replanted.

"Come and see back here," Vicky said. Tessa followed Vicky to the old stables, the wood of the horse boxes crumbling away, the doors hanging askew on rusty hinges.

"You know, Vicky. If this was all cleaned up it would make a marvelous studio and workshop for you." Tessa was thinking aloud.

"Oh, Tessa. That's just what I was thinking."

Vicky's face glowed. "That little shed at Langley is so small. I'd pay you rent, of course. The great thing would be that I could work and have a salesroom on the same premises. If I got planning permission, of course," she said, grinning at Philip.

"Oh, I think something like a workshop for hand-crafted furniture would be well received," he said. "Anything to do with traditional crafts is acceptable in the Dales. Although, having seen some of your work, Vicky, I'm not sure that the word 'traditional' quite applies."

"I can be traditional, if I have to be," Vicky said, laughing. "I'll dig out some of my early work when the inspector or whatever he is comes to visit." Her smile faded. "Oh, Tessa. I'm a total idiot. Here I am, making my own plans for your property. No wonder Grandmother calls me impulsive. I'm sorry. Talk about putting you on the spot."

"That's all right. After all, it was my idea in the first place. Or was I just picking up on your thought waves?"

"Probably." They exchanged grins.

"What about me?" Jason asked, his expression sullen.

"What about you?" Tessa asked.

"I'd like to live here. Don't forget I'm staying in England."

"Staying or not, I couldn't afford to give you this large house to live in. Sorry, love, but I have to treat it as an investment. Although it's in super condition, it will still need a lot spent on it in upkeep."

"I'm hoping that you'll think of Thornton as your home for vacation time," Philip said to Jason.

"Vacation time?" Jason repeated.

"Yes, I understood that you wanted to go to university or to take your degree at a college of some sort."

"Yeah, that's right. I suppose."

"You'll have to live away from the Dales then."

"Look, let's discuss all this later," Tessa said abruptly. "I can't quite see the point of making important decisions regarding people's futures in a disused stable yard, can you?" She marched away to Philip's Land Rover.

"You haven't seen the basement flat yet," Philip said, frowning, when he reached the car.

"I've seen all I need to see at present. I take it I can come back again?"

"Of course."

"Fine." She got into the front seat and slammed the door hard. Vicky and Jason scrambled into the back.

"Where to now?" Philip asked as he started up the car.

"To Leyburn Market," Tessa said. "I thought that's what we'd planned."

"I thought you might have changed your mind," Philip said stiffly. He glanced across at her, but she kept her gaze straight ahead of her as they drove down the hill and then negotiated the one-lane bridge across the River Ure.

When they turned into the Leyburn road, the traffic moved at a snail's pace. There were cars parked on both sides of the road and people on foot perpetually crossing over. Many of them bore wicker baskets on their arms.

The entire town square, which on normal days was a car park, was filled with stalls and booths bearing old books, new pillows, fish, cheese, locally grown vegetables, lampshades, T-shirts, and leather goods. People milled about, shopping and exchanging gossip.

"I'd forgotten how exciting market day is," Tessa said, leaning out of the window to get a closer look.

"Do you want to get out here then?" Philip asked. "We could be stuck in this line-up for ages."

"No, I can wait. I'd never find you again in this crowd."

As they were sitting waiting for the traffic to move, Tessa caught sight of James Barton standing outside the Bolton Arms, in earnest conversation with another man.

"There's James. I wonder if he's thrown your luggage out yet?" she said jokingly to Vicky.

James handed some sort of paper to the other man, who was glancing up and down the street, as if he were nervous. His head was covered by a tweed cap, pulled down low over his eyes.

"Looks as if they're passing illegal betting slips or something like that," Jason said.

"This isn't America, Jason," Vicky said. "There's a betting shop just around the corner from the fish-and-chip shop."

The traffic slowly began to move. The two men parted. James went around the corner of the hotel and the other man crossed the cobblestoned square, walking directly toward them.

"It's Peter," Jason exclaimed.

"So it is. That's a strange combination: James and Peter," Vicky said. "I would never have thought those two would be friends."

Philip was silent. Tessa glanced at him and saw that he was frowning.

The traffic ground to a halt again. Peter was about to cross the street when he caught sight of them. He froze on the edge of the street, a look of horror on his face. Then he turned and hurried way, disappearing into the crowd.

Chapter Thirty-two

After several minutes of driving around looking for a parking spot, they found one in the square by the police station, and then quickly walked back to the market.

"Sarah asked me to buy some cheese," Tessa said to Philip. "I don't know exactly what to get. I know you like Stilton and blue Wensleydale, but what else? Come and help me choose.'"

They left Vicky and Jason at a leather shop, arguing over the respective merits of an ale tankard or a wine goblet made of hardened leather.

As they walked through the crowded square to the cheese van, Philip drew Tessa's hand through his arm. The warmth of her hand and the way her shoulder and arm pressed against him was like a balm, easing the turmoil of worry in his mind. Yet he was still troubled by the incident with Peter.

Tessa halted a little way from the van. "You're worried about seeing Peter, aren't you?"

"You're very perceptive. Am I that easy to read?"

"No. But I saw the look on Peter's face, too. He was dead scared. Did you know he has a lover?"

"So I've heard. What about it?" he asked, frowning.

"Sarah says there's a rumor the man has AIDS."

"Peter?"

"No, his lover."

They stood looking at each other, people having to pass around them.

"It may be just a rumor," Tessa said. "After all, Sarah is a bit of a gossip, isn't she?"

"She is, but secrets are hard to keep in the Dales. Does she know where Peter's lover lives?"

"Apparently he's in a cottage in the remote part of Coverdale somewhere. She says that a doctor makes weekly visits."

"I didn't know that. All I do know is that Peter has been acting very strangely recently. As if his mind is on something other than work, which isn't like him at all. When we get back, I shall have to drop in on him at the lodge and have a talk with him."

Philip didn't have to go to the lodge. As soon as they entered the house after waving good-bye to Vicky, Sarah told him that Peter was waiting to see him in the library.

When he turned to Tessa, Philip's expression was grave. "Forgive me, but this could be important. Go ahead and have your tea. I'll join you later." He walked briskly to the library.

When he pushed open the door Peter was standing by the antique globe, slowly twirling it around. He looked up. Philip could see that his face was drained of color beneath the outdoor tan.

"Sit down, Peter," he said.

"I would rather stand, if you don't mind, sir." Peter rarely called him sir.

"Very well." Whiskey rushed up to greet Philip, but he acknowledged him with a quick pat and then ordered him back to his basket by the hearth. "What is it you wished to see me about?" he asked, folding his arms and leaning his back against the bookshelves.

Peter was holding the tweed cap he'd worn as an attempt at a disguise. He twirled it round and round.

"I knew I had to come to you, but I don't know how to start."

"Let's see if I can help you," Philip said, not unkindly. "Has it something to do with our seeing you in Leyburn earlier?"

"Yes." Peter looked utterly wretched.

"You had just had a meeting with James Barton."

"He was giving me money."

Philip frowned. "Money? Why was James Barton giving you money?"

Peter swallowed hard. "It was my final payoff."

"Payoff for what?"

Peter stared at him, trying to speak but unable to do so. Then his eyes filled with tears. "I'm sorry. I'm terribly sorry. I should never have done it. But I was so desperate for money ..."

It came to Philip with a sudden rush. The cross! It was Peter who had taken the Thornton Treasure. He stared at the younger man standing before him. After a moment, Philip went to Peter and led him, as if he were blind, to a chair at the table. "Sit down. I'm going to fetch you a brandy."

"No!" The word came out like a pistol shot. "I don't want anything. I just want to tell you and then get the hell out of here."

"Very well." Philip sat down opposite him. "I'm listening."

Peter held his arm across his eyes as he struggled to control himself. Philip averted his face and called to Whiskey to come sit by him. The spaniel padded across the room and laid his muzzle on his knee. Philip ran his silken ears through his hands, speaking softly to him.

Peter took a checked handkerchief from his jeans pocket and blew his nose loudly. "Sorry about that." Two round spots of color stood out on his cheeks.

Philip shook his head. "You were saying that you were desperate for money," he prompted gently.

Peter nodded. "Andrew ..." He swallowed again. "My friend, Andrew, has AIDS. He's very sick. He'll last only a few more months, if that. I've had to hire a nurse for him. He's terrified of going back to the hospital. And then there's the rent for the cottage and all the extra medical equipment. They only give him the basics. I had to provide the rest of it."

"Why didn't you come to me?" Philip asked.

"Because you've already been too bloody good to me. Given me the lodge rent-free. Paid me more than you can afford. How could I come to you, for Christ's sake, and ask for money to keep my lover who was dying from AIDS? I was terrified you'd find out. I knew that you'd throw me out on my ear when you heard that."

Philip sighed. "It's a great shame you didn't trust me more."

"I couldn't risk it," Peter said. "If I lost my job I would've been up the creek."

"So you stole the cross."

"They made me."

"When you say 'they,' I take it you mean James Barton?"

"Aye, that's right. The bastard came to me and said that he'd spill the beans about Andrew to you if I didn't do what he asked."

Philip stirred angrily in his chair. "So it was blackmail?"

"Partly." Peter knotted and unknotted the handkerchief as he spoke. "He threatened me with telling you. Then he offered me money."

"How much?"

"A thousand pounds." Peter looked at him defiantly. "It meant that I could pay off the money I owed the bookmaker. I'd been betting on the horses to try to make some extra. The rest of the money I used to give Andrew some of the luxuries he needed to make him comfortable for the last few months of his life."

"If James gave you that much money, I take it that he wasn't in this alone. Was it a gang of some sort?"

"I can't tell you," Peter said sullenly.

Philip stood up. "I'm sorry, but you're going to have to tell me. I want names of all the people that you know were involved in this plot." He whirled around and leaned across the table bringing his face near Peter's. "I take it that you passed the cross on to Barton."

"Yes," Peter whispered.

"And he has sold it so some private buyer, some foreigner, who has spirited it out of the country." Philip spoke with controlled violence. He was so angry at the thought of the treasure that had been in his family for centuries leaving England that he came close to punching Peter in the face.

"No."

"What do you mean, 'no'?" Philip demanded. "I want more names and more information, or I shall phone the police and let them take over. Which would you prefer?"

Peter shrugged. "What difference does it make if I speak to the police now or later?"

Philip's eyes narrowed. "If you tell me the entire truth it might make one hell of a difference."

"That's not going to be easy."

"Dammit, man. It can't be any more difficult than telling me you stole the cross, can it?"

"James says she has long arms."

"What does that mean?"

"It means she can get at people, however far they go. He said she's done it before."

"Who is this anonymous 'she' you're speaking about?"

"I'd rather not say."

Philip was losing patience. "Well, you're going to stay here until you do. Does this woman have the cross?"

"Yes. James says it's perfectly safe. The plan was to give it back to me once the purpose of the theft succeeded."

"To give the cross back to you?" Philip repeated.

"Yes. Then I'd put it back in the case. It would just be . . . be found there one morning."

Philip shook his head in exasperation. "This whole thing isn't making any sense. I know you're not a fool, Wilson, so please stop acting like one and tell me who this woman is."

"I can't. I just can't."

"All right. Let's go down another path. You said the cross would be returned once the plan succeeded? What was the purpose of the theft, if it wasn't to sell the cross and make a great deal of money from it?"

Peter's eyes blinked rapidly. He turned his head away.

"I've reached the end of my patience, Wilson. Either you answer my questions or I telephone the police."

"The whole idea was to put the blame on Jason."

Peter spoke so softly that Philip barely caught the words, but the gist of what Peter said came to him clearly. "You mean that the cross was stolen solely to discredit Jason?" he asked incredulously.

Peter nodded. "It was felt that he and your brother were getting too close, that something was needed to get rid of him, send him back to Canada in disgrace."

The meaning of his words struck Philip like a hammer blow. "And you were a party to all this? God, I'm so disappointed in you. And don't tell me again that you had to do it for Andrew."

"I did. He comes first. Wouldn't you do the same for Tessa?"

Philip stared at him and then said, "Not until I'd explored every other possibility."

"I was afraid of losing this job."

"So you keep saying. You should have realized how much I rely on you here. You do the work of three men. Or you did, until this happened."

"I've been worried sick. I haven't been able to think straight."

"I'm not surprised." Philip was torn by a mixture of emotions: disappointment, frustration, but mostly anger. "There's only one woman diabolical enough to have plotted against Jason this way. Only one woman who would have any cause to do so. I take it that Sybil Hargrave was the mastermind behind all of this?"

Peter hesitated.

"For God's sake, Peter. Once I knew why, it doesn't take a genius to work out who. It was Mrs. Hargrave, right?"

"Yes."

"Christ in heaven!" Philip released a long sigh. "Thank God Steven is dead. This might have been the last straw for him. I never did understand why he continued to love that woman, despite all she did. God knows how Tessa will react to this." He paced to the bay window and back again. "So Sybil somehow found out about Andrew and your bookmakers' bills and used Barton as a go-between to both blackmail and bribe you. Is that correct?"

"Yes. I need this job. I couldn't risk your finding out."

"We've been through all that before," Philip said wearily.

"Many people would have told me to leave, once they knew I was living with someone dying of AIDS."

"I'm not many people. You should have known that. Have you been tested?"

"Yes. I'm clear so far."

"Good." Philip went back to the window and stared out at the stone terrace and the rose garden beyond it. "I think we've said all there is to say, don't you?" He didn't turn around.

"Aye, you're right there. I can't say how sorry I am. You've been good to me. You didn't deserve this."

Philip turned around. "Who knows what I deserve," he said, frowning.

"I'll go and pack up my things at the lodge."

"No."

A tide of red flooded Peter's face. "I didn't mean I was going to run off. I'll be there when the police come."

"Don't do anything until I've thought this thing through."

"But I—"

"Nothing," Philip said. "And that's an order. Just stay put until I come to the lodge. I need some time to myself to digest all this."

And to discuss it with Tessa, Philip thought, as he watched Peter leave the room. She had already suffered so much at Sybil's hands that he would have done anything to avoid having to tell her about her aunt's latest plot against her. But it affected both Tessa and Jason too personally not to tell them.

It occurred to Philip that he not only had to tell Tessa and Jason about Sybil's plot, but he also had to face Derek and apologize for having accused him of stealing the family cross.

This was turning out to be one hell of a day!

Chapter Thirty-three

Tessa was stunned by Philip's story of Sybil's plot to discredit Jason. "The woman's mentally sick," she said, shaking her head in disbelief. "To have hatched such a plot and played havoc with so many lives: Jason, Derek, you and me, Peter ... She is truly evil, twisted, isn't she?"

"No doubt she would say that everything she has done was done to protect her own. It's surprising how many people consider that to be justification for doing something, however criminal it might be."

"Oh, Philip. I suppose there's no way we can hide the truth."

"I've gone over and over it. If we just put the cross back without saying anything, the suspicion hanging over Jason and Derek—and even Sarah and her nephew—would always be there. No, the truth has to be told. I just hope it can be confined to the households of Langley and Thornton Manor. I shall have to have a very strict talk with Sarah. We don't want this spread across the Dales, like manure."

"What are you going to do about Peter?"

His gaze met hers. "I haven't decided yet. I was going to ask you for your opinion."

She held her breath, sensing that this was a most significant moment in their lives. Here was a very important decision involving Thornton Manor, and Philip was asking her for her opinion. Tessa hesitated for several seconds and then said, "Peter's going through a tough time. That's no excuse for his behavior, I know, but . . . you've also told me how much you value his work. You'd be lost without him, you said. I think you should think about both those factors before you come to your decision."

He gave her a slow smile that made her heart turn over. "Thank you, darling."

She needed no further encouragement to go into his arms. She was in need of comfort and so, she sensed, was he. They didn't kiss, but held each other close, her head on his chest, his cheek against her hair. She wished that they could go somewhere far away from all their problems and be alone together. They needed time for themselves, time to discover each other, time to discuss their future—if they had one together.

Philip drew away. "I wish I could stay with you, but I have to go to Langley. It's imperative that I get the cross back from Sybil before she hears about what's happened and gets rid of it."

"God, yes! She might just do that, to be vindictive."

"I also have to speak to Derek." Philip grimaced. "That will not be easy."

"I can imagine." Tessa looked down at her hands, rubbing her palms together nervously. There was something she must do, but she knew that he wouldn't want her to do it. "Philip . . ." She hesitated.

"Yes?"

"I want to be the one to confront Sybil with this."

"No. That's out of the question. I'm not subjecting you to that."

"It was my idea," she protested.

"I'm sorry, but it is not a good idea at all. Besides, you said you were never going back to Langley, remember?"

"I didn't realize at the time that I had unfinished

business." She pressed her hands against his chest, feeling the crispness of his shirt beneath them. "This is between me and Sybil. She has attacked my son to get at me."

"I think it's more likely that she did it to ensure that Derek and Jason didn't get too close," Philip said dryly. "But I think dealing with Sybil on an emotional level would be a mistake."

"Are you afraid that I'll not get the cross from her?"

"Partly. But I also don't want that woman to upset you any further."

"I'm a big girl, Philip. I can handle her. I promise I'll be as unemotional as possible with her. I *need* to do this," she said, pleading with him.

He studied her face. "Is it that important to you?" She nodded. "Very well. If it's what you want." She could see that he wasn't very happy about it.

"If I feel I'm not getting anywhere with her, I'll send for you immediately, okay?" She grasped the lapels of his sports jacket. "I just feel somehow responsible for this having happened. I want to be the one to return the cross to you."

He took her face in one hand. "And when that's done—and if we could possibly get some time alone together—we have a great many important things to discuss."

Tessa turned her face and kissed his palm. "Don't I know it!" she said.

Half an hour later, after they had told Jason everything, Philip went to Langley House with her. It was James Barton who answered the door, greeting them with his usual servility.

"Mr. Thornton, Miss Hargrave. What a pleasant surprise! Whom were you—"

Philip marched right past him. "Where is my brother?"

"Mr. Derek is in the wine cellar. Shall I—"

"Thank you, no. I'll find him myself." Philip walked across the hall.

James turned to Tessa, looking rather aggrieved. "He's in a bit of a hurry, isn't he?" he said, his impeccable accent slipping a little.

"Is my aunt in her bedroom?"

"Yes, she is, but she's not to—"

"Thank you." Tessa crossed the checkered tile floor.

"Mrs. Hargrave gave orders that she wasn't to be disturbed," James protested.

Tessa ignored him. She was about to start up the stairs when something made her turn around. James had his intercom out and was about to speak into it.

Letting out a yell, Tessa raced back across the hall, glad that she was still wearing the Reeboks she had put on for the walk around the market. James's pale eyes widened as she came at him. She grabbed the intercom from him and threw it on the ground. It smashed open, scattering batteries and parts across the floor.

"Bloody 'ell! What did you do that for, then?" This time his accent had definitely slipped.

"You just keep your mouth shut," she said, bending to pick up the smashed intercom.

Camilla appeared from the rear of the house. "What on earth is going on? I heard someone scream." She stopped short when she saw Tessa. "Was that you yelling? And what are you doing here?"

"It's all right, Camilla. I was just exercising my lungs at your exemplary butler here."

"What on earth for?" Camilla looked at James. "What *is* going on?"

He shrugged. "I have no idea, Mrs. Thornton. Miss Hargrave here seems to be having a bit of a brainstorm." He nodded at the broken intercom in Tessa's hand. "She just smashed that. Deliberately. Your mother won't be at all pleased."

Tessa was already walking away to the staircase.

"Where are you going?" Camilla demanded.

"Up to see your mother." Tessa continued up the stairs.

"You can't. She's resting. She hasn't been well."

Tessa leaned over the gallery railing. "What I have to say to Aunt Sybil will take only a few minutes," she told Camilla.

Camilla ran up the stairs. "I don't want you upsetting her," she said when she reached the top.

"If you don't let me see her," Tessa said quietly, watching James as she spoke, "there's going to be a scandal that could blow this family sky-high."

Camilla's eyes widened. "What sort of a scandal?"

"One involving the police. Philip is talking to Derek about it at this very minute."

Camilla's hand went to her throat. "Oh, God. What has Derek done now? I told him this morning that if he didn't get himself into a clinic I'd divorce him. What's happened?"

"You'll be glad to hear that this involves Derek only indirectly."

"What are you talking about?"

"I can't tell you until I've spoken to Sybil."

"I'll find out then?"

"That's right." Tessa walked away from her. "Wish me luck, Camilla."

Camilla followed her along the gallery. Tessa could hear her tapping along behind her. "Oh, God," Camilla gasped. "It's my mother, isn't it? She's done something awful again, hasn't she?"

"Don't worry. It's all going to work out." Tessa turned the corner and walked down the corridor that led to the main bedroom. When she reached the ivory-painted door, with its gilded moldings, she hesitated, her heart pounding. Then she knocked, at the same time opening the door.

Her aunt was lying back against the pile of pillows, reading a letter. Letters and papers were spread out all over the bed and another pile of crumpled pages lay on the floor, where Sybil had tossed them.

"Who is it? Whoever it is, I don't wish to see you. I said I wasn't to be disturbed while I went through my papers."

Tessa came into her view, walking to the foot of the bed. "It's me, Aunt Sybil."

"What appalling grammar!" Sybil glared at her. "What are you doing here? I thought I was rid of you."

"You and I have some unfinished business. I'll take only a few minutes of your time and then I'll go." Tessa spoke briskly, as if she were attending a business meeting. "Peter has confessed everything to Philip."

"Peter who?" Not even by a blink did Sybil's expression change.

"Peter Wilson, the man who manages Philip's grounds."

"Ah, yes. What does this Wilson man have to do with me?"

"A great deal, it appears."

Sybil shook her head, smiling blandly. "My dear girl, I don't think I've exchanged more than a few words with the man."

"I believe that. But you used James Barton as a go-between. You told James to blackmail and then bribe Peter."

Sybil looked away for a minute and then shook her head at Tessa. "My goodness me, I fear you have been watching too many American television shows. I've never heard such a silly story. Blackmailing Peter Watson—"

"Wilson."

"Wilson. Watson. Whatever the man's name is. What had he done that I should blackmail him?" Sybil smiled sweetly at Tessa, as if she were trying to humor her.

Calm and businesslike, Tessa reminded herself as she fought her anger and frustration. "Let's not play games, Sybil," she said. "You blackmailed Peter and then bribed him to steal the Thornton Cross."

This got a response. Sybil's tongue flicked out to lick her lips, as if they'd suddenly become dry. "Why would I do that? I have sufficient money of my own, thank you, without having to resort to stealing."

"That's an easy one to answer. You did it so that Jason would be blamed for the theft."

A hit. A palpable hit! thought Tessa as she saw the paper in Sybil's hands start to shake.

Sybil put down the paper and clenched her hands into fists. "Jason took the cross. Steven knew he had." Her eyes suddenly filled with tears. "That's what killed him."

"No, Sybil. You took the cross." She wondered whether Uncle Steven had guessed that Sybil was behind the theft.

"It was *Jason* who stole the cross," Sybil repeated, her fingers rustling aimlessly in the papers. "Jason took it." It was as if she had convinced herself that this was the truth, to avoid facing the reality of what she had done.

Tessa came closer to her. "No, he did not," she said quietly. "Peter has confessed everything. If you don't return the cross Philip will be forced to go to the police."

"Police?" Fear filled Sybil's eyes. "Philip would never involve the police."

"Yes, he most certainly would. Peter will give them a statement. Then they'll arrest James, who will no doubt tell them everything in order to save his own neck. It will be in all the newspapers. Can you imagine it? *Mistress of Langley House plans theft of ancient treasure.*"

"Philip wouldn't let them do that."

"Philip would do anything he had to do to get the cross back. And don't forget it belongs to your own son-in-law's family. Just imagine what a dreadful scandal it would be once it became public."

Sybil shrank back against her pillows. "It can't become public. It has to be hushed up."

Tessa steeled herself against pity. *Remember what this woman has done to you,* she reminded herself. "There's only one way to hush it up. Give me the cross, Sybil. I know you have it. If you give it to me now, Philip will not go to the police."

"How do I know that?" Sybil whispered.

"Once the cross is returned, there won't have been a theft, will there? So there would be no point in going to the police." Tessa held her breath as Sybil's devious brain was trying to work this out. "Where is the cross?" she asked very softly.

Sybil stared at her, her lips pursing as she sought for a way to get out of the inevitable. Then she turned over on her side, facing away from Tessa. "Under the bed," she said harshly.

"This bed?" Tessa almost laughed at the absurdity of it.

Sybil nodded, but didn't turn to face her.

Her heart beating fast, Tessa knelt down. She couldn't see anything because of the wooden steps that stood at the side of the bed to enable Sybil to climb in and out.

She moved to the other side of the bed. Kneeling again, she saw, toward the middle of the floor beneath the bed, what looked like a folded blanket. Lying flat on her stomach, she was just able to touch a corner of it. She stretched as far as she possibly could, and her fingers grasped the blanket. Slowly she dragged it toward her until it was in her grasp.

On the bed, Sybil remained utterly silent.

Tessa sat on the floor and lifted the parcel onto her lap. She unwrapped first the blanket and then a large piece of brown paper to reveal a large white box. It must have held a dress at one time. Tessa lifted off the lid. Inside was something wrapped in several sheets of white tissue paper.

It's like a game of Pass the Parcel, Tessa thought, a bubble of hysterical laughter catching in her throat. Her fingers tore at the tissue . . . to reveal, in all its simple beauty, the Thornton Treasure.

She ran her fingers over the golden figure of Christ, the three large hand-cut jewels in their medieval settings. "Thank God," she breathed, meaning it in its true sense, as a prayer of heartfelt gratitude.

Carefully setting the cross back in its bed of tissue, she replaced the lid on the box and scrambled to her feet.

Her aunt was in exactly the same position as before, so that she was facing Tessa, her eyes open and unblinking.

"I have the cross," Tessa said. "I'm going to return it to Philip right away."

Sybil's eyes blazed . . . and then the light died. "I was going to give it back to him at the right time," she said in a monotone. "I had no intention of harming Philip."

"I know that. I was that one you wanted to harm. But you didn't. In fact, by stealing the cross you have managed to bring Philip and me even closer to each other than we were before." Tessa smiled at her. It was not a smile of triumph or exultation, just a small satisfied smile. "You can't hurt me or mine anymore, Aunt Sybil. We are now beyond your reach."

Tessa tucked the box beneath her arm and left the room, quietly closing the door behind her.

Camilla was waiting outside. "What's that?" she asked, looking at the box.

Holding it protectively against her waist with one arm, Tessa removed the lid and lifted the tissue. Camilla looked inside. "Oh, my God." She looked at Tessa, her eyes round with horror. "She had it all this time?" she whispered.

Tessa nodded. "It was hidden under her bed."

"Does Philip know?" Camilla asked.

"That's why he's here. He's telling Derek at this moment."

Camilla began to cry. "Oh, God, Tessa. What can I say? I'm so sorry. She must have completely lost her mind. How on earth—"

"No doubt Derek will explain it all to you. Don't worry about it. It's all over now." Tessa began to walk away and then stopped. "One word of advice, though."

"What's that?"

"Get rid of your butler."

Chapter Thirty-four

The two brothers stood looking at each other in the dim light of the wine cellar.

"I've been telling Camilla for years that her mother was crazy," Derek said. "Now I'm convinced of it. I just hope that Tessa doesn't make a bollix of it. You should have dealt with it yourself."

"It was important to Tessa that she do this herself." Philip eyed his brother. "What lies between her and Sybil goes back a long way."

"You're right there." Derek cleared his throat loudly to cover his embarrassment.

"As I said before, I owe you an apology for having suspected you."

"Damned right, you do."

An awkward silence ensued. Philip felt annoyed at himself for not having found a way to do this gracefully, but he never had been able to communicate well with his brother. "At least it means that Jason's name has been cleared."

"Yes, yes. I'm glad of that. I hear he has thoughts of staying on here."

"Yes. Do you mind?"

"Well ... I think it might be awkward."

"Not really. He intends to study estate management. He'll probably have to go to Newcastle or Scotland for that. I told him that he's welcome to make Thornton his home."

"Good of you," Derek murmured. "Might be a bit dodgy at Langley for him."

"Quite."

Derek's face suddenly came out in red blotches. "Camilla's given me what you might call an ultimatum. 'Dry up or get out.' " Derek grinned sheepishly at Philip. "She seems to mean it." His mouth trembled. "Won't be easy."

"No, it won't," Philip agreed. "But you can do it, Durr." It had been many years since he'd called his younger brother by his childhood name. "You don't want to lose Langley, do you?"

"No."

Philip looked at his watch. Tessa had been upstairs for more than fifteen minutes. He really should go up and see what was happening.

Derek lifted one of the bottles of Pommard from the rack and wiped it clear of dust with a cloth. "I've a good mind to take this up with me for a final send-off."

Philip said nothing.

Derek held the bottle against his chest for a moment, and then put it back in the rack. "Talking about losing estates, what are you going to do about that bloody tax money you owe for Thornton?"

"A good question. The answer is, I don't know yet. This inheritance tax seems designed to take away the very homes our ancestors have nurtured over the centuries."

"You'll have to think of something pretty bloody quick. They won't be willing to wait much longer, will they?"

Philip shook his head.

"I think it's time you took my advice. After all, I am heir to the bloody place. You'll have to open Thornton Manor up to the public. Hire it out for conferences and such. After all, Lord Spencer does it at

Althorp and he's Prince Charles's brother-in-law, at least for now."

"Althorp's a huge mansion, with pots of room," Philip said, annoyed. "Thornton's nothing like Althorp, as you damned well know. The rooms are small, not at all designed to deal with large groups of people." The thought of having conferences at Thornton was so appalling that he wasn't willing even to discuss it.

"Why don't you sell it?"

Philip straightened up, almost jolting the wine rack beside him. "Sell Thornton?"

"Not Thornton, you fool. The cross. Must be worth a million. That would pay the inheritance tax, at the very least. There should even be some left over."

Meaning, Philip thought, that he—Derek—might get some of the residue. "You're right, but I hate to think of someone in some private mansion a thousand miles away gloating over it. The Thornton Cross is not just part of our own personal history, but that of Yorkshire as well."

Derek shrugged. "It was just an idea. After all, you can't afford to insure it. This time you got it back, but it could be stolen again. Next time, it could be gone for good and you wouldn't have made a brass farthing out of it."

"Are you down there, Derek?" Camilla's high-pitched voice came wafting down the stairs to them.

Derek raised his eyebrows at Philip. "I'd better go. Yes," he shouted back. "Philip's with me."

"Come up," Camilla called. "I have to talk to you." There was a panicky edge to her voice.

Derek rolled his eyes. "I think she's found out."

"That's probably a good sign. Tessa must have told her."

Derek went to the foot of the stairs, and then turned to his brother again. "About Tessa," he said.

"Yes?"

"Is she going back to Canada or staying here?"

"Believe it or not, it's been so hectic for the past two days I haven't had time to find out, but I fully intend to do so tonight."

Derek gave him a wry smile. For a suspended moment, Philip had the strange feeling that he was looking at his father.

"It was always you Tessa really wanted, anyway," Derek said and, leaning heavily on the banister rail, began to climb the stairs.

Tessa and Camilla stood in the kitchen passage. Tessa was holding a large white box. She smiled when she saw Philip, and then held out the box to him.

He remained very still for a moment, and then he took the box from her. "Thank you," was all he said, but the brightness in his eyes was her reward.

"Aren't you going to open it?"

"Not here, no."

Tessa looked from Camilla to Derek. "No," she murmured, "there's no need, is there? Can we go now?"

"Certainly. Oh, one more thing, Derek. Just a reminder. Deal with Barton, or I will."

"He's in the office," Camilla said grimly. "I've told him to wait there until we come."

"I'll deal with him by myself," Derek said.

As they began an argument as to who should deal with James Barton, Philip and Tessa took the opportunity to slip away.

Tessa had hoped that Philip might take advantage of their being alone together in the car to talk about some of those important matters he'd mentioned earlier. To her disappointment, he seemed strangely preoccupied. He barely asked her about her meeting with Sybil, just telling her that he'd be interested to hear all the details tonight. Then he looked at his watch for the third time, muttered, "Four-fifteen," and put his foot on the gas.

Her heart sank with disappointment, and as they sped silently back to Thornton Manor, resentment slowly built inside her. After all, she had dealt adroitly with Sybil and retrieved the cross for him without any family scandal.

As soon as they got back, he strode ahead of her into the house. With a cool, "Excuse me, I have to make an important telephone call," he disappeared into his study.

Jason rushed into the hall. "What happened? Didn't you get the cross back?"

Tessa flung her leather shoulder bag on a chair. "Yes, we got the bloody thing back."

"Hey, no need to bite my head off! I should've thought you'd be pretty excited. Instead, you look as if someone died."

Tessa smiled and put her arm around him, hugging him to her side. "Sorry, love. I'm truly thrilled that we've got it back."

"Not as much as I am. After all, no one thought *you* had stolen it."

"You're right. It must be a big relief for you."

"What did your aunt say when you accused her? Did you have a huge fight? Boy, I wish I'd been there."

"I'll tell you everything about it in a minute. I'm dying for a cup of tea—or something stronger."

Jason peered at her face. "Have you and Philip had a fight?"

"Not exactly. He's just acting very strangely and I'm mad at him, that's all."

"I thought he'd be happy about getting the Thornton Cross back."

"I did, too, but something's eating at him. As he

doesn't seem to want to talk about it, I don't know what it is."

"Doesn't sound like Philip," Jason said, frowning.

"Probably something to do with Thornton itself. He was talking to Derek. Who knows? Something Derek said might have upset him."

They were sitting at the large pine table in the kitchen, having tea, when Philip came in about twenty minutes later.

"Ah, this is where you are. I've been looking for you." He was grinning at them like a Cheshire cat, totally transformed from the silent, preoccupied Philip she had driven home with.

"What's happened?"

He cast a frowning glance at Sarah's back. "Tell you in a minute," he mouthed. "Have you finished tea?" he asked.

"We have. Sarah made my favorite coffee walnut cake. Thanks, Sarah, that was great."

"Glad you liked it. You want some tea, Mr. Philip?"

"Good idea." He went to fetch a tray from the dresser. "Give me a small pot of tea and a slice of Tessa's cake and I'll take it out onto the terrace. Too nice to eat indoors."

"You go on out and I'll bring it out to you."

"No, I'll take it with me. You've got enough to do without having to carry trays around."

Sarah set the tray with a small brown pot of steaming tea, made the old-fashioned way with loose tea leaves, a jug of milk, and a plate of hot wheaten scones, with an earthenware jar filled with Thornton's own creamy honey. She handed Tessa a separate plate bearing three large slices of cake. "In case you and Jason want more."

"There's enough food here to feed an army," Philip complained, but he was smiling.

In fact, he hadn't stopped smiling since he first came

into the kitchen. Tessa was so bursting with impatience that Philip didn't even have the chance to pour his tea before she demanded, "What on earth is going on? You hardly speak a word to me on the journey home. And now you're acting like a cat with the cream."

"Actually this is milk," he said, smiling as he poured the milk into his teacup.

"Milk or cream, it's going to be all over your head if you don't tell me what's happened."

"Patience, patience." His eyes danced with a mischievous light. "All will be divulged."

"Shall I go?" Jason asked, looking from one to the other of them.

"No, no. This will be of interest to you, too, Jason. In fact, the whole idea was prompted by something you said to me."

"Something *I* said?" Jason looked bewildered.

"Yes. The first time I showed you the Thornton Treasure you said something about it being a shame that it was locked away, so that no one else could see it. Your mother had said much the same thing earlier to me." He glanced at Tessa. "I probably snapped at her at the time," he said wryly.

"You did."

"Anyway, I realize that I can't possibly afford to insure the cross. Derek said today that it could easily be stolen again and that it would be better to sell it before that happened. He was right. There's been that recent crop of thefts from houses and castles in Scotland and England. And only last week thieves stole a magnificent medieval chest from a church in Norfolk. Unscrupulous foreign collectors are willing to pay large sums for such treasures, no questions asked."

Jason shifted impatiently on the wooden garden bench.

"So," Philip continued, "I have decided that I

would far rather have the Thornton Cross on view to the public than hidden away in some private collector's house thousands of miles away from Yorkshire."

"You're going to sell it?" Jason said.

"Not exactly." Philip paused for effect, well aware of his audience's impatience. "I just made a telephone call to my contact at Inland Revenue. We have come to a tentative agreement, subject to confirmation, of course. They will take the cross in lieu of payment of the inheritance taxes that are owing on Thornton Manor."

"Oh, Philip, that's wonderful," Tessa said, knowing what it must have cost him to come to this decision. No wonder he'd been so preoccupied on the journey back to Thornton. "But what will they do with it?"

"Ah, that's where you and Jason come into it. I told Redding—the man at the tax office—that it must be put into a museum open to the public, as it is part of the history of Yorkshire. Redding is going to work it out, but he thinks that the York Museum would be very happy to have it."

"Hey, that's great," Jason said.

"I thought you'd be pleased," Philip said. He turned to Tessa. "What do you think?"

"I think you're marvelous." She jumped up and leaned over to kiss him on the cheek. But as her mouth came down, Philip turned his head to meet her lips with his.

Our first public kiss, Tessa thought as she heard Jason's appreciative whistle.

Philip smiled at her as she sat down again. "Now I know I did the right thing."

"I don't suppose Derek will be too happy about you exchanging the cross for the taxes," Jason said.

"Why do you say that?" Philip asked.

"Because he wanted you to sell it. I guess he thought he might get some money if you sold it."

"You have a singularly astute mind, my dear nephew. Yes, I suspect that Derek will not be at all happy about it. But, despite his wish for money from the Thornton Manor estate, I also suspect that he wouldn't have wanted the cross to leave this country. Besides, he has other, more pressing matters on his mind, at present."

"What?" Jason asked.

Philip looked at him speculatively. "I think that, as Derek's son, you should know—and will also be glad to know—that he intends to admit himself to a clinic."

Jason reddened. "Thanks for telling me," he muttered. "It's been worrying me."

"I'm sure it has. It has been worrying all his relatives. I'm sure that Vicky, too, will be very relieved. It is very hard to see a parent abusing himself with drugs or alcohol."

Tessa knew that Philip must be thinking of his own father, who had almost lost Thornton Manor through his drinking and gambling, and then left it in a dilapidated state to his son, without any money to maintain it.

Philip stood up. "Jason, would you mind very much if your mother and I deserted you tonight?"

Jason looked puzzled. "No, of course not. Why?"

"I want to take her out for a celebratory meal. I know we should include you, considering we are celebrating the return of the Thornton Treasure, but—" Philip broke off, frowning. "Where is it, by the way? I take it you brought it in from the car, Tessa?"

She clapped her hand to her mouth. "Oh, my God, no I didn't. It must still be there."

They looked at each other and then burst out laughing.

"It's just lying in the car?" Jason asked. "You idiots." He took off, racing around the house to the stables.

"Idiots is right," Philip said, his laughter dying away. He looked at her, his eyes filled with a brilliant light. "Would you like to go out on our own for dinner tonight? Jason won't mind, will he?"

"No, I'm sure he won't. He'll probably go to the pub with Vicky. I think Vicky could do with a good chat with him tonight. She's going to be pretty upset about her grandmother's involvement with the theft of the cross. It's not fair, is it? Grandparents are supposed to be special."

"Her grandparent is certainly special, but not in the way you mean."

Tessa caught sight of Jason coming around the corner of the house. "Here he comes." He was walking carefully across the grass toward them. "Thank God, he's got the cross. Can you imagine how we'd feel if it had been taken from the car? Especially after all I went through to get it."

"I'm looking forward to hearing all about that tonight."

Jason came up the steps, cradling the white box in his arms. "It was lying there on the back seat. You hadn't even locked the car," he said, sounding like a reproving parent. "I'm going to put it back in its case."

"Thank you, Jason," Philip said. "I think that would be best."

Jason's expression became even more concerned. "What about Peter, though? Will he be back in the house again?"

"No, he won't be," Philip said. "At least, not today. I asked him to stay in the lodge until I came to see him."

Jason sat down, resting the box in his lap. "What are you going to do about him? Will you turn him over to the police?"

"No. I don't want the police involved, for obvious reasons."

"Yeah. You'd have to tell them all about Aunt Sybil, wouldn't you?"

"That's right. What would you do about Peter, Jason?"

Tessa was surprised. For a second time today, Philip was asking for someone else's opinion.

Jason also looked surprised. "Me?" He shrugged. Then, when he saw that Philip was waiting for his response, he said slowly, "The guy was obviously under a lot of stress, because of his—his lover and the AIDS thing. And he wasn't given much choice, was he? Steal the cross or he could be fired from his job. Mind you, I think he was nuts not to come to you right away and tell you."

"So do I. It sounds to me as if you think I should go easy on him."

"I didn't say that. He deserves to be fired—or worse. How can you trust him now?"

"A good point. Should I give him another try, do you think? Or just let him go?"

Jason considered this. "I think it'd be safe to give him a try. He's a hard worker and he knows the estate well. And I think—" He stopped, his face going red.

"What?" Philip asked.

"Now that you know about his lover, couldn't he stop having to hide him away? Wouldn't it be easier if he lived with him, near where he works? It can't be for much longer, can it? How would it hurt?"

"How, indeed?" Philip said with a faint smile. "Thank you for your advice, Jason."

"Sure. Anytime," Jason said, not quite sure why his mother was smiling at him in that weird way. "I'll put the cross in its case."

"Good." Philip watched him as he went through the

kitchen garden and into the house. "You have a fine son there, Tessa Hargrave."

"Yes, I know," Tessa said, blinking away tears. "It wasn't always easy, but ... I think he's going to be okay." She touched Philip's hand. "In just one month, you've exerted a tremendous influence on him, Philip. Thank you for caring so much about him."

"I have two reasons for doing so. He is your son and he is my brother's son. No, three reasons. The last one more selfish than the first two. With training—and some years of experience on another estate—I'm hoping that Jason will help me manage the Thornton Manor estate one day."

"Do you really think he could?"

"I wouldn't have said so if I didn't think so."

"He truly loves this place, doesn't he?" Tessa looked out over the gardens, the sloping fells rising beyond them.

"He does. Strange, when you think that he hadn't set foot in England until a few weeks ago."

"Yes. Canada has always been Jason's home. I grew to love Canada over the years. I'll always be grateful to my adopted country for what it has given me."

"Yet Jason seems to love the Dales as if he'd been born here. As does his mother, I believe."

"You know I do. I always have done. But it wasn't until I came back to England that I realized how Thornton had always symbolized the true meaning of home for me."

Although she hadn't intended it that way, it was a perfect opening, but to her disappointment Philip scraped back his chair and stood up.

"I must go and see Peter," he said with a little sigh. "He's waited long enough. He must be a bundle of nerves by now."

"What will you tell him?" Tessa was beginning to

think that everything was more important to Philip than she was.

"I shall take the advice of my advisers. Tell him I shall give him another chance. Ask him to bring his friend to the lodge."

"That is kind."

"No, no. Not at all. Very calculating of me, really. Peter will work much better if his mind isn't over in another dale, worrying all the time about his friend ... and perhaps we can help to share the burden of caring for him." He looked down at Tessa. "Will you excuse me leaving you for a while?"

"Of course. What time do you want to go out?"

"Let's say seven. Will that be enough time for you?"

Far too long, she thought, wondering how on earth she was going to pass an hour and a half. "That's fine," she said. "We have lots to talk about," she added, desperate to get some sort of a hint as to what was on his mind.

"We do. It's hard to believe that Steven was buried only yesterday, isn't it? I feel as if weeks have gone by. Remind me, when do you intend to fly back to Canada?"

The question took her by surprise. "I'm booked to go back in three days."

"Right. That's not long at all, is it?" He got up and began piling the dishes on the tray.

"Leave that. I'll do it," Tessa said.

"Thank you. See you at seven, then."

He walked away, leaving her feeling far more unsure of the future than she had been only a few minutes before.

Chapter Thirty-five

As it happened, Tessa did not have enough time to get ready for her dinner with Philip, because Jason wanted to hear all the details of her meeting with Sybil.

"I have to go now, Jason," she said when she'd answered most of his questions. "I've got about forty minutes to have a bath and get changed."

"Big date, eh?" he said, grinning at her.

She made a face at him. "Our first."

"No. Is it really? Wow! You two don't move very fast, do you?"

"We haven't had the chance, have we?"

"Have a good time." Jason switched on the television.

"Thanks." She went out into the hall, then went back into the small sitting room that acted as a television room. Philip didn't like having television in any of the main rooms. "What shall I wear?"

"How should I know? Is it a posh place?"

"I should imagine so."

"Not a pub supper or the fish-and-chip shop in Leyburn?"

"Hardly. Quit wasting my time, Jason."

"Okay, okay. I don't even know what clothes you've brought with you this time."

"Should I wear black, because of Uncle Steven?"

"No, he liked bright colors. Did you bring that tropical green cotton suit thing?"

"As a matter of fact I did. God knows why. It's hardly suitable for a funeral. Or after a funeral, either."

"Wear that." Jason turned back to the television, now immersed in watching the soccer results.

Football, Tessa reminded herself, *not soccer.* "Are you seeing Vicky tonight?"

"Yeah. She called. She wants to come over here. There's a great sci-fi flick on the telly tonight." It occurred to Tessa that Jason was becoming very British.

"I thought she might be going out with Kevin."

"No. She likes him, but she's off men for a while. She said brothers don't count." He grinned at Tessa.

"Do you like having a half sister?"

"Sure, I do. Especially one almost my own age. That's cool."

"Tell Vicky I'll be speaking to her soon."

"You can see her when you get back from dinner. She'll still be here."

"Fine," Tessa said, leaving the room. She wasn't sure that she'd be in the mood for seeing Vicky when she came back. It all depended on Philip's mood, of course.

When she ran down the stairs it was almost a quarter past seven. He was waiting for her in the great hall, standing by the oriel window, looking out through the mullioned glass.

"Sorry I'm late," she said breathlessly. "Jason caught me just before I went upstairs."

"No need to apologize."

Philip was dressed in a lightweight formal suit of charcoal-gray, with a white shirt striped with pale gray and a cranberry-red silk tie.

"You look absolutely splendid," she told him.

"Thank you. And so, may I say, do you."

His mood was even more formal than his suit. Had Tessa not known him better, she might have said that he was extremely nervous about something. But Philip was always in control of the situation, so it must just be her own tension that was affecting her.

"Now that I see you, I wonder if this is dressy enough," she said nervously. "Perhaps I should have worn the black dress I wore to Steven's funeral."

"Definitely not," he said vehemently. "You look young and summery in that fresh green. In fact, you look as you did when you were sixteen."

She laughed. "I wish."

He looked at his watch. "Shall we go? I reserved a table for seven-thirty and it's now twenty minutes past."

He held the door open for her and then led the way out to the car.

"Where are we going?" Tessa asked as he raced off down the driveway. "Or is it a secret?"

"Not at all. I'm afraid we didn't have sufficient time to go very far. I should like to have taken you to the Box Tree at Ilkley. But there's a very acceptable restaurant in an old inn near Richmond. The food is good and it's usually quiet. At least it was when I was last there, in March."

The inn may have been quiet when Philip was there in March, but now, at the height of the tourist season, the car park was crammed, and people overflowed from the bars into the gardens at the rear, spilling laughter and music—and beer—with them.

When he got out of the car, Philip stared at the old inn. "Damn. This wasn't such a good idea, was it?"

Tessa tucked her hand into his arm. "It looks lovely. Come on. Let's have a nice meal and then we can go and find somewhere quiet afterwards."

The strained look eased a little. "You're right."

They pushed their way through the busy bar into

the central hall. Brass and copper winked at them from the old oak beams. The maître d' approached them. "Good evening, Mr. Thornton. Madam. Allow me to find you a seat in the private bar, where it is a little less noisy."

"I hadn't expected to find you so busy tonight," Philip said.

His disappointment increased Tessa's tension. *For heaven's sake, it's a Friday night in August,* she felt like saying. *What did you expect?*

"It's very warm, sir. The heat brings people out, I suppose."

"We'll go directly to our table, I think, rather than ordering in the bar."

"Very well, sir."

The restaurant was delightful. Low ceilings, soft lighting, small tables set with shell-pink tablecloths on which stood shining silver tableware, candles, and vases of fresh summer flowers.

"This is better," Philip said as the maître d' held Tessa's chair for her.

As soon as they had been given the menus and had their drink orders taken, Tessa leaned forward to run her fingers across Philip's forehead.

He gave her a quick smile. "What was that for?"

"I'm trying to get rid of that frown. Relax. I've never known you to be so edgy before."

"I had hoped—"

"It's lovely here," she said firmly.

"I wanted it to be perfect."

Their eyes met. "We're here together," she said softly. "That's as perfect as it can get for me."

He gazed at her for what seemed a long time.

"Now, that's wrong?" she demanded.

"I was just thinking how strange it feels to be sitting across a table from you, after all the years we've spent apart. We know each other so well and yet we've never had dinner out together before."

Tessa knew what he meant. It was as if the grown-up Philip Thornton had taken sixteen-year-old Tessa Hargrave out for her first special grown-up meal.

God! she thought. *Will we ever be able to get over that hurdle?*

The waiter brought their drinks, a Tio Pepe for Tessa and a Perrier for Philip.

They were about to resume their conversation when the waiter returned to take their order. When he left them, Philip held up his glass. "I'll drink to you again, when we have the wine, but for now, here's a toast: To Tessa, who has brought great change and excitement to our lives." He smiled at her over his glass and then drank from it.

"Thank you. I don't know about me bringing them about, but there certainly have been changes for us all this summer. I think we should drink to Uncle Steven. If he hadn't written that letter to me in June, I would never have come home."

"You're not sorry you did, are you?"

"Not anymore. I was, when Jason arrived and caused such a turmoil. And then when ..." she faltered, searching for the right words, "when we had that violent disagreement over Thornton, I was sure I had made a big mistake."

"I was being ridiculously hypersensitive. Thornton means a great deal to me. I was sure there was no way to avoid selling it." He leaned forward. "That's one matter I wanted to talk to you about, Tessa. Thornton. We've solved the problem with the inheritance taxes, but the question is: Where to now? You said you had some ideas. If I promise not to explode, would you be willing to share them with me?"

Tessa bit her lip. Was that why he'd invited her out to dinner, to discuss ideas for saving Thornton? "I did have some ideas ... but when we parted after my last visit, I was so mad at you for taking Jason's side against me, they all flew out of my mind."

"I'm glad you've forgiven me for that."

"Besides, you were so angry with me for suggesting that you might have to explore ways to open Thornton to the public to make money, I thought there was no point in thinking anymore about it."

Philip looked suitably contrite. "Once again, I apologize. It's hard for me to accept that there might not be any other alternative."

"I understand that," Tessa said, still not sure what he wanted from her. "I should imagine there are plenty of things you could do with Thornton, if you set your mind to it. Personally, with my uncle's death and the funeral, I haven't really had the time to think about it recently."

Her voice was sharp with annoyance.

"Would you be willing to do so?"

She stared at him. "Are you offering me a job as a consultant to develop your stately home?"

He stared at her, a white pinched look about his mouth. "What have I said to upset you so much? I thought you wanted to discuss Thornton with me."

She slammed down her sherry glass, so that some of the pale gold liquid splattered the tablecloth. "Certainly, I do. What do you want to know?"

"I want to know if you would be willing to help me build up Thornton again? I'm not sure I could do it alone. You see," he said softly, his long fingers adjusting the silverware, aligning large and small knives, "I'm not only ten years older than you, I'm also rather old-fashioned. I need to be dragged into the twentieth century, let alone the twenty-first. But I fear that it wouldn't be at all fair to ask you to do the dragging. It would mean you would have to leave your home in Canada and your job." He leaned his elbow on the table and rested his forehead in his hand. "If you were to accept my offer, it would be on your own terms, of course."

She was utterly, totally lost. What on earth was he asking her? To be his consultant? His companion? His mistress? His business manager? His wife? What?

Philip was usually so articulate, but tonight he was incomprehensible. She was about to say so, when their first courses arrived.

When they had gone through the rituals of ground pepper and the wine pouring, and the waiters had retreated, Philip spoke again. "You haven't responded to my question."

She picked at her Salade Niçoise. "To be honest, Philip, I can't understand your question. What is it you're asking me?"

He looked bewildered. "I should have thought that was absolutely clear."

"Well, it isn't."

"I'm asking you to stay on in Yorkshire."

"Ah, I see." She stabbed her fork into a piece of anchovy and ate it.

"On your own terms, of course."

"So you said before."

"We could draw up contracts, if you wish. I wanted to make that very clear."

Her fork clattered onto her plate. "Well, I'm afraid you've failed. As far as I'm concerned, it's as clear as mud."

Philip sighed. "What I'm trying to say is that you may choose to live in your new house. Kirkby House, I mean."

"Ah, I see," she said once again.

"But you are most welcome to live at Thornton, if that is what you wish," he hastily added.

"Damned nice of you."

"What the hell's the matter with you, Tessa?" he

said, his voice rising, so that people turned to look at them. "Here I am, trying to propose to you and all you can do is make sarcastic remarks."

"Is that what you were trying to do, propose to me? You could have fooled me!" Tessa stood up so abruptly that she jogged the table, toppling her wineglass and spilling wine on her skirt. She could feel it seeping through to her legs. She stood staring at his white face. "All these years, all these years I've dreamed of . . ." She choked up, unable to say any more.

Aware of startled faces staring at her, she dashed from the dining room, blindly seeking the ladies' room. When she couldn't find it, she pushed open the door to the car park and ran outside.

Having told the maître d' that he'd be back tomorrow to settle the entire bill, Philip ran outside. He saw Tessa sobbing over the bonnet of his car. He had never been so perplexed in all his life. Nor so afraid. In some way, he had made a total and absolute botch of it. Because of that, he had probably lost her forever.

That possibility precipitated him to the car. Ignoring the interested gaze of outdoor drinkers, he took Tessa in his arms, dragging her resisting body against him. "I love you, Tessa," he said over and over again, kissing her repeatedly on whatever part of her face he could find, eyes, ears, nose. "I love you, my own sweet darling. Whatever mess I've made of this, I love you and want to marry you and you to marry me. I've loved you ever since I first saw you in that awful gym slip and the hat with the elastic that cut into your neck and your large brown eyes in your thin face. I loved you then, I love you now, I'll love you forever."

He was vaguely aware of people laughing, of the salt taste of her tears on his lips, of Tessa's hands clutching at him, and then of her mouth eagerly opening under his.

It was then that the first cheer went up.

"Let's get the hell out of here," he said, grabbing her hand and pushing her into the passenger seat of his car. He drove out of the car park, tires squealing and onlookers cheering.

He thought at first that Tessa was still sobbing, but then he realized that it was laughter that was bubbling in her throat. Then he joined in and they both found they couldn't stop. The car swerved from side to side on the narrow road.

"Pull over!" Tessa shouted. "Pull over, Philip, before you kill us both."

He did so, drawing into an unpaved track leading up to a farm.

"Oh, Philip," Tessa said, gazing at him and slowly shaking her head.

"I made an absolute balls of it, didn't I? I thought I had it all worked out perfectly. A modern proposal. I knew how important it was for a modern professional woman to retain her independence, to have a marriage contract, not to feel pressured to give up her career to become a housewife ... Where did I go wrong?"

Tessa put her hand to his cheek. "Oh, my poor darling. You forgot one thing. You forgot that I've loved you practically all my life. You forgot that I'd never had a romantic proposal. My last marriage was a farce, remember, with my dear aunt buying a husband for me. I wanted to be young again, to be swept off my feet with romance, not wooed with contracts and business arrangements."

Philip put his head in his hands. "God, I'm a bloody fool. That's the way I wanted it, too, but I thought you'd think I was an old-fashioned chauvinist if I did."

They looked at each other, both veering between laughter and tears.

"Is it too late?" Philip asked. "Is it utterly spoiled for you?"

"No," she whispered. "Take me home."

He drove fast, but not as insanely fast as before. It was dark now, but the moon hung high in the dark sky, slipping in and out of the clouds. When they reached Thornton, Philip slowed down, prepared to get out to unlock the gates, but before he had time to open the car door, Peter was there to open them.

Philip leaned from the car window. "Everything all right?"

"Yes. I'm just getting everything ready for the big move tomorrow."

"Good. Thanks for opening the gates, Peter."

"Thank *you*."

Tessa's vision blurred with tears when she heard the wealth of meaning in Peter's voice.

"Where to now?" Philip asked when he'd pulled the car up at the rear of the house and they both got out.

"The garden."

He put his arm around her, guiding her in the dim light from the rear coach lamp, across the stable yard and onto the lawn. Light streamed across the grass from three windows at the rear of the house. They avoided it instinctively, stepping into the pools of darkness at the sides of the lawn.

The air was filled with the rustling of leaves in the summer breeze, the squeak of bats, the sweet scents of nicotiana and stock from the flower beds that lined the paved walkway. He was leading her by the hand now down the trellised walk. She knew where he was going. To the arbor at the end of the walk. The old arbor that sat atop a grassy bank overlooking the stream that meandered at the foot of the flower garden.

"Is this better?" he asked when they came to the arbor, which was swathed with fragrant honeysuckle. He dusted off the wooden bench she remembered from the first day she had seen Thornton.

She sat down. "This is perfect," she whispered.

His arm went around her, drawing her to him in the scented darkness. She put her hands under his jacket, pressing them against his back.

"My darling Tessa," he said against her mouth. "I have always loved you. Will you marry me so that we can live the rest of our lives together?"

"Yes, my dearest, dearest Philip. I will marry you. I want to be your wife. I've always wanted to be your wife, and to bear your children."

He drew away a little from her at that. "Forgive me, darling, for not having asked you in time for that to happen. To have a child with you would have made my life truly perfect." His voice held an ineffable sadness. "We shall have to be satisfied with Jason."

"Speak for yourself," she said. "I'm not even forty years old yet. Lots of women have children after they're forty." She strained to see his face in the moonlit darkness. "Would you like a child?"

"Our child? Yes. But I—I ..." He was searching for the right words. "I wouldn't want to endanger your health in any way. You're far too precious for me to risk that."

"You wouldn't. But we should start trying very soon."

"How soon?"

Her hands were already slipping his jacket from his shoulders and down his arms. "How about now?" she whispered. She knelt on the soft grass above the stream and laid his coat out on the bank. Then she lay down on the coat and held up her arms to him. At first he knelt beside her, staring down at her. Then he reached out one hand to curve about her breast.

Murmuring his name deep in her throat, she drew him down, her body straining upward to his, as she felt the weight and warmth of him upon her.

No one saw their long-awaited coming together but

the moon riding high in the night-blue sky and a slow-winking owl perched in the gnarled old oak tree by the water's edge.

From the orchard on the far side of the stream came the trill of a nightingale as it poured its sweet song into the warm darkness.

Epilogue

As Tessa stood in the ancient church of St. Michael and All the Angels, she glanced across the aisle to the ancient Thornton pew and the family members seated in it. Camilla was surveying everyone with her new expression of haughty disdain, now that she was—since Sybil's death in January—the mistress of Langley.

She would never be mistress of Thornton Manor, though.

Derek sat hunched in the wooden seat, looking as if he'd rather be anywhere but here.

He was no longer the heir to Thornton Manor.

This child, this son she and Philip had created with their love, his downy little head resting against her breast, his bright eyes looking up at his proud father, was the ultimate payback to Derek and Camilla. But somehow, thoughts of payback or revenge no longer mattered to Tessa.

She saw Philip's expression as he looked down at them both, his wife and son, enfolding them with his love. Two months ago, when their son had been born, Philip had wept with joy. It was the first time Tessa had seen him weep. "I don't care what we have to do to preserve Thornton," he told her later. "I want my son to grow up here, in his ancestral home, and his children thereafter." One of Vicky's wealthy friends had booked the great hall and the gardens for a wedding reception at the end of this month. And an Antiques Fair was to be held at Thornton in October.

There were going to be a great many changes at Thornton, thought Tessa, and she knew that they wouldn't be easy for Philip. But as she stood beside him before the rector of St. Michael's, and saw the pride in Philip's face as he smiled tenderly down at their baby, she knew that he would be willing to accept any changes that were necessary to secure Thornton Manor for his son.

The organ pealed out. Tessa exchanged smiles with Jason and Vicky, who were to be the baby's godparents.

Jason had driven down from Newcastle last night and would return to the polytechnic college there this evening. He had not taken the fact of his mother's pregnancy well at first, but when the baby had been born, and Philip reminded him that he was both the baby's cousin *and* his half brother, his sense of kin had prevailed. It was Jason who had suggested the baby's first name.

Vicky hadn't had as far to come as Jason. She lived in the basement flat in Tessa's house in Middleham, right next to her studio and workshop. Tessa saw her grin and wink at someone in the congregation. Probably Kevin. They were still good friends. Despite the fact that Vicky was enjoying herself thoroughly and had no wish to settle down, Tessa had the feeling that Kevin might just win out in the end. He had all the patient enduring qualities of a true Yorkshireman.

As she smoothed down the long lace christening robe that had been worn by her son's father and grandfather, Tessa knew that all that mattered most to her was now within touching distance. She was with the people she loved.

Soon they would return to Thornton for the christening party, where their friends and relatives would congregate to eat smoked salmon vol-au-vents and toast the baby's health with champagne.

Later, when everyone had gone, they would be by themselves. She and Philip and baby Steven. And Tessa would silently give thanks to Uncle Steven—as she did every night—for having brought her home.